SHE WHO BROUGHT DEATH

10 9 8 7 6 5 4 3 2 1

Cover art by Christian Bentulan
Map design by Madison Rene

ISBN 979-8-9884246-3-5 (paperback)
ISBN 979-8-9884246-2-8 (ebook)

www.MadisonReneAuthor.com

Published by Jade Quill Press

A NOTE FROM THE AUTHOR:

She Who Brought Death is a high-stakes romantic fantasy novel. As such, please be advised that you will find some challenging themes within its pages including, but not limited to: violence, blood, death, sexual content, sexual assault, infidelity, PTSD, anxiety, maternal death, homophobia, and plague.

For Emilia,
May you always stay strong and accomplish whatever you set your
mind to.

ZENOCH
KATSAO
KOHARI
THOMANI
SANIN
YONA SHORE
ANANSI
SILOS PEAKS MINE
DALTIUM
IVALIA
VELSPIRE
LIVASHIRE
SALLAIS
MALABRIA
SOLARIS
BRIMON
PORT KYANOS
KRYSTOPOLIS
SANVOLK
MT. SKIA COAL MINE
BLACK RIVER
ELFIN SPRING
PALTHESI
ASTURIA
VENOS
LUNUCA
KIKIONI

EASTERN SEA

DANAECA

SHE WHO
BROUGHT
DEATH

MADISON RENE

JADE QUILL PRESS

L ife as we knew it was different. Days were infinite, with no beginning or end. There was no night, no slumber, only life and awakening.

A young woman lay on her stomach on the beach, lazily tracing her finger in the sand and taking in the fine granules that stuck to the pad of her finger. Her ebony locks fell in sheets over her slender shoulders as she concentrated on her work. She had been at it forever, or at least it seemed that way. Time was immaterial, after all.

At last she let out a heady sigh, puffing hair from her eyes. She leaned back on her elbows to admire her creation: a setting sun, and not one, but two glowing orbs rising to take its place. She always dreamt of what life would be like if the light were snuffed to be replaced with darkness. She imagined it would be peaceful.

A frown furrowed her brow as she further observed her work. She'd drawn two figures holding hands, bliss etched on their faces, except—wait.

She lowered a hand to smudge part of her drawing. His hair was incorrect; it should have been long on the left side of his head, not the right.

As she finished creating the final strokes, a voice, high and shrill, rang through the crisp, tepid air.

"Saava! Saava!"

The dark-haired woman rolled her eyes. She would recognize her sister's drawl anywhere. With deliberately slow movements the woman, Saava, turned, twisting her hips so that she sat facing the newcomer. Where Saava was pretty, her sister was beautiful. Platinum blonde hair fell in waves over her shoulders and cascaded down her back, her bronze skin glistening in the Everlight. Her eyes were blue, striking, nearly as sharp and cold as her lips pursed together in thin burgundy lines.

"Good heavens, what are you doing out here? Do you not pay any attention to invitations?"

A groan escaped her. "Sister, your engagement party would be splendid with or without me. Why do you care if I make my presence known?"

Her sister's lips twisted. She drew a step toward Saava, pale-blue gown of spun silk trailing her.

"Because you are my sister." The blonde flourished a hand. "And the daughter of the Supreme Lord, or have you forgotten by spending all your time out here *creating nonsense?*"

Saava couldn't suppress her shudder at the way her sister sneered over her work. Every resident of Aeterna had their magical talents—it was what made them unique. Most were found useful. Her father, the Supreme Lord of Aeterna, was able to illicit joy to those around him through basking in his aura. Her mother, Lady Elicia, dominated the water and kept the Endless Sea flowing over the edges of Aeterna. Saava's sister harnessed the shackles of death; a power so revered that she earned the title "Goddess of Death." Her magic could cause life to cease. While it may seem odd that such a gift was revered, in an eternal world it was a blessing. Many of the ancient residents could attest to the problems posed by too long an existence.

In contrast, Saava created. She created roads, buildings, art, literature. Anything she put her mind to, she could bring into being, yet not in a physical form. Her gift was stunted, limited. Some, such as her mother, made excuses for her, insisting that her powers had yet to come to fruition. "She's still young, allow her to bloom," she would often say. But much time went, and her magic infuriatingly refused to surface. Thus, she stood on the sidelines while the Goddess of Death radiated among her parents, their friends, and all of Aeterna.

"I can't help it," Saava responded sheepishly. "If I don't get these things out of my head I feel like I will explode. It . . . calms me. You wouldn't understand."

Her sister huffed. "You're right: I wouldn't."

When it was clear that the blonde would not leave without Saava's accompaniment, she reluctantly rose, smoothing down her golden shimmering dress. A dark scowl crossed her sister's features as she spun on heel, barely glancing over her shoulder as she uttered, "Now come; I mustn't keep my fiancé waiting any longer than necessary."

Saava's shoulders sank, head dipping as she meekly followed, bare feet collecting sand and tracking it into the grassy meadow. She spared a final glance over her shoulder, at the artwork she had left in the sand. At the moons and darkness she created, and, finally, toward the Endless Sea beyond: a glittering cerulean body which swelled and sank with the waves. It poured down the side of the continent, like a spout, into the void below. Wrongdoers were cast over the side, banished from Aeterna forever to join in the eternal darkness. None knew their fate, or what was down below, but Saava secretly yearned to, and wondered many times what could await them if they dared to explore.

Only the wrongdoers knew, and a forbidden part of her yearned to be one of them.

1

NEVIA

Warning bells echoed through the night, sounding from the tower just shy of Nevia's bedroom window. The empress sat up with a start, eyes wide, heart threatening to rip free from her chest.

Footfalls echoed outside her bedroom door, combined with shouts and wailing. She kicked off her covers and snatched her dagger from her nightstand, not even bothering with slippers as she strode out from her bedroom.

The metallic tang of blood assaulted her nostrils the moment she stepped foot into the carpeted hall of the Velspirian palace, her guards, normally stationed outside her door, absent. She jerked her head up, horrified, to find that one lay bloodied and dead a short distance from the bannister. The other was soon to join his comrade, appearing worse for wear. Heart hammering, Nevia stole a glance toward the wreckage surrounding her: shattered twin doors lay unhinged outside a balcony, lush carpets and ivory decor no match for destructive force.

An enormous winged creature filled the corridor, its body covered in blue-black fur. Bulbous yellow eyes swiveled before fixating on her, jaw yawning open to unveil many dozen sharp teeth. These monstrosities had no name, being unlike anything they had seen before, but they had lovingly received the title of "night creatures," as they only struck well into the night, and bore similarities to the creatures of myth labeled with the same name.

Nevia let out a gasp as she pressed herself against the wall, hands running along the length of the stickiness, her jewel-hilted dagger clasped tightly in one of them.

"Empress!"

She twisted to meet the gaze of Renault standing a few paces from her left, face pale, long ebony hair plastered to his forehead by a thick sheen of sweat. Her personal bodyguard, loyal servant, and elder cousin to the late Emperor Darius II. He jabbed his sword into its side, seeking purchase on its soft underbelly where it would be most vulnerable. It let out a sickening squeal, twisting itself to rake its claws across his face, only for Renault to leap back several paces.

Nevia clutched the dagger tightly in her fist. Taking aim, she threw.

The blade landed, not in the chest where she planned, but in its eye. Its cry was shrill enough to shatter a mirror at her back, causing her to scream as she covered her head from the showering glass.

"Empress, no!" Renault lowered his sword and jolted toward her, but it was Elante who made it to Nevia's side first and threw her arms around her.

Nevia lifted her head just in time to find her other sentry finish the night creature off, silencing it for good by running his sword along its neck. The sight was horrific, and she could hardly imagine the hall looking as it once did ever again.

Her handmaiden, Elante, spun her around, forcing her to face her before squeezing her as tightly as she could. "You gave us such a fright!" her handmaiden chided. "What in Saava's name were you thinking, charging out into the hall like that when the warning bells sounded? Did you *want* to get yourself killed?!"

Elante was shaking all over. Despite being chided, the empress stroked Elante's silky dark hair soothingly, tucking loose strands behind her ear before cupping her face.

"Someone had to do something," she responded, which incurred the darkest scowl from her personal guard, now at her side.

"Your handmaiden is right, Empress," Renault countered, towering over the two women at his impressive height. "Leave such matters to your imperial guard. That's what we're here for. Your job is to remain safe."

"I'm not going to just cower in my room while people are risking their lives!" Nevia insisted.

Renault folded his arms over his chest. "Then you're making my job pointless."

"Enough!" Elante wormed her way between the two, pressing a hand to their chests. "What's done is done. But, Your Highness, you need to develop a stronger sense of preservation, lest I fear the rebels will delight in your demise and get what they want."

Nevia's lips thinned at the mention of the rebels: a small group of imperials, mostly Velspirians, who were traditionalists and despised having a woman, let alone a foreigner, sit upon the throne when more noble blood could be found, specifically Renault. He was the last descendent of the Androvich line and perfect for the throne, but Darius, her late husband, left the empire in her hands. Further, some of the rebels went so far as to blame her for her husband's death and insist she be punished.

They weren't entirely wrong—the war in which he died, after all, *was* her fault.

The empress closed her eyes, balling her hands into fists at her sides. Elante had mistaken this as tiredness, draping an arm over her and started to lead her away.

"I will get her back to bed," Elante reassured Renault, brushing the empress' thick platinum hair over her shoulder.

Renault looked reluctant to let the two women go without an escort, but nodded gruffly all the same. His gaze faltered to the monster's body, then darted around expectantly for anyone willing to help him do the bloody job of cleaning it up.

Everyone else had already scurried away.

The moment they arrived in Nevia's quarters, the empress collapsed in her favored chair beside the fire. While it was not particularly chilly in the early part of autumn, her blood ran cold in her veins from the night's events. Her gaze bore into the crackling flames, saying nothing as Elante bundled her in a plush blanket and began working a comb through the snares of her platinum hair.

"I shouldn't be here."

Elante's motions ceased. "Whatever do you mean, milady?"

"You said it yourself." Nevia waved a hand through the air. "The rebels want me off the throne, are going to find ways to try disposing of me, and eventually the rest of the people will let them. Who knows? Maybe someone sent that night creature in here to kill me."

Elante pinched her full lips into a frown. "Surely you don't really believe that."

"It's very possible."

Elante fumbled with the folds of her skirt, looking as though she wanted to say something, but instead began collecting Nevia's hair into a large bun atop her head. Carefully she smoothed it, tucking it into place with several pins before wrapping it in a silken scarf for protection.

"Well, I think," Elante said slowly, tying the ends of her scarf together, "that you need to rid such ideas from your head, and instead think about more important things. Like what you're going to say to lover boy when you see him next week."

Nevia whirled around in her seat. Next week. The council to discuss the night creature sightings across all of Danaeca. The empress had nearly forgotten, and she had called for the council herself.

"Ardan's not—I mean—" Her eyes fluttered. "It isn't like that, between me and him. It would be most inappropriate."

A playful smirk twisted Elante's lips into something sinister. "Mmm-hmm. Sure."

"I'm serious! Please don't speak such things."

It was partly true. Over the many months leading up to the Nephyl War she had developed a close bond with one of the clansmen: Ardan Kyaroe. He was brave, witty, incredibly kind, and impressively attractive, and Nevia, stumbling and desperate to cling on to stability during the greatest tribulation of her life, found herself falling in love with him. However, it had been three years since she had seen him, and in that time she told herself it was not love but infatuation. She had missed Darius, and at that time Ardan was the closest, kindest man she could pour her affection into.

Yet those caresses, those fiery kisses of passion that warmed her soul and made her toes curl. It had felt so real, but was it? She was both eager for and dreading the discovery. Seeing him again after all these years would help her decide, but she was afraid. No amount of warring against night creatures could prepare her for facing her heart.

The mirth faded from Elante's eyes as she pressed a kiss to Nevia's cheek. "Okay, I will stop, but I hope you know I'm only wanting what's best for you. I think it's good for you to find love somewhere, after. . . ."

She did not speak on, but Nevia already knew what she was going to say. She bolted from her chair, allowing her blanket to crumple at her feet. "No, this is exactly why I should stay where I am, as I am. Darius' death is my fault, and I must bear the consequences of my actions."

"Verrine killed him! Not you. We've been through this."

Suddenly Nevia's lips grew numb and tingly, her heart hammering in her chest. She drew in slow, steady breaths, trying to calm her raging heart and still the listlessness within her. These spells happened sporadically since the war, and it had been a struggle, but slowly, tenderly she was beginning to overcome them.

She still had many scars to heal from.

"It's been three years, Elante," Nevia whispered, eyes still closed. "And I can still see his face, hear his voice. I remember the words on his lips. He died to protect me, after every way that I hurt and betrayed him."

Elante ran up behind Nevia and grasped her forearms. "He left you no choice. Don't you see? He mistreated you ever since he wed you, but I think you just didn't see it until things got really bad."

Nevia inhaled sharply and turned to meet the gaze of her handmaiden. Even at twenty-five years of age, she considered Elante so wise. She smiled wistfully. "We both are responsible for how things ended. Our union was never meant to be, but now I must face what it wrought. While you're right, I should've handled things differently. If I could go back and change that, I would do it in a heartbeat."

Tears began to well in her eyes, which she tried desperately to will away. Elante must've sensed her distress, as she began to drag her from her sitting parlor to her adjoined bedroom. It took little prompting for Nevia to collapse into the satin sheets, allowing her handmaiden to bring the covers to her chin as if she were a small child and bid her goodnight with a pat on the cheek.

"I'll see you in the morning," Elante said.

"See you."

And yet with Elante gone, Nevia only had tormenting thoughts to plague her: of the horrors of the night creature assaulting the palace, and memories of her garments drenched in her husband's blood the day he died in her arms.

2
ARDAN

Cold winds swept through the Sanen encampment as the chief observed his clansmen take down the final tent, neatly wrapping the leather exterior to pack with the rest of their equipment. The seasons were shifting, and it was time to follow their game as they migrated to escape the deep cold of the Zenochian winter. Traditionally they packed up and moved twice or thrice per year, and Ardan was well accustomed to it by now. Nomadic by nature, he could hardly envision a life of stagnancy, staying in one place for years on end—if not one's entire life.

The mountains, while in a perpetual state of winter, were among the very few regions in Danaeca untainted by imperial influence, a place free from societal expectations and technology.

Their way of life was primitive, simple to some, and yet Ardan would trade it for nothing.

Except, of course, maybe *her*.

He smiled, long midnight black hair whipping in the breeze, thoughts straying to his dear Nevia. He had tried to write her a letter, but never could he bring the right words to paper. They had parted ways on uncomfortable terms after the war, and he feared his letters could be intercepted by imperial officials. He did not want Nevia having to explain to the Five Lords of the Androvich Empire why a Zenochian chief was head-over-heels in love with her.

But such was true. The adage of distance making the heart grow fonder was a saying Ardan could attest to. That afternoon he would set sail to Velspire for a council with the other world leaders. The meeting's purpose of discussing the night creature assaults was certainly important, yet he could not suppress his excitement of seeing her again for the first time in three years.

Three years.

So much happened in that time, and yet so little. He had become chief of the Sanen clan after the former chief, Risanna fell in the Nephyl War. Despite his hesitancy in accepting the role of chief and following in his father's footsteps, he was pleased with the progress of his clan. Lost materials from the war and avalanche prior were replaced within the last year. While their population suffered a great loss, many women of childbearing age conceived shortly after the war, in hopes of preserving their heritage. Now the clan was overrun with toddlers, and another wave of children was on its way to arrive early the next year.

"So, what are you going to bring her? Ready to craft a roc?"

Ardan didn't need to turn to recognize the brash speaker but did so anyway. Standing an arm's length away, with thick pale dreadlocks pulled back by a teal kerchief, was Khatalia Alasa, former chief to the annihilated Kohari clan.

"No, Khatalia," Ardan said, chuckling. "I am *not* going to propose to the empress of the Androvich Empire. That would be absurd."

"But you know she'd love it," Khatalia pressed.

To say the thought had not crossed his mind would have been a lie; he had indeed wistfully dreamt of a future with Nevia. He had never known love until he met her, and after the weeks rolled to months, and the tribulations underwent together, she quickly became his world. Living without her these past three years had been difficult, at times intolerable. So often he concocted reasons to make his way south and steal a visit, but he knew it wasn't appropriate, not after the death of her husband.

While she may be the sole ruler of the empire now, it wasn't necessarily easy for her to retain her position, and even still there were those who opposed her rule. Whispered rumors of rebellion wound their tendrils even as far north as Zenoch. For her sake and the sake of the empire, he must not jeopardize the stability.

"I'm not too sure about that," Ardan concluded.

"She said that she loved you."

"That was then."

"Yes, and?"

"And what?! There's no 'and' about it!"

"Well, then, she still loves you! Simple!" Khatalia threw her hands in the air. "I can't believe you are this dense and consider yourself smart enough to be chief."

"And you're this arrogant and you're my second," Ardan grumbled under his breath.

Instead of wandering the snowy landscape alone and without belonging, Ardan invited Khatalia to join them. She swiftly strode her way up to being second-in-command, just like he had been to Risanna, yet despite their roles Ardan could not shake the sensation that she was at times the real chief and he the figurehead. Even now, as he was ready to sail away to Velspire, the clan was perfectly content to be temporarily in Khatalia's capable hands.

"Anyway," Khatalia drawled, rolling her eyes, "I just wanted to wish you safe travels, and please do give Nevia a good slap on the shoulder for me."

"I think you mean 'clap,' "Ardan corrected.

"No, I meant what I said. I understand the common tongue."

Their chuckles fogged the cool air. Ardan patted Khatalia's arm before gripping it firmly. "Please take care of them, and watch out for those creatures of the night."

Khatalia harrumphed, wrenching herself free and folding her arms over her ample bosom. "Those creatures are no match for my spear."

"Don't underestimate them." He shot her a warning glare. "I mean it. These are not bears and wolves. These things are enormous. Most fly and only come out in deepest night. Be careful, Khatalia. I can't lose you."

The words left his mouth faster than he could catch them, and immediately he saw the impact of his words as Khatalia's brows knit in worry.

"I will. I promise. After all, I was tied to a bloody helm for two days without dying. I think I can handle a dark creature of the night."

He certainly hoped so. With a final pat of her shoulder he snatched up his pack and left. The worry of an assault quickly fled to the back of his mind as thoughts of Nevia surfaced to the forefront. He could not wait to see her again, to hold her again, to feel the sensation of her warm lips against his.

3
QIRIN

Garments rustled as funeral patrons folded onto themselves in unison, prostrating before the final resting place of Teniel Rumaar, prime minister of the Feishin Kingdom. King Qirin could hear the strung jewels of Queen Liana's hairpin jingle softly at his side, reminding him of her abhorrent presence. He pressed his head against the cool marble flooring in the Shrine of Everlasting Peace, trying to will his mind into stillness.

How he would miss Lady Rumaar. Since he was born she had been serving his parents, and after losing his mother in the Nephyl War she had been a strong ally. A confidant, his friend—she provided sound guidance when his decisions were naive. Despite being groomed into the role of king from youth, he found himself ill-prepared for being sovereign to a once pacifistic society.

Once, but no longer. He saw to that the moment he lay claim to the crown.

A hand rested on his shoulder, arresting his attention and causing him to lift his head. The others had already risen—the prayer for safe passage to the Nether Planes already commencing. Qirin met the gaze of his queen. Her expression was somber, lips pressed tightly together. She rubbed circles along his back, offering comfort to soothe the unrelenting ache of loss, but he ignored her and rose to standing.

The patrons bowed to the royal couple as they left, but he ignored them as well. His thoughts were so jumbled, so clouded it astounded him that Liana's voice managed to pierce through.

"She was a remarkable woman, stolen away from us before her time."

"Indeed." His fists curled at his side. "We have the night creatures to thank for that."

Liana jerked her head toward the other guests to gauge reaction, as if he'd just sworn in the middle of a worshipper's assembly. Her deep crimson lips pursed. "Not here. We mustn't speak of them now."

"Then where?" He threw his face to the heavens, his long flowing locks of ebony cascading over his shoulders and brushing the dark ceremonial obi at his waist. "Pray tell, my beloved wife, where shall we discuss my prime minister's murderers if not in her final resting place?"

His words were sharp, callous, and rang too loudly amidst the departing assembly. People seemed to flee now, some looking at the couple with apprehension as they passed. Offering apologetic smiles while the crowd dispersed, Liana drew his hands into hers and brought them to her chest.

"Qirin, I know you loved her, and I'm so sorry for your loss—"

"Loss is something I'm used to," came his reply, refusing to meet her gaze.

"—but this doesn't mean you can say whatever you want, wherever you want. You may be a suffering young man, but you are still king to these people, and as such you must command the respect you deserve and hold yourself together. What will they say if they see you crumble?"

"That I'm not fit to be king, maybe?" Finally he jerked his head to meet her gaze, her eyes dark and fierce, cheeks flushed from both make-up and frustration. "Which is fine. They can greet the chopping block, just like all the others who tried to force my abdication during the war."

Liana inhaled sharply, loosening her grip on his hands and allowing them to fall. She brought a hand to her swollen belly, massaging it as she looked as if on the brink of tears. "I don't know what to do with you," she murmured darkly. "I'm just trying to hold things together. I want what's best for the kingdom, and for you."

His gaze trailed her hand, his jaw clenching in silent resentment at the unborn baby which she stroked. Her baby.

Their baby. He hadn't wanted children, at least not for a while. She said it was not intentional, but he did not believe her, not after everything else she had been doing to manipulate his kingdom in the way she wanted.

"Don't play coy with me," he snapped. "I know you just want what's best for yourself."

The queen gasped, backing away from Qirin as though struck. Perhaps he would have felt bad, would have apologized, had he not felt manipulated. He resented her and their marriage. He resented his mother for arranging their union against his wishes. Perhaps he should have ended the betrothal. It was within his power to do so, but they had already come so far—the wedding arrangements had been made, people already were saving the date. Ending it would not have only severed ties and ruin relations with her father, a wealthy, influential lord to the south, but further shake the faith of his people in him.

Something he did not need when he was already under such scrutiny. His personal happiness was a small price to pay to ensuring that power remained in his hands.

Though at times, he certainly questioned that decision.

Qirin drew in a quivering breath, preparing to blurt more obscenity, when a young man stepped forward and bowed deeply to the couple, dark pleated hair shifting over his narrow shoulders.

"Your Majesties?"

Qirin held the breath he drew, gaze flickering toward the newcomer. Ceremonial robes of a royal-blue decked the man, silver embroidery accentuating a phoenix emblazoned on his obi belt—ornate garb for a momentous occasion. Immediately Qirin regretted his lack of composition. Especially in front of him.

"Rito." Liana turned to face him, surprise dawning on her features. "I am so glad that you came to attend Lady Rumaar's memorial. She would've liked that. You have always been so cherished within the royal family."

Rito dipped his head. "As has the royal family been cherished by me." Finally his gaze locked on to Qirin's with an intensity that forced Qirin's compliance, despite wishing to be anywhere but in the room. "I do hope that I am not interrupting. You both just seemed distressed so I-I wanted to make sure all was well."

"We're fine," Qirin said, perhaps too tersely. "Leave us, Rito. This is a personal matter that we are trying to settle."

He may as well have snatched a hot poker and scorched him. The look of pain on Rito's face could not be concealed as the young man began to shuffle away. Queen Liana remained motionless at his side, refusing to turn in his direction.

"You need to grow up, Qirin," she said. "Get your head out of your ass and start acting like the man I know you are deep down."

Fury almost boiled over but his queen did not linger long enough to receive it. She shifted from him, black mourning silks shimmering across the floor in her wake. He watched her go, and, despite his desire to chase after her, stayed. None were left in the Shrine of Everlasting Peace except for him, him and the bodies of royals and honored lords and ladies laid to rest within. He strode across the chamber, slippered footsteps scuffling on marble in the silence, and knelt before a golden altar. Embellishments were etched into its glistening surface, as well as the names of his parents: the late King Athilan and Queen Arethusa.

"I miss you both," he murmured, placing a hand on the altar. His fingertips brushed against one of many embroidered brocades crafted in their honor. For a brief moment he was overcome with the temptation to lift the lid of his mother's casket, to peer at her loving face once more. Such was considered the gravest of sins, believed that those whose rest was interrupted would be forced from the Nether Planes to walk the face of Gaia forever. "I wish— I wish that I had been more prepared when you passed."

Tears welled in his eyes, which he furiously blinked away. He had been banished from the battlefield during the war—Arethusa insisted on keeping her two children safe behind the stone wall encompassing their island nation. While there was no way he could have defended his mother, he did harbor knowledge that the invasion was coming. He did not share this warning with her. If he had, preparations that saved their country could not have been made. She never would have permitted him to ready their arsenal within the heart of the palace and engage his soldiers in swordplay. As a pacifist nation, swordsmanship was an uncommon art form used only for show. Despite this, Qirin took it upon himself to train with his soldiers in secret. They thought it was to better their performance, but Qirin knew the truth. He knew the day would come when Darius' military would march on his shores, and unlike his mother, he would bear arms to defend his country. In his mother's care, they would have curled up to die.

Qirin made sure that his people never bent a knee to anyone else again.

He whispered his blessings upon his parents and Lady Rumaar before ascending the steps and exiting the shrine. Sunshine beat down on his shoulders and seared through his black garments of mourning. The leaves of the cherry blossom trees, barren this time of year, fluttered in the breeze at his back. He made his way down the winding path leading up to the Wind Palace a short distance upon the hill.

Qirin's face was drawn tight. He could not afford to allow the tears to flow from his eyes. Not here.

"Your Majesty!"

That voice again. Qirin's shoulders went rigid as the footsteps of Rito dogged him, falling a short distance behind him. He must have been waiting for him outside the shrine. The king closed his eyes, willing the tears away. "You don't have to call me that, you know."

A pause. "I know."

Rito strode forward and extended his hands, grasping for Qirin's within the confines of his wide bell sleeves. His round, boyish smiling face peered up into his. "But I must keep up appearances."

A heavy sigh escaped the young king. "I wish it weren't so."

Rito was near his own age, standing at least five inches shorter. His face was always bright; where Qirin was dark with broodiness and pessimism, Rito was light, the optimist between them. Yin and Yang, and yet the two always complemented one another.

"There's a lot of things that I wish for, Qirin."

Qirin's heart leapt to his throat. "Such as?"

Rito let out a weary sigh, allowing his hand to fall. It seemed his thoughts trailed Qirin's own, the young man shaking his head as if ridding the daydream.

The absence of his touch stung at Qirin's heart. Part of him wished to snatch the hand right back, to parade around the kingdom with him at his side. Wishing, beyond anything, that *he* could be his king second. And yet, it could never be so.

"Never mind. Are you still going to the mainland tomorrow?" Rito asked.

"Yes, regrettably so." Qirin turned his gaze toward the palace, its sheers whipping through the windows visible even from there. "Nevia wants to speak to all of the leaders of Danaeca about this night creature problem. Apparently it's not only us suffering from their unwarranted assaults. She claims that she and Zenoch have been dealt a heavy blow, as well."

"You sound dubious. Do you doubt her sincerity?"

The words, while true, sounded ridiculous in Qirin's head, causing him to still his tongue. No, he was a fool to doubt Nevia's sincerity. How could he after everything she had done during the Nephyl War? She had, after all, exposed her husband's lies, fled the comfort of her home and branded herself a traitor for exposing the grave truth: the empire was the culprit of initiating the war between Feishins and Zenochians, in order to invade the kingdom for its resources. Nevia stood up for him, and for that Qirin was grateful.

Thoughts of his prior conversation trickled into memory. He realized, begrudgingly, that Liana was right: he *was* being childish, if not shortsighted.

"I know she has a good heart," Qirin concluded. "Yes, I'm leaving, but I shall ask Liana to stay here. I don't want her traveling when she is so near the end of her pregnancy."

"A wise choice."

"Would you come?"

Both men were equally shocked at Qirin's offer. Rito began fidgeting with his sleeves. "I don't see much purpose in my coming with you."

"You're a family friend." Qirin waved a hand impatiently. "What other purpose do you need? I would like someone that I can trust at my side, especially seeing as my soldiers once before were happy to discard me at the first better offer. And Teniel is dead, so it can't be her."

When Rito still looked apprehensive Qirin's face shifted from requesting to something far more desperate. Pleading. He drew a breadth closer without realizing it. "Rito, please. I need you."

Pain laced its way across Rito's face as he turned to the Wind Palace ahead. "There could be talk."

"Why would there be? They have no reason to spread anything negative. I am simply requesting that my best friend comes with me overseas. How can that be wrong?"

"Well, there were the earlier rumors. . . ."

A groan escaped Qirin. His sister—his dear beloved Mila—sowed the idea that Qirin rejected his many presented suitors because his interests did not lie in them but rather the young man inseparable at his side. His engagement to Liana quickly subdued such gossip, and with both his marriage and upcoming child it was never uttered again. But he did not want to give them reason to doubt, to think him more blasphemous from their traditional ways than they already did.

A ridiculous law, he thought. It shocked him that his people clung so dearly to traditional beliefs when they had greater technological advancements than any other society. With Qirin's new ideology introduced over the past three years, including his end to the pacifist movement, the people would not take kindly to him taking a man as his partner. It may be just enough to tip them over the edge, and he could not stop his own soldiers from forcing his abdication—or worse.

"People will talk no matter what you do," Qirin said dismissively. "The choice is yours. I won't force you to come, but I do ask you. Not as your king, but as your friend."

When Rito looked hesitant Qirin finally added, "Please."

The guardsman let out a sigh, running his fingers through his fine hair. "Okay, I will. But don't be surprised if I ignore you in public just for the sake of—well. . . ."

"No surprise. In fact, I would expect nothing less."

"Thank you, Qirin."

He let out a breath he didn't realize he was holding. They resumed walking in the direction of the Wind Palace. "Don't mention it."

"Will Liana mind?"

"No, of course not. She cherishes our friendship, as do I."

Rito shifted uncomfortably, and even Qirin had the wisdom to remain silent as they bound up the palatial steps two at a time. When he expected Rito to trail him, however, he remained, lingering at the threshold and watching him with a clouded gaze.

"See you tomorrow then, Your Majesty."

Qirin shot a glance at the sentries stationed at the entrance, a reminder that there were witnesses. "Yes, tomorrow, Rito." With that he disappeared behind a flutter of pink sheers and the airy wall of jasmine and ylang-ylang fragrances.

4
NEVIA

Glossy emerald tiles sparkled beneath glistening chandeliers overhead. Her curvaceous figure was concealed by a blue ballgown woven from the finest spun silk that money could buy, around her neck wore a dainty string of pearls. She felt beautiful, looked beautiful, and she felt oddly haughty about it.

A wide array of guests fluttered through the ballroom, dressed in fine silks and brocades in a vast assortment of brilliant colors. They looked otherworldly, their features distinctly not human. Their bodies were proportioned differently, long and gangly, but what was most unsettling were the elongated pointed ears protruding from perfect hairstyles. Upon the head of each guest lay a bronze circle—a fashion statement to be certain, yet one glance in the tall mirrors on either side of the ballroom revealed hers was an exception. Ensnaring her platinum waves was a black crown of willow and thorns.

Someone gripped her elbow. "My love?"

She spun around and saw him: Ardan, and yet not quite. Long, even black hair was drawn back from his angular face and high cheekbones, hazel eyes warm. Her lips stretched into a fine smile.

"Niall," she greeted, grasping him by the lapels of his suit and drawing him close. "Isn't it all so lovely?"

His gaze was glassy and afar as he took in the sights, coming up to stand at her side. "Yes, it really is. Your parents did a fine job at arranging this ceremony. It's beautiful." A frown pinched her brow as she turned to the side to study him. He searched the crowd, almost as if searching for someone.

For *her*.

A laugh bubbled in her throat, causing several guests at the nearby refreshment table to shoot a glance at her in alarm. Niall jerked his face from the crowd, expression darkened with alarm. "What is it?"

"You seek my sister, don't you?"

His face said it all, the way it paled to a ghastly white. Her lips curved into a wicked smile, savoring his reaction. She allowed her words to sink in as she tread toward a nearby servant offering beverages to the guests, her gown slithering across the emerald tiles. She snatched a golden goblet from the serving tray wordlessly and inspected its contents. The amber liquid bubbled as she brought it to her painted lips with a smile.

"I asked her to come," she explained, "but she preferred to spend her time creating images in the sand. I think she doesn't want to see you."

Hurt disguised too late flashed in Niall's eyes, the expected reaction to her words.

"She was over by the Endless Sea, however. If you wanted to leave the side of your fiancé to go, you know, see her."

His hurt morphed to fury, and for a moment she hoped he would lash out at her, in front of all these people, exposing him for the traitorous soul he was. Instead, however, he swallowed down his reaction, throat bobbing beneath his voluminous cravat. "No, it would be most inappropriate, and I have no desire to see Saava. It is only you that I care to gaze upon tonight, my beloved."

The words, while flowery, could not have been farther from the truth. One look into his tortured, hazel eyes told it all. She wrapped one arm around his neck, the other holding her goblet out to the side. They spun in a half-circle, a slow dance to match the orchestra ringing through the ballroom.

"Perfect," she whispered, brushing her rounded nose against his. "As it should be."

"Your Highness? Your Highness! Please, you must wake!"

Nevia's leg was violently shaken, forcing open her eyes and earning immediate ire. All heat died when she saw Elante at her bedside. It took her mind a moment to catch up, to recall where she was, and, further, where she had been.

"Are you ill?" Concern contorted Elante's brow. "You're drenched in sweat, and you were lashing about in your sleep. I feared you were gripped by fever."

"I was?" Nevia asked, dumbfounded. She ran her hands along the length of her bodice to find her silk ballgown replaced by her nightgown, and there was no trace of her circlet or any evidence that she was dancing in a ballroom with lords and ladies. And with a man who resembled Ardan. "I mean, yeah, it was just . . . did Saava have a sister?"

Elante stared at Nevia as though she had sprouted a second head. "What?"

"A sister," Nevia repeated, feeling foolish. "I know only the Goddess of Creation is celebrated, but did she have an older sister in the legends?"

A frown furrowed Elante's brow when she realized that Nevia's inquiry was serious. "I don't think so—or at least not that I've heard of. I only know of the goddess Saava, and what the legends say: that she created Gaia out of a wish to have companionship, and sleeps eternally at its center, flourishing our planet and granting us life. I know of no other goddess, especially not one sharing a bond with Saava."

"Oh."

"Why the sudden curiosity?"

Nevia grew tense at the inquiry. A forbidden part of her did not think she should confess the dream to Elante. It was, for all intents and purposes, a figment of her imagination, yet it looked real, *felt* real. In the dream world, *she* was Saava's sister, and she did not know how, but the guests in the ballroom were no strangers to her. There was Lady Renora, fawning over Lord Gavin across the dance floor without success, and Maria, one of her favored servants, doling out champagne on a silver tray. Could she truly imagine something that vivid?

Nevia leaned back against her headboard. "Just a dream."

Elante was equally quick to dismiss it. Snapping her from her reverie, Elante helped to untangle the empress from her sheets and dragged her by the wrists. "Enough sulking! Come, come! Don't you know what day it is today?"

Nevia's mind skimmed the possibilities. It was well past the first day of autumn, and the Day of the Dead was not for several weeks. And then it struck her, cold dread settling into the pit of her stomach. Members of the council were flocking to Velspire for the upcoming meeting.

And Ardan. He was supposed to be arriving that day.

After her vision as someone else in another life, she was loath to see him so soon. She also feared the prophecy left to her on her return from the Feishin Kingdom three years ago. Never would she forget the way her heart sank at the burdensome revelation, the uttering of a prophecy she did not want to come true. The seer had cautioned her against trusting the warlord or the chief, as together they would bring the death of Gaia. Did this dream and the prophecy have some kind of connection? And what if, after all these years, her feelings for him were still intact? What then? She didn't want to think about it.

"You need to come pick your outfit."

Nevia shrugged, finding herself padding over to Elante nonetheless. "You always pick out my clothes. Why do you need my input now?"

"Because you're the one courting your boyfriend, not me."

The barbed assault flushed Nevia's cheeks with color as she followed Elante behind the dressing screen to stand in front of her wardrobe. "We are *not* courting. I've already told you!"

Her handmaiden merely offered a knowing kind of smile as she thrust open the cherry wood doors of the wardrobe, unveiling an array of gowns. This was not the whole of Nevia's collection, but was her most frequented attire. Nevia let out a slow breath, puffing unruly hair from her face. There were silks and taffetas, brocades and linens. Finally Nevia selected a golden dress with princess seams, gathered at the bust and form-fitted across her stomach, flowing out at her hips and cascading loosely around her legs to the floor. Vines were embroidered along the length of the bodice and flowing sleeves, yielding an autumnal flair. It was airy, beautiful, and regal.

Nevia smiled to herself in the mirror at her selection, while Elante worked deftly to lace her bodice and move on to her thick mane. Reining back her hair was not an easy task and often turned into an hour-long project. To her surprise, however, Elante sectioned her hair and began plaiting it, weaving sections from the scalp and then braiding the length until securing it at the end. Her favored braid. Nevia couldn't help beaming at her. Since becoming empress she was always expected to wear ornate, traditional hairstyles becoming of the empire, and a plain braid along the side of her head was not among such selections.

"You *are* empress, after all," Elante offered in explanation. "It should be your choice how to represent yourself. No sense in all the frills of styling your hair if you're going to hate it."

Despite her words, Nevia could see many reasons why she should still comply with all the fanciful styling, as she was indeed empress—and a foreigner from the North. Secretly Nevia wondered if she was being given so much freedom because Ardan was involved, but she didn't inquire, and Elante didn't voluntarily share, so the question went without clarification.

The two women snaked their way through the ornate Velspirian halls afterwards, haunting tapestries of Darius' family mocking her as she went. Nevia tried her best to block out the wreckage to her right, the hall that had been devastated after the assault from the night creature, and yet her curiosity got the better of her, and she couldn't help stealing a glance in the direction. The glass doors had already been replaced, the blood removed from the walls and floors. No remnant of the night remained, a visual relief and not a mental one. It was only a matter of time until the next occurrence, carnage that could not be simply replaced.

Downstairs they engaged in a quiet breakfast in Nevia's parlor. It was once the room belonging to her father beside the library, complete with his favorite leather armchair and many of his possessions. After the war Nevia was relieved to return home to find that Darius hadn't ordered the servants to clear out her father's cluttered space, and she personally saw to organizing it herself. Still intact, it was a shrine which housed memories of her father, even if he departed to the Nether Planes at her late husband's own hand to punish her.

The memories brought pain. She recollected how it felt to see him bravely walk up to the gallows, how his eyes briefly met with hers and she could do nothing to stop the procession. She felt responsible, even if she held no sway over the decisions Darius made, or her father when he decided to accept the charge of sorcery to protect her. It was all in vain in the end, the full truth finally exposed to the people after the war and all the death left in its wake.

A rap at the door was enough to cause Nevia to nearly drop the cup in her hands, pale tea sloshing onto her golden gown.

"Your Imperial Highness." A pock-faced messenger boy shoved himself in the ajar door, brown eyes wide and bright. "The Zenochians and their entourage have arrived. They are awaiting your audience in the foyer."

5

ARDAN

The palace was everything Ardan thought it would be and then some. The only time he visited the imperial capital was alongside Nevia during the war. Never had he stepped foot inside the Velspirian palace, or even approached it, for that matter.

They were ushered through the steel gates and along the clay brick pathway to enter a foyer with cathedral ceilings, rising at least two—if not three—floors above them. The walls were adorned with gold and ivory wallpaper, lanterns fixed on every wall. Ardan had seen such technology before in the Feishin Kingdom, lighting that burned from an energy source deposited from the core shards or, more formally, Nephyl, replacing the need for coal, wood, and candle. The technology had a complicated system, much too difficult for Ardan to wrap his mind around, but the technology was revolutionary. Life-changing for the societies that adopted it.

Footfalls of his fellow clansmen reminded that he wasn't there to sight-see, but was instead on important business. Zaire, the chief of the Thomani clan, strode up, brushing Ardan's side as he inspected a cluster of fresh orchids in the foyer, their petals sweet and filling the space with their aroma. His blond hair, a stark contrast to his native bronze skin, was cropped short and as fair as Nevia's.

"It's a nice place," he commented, lifting his chin and nodding toward a golden statue of a woman, eyes closed, holding an orb in her palm. Ardan didn't hold the same beliefs as the imperials, but he was wise enough to know who the statue symbolized and revered. "I never knew what it was really like in the empire."

Ardan couldn't help feeling bitter. "Understandably, considering they don't like to showcase it."

The clansfolk made their home in the mountains, not daring to migrate into imperial territory lest they were forced to veer from their way of life. The nomadic lifestyle was cherished by most of their peoples, despite its hardships and everlasting winters.

And yet, seeing such comforts, such luxuries, made Ardan partly envious. To think that Darius once claimed Nevia as his wife in these walls, hurt her, oppressed her—

It made his blood boil.

Finally the imperial guardsman returned from announcing their arrival, and at his heels Ardan caught sight of her: the lovely empress of the Androvich Empire.

She grew more beautiful than he left her, if such was possible. Her hair was styled exactly as he remembered she liked it. Her curvaceous figure was adorned in layers of fine gold, as warm as the maple leaves fluttering from the trees. Lips parted slightly, he was finally successful at snatching her ice-blue gaze for a spell, and in that moment he wanted nothing more than to sweep her into his arms and spin her around, to hold her and press a kiss to those elegantly painted lips.

And yet, he suppressed his desires. Catching the warning glare of the raven-haired guardsman at her back reminded him that they were indeed being watched.

Carefully.

Nevia, wisely, was not warm or inviting toward him. She held her hands clasped in front of her, turning her attention from Ardan onto the two other men at his side. Perhaps she had known them from the war, but Ardan realized that she probably had little in the ways of introduction at that chaotic time.

"Your Highness." Ardan gestured to his left. "This is Zaire, chief of Thomani, and—"

"Chief Johari." Nevia suddenly drew forward, beaming. At his right stood the tall chief of Katsao, his pale dreadlocks hanging loose down the full length of his back, a broad smile on his dark-tanned face. He extended a hand, and she wordlessly accepted.

Johari had been the chief of the Katsao clan for nearly two decades, long enough to have known everyone quite well in his clan, and more than long enough for Nevia to have known him, heralding from the Katsao clan before immigrating to the empire.

"Nevia, it has been so long," he murmured, stroking the top of her hand with the pad of his thumb. "How good it is to see you again after all these years."

"Likewise. I'm sorry, for having left and never coming back. I —"

"Wouldn't expect that kind of trip on the Androvich empress." His smile was genial, kind. He brought a hand to tilt her chin upward. "It is fine, my dear. It brings me joy to see Natashka and Eja's daughter well."

She swallowed hard, and Ardan didn't need confirmation to know that she was on the brink of tears. Finally she drew back from the Katsao chief and paid her respects to Zaire, before it was Ardan's turn. He straightened, and ran a hand down his woolen coat, fixing her with one of his most charismatic smiles.

Her steps were excruciatingly slow as she approached, and he feared the very real possibility of his heart leaping from his chest with as hard as it pounded against his ribcage.

She halted before him, dipping her head respectfully. "Ardan, it is so nice to see you."

Her words, voice, were music to his ears. He took her hand, bringing it to his lips to brush a kiss on her knuckles. "It's nice to see you, Empress. I've missed you so much."

Her gaze averted his, and Ardan quickly got the message. They were in a room full of imperials; he would need to be cautious. He released her hand and cleared his throat. The collar of his woolen coat suddenly felt stifling in the warmth of the palace—and perhaps the tension of the room, as well.

"I'm sure that you must all be weary after your travels," Nevia said. "But I thank you for coming, regardless."

A genial smile crossed Johari's face. "The pleasure, Your Imperial Highness, is ours."

Nevia retreated back to her bodyguard's side, head lifted regally. Ardan almost could not recognize the empress as the Zenochian woman he ventured alongside during the war all those years ago, and yet deep down he was certain it was still her—in there somewhere.

"Our council will commence once the others arrive." Nevia inclined her head in the direction of the hall whence she came. "In the meantime, I invite you to make yourselves comfortable. You need all the restoration you can get after your arduous journey from the mountains."

Something flickered in her eyes, then, and Ardan perceived it as recollection, their own journey through the mountains together perhaps a bit too fresh for comfort. Before Ardan could steal another word she was gone, the dark-haired guardsman close at her heels. He clapped her on the shoulder and began speaking to her lowly, words indecipherable in the distance.

"That's his cousin, you know," Johari uttered in Ardan's ear.

Ardan lifted a brow. "Whose cousin?"

"The emperor's. His older cousin."

"Ah."

Something burned in Ardan's chest at the revelation. Thankfully he wasn't left to linger on it long, as a young servant girl, tall and slender, bearing the characteristic Velspirian traits of dark hair and high cheekbones, approached. "If you will allow me, Chief Ardan, I will show you to your rooms."

Having taken a heartbeat too long to answer, Chief Johari answered in his stead. "Yes, please, seeing us to our rooms would be very nice. Thank you." He merely shot Ardan a look that said *What the hell is wrong with you?* and followed the servant down the hall.

Their footsteps were cloaked by the burgundy runner beneath their boots. Ardan craned his neck to gaze at the crystalline chandelier overhead, marveling at the prisms it painted along the walls. They wrapped themselves around the palace and arrived in another hall. While he should've been paying attention, should've been mapping out the hall and listening to the servant prattle off where such-and-such was located, his main thoughts resided with *her*, thinking to himself that he would have to seek her out and set things right.

If it wasn't already too late.

6
NEVIA

That evening the empress took her supper in her room, not wanting to mingle with the Zenochian chiefs. Most specifically one. Whether they missed her presence, she didn't know, but being left to her thoughts while dining on chicken and potatoes did not do much to ease her nerves.

Afterward she paced the length of her room, mind whirling endlessly before she forced herself to sit down and read in hopes of distracting herself. The effort was not successful. Her eyes skimmed the same paragraph three times before finally setting the book down. She resorted to staring into the bristling flames of her father's fireplace, thinking about what to do with Ardan.

She didn't expect her heart to skip at the sight of him that afternoon, or the butterflies to claim her stomach at his voice, the shudder that crawled up her spine as his lips caressed her knuckles. Perhaps what terrified her most of all was the realization of how much she missed him, how much she yearned to spend time with him again. To feel his touch, his passion—

A shuddered sigh escaped her lips, hating herself for thinking such things. She didn't want to desire him; it was too complicated. He was the chief of Sanen now. It was probably expected of him to take on a wife and family of his own in the clan—if he hadn't already.

The thought made her sick.

A rap at the door, loud and strong, nearly made her jump from her skin. She smoothed her hands over her hair nervously, clutching the folds of her gown to keep her fists from shaking as she rose from her seat.

"Enter."

The door creaked open, revealing perhaps the one person who was going to make the situation considerably worse.

"Nevia—erm, Your Highness." Ardan stole a glance around her sitting parlor, as if seeing if she was presently holding an audience for anyone else before he lowered his guard. "May I come in, or would it be inappropriate to have a private word with the empress before the council is held?"

Her mouth went dry. Her fingers clutched the sides of her father's armchair to keep herself stable before finally rising from her seat and gesturing for Ardan to enter, wordless.

She stood there motionless as he passed her, carrying with him the warm scent of pine and citrus. As if she were afraid to move lest her own body betray her.

Even now, without the need for false pretenses, she found herself upholding the facade of an indifferent empress.

"What can I do for you?"

She could've cursed herself for how haughty her voice sounded. The hurt that flashed in his gold-green eyes, which once claimed her broken heart and repaired her soul when it was fragmented.

"I just wanted to see you. It's been—I mean—it's been a while."

Nevia nodded, not trusting her voice again. A long silence lapsed before he closed the distance between them in three strides.

"I missed you so much, Nevia."

They were mere inches apart, then. She lowered her chin, gaze boring into the ground as her breath quickened, the laces of her bodice suddenly feeling too tight. Her thoughts flitted back to her dream and the recollection of him being someone else she, as Saava's sister, loved, but didn't return her love. Did this have anything to do with the warning the seer gave her years ago, or was this merely her imagination gone rampant?

"And I've missed you." Her words escaped as a whisper.

"Please, I can't help feeling that you're upset with me. Are you?" Ardan knelt before her, reaching for her hands. She didn't have the heart or sense to tear her grip from his. "Tell me what I did wrong. I swear I'll make amends. Was it because I failed to write to you?"

"No, don't be silly. You didn't do anything wrong." Her laugh came high, shrill, uncharacteristically so. "I've just had a lot on my mind." She fumbled for an excuse, until, finally, one resonated. "It's just, these night creatures. The damage they're wreaking. They attacked just last week, the damage pretty sustainable. No matter how hard I try, I can't stop hearing the shrieks, feeling and seeing the blood splatters on the wall and my face—"

Understanding dawned on Ardan's face then. She felt guilty for misguiding him, but she would have to embrace this falsehood; it was the easiest way to handle the situation.

For now.

"Ah, I am so sorry. You shouldn't have had to face that."

"It could've been worse." Nevia tried to shrug the caring comment off. "There could have been more deaths. We caught it in time. But it was terrifying. I stumbled upon it in the hall when I heard the warning bells go off, in my nightgown and with a single dagger. I thought I was going to die."

Ardan's lips twisted, visibly pained. Gripping her arms, he drew Nevia closer and tucked stray hairs behind her ear affectionately. "You're very brave."

"Or stupid," Nevia said with a miserable laugh. "I got quite an earful from Elante and Renault after that."

"Renault?"

"My bodyguard."

"Oh." Ardan's body relaxed, and it was obvious, at least to her, that he feared Renault was as important as Elante to her. Someone who could've replaced him in his lengthy absence from her life.

"There's no one in my life like that," Nevia found herself offering. "Like, relationship-wise. If that's what you're implying —"

"No, no, no. Nothing like that. I mean, it's none of my business—"

Nevia arched a brow. "It isn't?"

A nervous laugh escaped his throat as he scratched the back of his neck. "I mean, okay, you caught me. I *was* wondering if, after all these years, you *did* find someone else, and for that I couldn't blame you. But I'm not going to lie: I would've hated him."

Nevia couldn't help herself from smirking at the thought of Ardan being jealous. So his feelings for remained her. "But what about you?" she dared to venture. He tilted his head in confusion, so she chose to elaborate. "I don't suppose you've settled with a wife and child of your own yet?"

He held up his hands. "Busted."

Her heart nearly floored, before he burst out laughing and brought her into a crushing hug against his chest. "Just kidding! After what I told you on the Feishin docks that day, do you really think there could be anyone else for me except you?"

She shoved him away, scowling, yet she couldn't keep the smile from her face for long. "You shouldn't tease me like that! I seriously thought you were married!"

"But I can't help it! You should see your face when you're flustered."

Briefly Nevia's thoughts fled to tossing the nearby throw-pillow at him, but instead she chose to lean in and clamp her mouth to his, pulling his strong, lithe body close against her curvaceous one. In response he held her tighter, tongue running along her lower lip, as if seeking entrance, which she easily granted.

Soon her back was pressed to the door, her arms wrapped around Ardan's neck. It had been so very long since she had known passion. She'd dreamt of these moments, fantasized their bodies entwined as one, the taste of his lips, the feel of his touch. Many flirted with the widowed empress, some going so far as blatantly offering to warm her bed, but she refused their company. It was simple to turn suitors down under the guise of mourning and wishing a life of celibacy after the emperor's death, but a part of her was holding out for him. Ardan. She wanted him. Wanted *more* of him. And yet, she was afraid to ask for or receive it. Even after all these years.

If it wasn't for the damn prophecy, and that obnoxious dream.

Her thoughts started to mute, however, as his hand wound around her waist, teasing at the laces of her bodice before grasping at the curve of her rear. She gasped, his touch igniting an all-consuming fire within her. She ran her fingers through his hair, interlocking them at his roots and giving a gentle tug. He moaned against her lips, arching his body over her and bracing his weight with an arm over her head pressed against the door.

This moment. She craved it. And again, she wanted more.

A knock at her back gave them a start, causing them to tear away from each other. They both locked eyes. Nevia would've laughed at the ridiculousness of it, had the voice on the other side not expressed such urgency.

"Empress, you must evacuate! The night creatures have attacked again, and there's six of them!"

7
ARDAN

Ardan's heart was still pounding from the ecstasy of Nevia's touch and pounded faster still at the news. More night creatures? Now? Eyes wide, he turned to Nevia. All the color that had risen to her face from their antics had faded, leaving her as pale as a ghost. Ardan shifted so that he was no longer pinning her in place, and it took her squirming to finally cause him to lower his arm.

"Where are they coming from?" Her tone was authoritative, commanding, the woman he loved slipping into the mask of the empress again. While the stark difference in her personas could be considered alarming, he knew deep down it was still her, withholding the same core beliefs and morals that comprised her.

Nevia cracked open the door to find the armored soldier who cried the alarm, face drawn, eyes wary. His black hair was cropped to his chin, burgundy uniform slightly different from the rest, with a black cape draped over one shoulder. Ardan easily recognized him as Renault. His mind again settled into a distinct impression of distaste—and he considered himself having a good judge of character.

"We're holding them at the gates," Renault said, words rushed. "They're not in the palace, but it's only a matter of time."

A frown furrowed Ardan's brow. "They are not just flying over your guardsmen?"

The man directed his attention to Ardan, his gaze flickering a moment too long on his lips. Was it evident what Nevia and he had been doing?

"No, these are different than any we've been attacked by. Much larger. At least they haven't demonstrated the ability to fly yet."

Panic clawed its way up Ardan's throat. He lifted his chin in defiance, a mock act of bravery. "I will join the fight."

"No!" Nevia clasped his wrist, her reaction surprising both men. "You mustn't. You could die."

"And your men won't?"

He hated himself after he spoke the words, calling out her affection in front of her guard. Why else would she prioritize his life over that of her men, if not out of personal concern?

The guardsman leaned casually in the doorframe, throwing Nevia a cool stare. "We have the situation under control," he supplied. "Or, at least for now. We are readying the ballistae as we speak, but it's going to take some time. We do not want to jeopardize your safety. You must go to the place we've arranged for such assaults post haste, Empress."

"But, my subjects, the council, Elante"—she turned a pleading face toward the man, who merely folded his arms over his broad chest and scowled down at her—"you can't ask me to leave them all, Renault."

"You would serve no purpose in dying here, and I will send your handmaiden right behind you, if it is any comfort." A tenderness fell over his features then, locks of raven hair framing his face. His gaze lingered on the lines of her face. "Please, Empress. We already lost Darius. Don't make us go through such a loss again. I cannot lose you, too."

A guilt trip, and yet a successful one. His resolve was unwavering. Nevia looked as though stricken, but smoothed her palms over her embroidered dress and calmly looked at her worried subject. "Fine, but be safe. Take those monstrosities down."

He bowed, shot one final glance at Ardan, and stole away from the hall. Ardan watched his back disappear behind the corner and looked out into the hall to see if other traces of life—friend or foe—were present. When assured the coast was clear he stepped out into the hall, the empress at his heels.

"So, evacuate, but to where?" he wondered aloud, but Nevia was already grabbing his hand, dragging him further down the hall and around the corner, past dozens of closed doors and polished suits of armor.

"There's catacombs below the palace," Nevia rasped. "We're going down there."

Catacombs. That certainly sounded ominous, but Ardan said nothing and kept pace with the empress, stealing his way down plush burgundy carpets and past frantic souls. At last they halted before a set of stone statues resting along either side of a tapestry depicting Darius' father. Ardan would've been challenged to have not known Emperor Rufus' face, the founder of the Androvich Empire. His name and likeness stretched as far north as Zenoch.

Nevia wrenched his portrait aside, exposing a bland stone wall. She shoved three stones in a sequence, seemingly solid, uniform, and unmovable, and watched as the stone wall swung inward to unveil a stairwell with the groans of gears.

It led down into the dark depths of the palace, must permeating the air in cloying waves. Ardan's face must've shown his apprehension. Nevia snatched up one of his hands, shoved a kerosene lantern into it, and led him below.

The air grew colder the further they descended into the catacombs. Thick layers of a slimy green algae coated the stone walls, reflecting the light from the lanterns in their hands. The staircase, slippery with the same damp ooze, continued to sweep downward in sets of landings and stairs into the unending darkness.

Finally Ardan's ears picked up the sound of trickling water, and after another dozen steps they came to a finality. Lifting his lantern, he found skulls lining the walls, with niches further along the way providing a resting place for the fallen. Both marked and unmarked tombs lay spread within the cavity, the tunnels looking as if they went on infinitely. He wondered to himself how far the catacombs went.

He lowered himself to the bottom step, bracing his elbows on his knees. "We can wait here for your handmaiden, if you want," Ardan offered.

All the composure she had carefully knit together vanished then, as she dropped to Ardan's side and buried her face into her forearm. She let out a quivering sigh.

"I just don't understand. Why do they attack? Where are they coming from?" She lifted a tear-stained face to him, eyes glassy and wide. "Was this because of what we did, all those years ago?"

Ardan scooped Nevia off the cold stone floor and into his lap, holding her tight out of love and empathy. She had suffered so much, and had been so strong. Now the rest of her loved ones were being threatened, never knowing which night would be the one they would awaken to more deaths.

"I don't know," he admitted. "One day I hope we will. But for now we just have to do what we are doing: fight these monstrosities off whenever they come, and pray to whatever deities you worship that we kill the last one eventually."

Before they kill all of us, he added in his mind, not allowing the negativity to escape his lips.

They held one another mutely, with only the dripping of water breaking the eerie silence for what seemed like an eternity. Tiredness started to claim Ardan, and he felt that he could've succumbed to sleep in the arms of his beloved, the two resting against the stairwell. He repositioned himself, shifting his leg beneath them to stave off the painful tingling in his right foot. Nevia's head lolled against his chest, and it was then he realized that she had fallen asleep.

She looked so angelic there, he could not help thinking, with soft, loose curls framing her peaceful visage. He pressed a kiss to the top of her head before tucking it under his chin. How he loved her, and was determined that he would never *ever* let her go.

8

NEVIA

To say that Nevia was confused would have been understating. Where was she? Where was Ardan? Instead she was in the gardens, enjoying a pleasant, sunny, cloudless day instead of within the depths of the underground. No breeze rustled her platinum waves, and the warmth of autumn's colors painted no tree on either side of her. It also wasn't her garden, and yet she knew it somehow was.

In her lap was the flute made from cocuswood, the one she had procured from a Zenochian merchant at the Saavis festival four years ago. She blinked, surprised to find it was unscathed, as if it had not fallen from her window and broken in two shortly after its purchase. Wrapping it in both hands, she slowly rose from her seat on the stone bench, brushing through tight rows of beauteous rosebushes and sweet alyssums to find her way to the steps of an expansive palace, its splendor making Velspire's own palace pale in comparison.

She remembered, then, that she had been waiting for her sister to accompany her. They were going to play music together: her the flute while her sister strummed her harp. After waiting ages, she never arrived. It seemed reasonable, then, that she should go check on her.

She followed familiar twists of halls, knowing the faces of the servants she passed; men and women all dressed in finery and all with ears stretching thin and hair worn long. When she passed the expansive ballroom, its midnight curtains drawn closed, her mind sharpened with recollection. She *had* been here before. Or, at least in the form of a dream.

Panic clawed its way up Nevia's throat. She was back, in the mystical world of her dreams—yet it was so real. Everything was so real.

Her feet propelled her forward, guiding her up to the second story and halting before an oaken door sweeping up to the ceiling. Hand-painted murals adorned the wood surface: forests filled with woodland creatures and Saava, dancing in a circle amongst them. It took little imagination to discern who created it.

Just as Nevia was about to knock and announce herself she heard moaning and heavy breathing from the other side. Nevia's fists balled at her sides. She suspected what was happening long before she eased the door open. The sight made her blood run cold, catching her sister in the heat of the moment.

Saava was on her enormous canopied bed, back to the door, and through the drawn sheer curtains Nevia could tell that her sister was naked. She sat mounted on another, engaged in a rather intimate moment with her companion. So engaged in their activity, neither noticed they had company, and Nevia was able to take two steps into the room and slam the door so hard it shook the walls.

Saava gasped and immediately leapt up, sweeping to the side and grasping for the covers. Nevia saw him then. His face. *Ardan's* face. She watched him try to conceal his nakedness, but it was far too late. The damage had been done.

"Is this how you celebrate the eve of our wedding?" she demanded of him, shooting a fiery glare. His hazel eyes lowered in shame, too stunned to move from the bedcovers that he seemed desirous to disappear within. "With my *sister?!*"

"Sister, please."

Nevia turned to Saava. Her rosy lips were full and pleading, eyes wide behind raven sheets of silky locks framing her face and brimming with tears. "Please understand. We were in love before Father announced your engagement. We've tried—we've tried to end things, but it isn't that simple."

Nevia, livid, drew a step forward, rage so strong it seemed ripe to tear Saava apart.

"If anyone is to blame, it is I," said her fiancé, lifting a hand as a shield. "Sable, I am so sorry. You have my utmost respect and I will do everything to cherish you as my wife, but"—he turned his gaze unto Saava, a look so full of passion and love it made Nevia ill—"Saava claimed my heart, and I can never take back what is hers. Please, forgive me."

Nevia swallowed, shaking with fury. She couldn't speak, couldn't form words. Ardan once gave that look to *her*. It belonged to her. All of it. Not Saava.

She knew they had been prior lovers. Saava would regularly sneak off, bring in a . . . guest. She saw them together, but she expected Saava to step down and fade into the shadows like she always did. She loved taunting them. She loved seeing the pain in their eyes that she got what Saava desired, as she always did because she was the favorite of Aeterna.

But this broke the mold of her ire. And she hated it.

"You have no right to speak to me," Nevia seethed, glaring first at Ardan's double before whirling on Saava. "And you—"

She took quick strides to Saava and threw forward her hands. Forceful bonds of black smoky tendrils snaked from Nevia's palms and encircled Saava's wrists, waist, and throat. Panic filled Saava as she became enervated, pallid, corporeal, as visibly weak as her pitiful domain of power. Her eyes imploringly searched Nevia as her lover begged for sanction. But instead of eliciting pity, his begging fed her glee. Nevia smiled wide.

When the color faded from Saava's face, the energy of her form flowing off in waves, Nevia let her magic falter. Saava collapsed back onto the bed, her face as pale as the death magic that she was exposed to. Her lover braced her upright, as Saava was too withered to hold her composure and poise, his shoulders slumped in defeat.

Nevia watched this touching scene unfold, and it surprised her to find tears dampening her cheeks. She forced them away as she spoke, voice cracking. A show of weakness.

"You will pay for this, Little Sister."

Nevia then fled the room, storming off at a furious pace so that none would catch her crying miserably. Safely tucked away in the confines and sanctuary of her own estate, she did so unconstrained.

The Goddess of Death—so beautiful, so venerated, and yet could never really, truly be loved.

9
ARDAN

Ardan swore under his breath as he tried to steady Nevia during her convulsions. He gripped her shoulders and called her name, but she didn't come to. Her eyes were white, rolled back in her head. Wherever she was, her mind was locked away, inaccessible through the curtain of unconsciousness separating them.

He slid his arms beneath her knees and neck, effortlessly scooping her to his chest as he rose to standing. Her head lolled, an arm falling loose and dangling. He began to panic, throwing a glance in the direction of the stairs they came from. Would it be sensible to go back up to get some help? It did not seem normal for her to enter such a state in her sleep, and it was odd that he could not bring her back to her senses.

He hadn't climbed more than a handful of steps before life finally started to stir in his arms, the godsend Ardan yearned for. He lowered the empress and himself back onto the ground, his back propped against the slimy wall notched with skulls as he gingerly brushed Nevia's hair from her face.

The empress' eyes snapped wide, and just as suddenly she leapt back from him. She slunk into the opposite corner, watching him with wide, fearful eyes. Ardan voluntarily stepped back to ease her tension, yet was taken aback by her reaction.

"Nevia," he intoned, carefully extending a hand tentatively out to her. "It's okay. It's just me, Ardan. I love you. You're safe."

A shadow of doubt passed over her face. She drew in a long, deep breath, breaking her stare to take in their surroundings. The stone column at Ardan's back, the staircase leading back up to the palace. Finally she met his gaze again, and this time there was faint recognition.

"Ardan." She tested his name on her tongue, hesitantly, weakly. He nodded in response, unable to contain himself by scooting over to her and snatching up her hands in his own. Hers were cold.

"Yes," he confirmed, and he watched her body relax. "You were asleep for some time and started shaking so hard. I thought I was going to lose you."

His relief was insurmountable. In that moment he wanted to kiss her, to pin her to his chest, to celebrate that she lived, and yet before he could act on any of those impulses she withdrew from his grasp and rose, bracing a hand on Saava's stone back to steady herself.

"Where are we now?"

"Still in the catacombs. We're waiting here until it's safe to go back up from the night creature's attack."

She frowned, still seeming distant and on edge.

Ardan slowly rose to stand, coaxing Nevia to follow. "Perhaps a little walk will refreshen you," he offered. "If nothing else it will help to pass the time while we wait."

He was rather curious to examine the tombs that went further into the catacombs, and, seeing as it was mostly a long, narrow tunnel, he felt the risk of getting lost was minimal. He started to move, and eventually, slowly, Nevia followed, still seeming quite distraught. A shudder racked her frame, as if chilled. Ardan had naught to offer but the clothes on his back and his own warmth. Eventually he chose to settle for the latter, reaching over and wrapping an arm around her shoulders. She tensed at his touch.

"Is this okay?" he asked.

"Of course it is," Nevia replied, voice tight.

"Then what's wrong?"

She drew in a sharp breath, but did not initially respond. Ardan continued to wait, their footfalls and the occasional drip-drop from a water vein being the only sounds to pierce the monotonous silence, yet she did not offer anything until they rounded a corner at the very end of the corridor.

"Does the name Niall mean anything to you?"

Ardan turned a curious glance at Nevia, still tucked in at his side. "Should it?"

"I had a vision that your name was Niall." Her voice came out curt, terse. "And you were cheating on me with my sister."

At this confession Ardan stopped walking, his arm falling from Nevia's shoulders. "I didn't know you had a sister."

"No, I don't."

"Then why do you think I would cheat on you with your imaginary sister? You really think me that unfaithful, after our conversation back in your room?"

"No! No, it's not that—"

"Then why are we even having this conversation?" He didn't even try to mask the hurt from his tone. To think this was why she had been treating him so coldly throughout their entire walk. It was unfair for her to hold him accountable when the reason was nonsense. "Are you implying that I'm someone else? That I've been lying to you?"

"Why are you so defensive and accusatory?!" Nevia's voice rose an octave as she threw her arms in the air. "I'm trying to be honest with you, and you're jumping down my throat."

Ardan let out a dry laugh devoid of humor. "No, Nevia. You stealthily tried to find out if I have a secret identity because you think I'm capable of cheating on you. If you're so worried, why not come out and say it? Don't play games. Is this what it's been about all along? Is that why you've been treating me so coldly?"

"No! I was told not to trust you."

His blood turned to thick, cold sludge in his veins. "You were told not to trust me." His throat was painfully tight, the acrid air, once breathable, feeling as though it would suffocate him. "By whom?"

"It doesn't matter," Nevia said dismissively. "I was just warned of this, and then I started having these visions."

It felt as though Nevia ripped his heart clean from his chest and stomped on it. Mouth agape, he stared at her, and, when her gaze met his, pain laced with guilt was visible.

"I know you've been through a lot," he said, tone terse but as pleasant as he could manage. "You were mistreated by that monster of a man who was once your husband, and for that I am horribly, terribly sorry. But, Nevia, I can't pay for his crimes. It isn't fair to me."

Nevia tossed her hair over her shoulder, clearly irritated. "I'm not trying to make you pay for *his* mistakes. I'm just trying to say there's something wrong with our relationship, and I need to find out what it is before we go any further."

He sucked in a breath. He saw this coming, but it didn't make the news any easier to swallow. He looked at her with a heavy heart. "The problem is that you don't trust me. You're willing to sow doubt between us when there is nothing there. I love you, Nevia, and I think I have only treated you with respect. If I haven't, I'm sorry."

Her gaze faltered, confidence wavering. "No, you have."

"But it seems that maybe I was mistaken in thinking that we were in the same place with our feelings," he continued.

"That's not exactly true," she half-whispered.

They returned to the bottom of the stairs, though this time he didn't offer his hand, or even glance back. "Then I think, as you said, you need to sort out what is wrong with our relationship. From my perspective, it is simply a matter of trust. Which I do understand to a point. After everything you've been through, how can you trust again?"

A wet rush of warmth descended upon his eyes as tears threatened to build, but he wouldn't allow them. To display such desperation in front of Nevia would be unfair to her. Nevia, however, didn't hold the same hesitation. He heard her sniffles at his back, and while it shattered his heart he didn't know what to say. She accused him wrongfully, and he was hurt. Very hurt. Even if he could understand what she went through that made her doubt, it was not his guilt or blame to bear.

Up ahead in the darkness they heard shuffling, and a single pebble bounce off stone.

They were not alone.

Ardan threw out an arm to halt Nevia's progression. "Hello?" he called out.

"Someone there?!" A feminine voice echoed against the stone from a distance, causing Nevia to forcibly lower Ardan's arm and rush around him.

"Elante!"

Ah, of course; this must've been the handmaiden that he had heard so much of. He approached at a steady gait, footsteps echoing off the stone walls, feeling like an outsider intruding upon their tender moment. The two women turned to face Ardan, the handmaiden's smile wider.

"So this must be Ardan." Elante's lips turned upward further in mischief.

"And you must be the infamous lady-in-waiting, Elante," Ardan greeted in return, merely dipping his head, no longer having the energy or heart to indulge her after their quarrel, which caused the young woman to bubble in warm giggles. Nevia pressed her lips together, seeming entirely unamused as she gingerly grasped the upper arm of the young woman.

"We should head back before others worry about us even more," Nevia said.

A frown furrowed Elante's brow, perhaps catching a whiff of the tension in the air. "Are you both okay? Did something happen down here?"

Ardan and Nevia shared a dark look.

"It's a long story," Nevia confessed. "Let's just go back. I need to assess the damages of the assault."

Compassion softened his heart marginally as he realized the empress had much more to worry about than her love life in that moment. Another night creature attack, in such quick succession of the last one. He attempted to convey as much, but she refused to look his way. Dejected, wounded, and still confounded over what had occurred, Ardan followed along in their shadow to the palace's surface to see what was left of it.

10
NEVIA

The burgundy rug outside the council room was becoming more threadbare as Nevia paced along it. She heard voices, loud and angry, on the other side of the doors, and she dreaded bearing the brunt of their ire the moment she entered the room. They would have questions, and she no answers. Anger began to rise too in her. There were so many answers that *she* wanted to demand, yet there was no one to demand them from.

With one final sharp intake of breath, Nevia wrapped her hands around the cool brass handles, pressed down, and swung open the doors in one fluid motion.

Brilliant light greeted her, along with the many dozen faces lining either side of the council table. A hush fell over the room as she entered, and quietly, carefully, Nevia tread to her place at the head of the gathering, raising herself on her toes as she crossed the tiled floor in attempt to keep her heels from clicking and not draw even more attention to herself.

"Ah, Your Imperial Highness, perfect timing," Prometheus, her grand advisor, greeted. He rose, offering to clasp her hand briefly before he resumed his seat at her side. "Young Xander here was just suggesting we halt the distribution of Nephyl in the event that it's correlated to the assaults, but the king has dismissed the idea."

Starting the council with a bang. She should've expected no less. Nevia folded her hands neatly in front of her, the many rings adorning her fingers glinting from the overhead chandelier. It had been several days since the second night creature attack on Velspire, and they all had been sitting on pins and needles waiting for the next.

At her immediate left sat Qirin, King of Feishin, his golden hairpin a stark contrast to the raven locks being held in place, his hands clenched into fists on the table. "Like I said, my country relies on its mining and distributing of core shards, and I will not halt production on a mere assumption," he stated.

A frown pinched Nevia's brow as she turned sharply to face a dark-haired young man down the length of the table. "And may I ask why you're here today, Xander? I strictly recall this meeting being by invitation only."

She did not invite him. He was neither one of the Five Lords nor a world leader. He was a figurehead, someone that became the face of rebellion that defied Nevia's rule. Most specifically, their qualm lay on her latest acceptance of magic and the distribution of Nephyl. Unlike Darius, who had been eager for the resource, Xander felt it had no place in their society and it was cursed. Trouble followed the core shards, he had argued, and when they started arriving in bundles from Feishin shores the rumor was spread that Nevia was a witch seeking the shards for her own purpose. The notion was absurd and most dismissed it as such. However, there was the unspoken rule that there is always traction for the absurd.

Worse yet, Xander's father was one of the wealthiest men in Ivalia, as well as a personal friend to the late Emperor Rufus. The Bakalov name held far more sway than the Byllily-Androvich one, especially when it came to select groups who decided to wreak havoc in Xander's name on the basis of his claims.

Xander Bakalov sat primly with his hands folded upon the table. "I was invited by him."

All eyes fell in the direction that Xander jerked his head, at a man who was fiddling with his pocket watch and paying little attention to the conversation. When he noticed all eyes were on him, however, he straightened, offering Nevia a salute. "Empress!" he cried, rising from his seat.

Nevia bit her lip, suddenly wary, as he made his way around the table, arms open wide.

"Oh, it is just so good to see you!"

He crushed her in a hug which threatened to close her windpipe. Nevia returned the embrace with an awkward pat on the back, hoping he would release her so that she could breathe again. When he pulled away he held her at arm's length and threw her a lopsided smile. "You haven't aged a day! Looks like the low-stress environment without that old dingbat has suited you well, eh?"

A throat cleared, loud and sharp across the table. A middle-aged man sporting long, silky auburn hair was rapping his fingertips on the tablecloth, eyes narrowing to slits. "Vladios." His tone held a warning, but also tiredness.

Nevia smiled shyly in the direction of the lord towering over her. If it were any other lord she would have shrugged him off, but this was not just any. It was Lord Vladios of Malabria, one of the few that had been kind to her when all the others mocked her, and the man she owed much to in the war when he turned against Darius to support her.

Vladios offered her a wink before sauntering back to his spot, wedged between the auburn-haired man and another lord.

It became clear, then, how Xander was invited. If Vladios' mannerisms were any indication, he had been drinking, and heavily, at that. He was a laughing stock to many, and it was little wonder why. She wished he would drink within reason, if not for his health than his reputation.

"Anyway," Nevia murmured, tearing her attention from the drunken lord and back onto Xander. "It's probably best you're here, as I have it on my agenda to discuss the development of the rebels."

An amused smile twisted Xander's lips as a brow shot upward. "Rebels? What rebels?"

The empress nearly reached across the table to throttle him. "Groups of nincompoops who start riots in your name, demanding that I surrender my throne to Renault because he is the last living Androvich and that I'm profiting by sitting here." Her words came out forced, but she didn't care. She was angry, and he deserved to be on the receiving end of it.

Xander flicked the curls on his neck away from his mandarin collar. "Well, I certainly didn't appoint them. Don't know why they're doing that in my name."

Nevia grit her teeth, and was almost ready to say more before a steady hand fell on her shoulder. Silencing her, comforting her. Nevia glanced to her left to find her personal guard, Renault, whom she almost forgot was there until then. He subtly shook his head. *A battle for another time,* he mutely suggested, seeing the challenge in the way his dark eyes narrowed on Xander. This battle wasn't over, even if the conversation was. Which it certainly seemed that way.

She lifted her gaze to the auburn-haired man: Lord Torquil of the province of Asturia. He sat back in his chair, face pensive. The three years post-war had treated him kindly. His once chronic dark circles were gone, likely from no longer losing sleep over his daughter, a seer, possibly being burnt at the stake if discovered by authorities—one of the many promises Nevia made when accepting her role.

The other four of the Five Lords of the Androvich Empire sat on either side of Torquil, men that had been in power far longer than herself. Save for one.

The newly appointed Lady of Ivalia tilted her head as Nevia's gaze fell on her. First female to ever rule one of the provinces, and the second female in power in Danaeca, only second to Nevia herself. Lady Galina turned, offering Nevia a warm smile before speaking up, arresting the attention of all present.

"Regardless"—her tone was deep, commanding silence—"I think we can all agree here that the night creatures are a problem, and they need to be stopped. In my opinion, if Nephyl is indeed involved, we should suspend its distribution and use immediately."

Qirin cleared his throat. "If that is true, then why weren't these attacks occurring before? We Feishins have been harvesting Nephyl for decades, and no one saw a night creature until last year. I object to the idea of Nephyl being behind it—"

"Even if you have tripled the production since you claimed the throne?" Xander countered.

An uncomfortable silence yawned over the council chamber. Nevia swallowed, looking over the sea of faces, leaders who turned to her for an ultimate decree.

"There's so much that we don't yet understand," Nevia said in answer. "There might be much more to all of this than we know."

"I can agree on that point." Qirin tilted his head. "So we can dismiss this and move on?"

"Well, I have concerns about that," Prometheus spoke, pushing spectacles up the bridge of his long, gnarled nose. "The night creatures have only been discovered last year, their purpose unknown. It coincided with the development of our Nephyl-powered energy generator, so in theory it could very well be the core shards attracting the creatures, as our young friend pointed out."

Ardan frowned. "Could halting the mining and distribution of core shards stop spawning the creatures?"

"Perhaps," Nevia said. "But they aren't only attracted to the core shards, as they're attacking Zenoch that isn't even using them, right?"

"Well, we have some," Ardan responded. "But they aren't commonly used, no. Mostly for heat."

"I don't think we should simply stop producing core shards if we don't know for certain that they're the source of the problem," Vladios piped up. "Technology has made leaps and bounds thanks to them. Ending their production now on a baseless theory would be an utter disgrace."

Tension ran thick. She opened her mouth to retort, but the lord of Asturia beat her to it. "You have to understand these are desperate times." His lips turned downward in disapproval. "People are dying. Our military forces cannot withstand a weekly assault. Who knows what else could happen if we continue allowing the core shards to be harvested and distributed? We cannot rule out the possibility of discontinuing their use for a spell and see if the night creatures abate."

A deep sigh heaved from Nevia's chest. Such considerations, such heavy burdens, and everyone looked to Nevia to make the final call. She dipped her head. "We need to increase security, especially at night."

"With all due respect, Empress," Renault muttered softly. "The last attack wiped out some of our specialized units. We don't"—his face reddened—"we don't actually have the numbers to increase security."

Silence fell again, with the exception of the scuffling of a chair's legs against the tiled floor. Either no one had any suggestions, or no one felt it was their place to offer them.

"What about—" Vladios started, but then stopped, as if thinking better on it.

It went on like this for some time, tit for tat, arguments, prattle and fruitless suggestions without end, until Ardan cleared his throat. "We have extra guardsmen up north. Let us help you."

Nevia's face turned red in shame. Ardan, of all people to offer help. Ardan, whom she'd hurt, whom she couldn't bring herself to meet eyes with. "No, you don't have to do that. You need to protect your own—"

"The creatures don't bother us much," Ardan interjected. "And we have the other clans to rely on if we need anything.

Combining our efforts, I'm sure we can provide a small aid to the empire."

Eyes turned to Nevia, awaiting her verdict. Finally she relented. "Only a few."

Ardan nodded curtly, then sat back, leaning casually in his seat as he allowed the rest of the conversation to flow. Nevia couldn't help feeling he was probably trying to win something, gain her favor somehow. *Or maybe he's just genuinely a nice guy and I'm being too harsh on him,* Nevia chided inwardly. "And as I stated previously"—she locked eyes with Qirin as she spoke—"we need to halt the distribution of core shards until this matter resolves."

Qirin's fists fled the table and into his lap, his jaw clenched tight as he turned his face away.

"In the meantime," she continued, ignoring the sulking king, "I ask you all to please be patient, and do be careful. Let's lay low on the core shards for now, increase nightly watches, and see how that goes."

"I've been enforcing a curfew in Asturia," Torquil supplied. "That has helped with civilian casualties, even if it hasn't decreased assaults. Perhaps that is something that would assist you here?"

"Yes, that is a wonderful idea," Renault piped. "Dusk to dawn. That should at least keep the civilians off the streets and safely in their homes."

Nevia was shaking her head before he even finished speaking. "They entered our own palace, Renault. Do you think they will not seek people from their homes if there's no one on the streets?"

"Guardsmen will be on the streets," Renault said. "Replacing civilians. Guardsmen that are prepared to take on an assault of night creatures."

"We should also ready the cannons," Prometheus supplied. "They could be useful."

Nevia bit her lip, hating the idea. It reminded her too much of warfare, but nodded in agreement to his plan nonetheless. They were, after all, at war again, only this time unified against monsters of the night.

The Feishin king was the first to shove his chair back, placing his palms on the table as he rose. "Well, it sounds like we have a plan. If we are quite finished, I believe I will be seeking some fresh air."

"As will I," Xander added.

And like that, the council was seeing themselves out, not seeking or awaiting dismissal from their empress. She watched them go, and didn't begin to rise herself until she saw Ardan shuffle toward the door, his lithe physique a stark contrast to shorter, stockier frames of imperials surrounding him.

Nevia ran her tongue along her lips, finding them dry. She had to talk to him and set things right. The vision was undoubtedly confusing, and she still did not know how to process the revelations of the perceived past and present, but there was no sense in maintaining such tension between them. Especially if he was going to be supplying her with additional forces, and if she would be seeing more of him during his stay.

Hands clenched, she steeled her nerves and began to stride over to him when her bodyguard skirted around her. He stepped directly in her path, a warm smile etched on his genial face.

"Well done, Empress. A very motivating conversation."

Nevia bit her lip, dubious. "Was it?"

His hand fled to rest on the hilt of his sword as a soft chuckle escaped his lips. "But of course. I've never seen the Feishin king so eager to dismiss himself, and the lords were quite agreeable with you. You've grown since you've taken up the mantle of the empire, all on your own. I'm very proud of you."

Heart skipping, she lifted her pale eyes to meet his, dark and entrancing in contrast. Comforting, familiar. He bore all the salient characteristics of his cousin—dark hair, chocolate eyes, the olive skin and pronounced cheekbones. She swallowed. "Thank you, Renault. That means more than I can say."

He leaned in and, to her surprise, brushed a curl from her face, knuckles barely grazing the tender flesh of her cheekbone. "It is the very least that I can do for the empress I would give my life for."

The air seemed to grow thicker, more challenging to breathe, and suddenly Nevia felt the room sway. She placed a hand on his arm to steady herself, his muscles taut beneath her fingers. A frown furrowed his brow as he reached over to feel her forehead and then rested it at the tender spot between neck and shoulder. "Empress, are you unwell?"

"I just need air," she rasped, releasing his arms and removing herself from their interlocked stance. "My apologies. I suppose this hit more nerves than I thought."

A bushy brow arched. "This?"

Nevia, frazzled, tossed a hand to gesture around. "This. All of this. The council. The discussion. The promise of more death coming our way."

A dark look flickered across his face. Was it disappointment? "Yes, yes, of course. It is certainly a heavy topic. Shall I escort you to the gardens so that you may enjoy some time in the fresh air?"

The thought made her heart pound harder, and she found herself frantically shaking her head. "No, it's quite alright; I can see myself there, thank you."

With that she marched around him and led herself out, accompanied by the harsh clicks of her high-heeled boots and tumultuous thoughts.

11
QIRIN

The council fell flat on its face, in Qirin's opinion. No truths were unveiled, only speculation, and worse yet he was ordered to halt the distribution of core shards without any compensation. It frustrated him, especially since the night creature assaults should not lay on the Feishin Kingdom. After all, they had been using Nephyl for years without issue. A night creature had never been observed or idealized except in myths and tall tales passed down by generations of mouths and ink-stained hands. Never present, never a threat.

There was much for the young Feishin king to be angry about. This was merely another burden that would rest on his shoulders alone to resolve.

Pleasantly crisp autumn air greeted him as he exited the confines of the palace, too restricted and claustrophobic for his liking. Sculpted shrubbery lined the brick pathway leading him to a marble fountain in the center of the clearing twice the size of any person. There he stood, listening to the babbling water as it spouted from their goddess' open palm and cascaded into the pool below. Coins littered the inside of the fountain. The tradition of wish-making was not lost to him, yet Qirin scoffed at the foolish notion.

It was there that Qirin saw him, approaching the fountain from the opposite side. His smile, tentative yet sincere, was warming. His footsteps were muted over the short blades of grass.

"Your Highness." Rito bowed in greeting, dark hair sweeping over his shoulder. "I didn't expect to find you out here."

Qirin rushed toward him, his black kimono catching in the wind. "Nor I, but it is quite the pleasant surprise. Is it not?"

Rito brightened, cheeks reddening. "It certainly is." He tilted his head, dark braid swishing behind his back. "Did you come to wish, too?"

A scoff escaped Qirin before he could rein it in. A sideways glance at Rito's wistful face made him realize that he was serious, forcing him to bite his cheek to keep himself in check. "Wish?"

"Sure." The young guard thrust his hand into his pocket, procuring two gold coins in the Feishin currency. "It's a Velspirian tradition, apparently."

A laugh escaped Qirin, a true, genuine laugh. He tilted his face to the heavens, his face bathed in the pale light of the two moons. "Gods, I missed you, Rito."

A chuckle escaped his friend, then, giving him a wink before flipping a coin. The two men side by side, an arm wrapped around one another, watched it flip through the air, only to land in the water with a *plink!* Qirin braced his hands on the stone edge as he leaned in precariously close. "So, what did you wish for?"

Rito strode toward the fountain, watching the gentle splashes briefly before running his fingers through the clear surface of the water. "I can't tell you or it won't come true."

"You and your secrets."

At this Rito arched a brow, only moments before flicking water into the Feishin king's face, making him scowl and swat at him. Soon they both were laughing, and for one solitary moment Qirin nearly forgot about his life back at home. The duties, demands, the abhorrent situation he found himself in. When the memories resurfaced he let out a heady sigh, gaze darkening.

"You know something, Rito?"

The guard lifted his head, his reflection rippling in the water behind them.

"I hate that I'm king."

A sorrowful expression clouded the otherwise jubilant young man, his gaze shifting to the ground, thoughtful. "You're a great king. You've brought your people leagues from where your mother left them in just a few short years."

Qirin huffed, folding his arms in his bell sleeves. "That was all Lady Rumaar's doing. Without her I am nothing."

Rito sprang up from his seat, striding over to stand in front of his dear friend. "You've always strived for perfection. It's what I've always loved about you. Perhaps, though, you could try accepting things as they are more often, and not always strive for that level of perfection so unattainable."

At this Qirin's nostrils flared. "If I settle for less I'll be dethroned. I can't afford to be anything less than what I am."

"You know I wouldn't let that happen."

The gentleness of his words, the tone of his voice—Qirin didn't know what overcame him when he crossed the distance between them, cupped Rito's round face in his cold hands, and pressed a kiss to his lips. There was an urgency in it, much unlike the tender kisses they once shared in private before he rose to the throne. Rito softly returned the affection after some initial hesitance, wrapping his arms around Qirin's waist and drawing him closer. When Qirin's tongue stroked at his bottom lip, seeking entrance, Rito granted it. The taste of his true soul mate, his first and only love. Qirin's hands left Rito's face as they entwined in his hair.

Time seemed to stop, and yet had continued on. Their kisses were the familiarity that Qirin sought for ages, yet had been entirely unattainable. Living a lie, living with her—it was intolerable. To pretend to love his queen, to not see Rito standing there, so close and yet so far. It had become torture, and no longer could he encage his feelings for the man he so desperately loved. Yearned for.

"Qirin?!"

The shrill voice of the empress rang out into the garden, much to Qirin's annoyance. He would've been delighted to ignore her, but Rito was not as belligerent. The servant tore himself away from his king before sweeping into a deep bow. "Empress."

Qirin rolled his eyes, annoyed by Rito's subservience, and turned. Her look of abject horror, posture slumped, mouth agape —all further drew out his irritation.

"Yes?" Qirin hummed. "Can I do something for you?"

"What were you—how could you—" Her eyes fluttered closed, brows knitting together as if in pain. When she opened her eyes they were ablaze. Qirin was all too eager to accept the challenge with the pent-up rage burning within him. She turned to Rito with surprising calm. "Could you excuse us for a moment, please?"

Rito bowed, slipping back into the manicured foliage of the gardens. The moment his slight form disappeared through the palace doors, the Androvich empress rounded on him, seething. "Qirin, what the hell?"

"What I do is none of your business."

"Oh? And I suppose your *wife* knows that you're passionately engaging in kissing your bodyguards?"

"He's not my bodyguard!"

Nevia threw her hands in the air. "Clearly!"

"Look." He gripped her forearms, uncaring that his nails burrowed into her bronze flesh. "This does not concern you. If it bothers you just look the other way."

"You're cheating on Liana," she whispered, eyes wide.

Qirin's eyes flashed dangerously. "No, I am cheating on Rito."

"But you're married to her! She is carrying *your* child!"

"Maybe." Qirin shrugged a shoulder, and he almost resented himself at how heartless he felt. "Or perhaps it's Lord Jing's. I don't know, and I hardly care. There is no love in our marriage, only manipulation, and two can play at that game."

Nevia's lips thinned, wrenching herself free from Qirin's grasp and stepping back as she shook her head frantically. "I thought I knew you."

He let out a mirthless laugh. "After meeting me briefly a couple of times in three years? I don't see how. And like I said, this doesn't concern you."

"No, it really does. If this is the way that you operate a marriage, how am I to trust how you operate a society?"

Anger had been rising in him, and now that the floodgates had opened for him to channel those feelings, he was finding it difficult to reel it back in. "My love life has nothing to do with my capability of running a country."

Nevia folded her arms over her chest. "I will not have this infidelity in my palace."

Fury ignited Qirin's eyes. "Even you can't control what I do behind closed doors in *your* palace."

"No, but I'm sure that the people of your kingdom would not be pleased to hear that their king is unfaithful to their queen, especially to a man, no less. Is that not frowned upon in your country?"

Now she had gone and said the wrong thing. He could barely contain himself from physically lashing out, instead settling for stabbing a threatening finger at her. "Don't you dare blackmail me, Nevia. You utter this to anyone, and I swear to the gods—"

A pathetic laugh escaped Nevia's throat. "Now look who's blackmailing."

Furious, Qirin brushed passed her, storming down the brick path back toward the palace. He stopped just before entering, hands grasping the brass handles of the glass doors. "This conversation is over. You'd better not try to tarnish my name, as I can do the same."

Threats to counter threats.

Despite his bravado, hot tears stung his eyes in blinding smears as he fled back to his suite. Nevia had struck a chord with her words, perhaps having a greater impact than she realized. He was very familiar with the harsh reality that others would not accept his feelings for Rito. A forbidden relationship or not in the Feishin Kingdom, he couldn't change how he felt.

Even with every lie he lived with, his love for Rito was true. It was the one thing that he refused to sacrifice.

12
NEVIA

The next morning Nevia stood in the center of the foyer, seeing all of her guests off. It would be quiet again within the palace, but Nevia didn't particularly mind it. Her heart needed a break, especially after earning the ire of Ardan and Qirin within a week's time. Perhaps a new record for her.

As she kissed Johari's cheeks in farewell guilt settled into the pit of her stomach, carefully averting her gaze from Ardan standing a few paces away. She could not meet those twin swirls of green and gold, could not do that to her already aching heart. She desired to embrace him and let go of all her doubt and conflicting emotions, and yet she could not forget what she'd witnessed. The continued dream seemed too genuine, too real. She felt there must be something more behind it, especially when coupled with the prophecy she left the Nephyl War with.

From her periphery she noticed the Feishin king with his entourage, and when she turned she was greeted with a glare. Qirin's arms were folded neatly in the sleeves of his dark kimono.

"Thank you for your hospitality, Empress." The words rang with mockery, as if a threat were threaded through his words.

Consumed with more guilt, Nevia stashed it away with the rest. How she had blackmailed him was terrible and unlike her. Had she not once been divided by love herself? Even still, she couldn't help being repulsed by his mistreatment of Liana. Maybe it reminded her too much of how Darius mistreated her, reopening wounds not yet fully closed.

"And I thank you for coming," she responded tersely. "I wish you a safe voyage."

He ignored her, focus across the room. Nevia traced it to Rito, emerging from the main hall carrying the king's luggage. Qirin appeared challenged by trying to swallow down raw emotion. Whether fear or sorrow, she could not tell.

The rest of his Feishin soldiers gathered around the pair, the escutcheons pinned to their shoulders glinting with an ethereal light. It was not until they shifted away to speak with Zaire that Nevia realized what it was: Nephyl. They were wearing Nephyl like a badge of honor.

The foyer held so many voices and conversations which echoed off the enormous empty walls that it made her head spin. People were laughing, fraternizing, and shaking hands. They were not leaving fast enough for Nevia's fancy. She thought about retreating, yet she knew her place was there. They came to see her from such distances that it was the least she could do to see them off.

Venturing a glance at Ardan, she found him to be staring right at her. She could not look away fast enough, or feign disinterest, as he took the initiative to approach her through the crowd of lords and guardsmen. He came to a halt and bowed.

She should have been glad, pleased with the opportunity to speak with him, even, and yet she could not find it within herself. Every warning bell was going off in her brain. As much as she wished, she didn't think she could be foolish enough to so readily discard her reasons for creating distance.

As much as she greatly desired to.

She lifted her gaze to meet his imperiously. "I suppose this is farewell, then?"

A chuckle dark and sorrowful escaped him. "Is that what you want? Me to leave?"

Her facade cracked. "I didn't mean it that way."

"Apologies, then, Empress." There was something lacking in his tone, and she didn't like it. Perhaps he was still trying to keep up appearances in front of everyone, but in the past it was different. Prior he appeared indifferent, not cold and distant.

Wounded. She could respect that. But she was hurt, too, and to expect her to feel otherwise was unfair.

"Traversing the mountains in excess is of no great pleasure to me." He avoided her gaze as he spoke, instead settling on something over her shoulder.

He paused, and she chose to prod him. "And?"

"And you need more protection." Not her specifically, she realized—but her people. Her heart dipped. "Which is why my companions and I will be staying here until more reinforcements can be sent down."

Her mouth went dry. There was no way he could stay. That would only make things much more complicated. To see him every day, to have the memories of what was, and dreams of what could have been and still could be. It would be torture. Seeing him off as it stood was already bad enough, but to willing choose rejection every day would be nigh impossible.

"I would be fine without your protection," Nevia said, perhaps too quickly. "I am safe enough."

"Right." Ardan gestured behind her. "You have your personal guard at your heels, after all."

There was no way that she mistook the bite in his voice, and she soon realized what arrested his attention earlier. Black cloak pooling at his feet, Renault leaned against a wall casually, peeling an apple with a dagger. Despite the appearance, she knew none of their interaction went unnoticed. Perhaps scrutinized.

She tried to speak, but no words would come. Everything that needed to be said was already uttered. There was nothing left for them now.

Ardan gave her a bitter smile, one that did not quite reach his eyes. His hands, rising slightly, fell back to his sides, as if he thought better of it. With a curt nod he strode away, accepting her silence as dismissal.

It could not have been farther from reality.

She wanted to yell at him and beat her fists against his back and tell him how wrong he was, how much she still loved him. But she couldn't, not in front of everyone. Instead she stood there, trying to will her heart to stone, allowing the foyer's commotion to fall on deaf ears while desperately trying to rein in her emotions.

She was drowning, and there was no one there to save her.

Her vision swam, darkness crawling within the deep periphery of her gaze. Lightheadedness became vertigo. She reached out for the person nearest her for stability.

That person happened to be her handmaiden.

"Your Highness?!" Elante reached for Nevia's hands to steady her, and that's when Nevia saw it: inky black tendrils, oozing from her own fingertips and ensnaring around Elante's. They snaked up her wrists, beneath her sleeves, forcing Nevia to break contact with a gasp.

The empress blinked, and the tendrils were gone. The darkness was nowhere to be seen, and her symptoms abated. She lifted her hands to her face. Nothing. Her bronze skin looked just as it had before, with no signs of the darkness she just witnessed. She turned wide, tortured eyes onto her handmaiden.

"Did you see?" she whispered stealthily.

Elante's freckled face scrunched. "See what?"

She was losing it. The visions, the darkness. It was all in her mind: a sick, twisted, separated, and different reality that was surfacing after everything she had undergone. It frightened her. Nevia shook her head and slowly backed away from her handmaiden, retreating away from the crowded space.

"Thank you, my friend. I just—I—"

Nevia spun on heel, finding herself surrounded. Renault was hovering over her within moments, worry etched in the lines of his face. Time seemed to slow, the lines of conversations blurring into garbled white noise, muted over the roar of her pounding heart. She saw the Zenochians and Feishins departing, and suddenly she could see them back on the battlefield again, recalling all too clearly that horrid day when so much blood was spilt. A memory of Darius' ghastly pale visage flickered in her mind, bleeding and dying in her arms amidst the coastline of hundreds of bodies.

It was all far too much, and she felt like she was running out of air.

"I need to be alone," she rasped, shoving aside Renault and Elante to make her escape. Much to her relief, no one followed or try to stop her once she opened the double doors leading outside.

Tears stained her face as the cool air greeted her in the palace gardens, a gush of relief filling her lungs. She strode quickly to the fountain, the very same where her and Qirin had their falling out just the night prior, and sat, grasping her knees with shaking palms.

She didn't realize her scars from the war ran so deep. Evidently, they did. And now she didn't have the one person who always understood her, who loved and supported her at her side.

Because of a prophecy, a vision, and her voicing stupid, irrational words.

She missed what Ardan and she shared. To have it all back would have been a blessed luxury, but she could not erase the images or take back words callously thrown. Their time apart only made the injury she dealt fester. To make matters worse, he implied her affections lay elsewhere.

Such was utter rubbish, foolishness. Of course she didn't feel that way for her personal guard. Renault was just there, a loyal companion, a very dear friend. There was nothing intimate between them.

Nothing. Not even the way her heart fluttered when he touched her cheek, or how she brandished his arm for support.

A frustrated cry escaped her as she dug her nails into the grooves of the fountain's stone seat beneath her. She wished the prophecy was never uttered, that they never discovered the core shards. She craved her father, her mother, Khatalia, and even Darius, as challenging and toxic as their relationship had been. She wanted so much that she couldn't have, and the want was killing her.

One frail piece at a time.

Guardsmen hearing her cries circled around like vultures, imploring her to speak, to tell them what was wrong. She screamed their dismissal, causing them to exchange puzzled glances and step one-by-one away, leaving their empress to her hysteria.

Another set of footsteps along the brick pathway approached her. Nevia drew in a harsh breath. "Please, leave me."

"No."

It was Elante, and Nevia well knew that she would not accept a dismissal no matter how she phrased it. Never had Nevia seen Elante so concerned, her face wan with a pastier complexion than when she was seasick. She swept over beside Nevia and wrapped the empress in her arms. This was exactly what Nevia needed.

"I'm such a fool," she murmured. She gave her best friend a tight squeeze while Elante soothed her, gently rocking her. "I keep hurting people. I'm making so many bad decisions and I don't know what to do."

Silence. Elante didn't try to tell her she was wrong, refute her words, or offer suggestions. She just held her, and let Nevia say what she needed to. Nevia was grateful. For this moment she needed acceptance, not correction, and it seemed Elante understood.

"I broke things with Ardan," Nevia confessed, to which Elante stiffened in her embrace. "And I threatened Qirin because he betrayed his wife."

Elante made a hum, but remained mute.

"And I keep seeing things, visions of a non-existent past. A bringer of death—"

"What does that even mean?" Elante blurted. Nevia lifted her head, then, meeting the quizzical gaze of her handmaiden. "The bringer of death. Are you trying to blame yourself for the war?"

"No, I—"

"Because it sounds to me like you're still haunting yourself about everything that happened in the past and trying to find ways to punish yourself." Elante stroked Nevia's hair. "Really, it's okay. You need to let it go."

Nevia closed her mouth. Was there more truth to Elante's words than she realized? Maybe she was blaming herself for the war, and that was what spurred all of these images. Maybe her subconscious was working against her, showing her alternate realities where she was death personified.

But that still didn't change the prophecy she received three years ago and how everything was coming to pass as the seer predicted.

There was one person who could perhaps provide her with answers, someone she had been meaning to speak with for some time.

"I need to speak with the imperial seer," Nevia spoke, rising. "If anyone has answers to all this, it would be her."

13
NEVIA

Traditional Ivalian law dictated that seers would be tried for witchcraft and, if convicted, face a public execution. When Rufus unified the empire, however, this law became nationwide. Seers and witches were forced to either live in fear or migrate to Zenoch. Maestra Annika, the head shaman of the seers, did just that, joining the nomadic clans despite holding different beliefs.

The true irony was that Saava supposedly blessed these seers with their foresight, the very goddess that the imperials worshipped. Innocents were killed regardless of age or position, and loved ones could do nothing but watch as they went up in flames. It was just the way it was, until Nevia took her husband's place on the throne.

Among her first decrees was the abolishment of anti-magic. Instead of being sent to the non-discriminatory pyre, seers would be revered and valued as imperial citizens, receiving the same education and care as anyone. People heavily rebelled at this change, particularly those devout to Xander's doctrine, but Nevia did not regret her choice. It allowed Orla, the daughter of Lord Torquil, to finally live a life beyond hiding within the stifling walls of the Palthesi manor, to be able to walk free and live as any normal girl. It also meant that the empire had the valuable asset of foresight, as much as a double-edged sword it proved to be.

Nevia made her way down a corridor of the palace, ignoring the staring faces of the imperial family portraits and the guardsmen at every corner. The imperial seer seldom left her quarters, so this was the first place Nevia sought her. She rapped her knuckles on the tall oaken door, the sound hollow amidst the pounding of her racing heart.

Rustles could be heard on the opposite side, and finally the door cracked open to reveal the freckled face of a teenage girl, wiry red hair bristling like an open flame. Her pale-blue, almost-white eyes lifted to meet Nevia's.

"Hello, Orla," Nevia greeted.

The girl opened the door wider, granting Nevia access to her quarters. A soft smile played on her wan lips. "It's nice to see you, Your Imperial Highness. Please come in and make yourself comfortable."

Incense burned on the mantle above an unlit stove on the far side of the room. The sitting room that belonged to Orla looked much like one of Saava's temples, complete with the burning of incense, golden statues of her in either corner of the room, and lots of greenery hanging from planters.

Nevia inhaled sharply, the pungent scents of patchouli assaulting her nostrils as she turned to watch Orla close the door. She had grown so much in the short time Nevia had known her. Her gift, once uncontrolled, had manifested into something extraordinary after her training under the head shaman, and she had served the imperial court with wisdom and grace for nearly two years. It was a great honor for the girl, earning pride within the empire's administrations and ire outside of it.

"Have a seat." Orla gestured to the throw pillows scattered about the floor. "I'm sorry that I don't have better accommodations for the empress."

"I don't need special treatment," Nevia retorted, perhaps too quickly. She sank into the cushion nearest the stove, where the essential oils burned the strongest. She closed her eyes, counting her breaths, taking note of Orla's seating herself next to her by the rustling of her gauzy, wrinkled skirt.

"Now then." Orla's voice was melodious, not unlike a song. "What brings you here?"

Nevia opened her eyes, question on the tip of her tongue. "Does Saava have a sister?" She folded her hands in her lap, displeased at herself for how eager she was for this knowledge.

Orla's lips pressed together, eyes narrowing a fraction. "Why do you ask?"

"So she does?"

"I neither confirmed nor denied. I just wanted to know why you want to know."

Orla was concealing something. Whether to shelter her secrets or to learn of Nevia's, she did not know. She met Orla's gaze evenly.

"I have been having visions, ones where Saava is in another realm, and I am her sister. Myself, and yet not."

Orla's face scrunched in surprise. She bolted to her feet and crossed the room. Procuring a leather-bound volume from a desk on the far wall, Orla flipped through the weathered pages frantically.

"What are you doing?" Nevia inquired, unsure if she should follow.

"The Goddess of Death," Orla murmured over the continued rustling of pages.

Nevia's curiosity could no longer sit idle. She strode to Orla's side, peering over the redhead's shoulder as she pored over a volume more ancient than any she had seen in the imperial library. The seer's slender fingers hovered over either side of the book, as if uncertain to snap it shut or unveil its contents, but she allowed the empress to see.

"I thought it was just a fable," Orla whispered softly. "But perhaps there is truth in stories. These were passed down from the first seers of Saava many generations ago."

She lifted the book for easier viewing, and Nevia's heart nearly gave way. An image of a woman whose resemblance to herself was uncanny greeted her. Platinum waves fell in wisps about her, with darkness pooling from her open palms.

"Where did you get this?" Nevia reached out for the book.

Orla didn't yield it, tugging it away and stroking the worn leather cover. "When I trained under Maestra Annika, when I first broke free of my house, she gave it to me," she answered. "It has been passed down for generations, or so she said. She told me she thought I should have it, someone with a future uncertain even to her. This future is one with many possible outcomes for Gaia."

Her eyes fluttered closed, lids nearly translucent. "I was so gripped by the story. Saava's dark sister, the bringer of death in the immortal realm of the gods. Only I never connected the dots and realized it could be you."

"Tell me," Nevia commanded, reaching out to grasp one of Orla's wrists. "Tell me everything."

A grim look flickered across Orla's face, frown wrinkling her smooth flesh. She took Nevia's hand, fingers frail and narrow, and thrust the heavy book into her hands.

"Read it," Orla whispered. "You'll find the answers there."

Sleep was evasive to Nevia. Every time she lied down, hair coiled in her silken bonnet, her thoughts would stray to Saava's mythical sister. The Goddess of Death, someone revered in the fabled land of the gods, and yet in their world the woman was all but forgotten. Why did no one seem to remember her? Saava was revered and worshipped, yet none ever whispered about her sister. Was it because she embodied death and not life, or was there something more than that?

The book unveiled little that she didn't already surmise from her own visions. It reinstated Saava's suffering at the hands of her elder sister. Anything Saava created, the Goddess of Death destroyed, a monster most foul concealed beneath a mask of beauty. She could understand why the stories faded with the passage of time. They were most unpleasant. No one wanted to read a story of their goddess being mistreated.

And yet, it was more than a story to Nevia. It involved her. The question that plagued her, however, was: how?

Her eyelids grew heavy, the room spinning overhead. Sleep was beginning to claim her, and finally, after fitful tossing and turning, she allowed it.

14
NEVIA

It was only a matter of time, she thought idly, her fingers running along the smoothness of her knitting needles. A project lay strewn in her lap, a scarf intricately woven in a variety of stitches. The rhythmic motion of knitting was soothing to the senses, and an excellent way to mask her trembling hands.

The ambience of rushing water in the distance greeted her ears, allowing her attention to fall upon the waterfall outside the extensive window to her right. A partitioning layer of glass separated her and the Endless Sea rushing to greet the Nether Planes, and she pondered morbidly how many "accidents" they would encounter if the glass was not there.

Wails reverberated off the walls, coming from the corridor beyond. Its sudden oncoming made her drop her needles, despite expecting it. Saava must have found her surprise, and now it was time for her to enter the stage.

Ivory columns rose high on either side of the hall, creating an archway at the start and stop of every window. She fell short a few paces away from the source of the hysteric wailing: Saava, kneeling on the ground, her frame shaking as her hands hovered over a facedown body. *His* body. She watched emotionlessly as Saava gripped his shoulders and wrenched him onto his back, revealing that his skin had turned a sickly shade of gray, eyes wide and inky black.

Horror and repulsion clawed at her chest at the startling revelation. Yet, counterintuitive to her initial response, she tossed her platinum waves and drew a step forward.

"What have you done?" she demanded, holding herself rigid in disapproval as her darkened gaze swept over her sister looming over new husband's dead body.

Saava's despair morphed to rage. Her head lifted, tears running freely as she ran up to her elder sister with godly speed, looking ready to rip her apart.

"You! It was you! You did this to him!"

"Don't be foolish, Saava," she answered with unearthly calm. "You know I would do no such thing. Why would I be the one to murder my husband? I loved him, after all. We were just wed a fortnight ago."

There was an edge to her own voice that rubbed her raw. Arrogance. Mockery.

As if knowing she won.

Saava grit her teeth, striking the platinum-haired woman across the face. The sound of flesh meeting rang through the corridor as the blow sent her reeling back against the wide pane of glass, her only barrier from the Nether Planes beyond. She lifted a hand to her burning cheek, staring upon Saava with fury burning within every fiber of her being.

"I've seen your work when you've ended lives," Saava spat. "This is what you do. This is your magic. You can't lie to me—"

"ENOUGH!"

The sisters, so engaged with one another, hadn't noticed the entourage of royal officials gathering a short distance away. Eyewitnesses for Saava's shortcomings. Perfect.

Standing tall and foreboding was a man crowned by golden vines perched perfectly atop raven-black hair. His tanned skin rippled along his strong, thick biceps, veins bulging along his forearms as his jaw clenched in anger. His eyes, sunlike and golden, made the elder sister shrink back in cowardice from their intense ferocity. Father. The Supreme Lord of Aeterna.

Face as hard and unreadable as stone, he approached the sisters, gaze flickering to the scene at hand. The moments ticked by as she watched, holding her own breath, wondering if he would buy it.

The lies she told him.

The supposed truth of her sister's sins.

A deep sigh heaved from his chest, dark hair slinking over the pauldrons atop his shoulders as he turned to his youngest daughter. "Saava, you can't hide it any longer." The man gestured towards the blighted corpse. "We know now."

"Father?" Saava blanched, turning to face the Supreme Lord of Aeterna.

He ignored her and continued. "Your mother and I have been patient. We thought perhaps you needed to come into your gift, as is common for many of us. We didn't know . . . didn't realize. . . ."

Saava waited moments for him to finish, but he didn't. He merely stared at the body of Niall somberly. Inky blackness began oozing from the corpse as the dark-haired woman swallowed dryly, eyes calculating, understanding. His unspoken accusation struck her hard. "You think I did this?"

"I told him everything," the elder sister confessed, folding her arms over her bosom. "How I've been covering for you. Pretending your magic was my own. I'm sure it helped to have a sister who shares the same gift, but I can't continue lying for you." She jerked her head in her husband's direction. "Not after this."

The lie came easily. The aftershock on Saava's face was something she could savor forever.

Her father filled the cavern with his mighty voice, intimidating, booming. "I cannot put to words my disappointment in you." Wroth as he was, his golden gaze seemed to burn greater. "How your selfishness brought this to pass. I cannot fathom why you chose to conceal your gift. The kingdom would've celebrated another Death-Bringer. There was nothing to hide from."

"But that's not me!" Saava screamed, frantic. "I don't have any magic. This wasn't—I would never—"

"I'm sorry that I betrayed your trust, Saava," the elder sister said, tone cold. "But you betrayed mine."

The sisters' eyes clashed, and in that moment she knew Saava understood. The bedroom. The couple's betrayal. The brutal promise she'd made to Saava.

Yet even she was surprised at how far she went to make the star-crossed lovers pay for wronging her.

"Saava, you are hereby banished from Aeterna. You are sentenced to eternal slumber in the Nether Planes."

Panic seized every muscle in Saava's face. She rushed to her father, black hair flowing behind her like a streamer.

"No, please! Please! You can't banish me. I didn't do this! I didn't kill him!"

He met her gaze, then, gold eyes shimmering with rage. "You defy me still?! Justice must be served, and the abuse of one's gift is intolerable. You of all people should understand this, Daughter."

Saava turned toward her sister and let out a shattering, piercing wail. She tried to charge the Death-Bringer, fingers stabbed outward like claws. Four steps were had before two guardsmen snatched her shoulders, binding her arms. Tears streamed down her face, ignoring the cloaked figure who approached from their left, but the elder sister did not ignore her. She was going to relish this.

Saava spat in her sister's direction, wailing as loud as she could, "I hate you!" before she was roughly turned away to face the newcomer. Face concealed, but not the blonde dreadlocks poking from her hood, the newcomer hovered a hand over Saava's cheek, stroking her gingerly. Her lips were downturned in pity.

"You will not feel a thing," the newcomer said, voice gravely and feminine. "You will merely be locked in a chrysalis, a stasis immune to all except death."

Saava fought against her captors to no avail. "No, no, please! I demand a fair trial!"

"The ultimate judge has already passed his judgment. There is nothing left to try you for," her father said somberly. "Farewell, Saava. I did love you."

Chills swept down her spine. Such callousness.

Saava's jaw slackened, and eyes widened. A whimper escaped alongside a look of tortured despair as the cloaked woman lifted her hand to place two fingers upon her forehead. Twisting could not let her escape her fate. She rasped, body shuddering, as the woman released her. In mere moments the struggling, despaired woman collapsed in the grips of the Golden Guard, still as death, but the elder sister knew Saava merely slept.

The Supreme Lord refused to look at the scene, turning his back and stopping in front of the glass wall to watch the torrential downpour of the waterfall. He clasped his hands behind his back.

"The chrysalis will take hold and envelope her shortly," he brought to voice. "It will continue to nurture her till the end of time. Parcel her and send her to the Nether Planes. The fewer people that are involved in her departure, the better."

One guard was immediate to bow to his command. "Yes, Your Excellency."

A brow of the elder sister's quirked up. "You don't wish to give your daughter a public farewell?"

The Supreme Lord's shoulders grew rigid. It was clear she struck a chord, and, if she were wise, she would not test her father's patience mere moments after sentencing his youngest daughter to an eternity in oblivion. "No. One silent farewell is enough. The shorter the duration of this, the better it will be for us all."

The world churned at her feet, the marble palace dissolving around her. She recognized this sensation, having been repeated during the other two visions she experienced of a past long-since forgotten.

Nevia was free falling through the bleak darkness, then was suddenly sitting upright in her bed. Cold sweat drenched her, leading her to throw the covers off her trembling body. She closed her eyes, shaking as she leaned back against the pillows at her head.

What did Nevia just witness? And what kind of a monster exactly was she?

15
NEVIA

Breakfast remained all but forgotten in the early daylight, her eggs and sausage left to grow cold as Nevia left her tray untouched in her sitting parlor to seek out Orla again.

With hair matted atop her head and knowing full well that dark circles rounded her eyes, she was certain her appearance must have been abhorrent. She didn't wait for Elante to help her prepare and instead scurried from her room with no preparations at all, save for a plain linen gown and her favorite boots. There was no time to lace up a corset.

She hammered on the seer's door, waited, and readied to pound again when the door swung open. If Nevia thought she looked bad, Orla looked more disheveled. Her loose hair frizzed and was sticking in all directions, her lithe form dressed in naught but a thin nightgown.

The young woman ran her tongue over dry lips, pale eyes lifting to Nevia beneath lowered lids. "Morning," she said hoarsely.

"Orla, can we talk?"

Orla ran a hand over her wiry locks before giving the empress a curt nod, granting her entry.

The sitting parlor was precisely as they had left it, save for the lack of burning incense above the now-burning stove. Nevia kneeled on one of the sitting cushions, folding her hands in her lap. "I had one of those dreams again."

Orla slipped to the opposite side of the room, shuffling through a stack of haphazard supplies. "What was it this time?"

"I framed Saava and condemned her to her slumber," Nevia blurted. The tension had been threatening to strangle her all night. The rest of the story followed in a flood: the murdering of her husband and the punishment of the Aeternum Supreme Lord, all because she framed her own sister.

"I-I think that's the real reason she's here," Nevia whispered. "Why she slumbers at the heart of Gaia. I think this—our planet —is the chrysalis that her father spoke of. She was sentenced here to an eternal slumber—because of me."

Orla, taking it upon herself, prepared a kettle on her wood stove for the pair while Nevia retold her dream and took up residence beside the empress, a steaming cup in either hand.

"It's a likely theory," Orla agreed, setting Nevia's tea before her.

"Theory?" Nevia scoffed. "It's the only explanation."

Orla brought the stoneware to her lips. "There's always more than one explanation."

The young seer appeared far more calm and collected at the revelation than Nevia. Perhaps it would've been different had she seen the grim scene herself.

"Who was the man that was killed?" she asked at last.

This was a question which startled the empress. It was not she herself that killed him, and yet she felt wholly accountable for the death of Ardan's double, as if done by her own two hands. To share this secret felt forbidden, in ways that were innately woven into her, and yet the way Orla's wide, orb-like eyes prodded her urged her to divulge.

"It was my husband, who was also Saava's lover."

"Did he have a name?"

Nevia nearly scalded her tongue on her tea before answering, "Niall."

"Hmm, Niall." Orla paused, thoughtfully stroking the side of her cup. "Did you recognize him?"

"I had seen him in earlier visions, yes."

A sigh escaped Orla, perhaps detecting Nevia's hesitancy. "I'm just wondering if you're the only one in these visions, or if there's anyone else in your life in them, too. I'm trying to figure out what's happening to you, and what Saava's trying to say."

Saava? Could this be Saava's method of communicating with her? Nevia hadn't thought of it this way, though it did make sense. No other explanation was sound as to why she kept receiving a narrative of a legend long-since past, a reality unknown to her until after the visions started coming.

Figuring out what was happening to her sounded wonderful. She wanted to know why she existed in another life as another person. She wanted to better understand who she was and her role in all of this, and yet telling Orla the entire truth made her vulnerable. Being so vulnerable rendered her terrified, as if uttering the words aloud would make it all the more true.

"It's no one. Just a man."

Had Orla been a mind reader, she would undoubtedly have feared the reaction the young seer would have. Luckily this was not within her skill set. Nevia partly felt bad for misguiding her, but she had to.

"Well," Orla said at last, pinching the bridge of her nose, "I don't know what this means."

Nevia's chin dipped. "Neither do I."

"But I really think it's important." Her white nightgown fluttered as she rose, spinning on heel to a cluttered table of parchment. Loose pages cascaded to the floor as she shoved them aside to procure a leather volume which was handed to the empress. "Write it all down. I want to keep track of these visions."

Nevia accepted the book, dubious, and rose from her seat with a noncommittal "I'll see what I can do."

"I'll do some digging and see if I can figure out what any of this means," Orla proceeded. "I have a few ideas, but I want to make sure I'm right before I tell you."

The empress tilted her head, interest piqued. "Can't you at least tell me what you're thinking? I won't hold it against you if you're wrong."

Slowly Orla lifted her gaze to meet hers, and there was no mistaking the small flames of indignation dancing within them. "No."

Nevia saw this as the end of the conversation. Despite her being the empress and Orla the young, humble servant, the seer had won this time. Nevia wasn't about to exude her will and force her to speak. She'd had enough of flaunting her title to gain what she needed. She gripped the door's handle. "Well, thank you for putting your attention to this."

Concern etched itself onto Orla face. "Just be careful. I can't explain it, but this all feels dangerous."

A laugh, dry and mirthless, escaped her. "We're just talking about how I'm the Goddess of Death and that I killed a man in my dream. Of course it feels dangerous."

The glare Orla shot Nevia as she left cut deep, and as she traveled down the hallway she viewed the visit as a total waste of time. There was something the redhead was withholding, and the more time that passed, the more desperate Nevia felt to receive it.

Her stomach reminded her that she had yet to eat, and briefly she pondered whether her abandoned breakfast would still be palatable. Of course, she could trouble someone to prepare her another meal, but she was loath to do that, much sooner be willing to scale the district's walls and find something in the forests than make personal demands. Besides, having been raised with the notion that every morsel was cherished, she despised the idea of wasting good food.

Nevia swept along the eastern wing and down a flight of carpeted steps. The autumn chill lingering from a chilly night reminded her that she should have finished dressing. To think of everyone witnessing their empress without proper garb, specifically the lack of a structured bodice to smooth and secure her, was torturous.

Echoes of laughter echoed down the hall as she retreated to her room, making her pause dead in her tracks alongside a suit of armor. She recognized the laugh. She would anywhere. While it should have propelled her to move on to her room faster, it instead made her legs unable to move, firmly rooted to the ground.

Should she try to hide? That would have been ridiculous. She was empress, in her palace. Even if wholly immodest, to face *him* of all people.

As two men rounded a corner Nevia allowed her platinum hair to spread over her breasts, relishing in the small amount of modesty it granted her. She tried to act poised and put together, but her form was off. The entire situation was incredibly awkward.

The words died in Ardan's throat the moment their eyes locked, causing Nevia's heart to flutter viciously within her ribcage. She didn't recognize the man she strode with: a tall Zenochian with coloring similar to that of her own. They exchanged a brief pleasantly before Ardan strode over. Toward her.

Nevia inhaled sharply, tucking stray locks of hair behind her ear. She didn't know why she waited for him, why she wanted to speak with him. She could have simply walked off, striding right past them. Or better yet, turned around and—

"Hello, your Imperial Highness." The greeting was unfamiliar, rigid, so unlike their previous interactions.

It was as if they were strangers all over again.

She bit her lip, unsure of what to do with her fidgeting hands. "You don't have to call me that."

"I do here." He tossed his head in the direction of the lengthy hall littered with sentries at every doorway. His gaze fell upon her then, taking her in. Nevia wished she could shrink away and disappear under his scrutiny, feeling her thin nightgown and hair did little to conceal her curves that he seemed to be enjoying. To make matters worse, he leaned forward to whisper in her ear, making her stomach twist in all the right ways. "Unless you want the rumors to grow, which they already might considering the way you're dressed out here."

Finally she met his eye, his smirk insufferable. "I was in a hurry."

A sideways smirk flickered across Ardan's face. "Of course."

She swallowed hard, ignoring the twinges within the lower quadrant of her core at their proximity, the familiar musky scent of pine.

"With all due respect," he said, lowering his face dangerously close to hers. "You might want to at least consider, you know"—a playful smirk crossed his lips—"wearing your nightgown right-side out."

A humiliated laugh bubbled in her throat, realizing it was true; in her haste, her clothing was indeed inside-out. She wanted to elbow him, *hard*, but not as much as she wanted to press her own lips to his, to feel his flesh on hers. To taste him—

"Well, while I have you here, I wanted to—" What? What did she want to do? Even she didn't know, and disappointment mixed with irritation caused her shoulders to dip in defeat. "To thank you. For coming to my aid when I needed it."

"I always will, Nevia." He professed it without a moment's hesitation, tone soft and husky. He lifted his free hand, and for a moment she thought he was going to cup her cheek, but he thought better of it. He cleared his throat and shifted away. "Anyway, I should probably go find my people and get them outside training."

Her eyes lifted to his. "Yes."

Something akin to pain flickered across his face before he said softly, so low that even she barely heard it. "Can I—can we talk later? I'd really like to discuss some things with you."

Her heart leapt into her throat, and she tried to keep her enthusiasm from her voice. "I would like that very much."

A dimple formed in his cheek when he cracked a grin. He took her hand in his, the callouses rubbing along her tender skin delightfully. She sucked in a breath, watching every move, as he slowly, painfully lifted her hand to brush his lips against. She delighted in the sensation, of his warm breath, the smoothness of his lips.

"Until then, Your Highness."

He dipped his head and strode off, Nevia watching him disappear around the corner. She felt like a foolish, star-stricken young girl madly in love, not unlike when she had fallen for Darius in the woods all those years ago.

Darius. Her first love, her emperor, her abuser.

Just as quickly as she thought of him she tried to absolve it, snuffing out his memory like a flame as she rushed to the safety of her room. She threw her weight against the door and let out a long sigh. There was so much on her mind, and she was an absolute wreck.

Arms grasped her, causing her to nearly leap out of her skin in alarm. There stood her handmaiden, lips pursed, giving her head a shake in disapproval.

"Highness, where have you been dressed like that?"

Relief flooded Nevia, grateful that it was none other than her friend, her confidant. And now that she had unloaded the heavy burden of her dream to Orla, she felt ready to take on her friend and any questioning that may follow. "Sorry if I kept you. I was . . . checking on things."

To her gratitude the servant girl did not detect her hesitation, more bubbly and chipper than Nevia had seen her in a while. "You have a lot to do. I get it; you're the empress, after all."

A pained smile twisted Nevia's lips. If she only knew the half of it.

Elante linked an arm around hers, playfully dragging her toward her dressing screen. "But they are going to have to do without you for an afternoon, because we're going into the city!"

16
NEVIA

Going into the city seemed like an awful waste of time. For leisure Nevia would've much preferred to hike through the woods, but Elante insisted upon hitting the Velspirian streets with the empress and an entourage of guards in tow. Those she didn't know on a first-name basis were respectful enough to maintain a generous distance to not overhear every word the girls uttered, but this was not the case for Renault. Standing a short distance away from Nevia, he left a discomfort, especially after their previous awkward encounter. Nevia still had been unable to process it or understand why her heart somersaulted in his presence. She had known him nearly as long as Darius, and closely for the past three years. Why was this development happening now?

No night creatures breached the capital's walls since the distribution of Nephyl ceased, though it remained unclear if that was indeed the forestalling factor. A forbidden part of her didn't want it to be linked. Nevia regardless hoped the orchestration of death and blood led by the creatures would cease. Nephyl had helped improve so many lives. She also did not think she could persuade Qirin to suspend production forever, too much profit tied into the export of core shards.

This concern, among many, was the driving force of Elante's decision to get Nevia out of the palace.

Their first stop was the corner bakery, the delicious aroma of fresh bread wafting into her nostrils upon entering. They selected a pair of one of Nevia's favorite delicacies of the region, fried dough with a cream filling, and Elante purchased a lengthy roll of golden-crusted bread for later. They barely stepped away from the counter before a flock of customers groveled at her feet, wishing to shake hands, touch her, and thank her for stopping the night creature attacks. When the situation grew rowdy, she turned to her personal guard, expression pleading.

"Help," she mouthed to Renault.

The man acted in fine response, quickly swooping in from the entryway to her aid. She couldn't help thinking he appeared like an oversized bat, dark cloak billowing and arms spread wide. His presence intimidating, he spoke in curt finality, "The empress has had enough visitation. That will be all." They dispersed immediately. It was magical, really.

The two women enjoyed their pastries as they strolled through the cobblestone streets of the shopping district, marveling at the collection of autumn gowns in the window of a clothing shop, before their discussion bled into conversation regarding the upcoming fall harvest, and what sort of celebration should be had in its honor.

"I am really not sure what to do," Nevia admitted. "In past years we have always acknowledged the fall harvest with a tournament and feast, but this year feels different. After the tragedies caused by night creatures it feels inappropriate to celebrate."

"That's all the more reason to do it," Elante encouraged. "We need to remind the people that life goes on, that we are still living, and what better way to do that than to throw the most elaborate autumnal festival ever?"

Elante went on about details, making suggestions for the feast and ideal guests of honor. At the mention of inviting the Feishin royal family, Nevia nearly choked on the last bite of dough.

"Let's go see the gift shop," Nevia stated abruptly. "I want to buy a gift for your nephew."

The change of subject went unnoticed, if only because Nevia brought up the four-year-old boy that Elante loved and cherished. The woman was hopelessly obsessed, stealing away to visit him any chance she received, spoiling him with as many goods as she could afford. Elante's cheeks flushed with excitement at the mention of him.

"You really don't have to do that." She coughed into her sleeve.

Nevia placed a hand lightly on Elante's shoulder. "But I want to. I want him to get to know the real me, beyond the crown."

A shy smile crept over Elante's face, lowering her arm from her face. "Well, you don't have to buy gifts for that, you know."

"I do know," Nevia reassured. "But what better way into a child's heart than with new toys?"

"Aha, so you have a personal ulterior motive!"

Nevia only smirked in response.

They rounded a corner en route to the gift shop, passing other shops within the district. Clothing shops with ravishing mannequins, and a music store that Nevia herself had visited years ago. They were almost there when they saw a cluster of individuals gathered outside one of the brick buildings. Curious, Nevia sidetracked their party to get a better look. On further examination, they were ogling over a poster pressed to the window. On it was the likeness of her face, and beneath it read:

Death to the heathen!

A shudder coursed through Nevia's spine. Why would anyone put posters like that up in the streets? Who could wish for her death so blatantly?

At her side Renault grew stock-still, and one glance at his face told Nevia all she needed to know. He marched between the dense crowd and ripped the poster from the window, crumbling it in one of his large, strong fists and tossing it to the ground at his feet.

"Who is responsible for this?!" he roared, turning to each cowering face in turn.

The crowd began to disperse, leaving mostly the two women and their handful of bodyguards. One young man in particular was emboldened enough to draw a step closer. Renault lifted a thick brow, pointing at the parchment between his feet.

"Did you make this?"

The man shook his head, dark hair falling limply in his face. "No, but I wish I did."

Several swords unsheathed at the very statement. Nevia lifted a hand, hoping they would lower their blades, but her feeble gesture went ignored—the man was at the center of their attention now.

"You would speak against the crown?" Renault demanded, sword drawn and pointed directly at the man's throat.

A hollow laugh escaped him. "Go ahead, we're dead anyway, thanks to her. She's bringing those monsters in to kill us all. So long as she lives, we will all be in danger—"

Nevia could not stand being on the sidelines anymore. She marched up to him, hands balled into fists at her sides. "That is absolutely untrue."

The man jutted his chin. "Oh, really? Then why are you encouraging the education of seers and inviting them in? Why are you bringing that bewitching material that is causing all of this?"

The core shards, Nevia realized. *He thinks the core shards are behind it, as do we all.*

Her moment of hesitation was all that Renault needed to lift his sword, preparing to strike the man. Panic seized Nevia all at once, and she was quick to wrap her hands around Renault's sword arm.

"No! That's not necessary!" She was panicking then, eyes searching the scrunched up face of the man who was her protector. Her friend, and perhaps something more.

The tension between Renault's brows softened, yet his eyes remained hard as he brandished his sword at the man again. "This man threatened you, and you would spare his life?"

"Yes." Nevia turned a sharp glance in the man's direction. He looked neither remorseful nor grateful, and Nevia couldn't help but pity him. "He has been misguided, surely by Xander's lies again."

"Lord Bakalov speaks truth!" the man intoned.

Nevia's forgiveness encouraged others to join him, and soon a cluster had gathered to chant "Death to the heathen!" And "No more core shards!" It was disturbing, alarming, and Nevia felt her heart grow heavy in sorrow. They were quickly ushered from the scene, albeit Nevia was loath to leave. If only she could make them understand, help them to see reason.

"I can't believe him," Nevia seethed when they were a safe distance away, treading between Elante and Renault as the gift shop loomed into view.

Elante nodded sympathetically. "I'm sure the man was just upset. He probably didn't mean—"

"Not him," Nevia snapped. "I mean Xander! He's causing all of this! He's making rebels!"

"Or perhaps," Renault piped, "Xander leaked the information from the council and learned that core shards may be connected to the assaults, which would further their beliefs involving you."

"That's ridiculous," Nevia grumbled.

No one said anything after that.

The bell chimed behind the two women as they entered the gift shop: a lovely establishment with warmth that exuded from within the moment they stepped foot inside. Every wall was tastefully adorned with gifts, fine porcelain to pottery, dolls to personalized journals. Behind the glass-walled counter were some of the shop's finer wares, including pocket watches and jewels. Tables draped in cloth of a forest green housed more merchandise, predominately specials that the salesclerk was trying to clear out of his inventory.

Nevia nearly choked on the many dozens of fragrances wafting upon them as they passed an aisle of scented wax and perfume. It seemed Elante felt similar, gauging from the way she cleared her throat and grabbed at the high collar of her gown. Passing through the haze of scents, they finally arrived at the back of the store where the toys and games were kept. There were many options available for young children, most hand-crafted while others were clearly manufactured from local factories. An array of colorful teddy bears caught Nevia's eye.

"What is he into these days?" she asked, lifting a bright green one from the shelf.

"Nolan likes just about everything," Elante responded, laughing. "Just don't get him another teddy bear. My sister might just gut you, empress or not."

They examined toy pianos and miniature checkers sets, and while doing so Nevia found herself wondering what it would've been like had Darius and she chosen to start a family. Would she too threaten well-meaning friends about gifting her child additional teddy bears? A part of her found herself yearning to find out what it was like, which struck her as odd, as she had never once really considered wanting a child.

"What about this?" Nevia procured a xylophone, the different keys painted in vibrant hues. Elante merely coughed beside her, but didn't deign to answer. Nevia took that as a no and despondently set it back down. What better way to bond with the boy than over one of her favorite pastimes if talent was fostered early? They could play together, first the xylophone, then the—

Nevia was ripped from her thoughts as Elante let out a gasp, clutching at a display shelf. Porcelain dolls tumbled to the floor, followed by the bears Nevia had admired. The empress' panic surged as she grasped Elante's shoulders to support her.

"Elante?!"

Her handmaiden feebly tilted her head in Nevia's direction, and the empress was horrified at what she saw. Her skin had taken on a sickly grayish hue, lips tinted with a purple rim. Nevia couldn't help but scream in alarm.

"Empress! What's wrong?"

Renault was beside her in seconds. Again, Nevia was grateful. She clutched at his arm, her lips fumbling for words.

"Quick, Renault, she's dying!"

Elante tumbled from her position supporting herself on the shelf to staggering to the floor. Renault looked stupefied, staring down at the handmaiden as though not recognizing her. He barely made a motion for her before Nevia bunched his cloak in her fists and shouted again: "Get. Help. NOW!"

Other customers became acutely aware that something was terribly wrong. They began darting out of the way and into cover. Some seemed glued to the spot while others rushed from the store in fear that a plague was spreading. Perhaps they were not wrong.

"You're going to be okay," Nevia soothed, brushing back Elante's hair over her ashen forehead. Renault stooped down to lift the handmaiden. Elante went limp in his arms as her eyes rolled to the back of her head.

There was no certainty. She had no idea if Elante would be alright, but she repeated it to herself like a mantra, over and over and over, as they left the store and even during the expedited ride to the palace.

She was going to be okay. She was going to be okay.

She was going to be okay. . . .

17
NEVIA

Nevia refused to leave her handmaiden's side in Elante's bedchamber, even when she was urged to for her own safety.

"We don't know the cause," the physician had said.

"You will do no good to her if you succumb and fall ill too," Renault further urged.

Neither of their protests did any better of convincing her, so there she stood, cloth mask over her face, for as much protection and good as it would do her. She watched the imperial physician do his work, examining her vitals and outward symptoms. All the while, Elante's condition seemed to worsen, her skin taking on a more violet hue.

What instilled Nevia with the most dread of all was that the whites of her eyes turned ink-black.

"Well?" Nevia asked the physician, following him to the vanity where he'd set down his supplies.

The physician let out a sigh as he lowered his own mask from his face.

"For now, she is stable," came his response. "I gave her something for the pain, and she is resting as peacefully as I can make her. However, I have never seen the like of her condition, and I do not know if this disease will worsen or subside. And as you already know, I suspect it could be contagious."

Nevia sucked in a breath. She had seen such a case before, but how could she explain this to the physician? It was another life, as another person, and worst of all it had come from her.

A hand rested on her shoulder. Warm, firm, comforting. Renault hadn't left her once, nor did she expect him to. Hard worry lines etched into his face.

"When did her symptoms first appear?" her physician asked, piercing the prolonged silence. "Was she acting oddly this morning? Yesterday? What were the first signs that something was amiss?"

"I don't know, I—"

I cursed her when I reached for her that day, Nevia recalled, the day when she realized Ardan would stay but she could not be with him. That must have been it. But instead of professing it, she met his gaze, steeling herself to maintain the calm, cool exterior of the

Androvich Empress. "She just started coughing and fell. I don't think she was showing any symptoms before that. It happened so suddenly."

His sharp gaze met hers above her mask, and for a heartbeat she feared that he saw right through her deception. Instead, he dipped his head.

"Well, I will continue to monitor her and watch for any changes. I do not know what ails her, so we can only treat the symptoms."

"But she will be okay?" Nevia asked.

A heady sigh escaped him, gaze falling back on the patient. "I don't know." His words were firm, but kind. It came as no surprise; deep down she knew he could not offer the validation she sought. He patted her shoulder. "I will step out for now and check in within a few hours. Should any changes happen before that, Your Imperial Highness, please don't hesitate to seek me out."

With that, he packed his things and left. She was left alone, with Renault at her side.

Renault. Her personal protector. Her confidant. One of her dearest friends.

She could alleviate the overwhelming panic consuming her heart and share it all with him, and he would still accept her. She knew it to be so. And yet when she had finally readied herself to open her mouth and confess her fear, he spoke first.

"Do you two want a moment alone?"

No. "Yes," Nevia said, cursing herself inwardly. She missed the opportunity to alleviate the weight on her heart, but it was easier to bid him goodbye, she realized, than find words to tell him everything.

Much to her shock, he leaned in closer to her side and brushed his lips over her temple, the sensation warm enough to set her ablaze. It lasted all too brief, and before she could process what happened he was already at the door, brows knit together. "I will be just outside this door. Please call upon me if you are in need of my services, Empress."

Her mouth went dry, fingers numb at her sides. She could still feel the burn where his lips pressed against her flesh, where the fine baby hairs of her temple stood on end. Clearly the action was made out of affection, but was it romantic or simply platonic?

And she was in no emotional state to figure out what *she* felt herself.

When she was alone she allowed her guard to fall and wrenched the mask from her face. There was no need for it, after all, if the affliction which plagued Elante was what she suspected.

The empress knelt before her friend, swallowing the hard knot in her throat. "I'm so sorry," she whispered, running a hand along the brown locks fanned over her pillow, the only part of her friend unaffected. "This—this is my fault. I'm so, so sorry. I wish that I could heal you."

Elante's eyes fluttered beneath her lids and her cracked lips moved, forming words that Nevia couldn't understand. The empress broke out into sobs, burrowing her face into the crook of Elante's arm and wrapping her arms awkwardly around her.

She lost track of how long she knelt mutely at Elante's side, soaking her bedcovers with her tears. She only stopped when the waterworks had run dry, head throbbing from the exertion.

It was consuming her. To tell someone, to share this atrocity she had sown—she so desperately wanted to divulge, yet was petrified at the notion. What if they demanded punishment, the burning of the witch everyone always thought she was?

Fear so strong compelled the dark empress to suffer alone, with only her condemning thoughts for company.

18
ARDAN

Ardan could not stop thinking about the empress since encountering her in the hall that morning. There was no mistaking the way she looked at him, the way she observed his every move. When their eyes locked he felt certain she desired to make amends from their previous disagreement, something he was more than happy to oblige. He hated the chasm dividing them, the innumerable barriers forcing them apart.

Despite recognizing the time had come, seeking the empress for a conversation was a near-impossible task.

Upon first inquiring after her, he learned that she went into the city with Elante. This made perfect sense at the time. She was, after all, Nevia's dearest friend, and it was reasonable that the two girls would venture off into the city together. How often was it that Nevia was able to set aside her imperial duties to do something of personal enjoyment? If anything, he was grateful that she found her way out of the palace, and took to preoccupying himself in her private parlor to wait for her.

And wait he did.

Yet the hour grew late, and she never returned.

A loud sigh escaped his lungs as he stretched his long legs, leaning back in her favored chair, gaze flickering toward the grandfather clock in the corner. Ardan told himself that he was being ridiculous; he could not merely sit there waiting for her indefinitely.

If the sentries thought it conspicuous that the Zenochain chief left her quarters, they did not let it show. Inwardly Ardan cursed himself as he turned the corner. It should've occurred to him how bad it would look for him to linger in her private domain, yet it did not. More and more he found himself acting on impulse, acting before thinking, and damning the consequences as he went along.

Or, at least when it came to decisions involving *her*.

His exploration of the halls led him to the second floor, where he saw the familiar dark figure of Renault swoop across the floor, comically reminding Ardan of a bat. The folds of his cloak billowed as he paced outside a room.

Ardan tried to swallow back fury rich and feral. Silently he came to despise this man, yet Renault had given him little reason to. He was Nevia's personal guard, and had become painfully close to her in the three years of her sole reign.

Three years that Ardan had not been there, but Renault was.

Wherever Renault was, Nevia was not far away, so he swallowed his pride, rolled his shoulders, and strode up to approach.

The guard stopped his pacing as soon as Ardan's footsteps echoed within earshot. He lifted his head of dark hair to meet Ardan's gaze, a slow smile playing on his lips. "Ah, Chief." Renault's hand slid to the hilt of his sword. A motion that did not go unnoticed.

Ardan merely dipped his head in greeting. "Renault."

"It is so nice to see you this evening. Can I help you with something? You look . . . lost."

Ardan halted in front of the man and sized him up. Renault's smile widened, unfriendly. He could detect malice, disdain. Mirth lurked behind his depthless eyes, as if mocking Ardan and taking personal pleasure in toying with him. Perhaps it was simply Renault's loyal devotion to Nevia which bothered him, but his feelings were ones that he could not quell. He loathed this man.

But what Ardan loathed most of all was that Renault gave him no reason to feel the way he did except for relating to the late emperor. It would have been easier to wrestle with his emotions if Renault Androvich gave him a reason for his disdain.

"I'm looking for Her Imperial Highness. Have you seen her?"

A dark chuckle escaped Renault's throat. "Ah, yes. I had almost forgotten about the affections you two share."

Ardan's hands balled into fists. He should have denied it, and yet he could not. He wanted to claim Nevia, to let him know she belonged to *him*, even if they had a dispute and their relationship status had become murky.

His lack of response seemed to further amuse the guard who chuckled darkly and tossed the hair from his face. "If I were you, I would be careful about how you seek her out. People might get the wrong impression. Or, rather"—he smiled dangerously—"the right one."

"I think," Ardan murmured tersely, "that it would be wise if you didn't make assumptions without hearing it from Her Highness' lips first."

"There's things that I understand without Her Highness telling me," he said simply. "I know her greatest dreams. Her aspirations. Longings . . . yearnings."

Ardan shifted his weight, growing more uncomfortable by the minute. "That's lovely. And I don't suppose you worry about rumors spreading about you two?" He was going way too far, yet he was committed—he had to see it through now.

In response Renault tilted his head, eyes glittering dangerously. "Oh, Chief, all I worry about is the reputation of my beloved empress being tarnished by one of her fellow clansmen she traipsed alone with before the war. I will not have it sullied. There is *nothing* else greater that could."

Ardan's temper flared, and he might have reeled back to loose a punch directly into the guard's smug, jeering face had the door at their backs not opened, unveiling none other than the empress herself.

Her face was a mess of smudged makeup, the tip of her rounded nose pink. She drew in a sharp breath and blinked, eyes widening as they flicked between the two men. Both started to speak as one, but she did not await for either of them to finish, instead forcing herself between them to march away.

"Your Highness—" Ardan blurted, concerned. He began to step toward her, but was halted by Renault's extended arm. Ardan gritted his teeth.

"You are dismissed, Chief," Renault stated, tone firm. "I will see to the Empress' needs now."

Ardan leveled him a glare, "But—"

"You may see Her Imperial Highness when she is in better spirits." He sidestepped Ardan. "Now, if you'll excuse me."

With that, Renault swept away, militant boots clicking as he closed the distance to Nevia's side. Ardan swallowed down his mounting frustration, heart sinking as he watched Renault's hand shift from the hilt of his sword to the small of Nevia's back. His fingers curled around her side as he gently coaxed her around the corner, out of Ardan's line of sight.

Perhaps there was more, Ardan thought dismally, behind Nevia's dismissal of him back in the catacombs. Her heart had been divided once, after all, between Darius and himself. Maybe it has happened again. Three years allowed Renault plenty of time to insert himself in his place. The confidant and friend to earn her love.

And Ardan was too late to win it back.

19
NEVIA

Keeping her dark secret to herself over the agonizing days threatened to consume Nevia. Eventually she settled on confiding in Orla. The seer, as young as she may be, was more privy to the situation than anyone. If Nevia could safely tell anyone besides Elante, it was her. Perhaps she could have shared with Ardan, but that ship had sailed. She failed to reach out as promised, and when she shot glances at him the next day he purposefully turned his head away and ignored her.

The door opened before Nevia's knuckles could even meet wood. The seer's pale eyes met Nevia's, as if searching her soul. Nevia drew a sharp breath, and there, in the doorway, told her everything. The words escaped faster than she could rein them in, and eventually Orla snatched up the empress' hand to tug her into the room.

"You don't want anyone to hear," she hissed, throwing a glance in the hall before snapping the door shut. Her skirt, as fiery as her hair, billowed as she turned to the empress.

"I can't lose her," Nevia bemoaned on the verge of hysterics. "Please, please tell me there's something that we can do to save her."

How the imperial seer went from prophetical advice to her personal therapist was unknown, or how a mere thirteen-year-old was expected to carry the weight of a grown empress. And yet such was their unorthodox relationship. Orla knew more than many others, if only because she was touched with the magical arts, and lived a life far from the average, mundane ones of her other affiliates.

Orla pressed her lips together, thoughtful. "Well, I don't know if this will tie in or not, but I heard from her—I think I know how we can save your friend."

Nevia blinked back her confusion. "Heard from whom?"

"Oh, don't be dense." Orla rolled her eyes, reminding Nevia that, despite her sagaciousness, she was still only a sass-filled teenager. "Saava. I had a vision of the future. It was bad. The skies were gray and the grass was dead. She told me she is dying, and if she does . . . we all go down with her." She shook out her frizzy mane. "She said only the Goddess of Death has the power to free her from her bonds, and we both know that's you."

Nevia sucked in a breath. That was a lot to take in. She recalled the prophecy given to her years past, saying that only she could deliver Danaeca from its path of death. She had thought that the seer meant the war, but could she have inferred to this? The empress rubbed the side of her head ruefully as she sat back on her heels. "Orla, I can't even save my best friend. How am I expected to save a sleeping goddess?"

Orla shrugged. "She didn't say, but the goddess doesn't lie. You must go to her in Gaia's Core."

Nevia's eyes fluttered closed. She recalled the popular myths circulating among seers. It was believed at the center of the planet "Gaia's Core" resided, where the goddess herself slept, sharing her wisdom with the world through those touched with magic. There was the profound question of whether it was even possible to descend to the very heart of Gaia, yet it seemed Saava—and therefore Orla—thought it possible.

Nevia raked her fingers through snares of platinum hair. "No one's ever been to the core of Gaia before. I don't expect I could be the first. I wouldn't begin to know how to even dig that deep into the earth."

Orla shook her head. "I doubt that you'll have to literally dig a hole. There's got to be some path, some hidden route. Maybe you're not the first like you think." She stood up, smoothing down her skirt. "But you'll figure it out."

Nevia lifted her chin in defiance. "And if I don't?"

A heavy sigh escaped Orla. "Then we will have a much bigger problem than just your friend dying. Saava's dying, too."

This was certainly relevant to them all. If their goddess died, Nevia did not see how their planet could go on. The empress' stomach dropped, dread causing her blood to run like sludge in her veins. "But how?" She shook her head furiously. "She's been sleeping there for thousands of years. How could she be dying?"

"We're the ones doing it to her," Orla responded. "Call me a liar if you want, but I know what I was told. The core shards are her magic source, and we're draining her by taking them."

Suddenly Nevia's thought's flickered to the night creatures, seemingly drawn to the core shards and struck wherever they were. What if they weren't coming of their own volition, but—

"Saava must be sending the night creatures to stop us," Nevia murmured. "They aren't quite the monsters we think they are. They're trying to stop us from depleting the goddess."

Orla merely shrugged. "I don't know about *that*. She only told me she's dying, and only you can rescue her."

With as many answers that were given, even more questions spurred in Nevia's mind. How was she, the Goddess of Death, capable of saving the Goddess of Creation? Was saving Saava going to be enough to save Elante, or was it too late for her? Was this quest relevant, or was she choosing to save a goddess and their planet over her best friend?

Nevia sniffed, caressing the golden brocade of the cushion beneath her. This was her greatest task as empress yet, and she did not feel that any amount of training could have prepared her for the task at hand. She swallowed roughly. "There has to be something more to all of this. Something we're missing."

Orla ignored her question, perhaps because there was no response she could provide. The seer strode to the door and threw it open. A dismissal. "You know where I am if you need any assistance."

I need lots, Nevia thought after her, but didn't bring it to voice, instead rising to leave the seer's quarters.

Her thoughts fled back to Elante, her body unmoving on the bed. Nevia's hands scrunched tightly in determination, nails biting crescent moons into her palms. *I will save you, Elante. Even if I have to give my own life to do it.*

She was empress, after all. She controlled the most powerful nation in all of Danaeca. She would save Elante, even if she had to rip a hole in Gaia to do it.

20
NEVIA

The days came and went with no change in Elante's condition, a blessing and a curse. On the one hand, Nevia thanked the goddess that her health wasn't failing further, but on the other she was disappointed that no miracle yet graced her.

That morning of the autumn harvest festival she hoped that it was Elante who knocked at the door to assist her. The thought was beyond all reason, and her heart sank when it was only the substitute handmaiden, a small girl with a pretty face and unknown name. She was polite and good at her job, swathing Nevia in her ceremonial ivory garb and lavish makeup, but she was not Elante.

No one could be.

That was hours ago, and the festival had already commenced. The empress sat in the pews of the grand cathedral, its ceilings towering above the heads of its ground-level worshippers, and balconies allowed further seating within the cathedral, enough to house thousands. Per tradition, tithes were paid to Saava, the Goddess of Creation, upon the autumnal harvest. Families of all classes sat, awaiting their turn to lay down their offerings. Normally one would bring something of value, monetary or sentimental. It was the act of selflessness that was cherished, resembling the sacrifices Saava made when she entered her eternal slumber and bestowed life to the planet.

A holy chant reverberated throughout the entire cathedral strung together in the Old Tongue, its meaning long-forgotten but its verses still retained. Nevia clutched the cocuswood flute in her hands, palms sweaty beneath her gloves. She was growing agitated and uncomfortable in her scratchy gown, with its many layers of skirts. A corset was fitted tightly against her torso, her substitute handmaiden not wielding a fragile hand when it came to doing her laces. The sheer veil traditionally worn by nobility was draped over her face, doing little to mask her stoic expression as she rose from her seat, her turn coming at last.

The flute had been expensive, special, and at one point very dear to her. It had been broken, but she had kept it to serve as a reminder of different times—better ones. She had been holding on to it for ages, but currently felt it time to let it go. To pass it on, despite its broken state.

Her footfalls fell mute on the assembly as she strode along the carpeted runner down the aisle, candles lit in tall, standalone brackets at the end of each pew. Her heart hammered in her chest as she shunted, averting her gaze from the many faces staring at her to the front of the ceremony.

Their foreign empress, following their traditions.

She halted as she reached the end of the aisle, lifting her gaze to meet the stone face of the goddess centered in the dais of the holy place, eyes unseeing, palms spread wide as if in greeting. She swallowed a painful lump in her throat as she knelt, chiffon skirt snagging at the grout between tiles. Carefully she placed the flute at the bare feet of the statue and clasped her hands together, dipping her head in respect before finally, cautiously, tilting her chin to meet the smooth lines of the goddess' impassive face.

Memories flickered through Nevia's mind, recalling the goddess in a much more lively form, her face much younger and meeker than that of the wise woman imperials portrayed.

A throat cleared beside her, piercing her thoughts and bringing her back. A clergy member stood to her left, eyes locked on her sternly, his thick white mustache dipping at the corners as if in an uninterrupted frown above his official show of disapproval.

Nevia threw a glance behind her shoulder, taking in the patrons dressed in a similar ivory garb, each bearing their sacrifices and awaiting their turn. The ceremony had to continue, and everyone was waiting on her. She mouthed her apologies and lifted herself, shuffling past the line of worshippers and back to her seat.

Renault sat waiting for her, an ankle propped over his knee. He looked very uncharacteristic of himself with his pale ceremonial garments, replacing the blacks and burgundy he generally wore. He reached for her hand as she drew closer, rubbing his thumb along her knuckles. Such displays of affection had become commonplace from him now, and she didn't know whether she enjoyed or despised the development. It didn't go unnoticed by her that he'd made physical contact before thousands, when such touch was quite forbidden in public. Perhaps it was a slip-up, or perhaps he simply did not care.

Another trait he shared with his late cousin. *Her* late husband.

"You seem distraught," he observed.

Hesitantly she allowed her fingers to slip from his, still relishing his touch as she folded her hands primly in her lap. She turned to face the sacrificial ceremony, schooling her face into indifference.

"I am concerned for my handmaiden," Nevia said tersely. While not a lie, it was not wholly the truth.

Renault looked ahead as well, following the next set of partakers. "Yes, her condition is regrettable. How is she?"

"They think she has days left," Nevia murmured lowly, forcing her heart to harden, so as not to feel the pain her words etched into her soul. "It won't be much longer if a cure isn't found."

His hand found hers in her lap, and she could only clasp it tightly.

"And there is no suggestion of a cure? Nothing has been found that may help her?"

Nevia sucked in a breath. She turned her gaze back, Renault's chocolate eyes solemn and searching. Concern was evident on his face. She could tell that it pained him. It pained him that she was in pain, not that Elante was dying because he barely knew her. He suffered because Nevia suffered. This made her feel terrible to be the source of another's suffering, and yet she was so grateful.

There was someone at her side that still cared.

"There is one lead," Nevia whispered, hesitant.

Her conscience screamed at her not to say another word, to keep it to herself, and yet she couldn't. She could trust Renault; he had proven himself a worthy servant, and one of her most trusted, loyalest friends. Perhaps even something more, if she would allow herself that bond.

The burden her heart bore was too great to carry alone; she had to entrust it with another. If not to find a solution, but to bring her own self some much-needed solace.

"There is some connection to her ailment and the Goddess of Death. And Orla has had visions."

Renault's face cracked, eyes widening a fraction. To his credit, however, he said nothing, waiting for Nevia to further explain.

"These visions—well, communications—have pointed me to enter Gaia's Core, and it seems I need to get there urgently. Not only for Elante, but for everything."

A frown furrowed Renault's brow. "For everything? What does that mean, Your Highness?"

Nevia opened her mouth, and then closed it. She wasn't sure how much she should really say, especially when surrounded by so many people. She was omitting much, but he did not need to know it all—just the basics. "There's more on the line than you know," she confessed. "This is something that I alone must do."

"No."

Nevia's ice-blue eyes clashed with his dark ones. "What?"

"You will not do it alone." His hand left hers to give her knee a squeeze. "I will come with you."

At this Nevia's mouth ran dry. Her heart soared at the thought of not being alone. Of being surrounded by comfort, love, familiarity, and yet as quickly as she relished the idea she was equally prepared to reject it.

"You can't."

"Why can't I?"

"You're needed here, in the palace. The night creatures—"

"Haven't attacked in weeks since the distribution of Nephyl ceased. It was as you claimed, Empress. They were connected to the night creatures, and now they are no longer a threat." He took both her hands, and this time she let him. "My place is by your side. I vowed to protect the rightful heir to the throne, and that is what I will do."

The fourth row was returning to their seats while the next shuffled into the aisle. The ceremony would take hours yet, but the clergy at the front had patience in abundance and practice with the masses. Nevia's eyes shifted back to her guard, searching Renault for any display of hesitancy, reluctance. There was none. She dipped her head in assent.

"You have my gratitude, Renault. Thank you. I would be honored to have you at my side through this."

Hand slipping from her knee, dragging unnecessarily long up the length of her thigh, he snatched up her hand again. He carefully met her gaze as he kissed it, lips lingering too long to be casual. A shiver coursed down her spine.

"Then we will ride at dawn."

At this Nevia arched a brow. "At dawn? Why, Renault, I don't even know where Gaia's Core is—"

"You may not, but I think I do." He gave her a wink. "The vault contains many secrets. You should check there. Archaic maps could probably help you."

Could it be that simple? Why, she did not even once consider the vault. Relief flooded her. Maybe there really was a chance that Elante could be saved before the curse consumed her.

"You have given me hope," she said, to which Renault flashed her a smile.

"That is part of my job, Empress."

She heaved out a slow breath, the boulder boring down on her feeling suddenly lifted. It felt even lighter when she felt Renault's fingers graze her right side, arm now wrapped around her the small of her back, hidden from view by the bench so that none could see. There it was again, that fluttering in the pit of her stomach, the fuzzy sensation in her lower core. But instead of willing it away, she relished it. Yearned for it. She wanted more. More of his affection.

"My job is to be by your side, to ensure all of your needs are met, Empress," he whispered into her ear. The words set her heart ablaze, its warmth spreading into her cheekbones. His lips grazed her ear, then, his teeth slightly, ever so slightly, teasing her lobe, so quickly that Nevia almost wondered if she imagined it.

Her doubt grew as he subsequently leapt to his feet, offering his hand despite the fact that the service was very much still in session. "Seeing as you have more pressing matters to attend to, I will escort you back to the palace," he offered. "Unless of course you would rather partake in the festivities?"

Her heart sank at the very thought of the festivities, the ones that Elante herself had orchestrated with her before her illness consumed her. There would be a feast, music, and dance in the central square, but Nevia couldn't stomach the thought of partaking in it, any of it. Not while Elante was suffering, and not when she had scalded Ardan and was betraying him even further by whatever was blossoming with her personal guard.

At long last she shook her head, causing a few stray curls to spring free from their pins. "No, please take me home. I want no part of any of it."

His lip curled, grasping her fingers snugly in his gloved hand. "As you wish, my Empress."

21
QIRIN

Tension had consumed Qirin since his return from Velspire, particularly in regards to his love life and the mining industry. Qirin wasn't merely angered by Nevia's threat—he was livid. Under normal circumstances he would have considered heeding her advice and halting all production of Nephyl. She was, after all, the one who put an end to the war and stood up for him at her own personal risk. They had been friends once, but now he could not think of a greater enemy, and would simply double the already tripled Nephyl harvesting to spite her.

The Feishin queen had acted aloof since Qirin's return, specifically after an unnecessarily strained dinner conversation when he refused to return her affection. Since then, she stopped making public appearances at his side which did not go unnoticed by the people. At formal weekly prayers in the Shrine of Everlasting Peace a handful of attendants asked about Queen Liana, and if pregnancy complications were the source of her absence.

"She is healthy and well," Qirin reassured. "She just didn't feel like gracing us with her glamorous presence. That is all."

The sarcasm was thick on his tongue, and he inwardly chastised himself for being belligerent. He watched with a hardened heart as the shoulders of his subjects dipped, disappointment evident on their faces. He was given a wider berth than usual, one he did not particularly mind. He liked having the luxury of his own space.

That evening was one such occasion where he enjoyed the tranquility of solitude. A servant had arrived earlier with an offering of his favorite evening tea, but Qirin was quick to dismiss him before he could be waited on further. The young king stood in front of a long mirror propped in the corner of his room, running a wide-tooth comb through his long ebony hair, allowing the silken strands to fall in sheets over his bare shoulders.

A rap on the door arrested his attention, and he took a moment before answering, annoyed at whoever was on the other side.

"You may enter." He could barely contain the agitation in his voice, dark eyes flicking into the mirror to catch sight of his visitor. His heart skipped a beat when he recognized him: the dark hair drawn back into a tight bun, the round visage of youthful energy.

The warm honey-brown eyes that he loved so dearly. Their gazes locked in the mirror's pane.

"Good evening, Rito," Qirin greeted warmly, setting down his comb and turning to face him. "What a pleasant surprise."

Rito bowed stiffly, long bell sleeves clutched in his palms. Such formality. Qirin so greatly wished to abolish it, ideally from every noble, but at the very least his dearest friend. The king clicked his tongue and crossed the room to him, grasping his shoulders and forcing him upright.

"Now now, what did I say about formalities between us? There is absolutely no need." He patted his shoulder, flourishing an arm toward the serving platter resting beside his bed. "Please, join me for my evening tea. I've missed you."

His loyal servant lifted his head, his expression pained. "I've missed you, too, but I can't stay. I . . . actually just came to say goodbye."

A laugh rose in Qirin's throat, dismissing Rito's claim and swooping over to the fine porcelain tea set. "Say goodbye? Pray tell, where are you going? Can I come with you?" He poured himself a cup and turned. Instead of taking a sip, he brought it over to his friend and offered it with both hands. "There was only one cup. My apologies. I wasn't expecting any company tonight, but we could share."

"Your Highness." Rito's tone was strung unusually high. "I thank you for your hospitality, but as I said before, I'm not staying. I'm leaving the Feishin Kingdom."

The smile faded from Qirin's face. His blood ran cold. "Why?"

"Don't you see? My presence is ruining your life. Your marriage is strained because of me—"

"It is not because of you," Qirin seethed. "It was doomed from the start. Liana and I were never meant for each other, and she loves someone else, as do I. It's mutual."

Rito was shaking his head in disagreement. "But I still think that if your heart wasn't divided it would be easier for you to be with her."

The light faded from Qirin's eyes, gaze lifting to lose himself in Rito's round, lovable face. "The fault is all mine, not yours." Suddenly Qirin grasped Rito's shoulders, pulling him in against his exposed chest. "Please, you must reconsider. Don't leave me like this. I couldn't bear to lose you, Rito."

The king could not see Rito's face, but could feel the hot tears fall freely on his shoulder. "This already hurts so much, Qirin," he said, voice thick. "Please, let me go. Let this be easy for both of us."

"No, I refuse it. You cannot leave me like this. I-I love you."

Rito shuddered in Qirin's embrace. Slowly he untangled himself from his arms and pulled back, considering his lover with a tear-stained face. He lowered his chin, refusing to meet his king's solemn gaze as he forced the offered teacup back into Qirin's hand. To Qirin, this was more than simply rejecting tea.

It was rejecting his love. Him.

Rito's dark gaze barely met Qirin's. "I'm sorry."

But Qirin would not be placated so easily. He tried to coax him, to grasp onto him, to keep him at his side, but Rito sidestepped his king with a gentle, sad shake of the head.

"I'm ending this for both of our sakes, for the sake of your future child—"

"It's not even mine!" Qirin screamed, voice shrill. Uncaring who heard, who believed the unspoken truth he had convinced himself out of pure malice. He ran his palms over the crown of his head, desperate. "Rito, give me a month. I will sort everything out. We don't even have to be together anymore, damn it, just don't leave me!"

Rito's mouth twisted, his next words taking him great lengths to utter. "As long as I'm in this kingdom I will always remind you of what could have been, but what cannot be. I need to remove this from your life. Consider this my ultimate service to you. My king, my love. My everything."

Warmth built behind Qirin's eyes, fists balling at his sides. "Rito, no, please. Don't go."

At that, Rito leaned forward, his lips brushing against Qirin's ear. "Be the king you were always destined to be. Live free, and please, please go and give your queen the chance she deserves. I know you don't believe it, but she really does love you."

"But I love *you*, not her," Qirin bemoaned, silenced only by Rito turning his head to press a kiss to his lips. A goodbye. To savor him again one last time. He pulled away, nodding with a sense of finality.

"Be free, Qirin. Be happy."

Rito strode to the door without glancing back, perhaps trying to make it easier on them both that they had to part. Qirin threw out a hand feebly to snatch him back. To keep him near in some way, shape, or form. However, his love slipped between his fingers, and he couldn't keep him except through order of the crown. But if he loved Rito, as he truly did, he would not abuse his power against his resolve.

No matter how much it pained him.

He let out a growl of fury, hauling the half-empty teacup against the mirror. Both shattered into a miserable pile of shards at his feet. His breaths came in, fast and harsh, as he took in the wreckage, raking a hand through his hair. Everyone he loved was being taken from him. His mother, Lady Rumaar, and now Rito. Even Mila, his sister, was overseas in Iddlegaard having wed a foreign prince, perhaps never to return to Feishin shores again.

His heart couldn't bear much more loss.

22
NEVIA

It had been years since Nevia had stepped foot into the vaults burrowed away deep within the palace. At first she was loath to breach the threshold of the catacombs again, the assault of night creatures tarnishing her memory of the place, but Renault was there to grasp her hand and reassure her that all was well. This gave her small comfort as they plunged further into the source of the empire's finest palatial treasures.

It was not heavily guarded. In fact, it was not guarded at all, something Nevia thought should change in the future. A metal gate was the only protection of the vault's wares, apart from the fact that it was housed within the unused catacombs hidden away. Few knew of the catacombs very existence, and even fewer knew where they led. Some forms of protection, she realized, served greater than sentry and borne arms.

Renault held the lantern close to illuminate the space before turning to Nevia and giving her a nod. She sucked in a breath, drawing a step forward as she fidgeted with her signet ring. The one Darius wore everywhere, the one piece of him she had left. She slipped off the ring and pressed it into the lock, turned and released the latch. Her personal guard gestured for her to enter first.

The air was musty, dry, and thick, dust coating every surface in a thick layer. Nevia lifted her lantern to examine rows of chests, along with shelves filled with boxes and crates. Silks and drapes adorned another shelf as she perused, absorbing all of the culture and history of Velspire even before the birth of the empire. Rufus Androvich collected so many objects during his conquest, though she wondered how many had already been here before he ever rose to power and claimed the place which once housed a shrine devoted to Saava.

"It's going to be something old," Renault mused aloud, tilting his head to study the shelves lining the vault's ceiling. "Did Darius ever mention anything about the Core of Gaia to you?"

Nothing that she recalled, but that did not mean that Darius was not aware of its existence. There was much he did not divulge. Instead of answer, she glided over to an elongated table taking up the center of the vault, brushing off a coat of dust with her sleeve.

Renault grunted, muttering under his breath before surprising Nevia by leaping onto the very table in front of her to gain access to the shelves lining the ceiling. "Better get busy looking, Empress," he said, voice strained as he shuffled through objects. "Don't want these lanterns to run out."

The vault soon became ransacked with their combined effort. Trunks were opened, jewels were spilt, and papers strewn all over the floor. Nevia's mouth fell as she watched Renault mercilessly tear into a chest, hurtling gems and precious stones haphazardly before tossing the entire chest to move on.

"It has to be here somewhere," he growled, leaping off the table and crossing to the opposite side of the narrow room.

Never had she seen him so uncharacteristically . . . aggressive. Nevia drew a step back, leaning into a collection of swords on a nearby rack.

"It's really okay," she reassured, wishing to placate him. "We'll find another way to the core if we must. I'm sure—"

He threw a glance in her direction, sweat plastering his dark hair against his face. He opened his mouth as if to speak before stopping abruptly, eyes falling on the sword rack by Nevia's side. He stabbed a finger toward it. "Did you check in there?"

Soon the pair was emptying the rack, unsheathing each sword and searching every scabbard. Nevia's fingers met with the golden hilt of a falchion—the very same that Darius' father had used to secure his empire—and lifted. The sword glistened in the light of their lanterns, but otherwise it looked as any ordinary sword would.

Defeat began to sink in, then, having exhausted their options. It was only through re-rummaging through a carton of documents, most pertaining to the legal boundaries of Velspire within Ivalia, that a weathered piece of parchment caught Nevia's eye. She plucked it from the rest and unfolded it, and on it was a small hand-drawn map and script in longhand reading:

Power's Source

"Well, I found this."

Renault was quick to snatch the paper from her, his eyes skimming the parchment. He moved back to the central table, brushing all of the random treasures onto the floor to place the paper upon it alongside a map of Danaeca that he'd unrolled from a nearby scroll.

"If I'm right," he murmured under his breath, "this sketch lands us . . . right about"—his finger landed at the heart of the Feishin Kingdom, the sketch of its stone border mocking her—"here."

"But that's just the Feishin Kingdom, isn't it?" Nevia protested. "Could the entrance to the Core really be there?"

Renault grumbled, crumbling the parchment in his fist, "I don't think this is what we're looking for." He threw it atop the rest of the treasures on the vault floor. "Come on, back to the search."

Her fingers fled to his shoulder before she could think. "We're not going to find anything, Renault."

A frown furrowed his brow as he turned to glance at her, the desperation in his eyes resembling something that could devour souls.

"We've already torn this place apart. Maybe it's best to gather intel elsewhere. Ask around—"

"It should be here, though! I just know it should be."

Nevia grimaced, removing her hand from his shoulder and kneeling on the floor to pour over the contents. "Why don't you help me clean this up and we'll talk to Orla after?"

"What would the child witch know?" he sneered.

Nevia's lips parted, jaw slackening. He must've realized the error of his ways from her horrified expression, as he lifted his hands defensively. "I mean—I apologize, Empress. I just am frantic. I want to help you, and there is no time to waste."

She felt it, too—that mad desire to find a way to save Elante from an untimely death from a disease that Nevia brought upon her. If Nevia was able to curse her best friend, there was no telling who she would plague next. It seemed her accursed touch was unpredictable. She had no interest in condemning Elante to death, after all, and did not know how to prevent it, or when her death magic would rear its head again.

That alone was enough reason for her to succumb to Renault's desire to continue the search.

They exhausted every nook and cranny, seeking the location of Gaia's Core for hours, to no avail. They were no closer to finding it than they were when they arrived, and only were left with an enormous mess. Nevia sank to the floor and hugged her knees to her chest, rocking softly as she watched Renault search through a box of old documents for the third time. Tears began to well in her eyes at the thought of Elante, feeble, cold, and dying in her small bed, darkness seeping and spreading beneath her skin. A darkness that Nevia cast upon her.

She was killing her best friend.

"I think we should go to the Feishin Kingdom," Nevia said at last, snapping Renault from his search to turn his wary gaze toward her.

"I presume this is because of the drawing?"

"I think"—she crawled across the dirt floor, fingers clutching the discarded note and spreading it open, running a thumb along the two words scribbled in rushed longhand—"this has to be important if it was concealed so carefully. Darius told me of his father's conquests, how he would travel around the world seeking his next path to glory. It wouldn't surprise me if he learned about the core and made a plan to one day go there."

Her eyes fluttered closed, pained. "It's our only lead. The Feishin Kingdom is where the core shards were first discovered. It would make sense if passage to the core is hidden there."

"And if it isn't?"

"Then we've wasted our time, and Elante will die."

Something broke in Renault, then, tension slackening from his rigid jawline. He stalked over to her side and knelt, clasping both her hands in his own, completely enveloping them.

"We won't let that happen," he breathed, placing his forehead to hers. Seeking the comfort, the warmth, spreading through her chest, she leaned in, taking in his scent of fresh rosemary and cedar.

"You shouldn't make promises you can't keep," Nevia murmured, all mirth fading from her tone.

His hand fell from hers, only to brace the back of her head, drawing her closer. His eyes glittered. "I only make promises that are in my control."

His lips grazed hers, and she was too stunned, too mesmerized, to prevent it, instead savoring the feel of his lips. Their warmth, their taste—

She sucked in a breath, bringing his lower lip between her teeth. A soft moan escaped his lips, repositioning himself on the floor to lift her into his lap. How she yearned for affection, for comfort, for release. It had been so very long since she'd been held and adored, and she relished it. His hands caressed her back, her curves, and she couldn't help biting down on his lip slightly when his hand fled to cup her breast, giving it a slight squeeze.

She could lose herself in this, in *him*, yet she could not help thinking about Ardan. The feelings she once harbored for him, and still did. The look of utter dejection on his face when she stormed away from him the night of Elante's affliction, and she never tried to make amends, never attempted to seek him out.

These thoughts allowed her to break away, noses grazing and breaths labored. Renault kissed her closed eyelids, running his palms slowly along her shoulders. It took every ounce of her strength to push herself away shakily, bringing herself on to her knees in front of him. "We can't do this, Renault. We shouldn't —"

"Of course, Empress."

His tone suggested otherwise, and the look of wistful yearning upon his face almost made her return to his lap. Her nostrils flared as she inhaled sharply, giving her head a light shake. How fickle was her heart, skipping from one love to the next so flippantly? She had never committed to Ardan. In fact, she had broken up with him. It was perfectly acceptable for her to pursue another lover, to seek comfort in Renault. Given his blood ties to the Androvich family, their relationship would not only be accepted, but celebrated.

A shudder coursed through her. This would have to be dealt with at a later time. Elante's well-being was her utmost priority.

And yet when Renault allowed his hand to slip into hers as they made their way out of the vault, she couldn't help interlacing her fingers into his.

23
QIRIN

R ito's departure compelled Qirin into seclusion, making fewer public appearances than usual and refusing to join in any communal meals. Not even with his queen, who was the last person he wished to see.

Even sleep was hard for the king to come by, the first few nights spent tossing and turning. By the third night deep sleep finally had enveloped him, being able to find some amount of comfort in restful oblivion.

Such only lasted a few hours, however, being interrupted by a bloodcurdling screech from outside the king's window. He bolted upright with a start, just in time to witness his windows being raked open by enormous claws. Glass shards showered the air as he rolled off his bed, retreating into the corner.

There, climbing into his bedroom window and standing before him on all fours and nearly as tall as himself was an abomination to every one of the senses. Muscles grotesque and shifting sickeningly in the pale moonlight as it grew closer, three bulbous eyes fixated on Qirin. A guttural growl escaped its throat, teeth dripping with blackened saliva. Its breath reeked of death.

Letting out another screech it charged, straight for the Feishin king, quickly closing the distance between them. Qirin barely leapt out of the way of its sharp claws, instead colliding with his dressing screen, causing both to topple to the ground.

The scuffling of paws along the bamboo floors alerted him of the creature's pursuit. His hands met with a large jagged shard of glass, remains of his bedroom window. It wasn't his katana, much as he would have preferred, but it would have to do given the circumstances. He dragged it across the monster's side as it approached, causing it to howl with rage. His hand smarted as the jagged edge sliced into his own palm in the process, but it was a small price to pay for the damage inflicted on the monstrosity. A single swat from the creature sent Qirin flying across the room, this time tossed into a dresser.

White-hot pain shot up his ribcage upon impact, the breath knocked from his lungs. He had no doubt a few ribs were broken. Despite the pain, he shot up to his feet. There would be no survival if he stayed, no sanctuary left within the room. He scrambled his way out the bedroom door and fled, down the hall and as far from his bedroom as possible.

The night creature was hot on his heels.

Skidding around a corner, Qirin ran on, through the tapestry-covered walls and into the grand foyer, the sound of their scuffling feet echoing off the domed ceiling. Barefoot and in nightclothes, Qirin threw open the doors leading out of the palace, the cool air a kiss of relief upon his flushed cheeks. He did not get far outside, however, before jolting to a halt. His path was barred.

Drooling and growling, a row of abominations stood preventing access to the serpentine streets leading away from the Wind Palace, scales dark and teeth gnashing, a breed similar to that of which he encountered in his bedroom. Weighing the odds, he found it better to lock himself inside with one rather than try to fight his way through four, thus he retreated.

Slamming the front doors shut, he whipped around to face the night creature that assaulted him. It had done a number on the two Feishin sentries that had been stationed at the door, leaving them in shredded remains on the bloodied tile floor. Slowly, as if savoring this moment, it padded down the foyer, closing in on the king.

Back pressed to the door, with four other night creatures waiting on the other side, Qirin steeled himself, ready to accept his fate. There was nowhere to run, no weapon on his person that he could use in defense, wishing he had not cast the glass shard aside in his bedroom. He only hoped the monstrosity would make it quick.

As if by a miracle the night creature halted, staggering back as it stretched its blue-black wings taut. It shifted, and it was then Qirin saw the spear embedded in the creature's enormous shoulder.

He traced the night creature's gaze to find a dark-haired man standing on the landing above them. Fury scrunched his face, long red hair spilling over his shoulder. The king's eyes narrowed, recognizing him immediately—Lord Jing.

Hailing from one of the wealthiest families in the kingdom and son of a nobleman who was once in King Athilan's court, Lord Jing was beloved, charming, and charismatic, many of the things that Qirin lacked. He also had once been in love with Liana, a love he was certain did not end upon their royal union.

And now Jing was here. In the middle of the night, in Qirin's palace.

It did not take much imagination for Qirin to realize why Liana had been so absent as of late.

"I will hold him off!" Lord Jing's voice fell deaf beneath the night creature's cries, the monstrosity switching targets and now fixated on the lord as it bolted up the stairs towards him.

Qirin's lip curled in disgust. "I don't need your help!"

The night creature brought an enormous paw to strike Jing, but the lord did not stand by waiting for the blow. With executed finesse he leapt from the landing, meeting the first floor without even slowing down. The sight made Qirin visibly wince, but Jing appeared wholly unbothered. He grabbed a javelin from one of the fallen guards on the floor before coming to stand by Qirin's side.

"I think you do."

Footsteps shuffled from their left. Reinforcements, finally! Qirin wondered where they had been all this time. He turned toward them, searching their terrified faces, spears held feebly, uselessly, in their slackened palms. The creature arched its back, threw out its chest and howled a long, prolonged note as it exuded all the breath from its lungs toward the reinforcements. The air grew thick, putrid, and acidic.

Qirin immediately felt the burn, sucking in a breath and covering his face with his sleeved arm. Whatever the monster exhaled, he soon realized, was not meant to be inhaled. It was a weapon, and his guards were falling to it.

Fingers encircled his wrist and tugged, propelling him away. Lord Jing was dragging him from the scene, cloth wrapped around his face. Diving between the legs of the enormous monster, the two men retreated further into the palace in hope of escape.

There was no time for rest. Jing dragged him by his elbow, jerking him over to the elevator at the end of the corridor.

The one which would lead them to—

Qirin's feet shuffled to a halt as the realization of what Jing planned to do hit him.

"It would be a disaster if we take it to the Nephyl mines," Qirin growled. "You are a fool."

Jing tilted his chin, pity clear in his dark eyes. "No, I am a hero, saving the life of Liana's ungrateful husband."

Under less dire circumstances Qirin would have come up with a heated retort, but he held his tongue. He drew a step to join Jing on the platform, folding his arms over his chest. The pounding of massive footsteps rattled the light fixtures and made the elevator sway beneath their feet. Jing cranked the lever, and they plummeted, fast and hard, from the white room down into the mine.

The surrounding terrain rushed by Qirin's eyes in a blur, and he wondered if they were going to crash at the bottom considering the breakneck speed at which they descended. To further worsen matters, the platform swayed violently in its cavity, weight bowing the fragile metal frame above their heads. Fear seized Qirin and made his tongue go numb as the night creature, pursuing them even now, dug its claws into the ceiling of the elevator, piercing through sheet metal. A swipe of its claws striking the metal chain suspending them sent them swaying. The king flung out his palms to grasp the brass railing, holding on for dear life as he was threatened to be violently ejected. They plummeted down at an alarming speed, much faster than he thought was intended for the platform.

The elevator jolted to the bottom with a sickening snap, tossing both men backward. They were battered, but they would survive. At least from the elevator collapse.

The miners gasped at their jarring arrival, all operations ceasing. Their panic quickly escalated into horror as they soon discovered that their king brought company to observe the mines. Barely able to fit through the elevator's cavity, the enormous canine-with-wings charged at them, mostly ignoring the screaming miners who worked viciously to escape its path. Some miners were more brave; instead of cowering they drew their pickaxes and makeshift weapons. Qirin would have joined them, but Jing urged him on, nearly wrenching his arm out of its socket.

"No, no time! You must go! Go deeper!"

Qirin and Jing fled further, garments and hair whipping around them. Without the common headlamps of the miners, their path was soon lit solely by the eerie glow of the core shards from the walls, surrounding them on either side and growing more and more abundant as they went. They had barely set foot in the cavity of Nephyl, the discovery site of the core shards, when Jing lifted a palm, halting Qirin in his tracks.

Qirin looked at Lord Jing in question. A pickaxe lay in his other hand, one that he must have procured from the miners in the main entrance. Qirin's gaze flickered between Jing and the makeshift weapon, watching as the noble broke off a solitary glowing crystal from the wall with his bare hand and ran a finger along its jagged edge.

The lord's eyes lifted to Qirin's, sadness within them. His lips twisted with bitter resolve. "You need to live for your child. For *her*." He started to turn. "Love her as I do."

It was then that Qirin suddenly understood, recalling the incident with the Zenochian girl who struck a piece of Nephyl and died. It had let out a devastating shock of energy, one of the very reasons that miners had to wear careful garments and ensure no metal came into contact with raw core shards. Nausea threatened to gag him as Qirin threw a hand out to stop him.

"Jing, no!"

It was too late. The man's tunic easily slipped from Qirin's outstretched grasp when Jing charged back into the tunnel, straight into the claws of the night creature. Such bravery and resolve was admirable. An act of selflessness, though Qirin would not delude himself for a moment in thinking it was for himself and not Liana.

A brilliant light filled the cavity, followed by wretched sounds that made Qirin's stomach drop. The core shards tinkled softly, the entire cavern shaking slightly.

Just as suddenly as it occurred, the light abated, the cavern growing still once more. No sound of a struggle or pursuit remained. Only dead silence.

Shakily Qirin rose, his bloodied palms streaking the Nephyl along the walls as he edged himself out of the sanctuary of the cave, back into the mine shaft. It wasn't long before he saw it: the bulky figure of the night creature, crumbled into an electrified heap atop the ground. The ground glittered with emerald shards, remnants of Nephyl that had undoubtedly been destroyed by the blast.

Holding a breath to prevent the putrid stench of charred fur and skin infiltrating his nostrils, he approached, waiting to confirm his suspicions by searching the body of the monstrosity. And there, beneath it, lay Lord Jing, his body worse burnt and nearly unidentifiable had Qirin not known to look for him. A throaty rasp escaped Qirin as he lifted a hand to his own lips, entire body shuddering as he leaned into the nearby wall for support. His legs caved beneath him, forcing him down the wall along sharp crystals, but the pain was not worse than his ribs, and was much less than the loss experienced.

As he looked upon the body of his rival, a man who had every reason to loathe him and yet sacrificed himself for him, Qirin realized how utterly horrid he had behaved. This man gave his life out of pure altruism and love. He was not unlike Rito in that regard, earning him the deepest respect.

"I will never forget your service," Qirin said, eyes fluttering closed as he dipped his chin. "Peace, Jing. May you greet my family in the Nether Planes. I promise you: I will take care of her. I will."

24
ARDAN

Sweat beaded along Ardan's brow as he dabbed his forehead with a towel. His breaths came in rapidly, his heart thundering in his chest. At his side stood Inigo, a fellow clansmen he had known from youth. Surrounding them were at least a dozen imperial soldiers, yet here in the training room they were all equals, fighting to defend this foreign country against a common foe: the night creatures. Ardan's presence, however, had been useless. Still no night creatures ventured to Velspire. Perhaps soon he would be returning home.

And all without making amends with the empress, Ardan thought sadly, reaching for his cotton tunic. He pulled it over his head, muscles taut, concealing his Kindred Spirit tattoo of a bear upon his shoulder.

His friend seemed to detect his shift in mood, a once jovial facade to something far more somber. He joined Ardan at his side, exiting through the training doors and into the fresh, cool air of the palace halls.

"Something is on your mind," he mused.

Ardan threw him a casual sideways glance. "There's always something on my mind."

"But this is different." Inigo rubbed his chin, surveying him with forest-green eyes. His facial structure with a broad forehead and long, sallow cheeks reminded Ardan of Khatalia. Were it not for his short-cropped black hair, he could have claimed the man to be related to her. "I'd say your mind is preoccupied."

"I'm just thinking it's time for us to go," Ardan said. "There's been no attacks. I think Her Highness can handle things without our interference." He lifted his eyes, not even bothering to conceal his sorrow as he said, "Our assistance no longer seems needed."

No further argument escaped his friend. Inigo glanced at the suits of armor as they passed, seemingly searching for something.

"I'll ready the others, if that's what you want."

Ardan wiped his sweaty upper lip with the back of a hand and sniffed. It pained him to leave, and yet staying there, watching Nevia be swept away by a man that was not him—he could not bear it.

Even if it wasn't time to go, it was time for *him* to go.

"Let me just speak with her," Ardan said finally, clapping his friend on the shoulder. "I'll see what she thinks."

Inigo offered a respectful nod before sauntering off in the direction of the nearby kitchens, its warm scent of spices and fresh bread wafting toward them. The smells made Ardan's stomach growl. Nothing sounded better than a nice hot meal after an arduous training session.

Except, of course, speaking with Nevia.

No one seemed to know where she was, and his inquiries over her sent servants scurrying off, only to never return and leave him hanging. He poked around the places he knew she often frequented that were available to him, save for her private rooms, because he felt those were not his place to explore. Especially after having made a scene last time he went looking for her there.

At last he encountered a familiar face, a flash of fiery red hair flickering as it turned the corner, her skirts billowing from behind her. He rushed toward her, nearly toppling a suit of armor in his haste. He snatched up her arm, leaving the imperial seer shell-shocked and pallid.

"Orla," Ardan said, breathless. "Sorry, didn't mean to frighten you. Have you seen Nevia?"

At the mention of the empress the imperial seer seemed more on edge, her hands fidgeting together with the drawstrings at the neckline of her low-cut bodice. "She's gone," she murmured darkly.

A frown contorted Ardan's brow. "Gone? Gone where?"

"It's too late to do anything about it." She inhaled sharply, releasing her drawstrings and smoothing her palms over her skirt. "She's gone to Gaia's Core."

"Gaia's Core?" When Orla didn't elaborate Ardan reached to grasp her hands. "Tell me, please."

Orla inhaled sharply. "Then you'd better come and sit with me. It's a long story."

Pain laced Ardan's face as he sat back against the table in Orla's sitting parlor, legs crossed beneath him. "Why didn't she tell me?"

Orla's hands leapt defensively. "Don't look at me! I just know she went to the core with Renault, and after being drawn in to Saava's mind without her awareness, well . . . I'm really starting to question everything I thought I knew."

Ardan pinched the bridge of his nose. Everything that Orla shared made a smattering of sense, and yet his mind was spinning. Nevia did talk of visions; that was the very reason that she broke up with him. But what Orla shared from Saava's mind was so far-fetched, so surreal, that he was hesitant to believe it.

"When did she leave?" he asked sharply. "You said she was going to the core. Where did she go?"

Orla bit her lip. "I don't have the specifics. She didn't tell me. Just that she had a lead to the Feishin Kingdom and was leaving this afternoon."

Ardan rose from the floor so fast that his head started to spin, forcing him to throw out his hands on Orla's ritual table to steady himself. "I must go to her."

The imperial seer glanced over at him uncertainly. "It's too late. She already left hours ago."

"So I need to hurry. How do I get there?"

"I-I don't know."

Ardan balled his fist and slammed it onto the table. "What do you mean you don't know?! You're a damn seer. You know everything!"

At this the girl rose furiously. "I do *not* know everything! That's *not* the role of the seer! We're just messengers. I don't know any more than you do."

Ardan spun from the room, slamming the door shut behind him, leaving Orla mid-sentence before she could reiterate the same useless knowledge he'd already known.

He'd come to tell Nevia goodbye, only to find she already left and he had to chase her down to stop her from doing something potentially abhorrent.

Before it was too late.

25
QIRIN

A week had passed since the assault of the night creatures upon the Wind Palace. The royal couple sat painfully silent over tea in the dining room, the dead leaves outside the open window fluttering in the breeze. Qirin sat on his knees, watching Liana's face with newfound tenderness. She was taking the news of Lord Jing's death better than anticipated. Averting his gaze, she brought her teacup to her lips and drank soundlessly. A low, heavy sigh escaped Qirin, lowering his shoulders. Best to get it over with.

"You are probably wondering why I brought you out here for tea," Qirin stammered, hands suddenly clammy.

The queen tilted her head in his direction, her fingers tapping the edge of the table. On her ring finger she wore a white-gold band gifted to her by Qirin that morning. In place of a stone at its center, a core shard glistened in the brilliant morning light. "A peace offering," he had called it.

"You do curious things from time to time, Qirin. This is one of them, but I expect I'm going to get my answer soon enough."

This was it. The time of his ultimate confession. He pressed his fists into his thighs to halt their shaking. "It is time that I came clean with you."

At this her fingers halted.

"I am not attracted to women."

Liana snapped her gaze up to meet his, then, face pasty-white. "Qirin, I—"

He raised a hand, commanding silence. "I have tried to fight it all my life, to wrestle with my feelings. I thought I could bury it away, to live the way I was expected. But it's been consuming me, and it was simple to make you the target of my resentment." He inhaled sharply. "I told myself lies to justify my actions. I convinced myself that you didn't truly love me, instead only wanting the power behind my crown. What's horrible is that I believed it."

Liana's eyes narrowed. "Why are you telling me this now?" Her voice was sharp, hurt.

As it should be, Qirin reasoned. "You have every reason to hate me. I could never ask for your forgiveness. I have been in pain, which I inflicted on you to make myself feel better. I am very, very sorry, Liana. You have been treated most unfairly. I should've realized that you, too, were suffering, unable to be with the one you loved, as I was."

A frown furrowed her brow, fingers running over the folds of her gown. "There was someone?" she whispered.

Qirin dipped his head. "Rito."

He watched her face's lines soften. It surprised him when she reached out and grasped his hand, folding it gently within hers. "It makes so much sense now," she said, partly to herself than to him. "I always wondered why your best friend shadowed you, why you both exchanged glances when you thought no one was looking. I didn't think much of it, as it's, well—"

"Forbidden, yes," Qirin finished for her. "That's why we knew it would never go anywhere, but it was where my heart lied, and no matter how much I tried I couldn't change how I felt. My love for him was—is still strong, and I will not lie to you: it always will be."

The Feishin queen bobbed her head in quiet understanding.

Qirin took the opportunity to continue. "We both were robbed from choosing the ones we loved, instead forced together by the wishes of our parents." He closed his eyes, pain lacing his features. "Now both of our beloveds are gone, and we have only one another to lean on."

Liana tilted her head, earrings tinkling softly. "Did something happen to Rito?"

"He left the island for good," Qirin said flatly. "He wanted to remove himself from the equation."

"You could've stopped him," Liana said. "Or gone after him."

"No, I'm not going to force my will on him," he replied. "This was his choice, and I need to be the bigger man and respect that. The thing is—you and I, we're still here. And I guess—well, I'm *hoping* that we can forge a new path forward, now that we better understand each other."

When she remained silent, he continued further with: "Maybe it will never be love, but perhaps we can reforge our relationship on trust and respect, maybe even become friends?"

Liana deadpanned, hands resting on her swollen belly. A heavy sigh escaped her as she tilted her face to the heavens. "Oh, Qirin, is that what you really think? That I don't love you?"

The words were not what he expected to hear. "Well, is it not the truth?"

She was already shaking her head before he even finished. "I've loved you ever since we strode through the gardens together for the first time. Lord Jing was my first love, true, but we knew that we could not be together after my father proposed me to you. We understood that."

Slowly Qirin's heart sank, feeling quite foolish for all that he rambled on about their hearts elsewhere and being trapped into a loveless marriage. It was like that for him, but perhaps such was not the case for her.

"But the night he died," Qirin prodded, "he was here. With you, in the palace—"

A cool breeze tousled Liana's hair, sternness sharpening her features. "He came to visit. That is all. I do not appreciate what you are insinuating. I would tread carefully, if I were you."

It could have been a lie, yet after Qirin's own confession he found little reason for her to say such.

"You mean that you and Lord Jing weren't . . . ?"

Horror flashed on her face. "You mean was I cheating on you with Lord Jing? Good heavens, Qirin, no! Is that what you thought?"

Shame made it so that he could not lift his face. "I was under this impression, yes. I-I was convinced that the child you carry is not mine."

"Absolutely not true." She was seething; never had he seen her so angry, and to say that he was not marginally taken aback would not have been truthful. "Do you think me that dishonorable?"

He reached out to snatch up her hand, only to have her draw it away. "Look, I understand you're angry—"

"That doesn't even scratch the surface of what I am!" Her glare was coarse as her eyes flashed to his. "If you thought this was happening, why didn't you ever speak to me and try to set things right? Why did you go on believing this?!"

No argument was sound when he thought about it. He was disappointed in himself for thinking so lowly of her, especially when she had given him no reason to do so.

She loved him. It was a difficult truth for him to swallow, and yet it rang with validation as he recalled all those tender moments she doted on him with affection, her disappointment when he did not return it. He recalled, most recently, the funeral of Lady Rumaar, and how she tried so hard to comfort him while simultaneously placating the people because he was unable to do so.

She was a better royal and partner than he was, and for that and more he felt deep shame.

Tears began to flow, beading at his chin. Now as he gazed upon his queen, he saw her in a new light, admiring her in a way that he wished he had sooner. While he could never love her the way she desired, perhaps he could love her in his own way. As a partner in ruling this kingdom together, in raising the child they created and would soon be arriving. But would she give him this chance, or was the damage he dealt too great for repair?

He opened his mouth to speak, and was perhaps saved from uttering more foolishness when a guard emerged from the curtain partitioning the room from the hall. The sunlight gleamed on her black leather armor and the exposed katana at her hip.

"Your Majesties." She offered both a bow. "I am sorry to interrupt, but you have a visitor."

Liana dabbed the corner of her mouth with her linen napkin. "Of course, send them in," she responded.

Qirin's heart leapt into his throat. For one traitorous moment, he hoped that Rito had a change of heart and had come back. Even to grace him with only friendship, maybe he decided to stay.

Maybe Liana would even understand and allow them something, *anything*. Maybe—

Qirin watched, hopeful, as a shadow emerged from behind the soldier. Aspirations were quickly shattered as the shadow split into two, and standing before him were two individuals he couldn't care less to see. Not on his soil, or ever again.

He felt as though his knees were kicked out from under him as he locked eyes with the woman who had quickly rose to the top of his list of enemies.

"Qirin," the empress voiced, tone authoritative despite being in *his* palace. "We need to talk."

Fury flared his nostrils. *She knows,* he thought irritably. *She knows that I disobeyed her and distributed Nephyl, and now she's come to tell me that I will pay the price.*

Would she start another war? He did not know, but one thing was certain:

The warrior in him was ready.

26
NEVIA

The empress couldn't help feeling that her very presence tainted the dining room if gauging from the way Qirin recoiled when he saw her, not hiding but embracing a loathing that made her take a slight step backward.

She inhaled sharply, an insurgence of anguish threatening to overload her senses. She could feel it, that culminating power. Would she lose control and unleash her death magic, right then and there? It would certainly make her next request that much more difficult, even if she was perhaps doing Qirin a favor by doing away with his wife he didn't love.

As if sensing her struggle, Renault clasped one of her hands in his, running a thumb over her knuckles to coax her, comfort her. She bit her lip, wishing he had not done this. The touch felt intimate, and the Feishin king thought so as well, with the way his eyes darted to their hands.

He made no comment as he rose from his kneeling, offering her a tilt of the head in a mocking bow. Nevia wasn't particularly surprised. Their time for pleasantries was long gone, made abundantly clear back in Velspire.

She tucked a lock of hair uncomfortably, stealing a glance at what had been tea time between the royal couple. She shouldn't have blackmailed him, and yet seeing Liana sit there, one hand protective over their shared child, without even knowing of his deceit struck a hollow chord in her that knew the hurt a spouse can do to their beloved. A desire to protect Liana of betrayal by the one she loved resurrected itself.

As if detecting the unspoken tension, Liana clambered to her feet, turning toward Nevia and giving her a curious, sideways glance. "I will leave you to your conversation, then." Her fingers brushed over Qirin's shoulder briefly as she passed him. To Nevia's surprise, he did not respond by cringing.

The king straightened his shoulders, waving at the now-vacant side of the table. "Please, have a seat. Make yourselves at home. Renegade, wasn't it?"

Nevia noticed her personal guard stiffen. "Renault, Your Highness."

"Oh, right. That's what I meant, yes."

Qirin's mask of hospitality was see-through, the fury of hatred lurking beneath. Regardless, Nevia hitched up her skirts and knelt at the table opposite the Feishin king.

"Thank you," Nevia said, "both for your kind offer and for having us unexpectedly like this. I don't like to drop in uninvited."

The servant at her left appeared flustered, having made a mad dash for the teapot but failed to beat Qirin to it. The king pressed his lips together, snatching up a pot and pouring tea for each of his guests, the amber liquid steaming. It smelled like citrus, and she did not have to feign interest when he offered a cup to Renault and her.

The three drank in silence, with only the wind chimes outside the window to break it. It had been the final days of the Nephyl War when Nevia had last been in the Feishin Kingdom. Just as before, she could not help marveling at its beauty. Sheer curtains fluttered in the gentle breeze, bringing with it the scent of jasmine from the outdoor gardens. Banners of the Feishin Lotus and an intricate brocade of a golden shrine and green diamond adorned the wall at Qirin's back, the only two walls devoid of lights powered by Nephyl energy. A frown furrowed Nevia's brows as she studied the brocade. It was clearly dated, faded by the sun and weathered with age. Green swirls were stitched to exude from the diamond, and, if gauging from the six stone pillars depicted out front, she was certain it was the Shrine of Everlasting Peace.

Qirin shifted slightly, suddenly cutting the tapestry from view. "Why are you here, Nevia?"

Nevia set down her teacup, with more force than intended. "I need your help."

The king's eyes met hers. "Oh, really?"

"Elante is dying."

"What a pity." His tone held none.

His aloofness made Nevia ball her hands into fists on the smooth table. "Please, Qirin, I know you're angry at me—"

"I offered my aid to the empress that saved my country from annihilation by exposing her husband's lies. You, however, are not her"—he jabbed a finger at her—"you threatened and manipulated me, and reminded me why I cannot trust any other country but my own. I revoke my offer to provide aid henceforth. You are not worthy of it."

Renault slammed a palm on the table, rattling the tea ware. "Oh, bloody hell! Don't you see how childish you're being? Let go of your petty grudge and listen to the empress for a damn minute. This is serious!"

Fury danced in Qirin's eyes. Before he could utter a retort, however, Nevia blurted: "We need to get to Gaia's Core."

Qirin's brows rose in question. "There is such a place?"

"Yes, and I think it's here." Nevia procured the piece of parchment tucked within her sleeve, the very one they found in the vault, the one they hoped would lead to their salvation. "We found this in Emperor Rufus' vault. Since the core shards were discovered here, and this map suggests the source is here, I think the only entrance to the core may very well be on this island."

Qirin's dark eyes glittered. "Show me."

Nevia smoothed it down and slid it across the table, the paper greedily seized by the Feishin king.

"It could be anything," Renault added gruffly, shooting Nevia a dark look. It seemed clear he was loath to divulge this information to Qirin, and Nevia could hardly blame him. But if they were going to save Saava and Elante, Nevia saw no other recourse.

She toyed with the hem of her sleeve, watching as Qirin frowned down at the paper. "And, by the way"—Nevia drew in a breath, the words paining her before uttering them—"Your secret is safe with me. I'm not going to go tell Liana."

"It doesn't matter, she knows," Qirin murmured, not removing his gaze from the parchment.

Nevia blinked. "She does? Then why—"

"Why am I still mad?" He thrust the paper toward her, the map flying off the table and between the two guests. "Because you blackmailed me, Nevia. Friends don't do that. You found my weakness and exploited it. How the hell did you expect me to feel after that? More than pleased to welcome back a toxic friendship? I think not."

Renault's hand flexed to the jeweled hilt of his sword, and Nevia could easily envision the situation getting unnecessarily bloody if it were to continue without intervention. She placed a hand on his, shaking her head softly.

Qirin was right; how could she expect them to make amends and resume their friendship? She was nearly as bad as Darius, even if the stakes were not quite as high.

"I was wrong." Nevia's chin dipped. "And I am sorry—"

Qirin rose to standing, the folds of his brightly colored kimono unfurling as he threw an arm toward the entrance. "Just get out of my sight. I don't ever want to see you again."

Nevia swallowed a painful knot, remorse digging its claws into her very heart. "Please, Qirin you don't mean that—"

"Oh, you bet I do. In fact, next time you are spotted on this island I will have you imprisoned. You can forget about our alliance."

Renault shot up, striding around the table and standing within mere inches from Qirin's face. "You're being an ass," Renault seethed between clenched teeth. "Your very decisions could cost a young woman her life, and the life of the goddess—"

A laugh, high and shrill escaped Qirin. "See if I care. I don't believe in some stupid goddess sleeping in the core of our planet anyway."

The empress was shaking, an ache throbbing in her chest. She wanted to pound her fists into Qirin, to scream in his face and tell him how puerile he was being. Instead she rose and offered a slight bow. "Then I guess we're done here."

Qirin regarded her briefly before gesturing to the curtained doorway. "Guess so."

She didn't offer Qirin a farewell. Instead she reined in her emotions yet again, swallowed the lump that was nearly a permanent resident in her throat, and marched out into the hall. She felt Renault lay a hand against the small of her back, following her lead away from the palace and into the courtyard.

No one said anything to them as they passed. Whether they understood the tension between the king and the foreign empress was uncertain. The copper gate was swung open and slammed behind them, effectively sealing them from the Wind Palace. Instead of continuing down the rickety path into town, however, Nevia hitched up her skirt and began to traverse up the grassy hill.

Renault jogged over to her side. "Where are we going, Empress?"

We. She liked the sound of that.

"To the Shrine of Everlasting Peace." She trained her gaze straight ahead, the golden onion-shaped rooftops of the holy site visible in the distance. "I wish to pay my respects to Queen Arethusa one last time, seeing as I'm no longer welcomed here."

Renault swore darkly, breathless from their fierce pace. "While I appreciate the sentiment, I would like to remind you that time is of the essence if you want to save your friend and—"

His remaining words were left to die in his throat as Nevia produced the parchment and placed it in his hands. She found it difficult to suppress her grin. "Oh, right, and going to Gaia's Core while we're there. The tapestry behind Qirin's head depicted something fascinating to me. For a society that doesn't believe in

Saava, I find it curious they would weave a golden shrine with a big green diamond beneath it. I think it's way more than symbolic."

Renault clapped her shoulder. Something akin to pride was reflected in his tone when next he spoke. "You sly empress, you."

It was true, and she normally would have felt bad. But Qirin specifically said that he did not want to see her again on the island, not that she had to leave it immediately. She did not need his blessing to enter their holy grounds. All were welcomed there, even a foreign empress of another realm.

"I told Elante that I would save her." Nevia set her jaw. "And I will do whatever it takes to keep that promise."

27
NEVIA

The shrine was much as Nevia remembered from Queen Arethusa's funeral, with its onion-shaped roof constructed from a lattice of stained glass, allowing a shower of rainbow colors to dance along the marble flooring. Lanterns powered by generated energy adorned each wall, allowing plenty of light despite the shrine's depth in the ground.

Caskets of the departed nobility lay on their own separate altars in even rows of gold. As she tread carefully through the silent tomb, she couldn't ignore the sensation of trespassing, disturbing something sacred.

"So what are we looking for, exactly?" Renault echoed her thoughts, running a finger along one of the caskets.

The empress had been wondering similarly since she observed the tapestry. Even if it suggested the core was beneath the shrine, there had been no indication where the entrance resided. She didn't know where the hidden entrance to Gaia's Core would be, but resolve kept her going. They just needed to look hard enough.

Nevia's footfalls echoed through the silent resting place as she strode over to the late queen's casket. Queen Arethusa's death had taken its toll on the empress over the years. While she did not know her well, Arethusa had offered aid when she was under no obligation to do so, and how was she repaid? By being duped and then killed on her own soil.

Nevia fell to her knees and dipped her head. "I'm so sorry," she whispered, running her palm along the embossed gold face of the casket. To think of what she would say if she saw the world now. Her daughter, wed and shipped off to the other side of the world. Her son, ruling over his inherited kingdom with an iron fist and a sword at his hip. The night creatures, threatening nations of every corner of the continent, including the Feishin Kingdom. It was a tragedy she was glad Arethusa was spared from.

Her guard's throat cleared, returning her to the present. "I love that you're worshipping the queen and all, but we have a mission that's rather time sensitive."

Nevia lost track of how many times he had reminded her of this, but it was plenty. It struck her as odd that he was perhaps more concerned about Saava and Elante's fate than herself, but reasoned this was how he dealt with stress. He was a soldier, first and foremost. He was used to strict regimens and deadlines.

"I wasn't—" Nevia protested, but conceded and rose. "I don't know, to be honest. I just know the door has to be somewhere in here."

"That's entirely unhelpful."

"I understand that!" Nevia waved her hands impatiently. "But I'm trying, alright? Why don't you make yourself useful and do the same!"

Anger flared his nostrils. She half-expected him to chide further with something witty, but instead he spun on heel to the opposite side of the shrine, getting lost between rows of caskets to further his search.

She passed the caskets, admiring the ornate engravings on each as she went. One casket, raised higher than the rest in the shrine's center, arrested her attention and prompted her to examine it further. Unlike others, this one was polished to a fine gloss. What further set it apart was the lengthly inscription along the casket's face. She ran a finger over the engravings, feeling the grooves etched there. In contrast to the other names in Tolsi, the Feishin's native tongue, this particular passage was one she had seen before, chiefly because she had seen it everywhere. The Feishin proverb: *Pass with a heart of peace and understanding.*

It made sense, she supposed, to pass on to the next life with a heart of peace and understanding. But it was curious to dedicate an entire casket to it, especially when none of the others hosted such. She remembered it well: The First King, King Feishin, originated the proverb, thus the people clung to it. The Feishin believed that through peace anything could be achieved. It made sense for an archway, but for a casket? A bit excessive. Perhaps he was trying to make a statement?

Nevia gasped, the obvious glaring at her.

A statement. That was exactly what this casket was making.

Nevia's fingers gripped the side, finding where the lip overlapped the base of the casket. Hesitation gave her pause. Was she really going to open someone's grave? It was disrespectful, at best, and outright harmful at worst. She recalled that the Feishins believed that the deceased would be ripped from the Nether Planes to haunt Gaia for eternity if their slumber was disturbed. Qirin could have her imprisoned for defiling the dead, which after their previous conversation he would have no reservation doing.

And yet the phrase made sense.

Pass with a heart of peace and understanding.

They must have known, she reasoned, *that the path to Gaia's Core lay beneath their burial grounds.* What better place to reach Saava's own place of rest? The meaning behind the proverb seemed lost over the generations, but to Nevia it could not have been more clear. She began to lift the lid of the casket.

It creaked loudly, lacquer snapping from being sealed so long. Renault swooped over to her, panic causing his complexion to pale. "What are you doing, Empress?!"

Nevia swallowed hard, running a hand along the script. "It says here to pass with a heart of peace and understanding."

Renault shrugged dismissively. "It's just a proverb. Everyone knows it—"

"I think it's more than that."

She started to lift it again, causing his eyes to nearly bulge from their sockets. His hand grasped hers, halting her movement.

"Wait." His eyes held wariness when they clashed with hers, but also concern. "You can't just—I don't think you should—"

She smiled, then, finding the bravery deep within herself that she needed. Gently she tugged her hand free of his grasp, readjusting her grip. "Trust me."

She began to pry it open.

But it was stuck.

She repositioned herself to get a better angle, but the lid would not budge. It was sealed shut.

"Let me help."

Renault came alongside her, putting all of his weight behind his efforts as he attempted to shrug off the lid. They heaved for several moments, until a snap resounded through the shrine, the resistance giving way and allowing the casket's lid to slide ajar. Nevia swallowed back her panic, steeling herself for whatever they were to find inside. Maybe, just maybe, she had been wrong. Maybe they would find only the rotted corpse of the First King, ruining his afterlife *and* being haunted forever.

That would certainly put a damper on her day.

"Well, I'll be," Renault said breathlessly beside her, giving her courage enough to crack open an eye to peer inside.

In place of a body, there was a set of stone steps, leading down into the depths of inky blackness.

Renault gave her upper arm a squeeze before pulling her into a sideways embrace. "You've done it!"

Relief flooded every cell of her body, a laugh bubbling in her throat. She flung herself into his arms, allowing him to lift her and spin her in a circle to celebrate their victory.

They were close, so close to saving Elante. Soon they would find Saava and everything would be righted. She gripped his hand, smiling from ear to ear.

They found it. They would succeed. Elante would live.

28
NEVIA

The narrow stairway led to a tunnel, cold, dank and, most especially dark. Even with the shrine's stolen kerosene lanterns in hand, it was still difficult to see more than ten steps.

They had been descending for hours. The tunnel became less structured as they went, widening in some sections and narrowing in others. A few were barely wide enough for Nevia to crawl through, while others seemed large enough for three men to walk abreast.

While Nevia realized Gaia's Core would be, true to its name, at the core of the planet, she did not conceptualize what the descent into it would be like. Her legs felt like jelly as they plowed into the inky darkness, the light above mere a pinprick threatened to be snuffed.

A blend of emotions coursed through Nevia as they further descended. What if Saava rejected them? What if they came upon a dead end? Worse yet: what if Nevia used her death magic on Saava herself, effectively killing the goddess she was trying so hard to save? None of these prospects were promising.

Despite the darkness cloaking her, the empress failed to conceal her anxieties. Renault wrapped an arm around her shoulders, drawing her close. He had been much more forward since their shared kiss in the vault. While she enjoyed being the recipient of this newfound affection, it made her queasy. It felt *wrong*.

Stabbing into the silence, Renault's voice broke out, hoarse from lack of use while simultaneously kindling with excitement. "I wonder what we'll find in the core."

Nevia raised a pencil thin brow, attempting to slow her pace so as not to trip on the rocky soil that was becoming more unsteady as they descended. "I don't know, the sleeping goddess, maybe?"

He continued at his furious pace. "Beyond that."

She lifted her lantern to peer into his face. It was aglow, and not merely by the light in her hand. Something burned in his eyes; if Nevia were to describe it, she would say it was aspiration.

"There must be a trove of Nephyl there. Imagine the possibilities! You would be revered, perhaps grow even more powerful than the goddess herself and become one of your own."

His words chilled something in her core. Perhaps it was how the truth unintentionally rang through his words, in that she was quite likely a goddess herself. Or at least a lesser form of one.

"I have no interest in power or Nephyl," Nevia stated, voice cold. "I am only here because I'm told that I need to, and that I need to save Elante."

He glanced over at her, then, face schooling itself back into a mask of indifference. "Of course, Empress. Forgive me. My imagination got carried away."

No further word of power or authority escaped him. In fact, no further words escaped him at all. He held his lantern high and continued down the path, Nevia a short distance behind. She could not help watching him with a new unease. Something about that abrupt shift in demeanor made Nevia squirm and suddenly feel uncertain.

He must just be excited, Nevia told herself. She could partly relate. She was excited to save Elante, too, and be the hero that saved Saava from her untimely demise.

Her concern faded further into the recesses of her mind as they took a sharp turn, nearly tumbling down the stretch of flooring before it started to level out. The ceiling of the pocket was no longer brushing their heads, and wider, allowing them to slow their descent, even if brief.

She lifted her arm to cast a beam of light within a radius around her. They stood in a cavern, dirt packed on either side. She lost track of how long they had been climbing downward, or how far down they had made it. Her legs felt like jelly, and when she began to take another step forward, Renault threw out an arm to halt her.

"I think this is far enough for now."

They couldn't stop, even though everything in Nevia's being screamed at her to do so. Now that she stopped moving, it took all of her willpower not to collapse to the ground and take a breather. "She's counting on us—"

"And we'll fail her for sure if we're dead," Renault countered, snuffing out his lantern to conserve oil. "Which is bound to happen if we keep going like this."

The harsh reality of his words stung, but it was true: they did need to rest. Even if brief.

Renault unfastened his dark cloak from around his shoulders, draping it around her as she allowed herself to slide down the cavern wall, resting her legs for the first time since they had stepped foot inside the passageway. An involuntary groan escaped her as she stretched out her calves.

"Rest," he repeated. "I'll keep an eye out."

"But we can't be long," Nevia said urgently.

His dark gaze clashed with hers. "We won't be."

She dug her fingers into the cold earth beneath her, rooting herself, grounding herself as she readied to lean her head against the wall. Her guard, warm and soft, brought her to rest against his chest instead. The rhythmic beat of his heart beneath his soft tunic is what allowed sleep to claim her, the warmth of his embrace thawing the chill that clung to her.

She awoke to the sound of droplets. No longer was she encased in the warmth of Renault's embrace, finding herself instead on the cavern's dirt floor. Loose curls tumbled over her shoulder as she rose. Her mind was refreshed, her body less so. The full ramifications of their trek felt heavily in her stiff calves.

They were fully cloaked in darkness, both lanterns extinguished. As if detecting her awakening, one of the lanterns was cranked on a short distance away, illuminating Renault's dark figure. His broad shoulders were dipped, head bowed until he noticed the empress' gaze on him.

"Good morning, Empress," he said softly. "I trust you slept soundly?"

Morning? "How long did I sleep?"

With that Renault stalked over and knelt before her, not deigning to respond. He dropped the lantern beside them to grasp both her hands to ease her up. Her muscles screamed in protest, yet she obliged and lifted herself to her feet. Their faces were mere inches from each other, his breath tickling her chin. "I have no idea, but you needed your rest. It hasn't been longer than a night, of that I'm certain."

A whole night?! Panic dug its claws into her as she tore herself away from him, snatching up his discarded lantern and moved in the direction of the cavern's decline. "We must get going, then!" she urged. "I never wanted to rest long, just enough to regain some strength—"

"That is what I wanted for you, as well."

Renault allowed himself to lean in, lips softly grazing her ear as he whispered: "But you looked so precious, so stunning in sleep that I did not want to disturb you."

A chill ran down her spine. Instead of being flattered, she couldn't help feeling disturbed. "You watched me sleep?"

His expression was unreadable, yet his gaze was clouded with the unmistakable expression of lust. "It is my job to protect you, Empress."

She couldn't suppress her shudder. This felt far more than mere protection. "We should go," she repeated, unable to quell the waver in her voice.

He caressed her cheek, sending another chill down her spine. "Of course, Empress."

And again they were off, delving deeper and deeper.

And deeper.

29
NEVIA

Nevia had no sense of time as they continued their trek. The only indicators were their stomach aches and dwindling rations, which she wished they had brought more of. They only had the supplies in Renault's pack, which was not plentiful by any means. Already they exhausted most of their supply; the journey back would undoubtedly be uncomfortable unless the goddess could provide her assistance. When she brought voice to this, however, Renault waved away her concerns, reassuring her that they had nothing to fear.

"She is the goddess of creation, after all," he replied jovially. "What is producing some sustenance for her saviors?"

Nevia thought he was getting too confident, but she did not voice it.

Not only about Saava's benevolence, but also their relationship. His hands fled to her, more frequently and more often. A reaction that, once welcomed, now became something that brought Nevia discomfort. Finally to the point that Nevia tore free from his arm about her waist.

The gesture did not go unnoticed.

His lantern stopped bobbing as he came to a halt. "Empress?"

Her heart pounded in her chest. "We need to talk." Her voice sounded thin, even to her.

She could barely make out his features in the dimness of the tunnel, one brow arched in question. "I'm listening."

A heavy sigh escaped her. No way to proceed except honestly. "I know that I'm conflicted and difficult to read," she admitted. "I'm going through a lot."

Something unreadable glittered in his dark eyes. "I know, Empress, I know. And I want to make it all easier for you." He lifted a hand to cup her cheek. "You see, from the very moment Darius brought you home, when I first laid eyes on you"—his hand moved from her cheek, brushing her thick locks over her shoulder, strands of her hair gliding through his fingers—"I was infatuated. And yet, my hands were tied. You were to be my cousin's wife, so of course you were off-limits if I wanted to keep my head, and then after his death I wanted to grant you space. To give you time to mourn."

Nevia inhaled sharply, none the wiser of his prior infatuation. The warm smiles, the excessive touching. She had thought he was friendly, not once thinking it was because he desired her. She partly wished the earth would crumble and swallow her whole.

"But now." His wide smile sent chills down her spine. "Now I am free to claim you. To make you mine."

A frown furrowed her brow. If his words were meant to make her feel warm and fuzzy, it was having the opposite effect. "Renault—"

"Never have I seen a woman such as you." He swept a hand to gesture toward her. "Your bronze skin. Your white-blonde hair. You're exotic. I have experienced many women, but none like you. I want you, Nevia Bylilly. All of you."

His hand found her waist in the darkness and drew her in. This now felt wrong.

All. Completely. Wrong.

"I don't know what to say," she whispered.

He lowered his nose to brush hers. "Then say nothing."

Cold air stung her nostrils as she inhaled sharply, lifting a hand to his chest to shove him away. "I am flattered by your affection, and I do care for you, Renault, I do—"

"Then was is it?" he snarled, the polite, sincere demeanor of her personal guard ebbing away into something darker, more ugly. "The people would celebrate our union! The empire would remain in the Androvich bloodline. Don't you see? It's perfect!"

He was right: it was perfect, thoughts that had been weighing greatly in Nevia's mind since the beginning of their kindling relationship. She shook her head. "No, it's not that."

"It's *him*." The amount of venom in Renault's tone made her recoil, and she did not need her imagination to know precisely who Renault was referring to.

Nevia's spine grew rigid, not wanting to bring Ardan into this conversation. "That's enough, Renault."

"And who do you think you are, telling me to stop?" he barked, throwing a hand violently into the air. He strode toward her, forcing her to walk backward. "Some pompous, arrogant bitch from the north who thinks she can just sit on my cousin's throne after he died and whore herself off to her native heathens?"

The insult made her gasp. A new side of Renault was being exposed. One that was more loathsome, more vile. Her heel snagged the hem of her gown as she backed away, causing her to lose her footing and stumble into the wall. Renault was on her within a heartbeat, towering over her and pressing his face into hers.

"Don't make me keep groveling for you," he growled, grasping a fistful of her hair. "Especially when I know you want me as much as I want you."

Something within her snapped, patience wearing to nonexistence. She snatched up his wrist, digging her nails into flesh hard enough to leave imprints. "Stop your nonsense," she demanded, tone cold enough to freeze the air. "I order you to unhand me immediately and stop this foolishness."

His laugh came out as a bark, spittle flecking her face. "Ah, there it is: using my cousin's authority against me again. Pray tell, how often are you going to keep relying on that little backbone he gave you? Is that all you can do?" And then he leaned in, lips brushing her ear as he whispered more callously, "And I can't help but wonder: will you use that same authority in bed? I cannot wait to find out."

White-hot anger flashed within her, spilling forth from her chalice of restraint. She slapped him across the face, the sound of meeting flesh reverberating against the barren walls. He was quick to recover, grasping her face tight enough to snap her jaw. The calm, kind face of her protector was gone, replaced by someone dark and feral, a man she could not recognize.

"I do love a good challenge," he growled, cinching her close. "You may not know what's good for you, Empress, but I do. I always have. It's my job, after all, as your personal guard, to keep you from any—"

His words ended with a grunt, as she slammed her knee into his crotch. Hard.

"I have never felt so repulsed by anyone," she spat, shoving him away and unsheathing the dagger at her thigh. She went nowhere without it, and today was no exception. She evened it at him, fixating it at the tip of his sternum, but to her surprise he only laughed.

"You would cut me down," he said mockingly, "when only hours ago you so willingly displayed your affection towards me?"

"A mistake," Nevia snapped, voice strengthening to match her resolve. "I see that now. I was conflicted and weak, and you exploited me."

Long sheets of dark hair fell over his face as he shook his head, shoulders slumped. "So ready to blame, when the only one you can blame is yourself." He lifted his chin defiantly, acting as if the tip of a blade wasn't ready to pierce him for any wrong move. Perhaps he thought Nevia was bluffing, but he was wrong.

Determination contorted her features, nose wrinkling. "I can blame myself for many things, but for your actions, using me to gain my late husband's crown? I think not."

It happened so fast. He snatched her wrist, disarming her in one deft movement and twisting her arm painfully till she feared it would snap. She was whipped around and pinned to his chest. The tables had turned, and now a blade was placed against her throat.

"I wasn't lying when I told you that I was infatuated with you," he murmured, running a finger along her cheek. "Like I said: you're a foreign beauty that I envision many a night sinking myself into. But you are also in my way. You sit upon the throne that should've been *mine*, dictating the people who should be following me, and as long as you sit your imperial ass there I will not have any leverage over the people."

So there it was. Her personal guard, the man who was meant to protect her from any threat, was indeed the threat itself. Her throat constricted. How betrayed she felt.

"So those moments," she faltered. "Those kisses, your words —"

"Flattery, mostly," Renault confessed. "But I'll admit in the heat of the moment I meant some of it. I was—no, am—obsessed with you, and I wouldn't mind having such a fine beauty rule at my side if you'll cooperate."

"This was all about power."

Something lethal infiltrated his voice. "No. It was about everything that Darius got—that I never did."

Suddenly Nevia found herself wishing it was a night creature she faced rather than the monstrosity standing before her. At her struggle she found his grip on her only tighten, the blade's edge biting into her skin. "What is it you want, then? Marriage?"

"Not quite. What I want is to tarnish your reputation, lay claim to you so that you have no choice but to wed me and make me emperor. After all, who wants a woman who whores herself to her bodyguards to rule them?"

Anger unlike any she experienced coursed through her. Hurt, pain, betrayal. Already she had lost so many, and now Renault, too? Someone she thought she cared for, only to have ripped from her the illusion made by this monster, who claimed it had never been real?

Dark tendrils erupted from her fingertips, and the moment she knew what was happening it was too late: it encircled the strong arms bracing her, the sword hand that held the blade to her throat. Choking rasps escaped her captor, and she took this opportunity to wriggle free. She twirled to snatch up her dagger, only to find there was no need for it: the magic was a weapon more potent, more lethal, than a blade ever could be. Unlike the slow infection that seized Elante, this was abrupt, more potent. Within a few moments he was convulsing on the ground, and she looked down at him without a single ounce of pity. The light from the nearby lantern streamed over his face, unveiling his ashen skin and ink-black eyes.

For the first time she was glad to be the Goddess of Death. Her only regret was that she could not inflict him again.

And again, and again, and again.

A slight gasp escaped Nevia as she shook her head, hands fleeing to her throat. What was she doing? What just came over her that would make her wish for the death of another living soul? What he did was wrong, yes, and she was angry. So very much so. And yet, to do this . . .

She watched the life fade from his eyes, the final breath leave his lungs as his struggling body grew still. Her knees gave way and buckled, tossing her to the cold earth below. Tears fought their way through. Tears of relief, anguish, guilt, and fury. She could not believe him. Could not believe his utter betrayal, his false devotion. She would never know his story, but whatever it was did not lessen the gravity of his actions.

Finally she lifted herself on trembling legs, dusting off her skirt before snatching both lanterns. With a coarse swallow she threw her attention back into the task at hand: the endless, spiraling darkness beyond that beckoned her.

She was alone now, and the only way to proceed was forward.

With the weight of the sins she now bore.

30
NEVIA

The echo of her footsteps propelled her forward when everything else felt it would give out. It became a rhythm, a consistent pattern that stilled the restlessness in her heart. She dulled out all thought. She had to, lest she succumb to the pain and despair twisting within her core, something which left her feeling raw and miserable inside.

It was the glow ahead that assured her the end was nigh. The light at the end of the tunnel. The walls were painted a sickly green from this brilliant light, powerful enough to tint her skin and tattered gown. She threw a hand to shield her eyes, so accustomed to the darkness. The earth smelt different here somehow. Newer, fresher. Cleaner. Restored. The pull of descent ceased, Nevia's footing steadying on even ground.

She halted before it. *Her.* In all her magnificence.

The goddess was encased in a face of crystal, its glistening surface emanating the very light that permeated the walls coated in core shards. The very core felt like one massive shard; Nevia could feel the energy radiating around her. The hairs on Nevia's arms stood on end, a chill running down her spine. There was no doubt that Renault was correct: there was enough power here to wield authority of the entire planet.

Saava's beauty was even greater in life than any dream. Dark hair was frozen in time, streaming around her as if flowing through water. Her perfect lips were tinted pink, lashes lush and thick, the perfect contrast to her pale skin. She was the embodiment of peace; it was hard to believe that she was in any imminent danger.

Nevia drew close enough to hear the gentle hum of energy around the goddess. The light within the crystalline shell pulsated, and, if studying it very carefully, she could see thin tendrils flowing from the crystal's center to dance up the walls.

It was power. Energy. Life.

Creation.

Nevia knew from the legends that Saava was the goddess of creation. Her powers gave life, her visions becoming reality. Mother of all mothers. And yet seeing her static and encased in a chrysalis of her own magic made her seem just as helpless and frail as any mortal.

This was greater than anything Nevia could have anticipated. She expected to see core shards, the clear connection between the two undeniable. But this alcove, the goddess herself—

The arduous journey almost felt worth it for the breathtaking sight alone.

As if drawn by magnetic force, Nevia walked forward, and before she could think it through she lay a palm over the smoothness of the crystal face. Initially cold, it started warming at her touch, and in that brief moment she felt a sense of connection unlike any in her existence.

The magic within the crystal sang to the magic within her, and she could feel it, then, awakening and culminating within her. As if detecting it, the energy of the core shard probed deeper, harder, pressing past any barriers that Nevia mentally erected to keep herself safe. It felt like twin forces, so similar and yet so different, desperately worked to meet, and it was too much for her mortal body to bear.

A cry escaped Nevia's lips as she wrenched herself away, clutching her hand to her chest. It seemed fine, even if she herself did not. And then she heard the sickening crack that echoed throughout the crystalline cavity, forcing her head to jerk up. What she saw stole her breath away.

No.

Nevia watched in the utmost horror as the place where her fingers once lay turned black, running like scorch marks along the crystal's face. The smooth surface cracked, the darkness spreading and fracturing the enormous core shard as fissures spiraled in all directions, not unlike a droplet of ink merging with water.

This could not be. She didn't come all the way to inflict her death magic on Saava, on the very core itself! Nevia desperately tried to reach out, to mentally contain it—but it was too late. The crystal's lustrous glow surged, growing even brighter than before, only to fade away like a candle snuffed by the breeze. Darkness blotted out the light as it traveled on a mad path of consumption.

Nevia ran her fingers through her hair, eyes threatening to bulge from their sockets as she watched the scene unfold in all-consuming despair. Her death magic spiraled out of control, the result more catastrophic than her worst imagining. She had one job: free the goddess and save her, and instead her death magic overtook her, spiraling into an abyssal blackness that she couldn't even remotely control.

The cavern went dark as the last vestiges of its ancient, inner light faded, the agonizing tingle of death and decay dissolving into the very air she breathed.

The empress collapsed to her knees, with only the eerie silence meeting her ears. She had singlehandedly ruined everything. Her worst fears were blighting Saava, and she succeeded in doing so. Hadn't Saava, in all her wisdom, foreseen this outcome? Worst yet —was that what she wanted? Maybe she had grown tired of sleeping in the planet's core. Maybe she wanted to be free. Maybe death was her only escape from a prison she had been confined to for two millennia—

Just then, in the depths of the darkness two pinpricks of light snapped into existence. Eyes, Nevia realized. Daring a moment of hope, she lifted her lantern to gaze upon the goddess' form. But where there should have been a diseased corpse there was instead a perfectly healthy woman.

And she was moving.

Saava tilted her neck, stretching out her tendons as she flicked her wrists. She sat up in the confines that had once been her coffin with wide, curious eyes, pupils shrunken but expanding in the dim light. With the core gone, there was nothing binding the goddess to her position, fueling the planet. She was now able to walk free, untethered. Unrestricted.

She turned, glancing toward the walls of dying Nephyl, taking in the damage that Nevia had done. The curve of her lips and the upward tilt of her chin, however, made Nevia rethink with the utmost horror.

She was not assessing the damage. She was admiring it.

This was only affirmed when she turned that chilling smile on to Nevia.

"You did well, my child." Saava's voice was melodious, as if her vocal cords each were an instrument. "Your purpose has been fulfilled."

In that moment, Nevia understood what she had done.

And realized the grave mistake she had made.

31
NEVIA

"Y**ou are no goddess." The words came out barely more than a whisper.

No immediate response came from Saava as she drew closer, those two glowing pinpricks focusing in on the empress. Crystal fragments scattered beneath her bare feet with her movement, the sound crunchy and brittle in the chamber, whispering of Nevia's failure.

A flame erupted into life on Saava's outstretched palm, dancing, spiraling and illuminating their faces. She was everything that Nevia had witnessed from her visions, save for the smile that twisted her lips in malice.

"I never claimed to be one." Saava halted in front of Nevia, standing a head taller. "It was you foolish mortals which gave me the title. Did it serve your need for a story to support your miserable existence?"

Saava's reply chilled Nevia to the bone. "Then what are you?"

She looked down at Nevia haughtily along the bridge of her lengthy nose. Her features, once sleek and elegant, now looked cruel, a creature of magnificent beauty more dangerous than the night creatures that walked in the dark.

"I owe you no explanations, my dear. But I do want to see the look on my sister's face when I tell you everything, so I suppose I will oblige."

Saava gestured toward the only escape from Gaia's Core, the very tunnel that Nevia had painstakingly traversed over the course of days. "Come, let us go for a little stroll, just the two of us?"

The suggestion made Nevia's stomach sour.

"I will go nowhere with you until you start explaining yourself," Nevia managed through gritted teeth.

Saava clicked her tongue, expressively disappointed. "How sad. It doesn't want to play my game. Well, no matter." She snapped her fingers, and a culmination of soil and rock unearthed themselves from the ground, rising to bind the empress' wrists and ankles. Nevia struggled, trying desperately to wrench herself free. She was entirely at the mercy of this woman, this goddess who seemed to care not for her creation. Saava flicked a finger, and the earth encasing Nevia's feet glided her along, dragging her to match the goddess' quickened pace.

Saava held Nevia's dropped lantern in her hand, extending it to illuminate the way. Her own generated flame bobbed at their backs, a ball of fire in the looming darkness. "Instead of answering your questions," Saava started, "I would like to hear the truth from your own lips. You already know, do you not?"

Nevia was conflicted. She knew the unspoken words on her tongue were a lie, had known, perhaps, for a long time. This acknowledgement must have been written clearly on the empress' face, as Saava let out a shrill laugh to echo.

"It's all true, then," Nevia blurted, eyes wide. "I am your sister, and I killed the one you loved. You were sent here to Gaia as punishment for my crimes, and now you want me to pay the price for all the pain I've caused you."

"Mmmm, you're so close!" Saava came around to walk backward, facing Nevia and grasping her face. A jagged nail dragged down her cheek, leaving her mark. "And yet not quite there, so I suppose I shall elaborate." She released Nevia's cheeks with a toss of her hand and straightened, now walking alongside the bound empress.

"It is very true: you stole my love from me, claiming him as your own. But it was not enough to me and Niall, no. You had to take things a step further: kill him, and frame me in the process." Saava chuckled darkly. "It's sad, really. You thought you got away with it, living your pretty little life with your pretty little lies."

Nevia swallowed dryly. She felt guilty. Horrendously so. Somewhere, in another life, she had done atrocious acts, and yet:

how could she punish herself for something she had no recollection of doing? It was unfair.

"We are done here and now, Sister. You will pay for *everything* you've taken from me, as will the rest of this little fantasy land I made up. Once I'm rid of them and they are no longer draining me of my mana, I will leave this shell and return to Aeterna, to take care of the real you. Once and for all."

The words gave Nevia pause, mind searching fruitlessly for connecting the dots. Her entire body seized in panic, yet it did nothing to halt her involuntary progression upward. "The real me?"

"You didn't figure that part out?" Saava waved a hand irritably. "You're not my actual sister. You're merely a shade, a fragment of my imagination, and only half as awful as a result. If I'm honest, I almost kind of liked you. I've watched how you handled yourself in that war and how you gave your husband what he deserved. Very well played, child. I am proud of you."

Nevia's heart floored. "I'm not real?"

"Well, that depends on your definition of reality." She smirked. "Can you claim that your dreams are real, your thoughts, your stories? Or only what is physically, tangibly there? This?"

Saava gestured wildly to the walls, arms whipping the musty air. "All of this? It's all in my head! I created you through my dreams, my imaginings.

"Amidst my moments of lucid dreaming over the past two thousand years, there were dreams—plenty of them. Many of which, my dear, involved you. Sable, my sister. My best friend, my worst enemy. My savior, my demise. Each version of you has had its variants over this planet's lifetime, but I must say I was quite pleased with my latest fabrication of you. Not only are you as close to my true sister as you could be, but you even have a taste of her gift! Ha! Who knew the power of the mind could be so potent?"

Nevia swallowed back a sob. This was all her creation. Her . . . dreams? Did this mean fate, events were already predestined, were mere fabrications by her, as well?

"Oh, don't look so surprised." She threw her hair over her shoulder and turned her back on Nevia. "You were just a means to an end, nothing more. Surely, deep down, you knew that to an extent."

"Then what are you going to do with it all?" Nevia ground out, and yet she already knew. When Saava confirmed her plan, it came as no surprise to her.

"Why, let them die, of course. I can't have you lot leeching out my life force as I return home. Don't want you dragging me back here to die."

"The real me would kill you when you return," Nevia managed, seeking to harm this monster of a woman in any way she could. "She's demonstrated that she can when she took Niall—"

Saava's eyes flashed dangerously, and in moments Nevia found her shackles extend, springing up to wrap tightly around her neck, crushing her windpipe. Her hair was yanked back painfully by

Saava's unrelenting grip, roots tearing free in several spots from the force.

"Don't. Ever. Speak his name. You are unworthy of it."

Tears burning while her icy gaze grew colder, Nevia threw a death glare at this creature hell-bent on revenge and willing to sacrifice an entire planet to do it. To think she was once called—and worshipped as—a goddess! To think Nevia, herself, thought this woman was worthy of praise and affection until mere moments ago. Now, she wasn't sure if she'd witnessed a greater monster.

"Why did you do it?"

Saava blinked in confusion. "Do what?"

"Make me. Us. All this." Nevia jerked her head to indicate their surroundings. "Why have us here to begin with? Do you profit from our worship or something stupid?"

Saava's lips twisted. "What a novel mortal concept. None of you were on purpose. As I mentioned, you are perhaps the sixth iteration of my sister that I have conjured. Your existence is comprised of my dreams, my hopes. My memories. My subconscious created you. It wasn't intentional, believe me."

"If you created us, can't you just take us out?" It was the question that burned Nevia's insides, and the one piece that confused her greatly about it all. Why did she need Nevia when she could just do the work herself?

"I create, child, that is what I do." Saava clenched a fist. When she slowly unfurled it, Nevia watched as a simple pink rose bloomed in her palm. "The only thing I cannot create is death itself. Only you, dear sister, can do that."

"But surely you could create disasters," Nevia interjected. "Surely—"

"You don't think I tried that?" Saava spat, snapping her alight eyes upon the empress. "Earthquakes, floods, wave surges, avalanches, warmongering lords, ambitions, fears—thoughts all manifest, and they cannot snuff you little imaginings out!"

All feeling left Nevia, dread flooding all of her receptors at once. "You caused Darius to start that war." It was a statement, not a question. Her eyes fluttered close. "His corruption. It was all you?"

"No, dear, don't give me that much credit. I just set him on his path, and he did the rest. No, I don't bend fate like that. That's Freya's powers." She flourished a hand. "The closest that I've come, I daresay, are those creatures of the night in my latest creative spurt, but my hold on them is limited. I can create them, but I cannot influence their will. Once they leave my molding hands, so to speak, they are on their own. I didn't realize they would be most attracted to the core shards that birthed them beyond all else. Without core shards, they have no interest to feed."

So that was the reason for the attacks. Nevia's head fell limp, her body still being forced to coast along in the darkness. They probably passed and buried Renault's corpse by then, a thought which brought a hard lump to form in her throat. She wondered if

Saava put him in her path, too, a hurdle to conquer and break her down.

"Where is this world?" Nevia asked, changing the topic. "This Aeterna that you've mentioned so many times? How do you plan to get back there?"

For a moment Saava's expression was wistful, playful and less lethal, much more like the Saava that Nevia remembered from her dreams. "If I told you that would ruin everything, wouldn't it?" She reached over and tapped Nevia's nose. "It's a world that only the immortal walk, creatures birthed from the elements. You will never see it. You couldn't. Well, actually, I don't know if you could or not. I've never seen a mortal there, so I would imagine not."

"You never saw a mortal before you invented them," Nevia grit out.

Saava's face fell. "That's true."

"You're rather unoriginal, really," Nevia further ventured, her gusto coming from seemingly nowhere. "Borrowing concepts, entire people from your past life. Could you really not come up with something more entertaining of your own design?"

A tick in Saava's jaw became visible at the insult. "You know what"—Saava whirled around, halting in front of Nevia. "I'm getting rather tired of this conversation. I think we will call it here."

When Nevia was about to ask why, or what else she planned to do with their time, the goddess thrust out her palms, and strong winds erupted, effectively snuffing the flame of Nevia's lantern.

They would have been in complete darkness, except for the glowing bobbing orb behind them, its light flickering off the cavern walls and bathing a streak of narrow light upon Nevia and her captor.

The sounds of snapping and stretching reached Nevia's ears, and she could make out an enormous, dark object filling the space between her and the goddess. Odorous, hot breath beat down on her, soon joined by a fierce roar.

"Hmm, sounds like someone is hungry," Saava mused, sidestepping Nevia. She tucked the rose into the empress' hair. "I think I shall leave you two to sort things out. It's not like I need you anymore. Goodbye, Sister Number Seven."

Nevia threw back her head, just in time for her confines to snap. She was barely able to throw out her hands to keep from colliding face-first into the rocky path underfoot. She scrambled up and sought Saava, but the woman was long gone, already forging her own path up and out of the earth that was once her prison.

And was about to be Nevia's grave.

32
NEVIA

The only parting gifts Saava left her were the orb which bounced and bobbled behind Nevia and the unlit lantern that rolled across the cavern floor. What the purpose was, Nevia did not know, when she was being left to die, anyway.

The night creature was soon on to her. With the light of the orb no longer being restricted, Nevia could now make out what monstrosity she was up against. It resembled an enormous mole mingling with a snake, large canines jutting from its jaw. Its scaly hide was slimy, color indiscernible in the dark. It let out a bloodcurdling screech. Its breath reeked of decay, beating down into Nevia's face and tousling her hair. Nevia ran her hands along the length of her bodice, her hips, fingers at last meeting the dagger hilted at her thigh. She tugged it free just as it charged, forcing her to leap blindly out of the way, into the wall opposite her.

She was quick to discover that what it lacked in agility it made up for in brute strength. Its scaly hide was barely penetrable. This became evident when she jabbed her dagger into its side. The creature showed no pain, unfazed. It was as if she merely pricked it with a needle, only the stab did not even draw blood.

Outmaneuvering was her only defense, but she did not know how long she could keep it up. Fatigue had already set in to her body from the climb down into the core—there was little left to expend on acrobatics to avoid one of its sharp, disgusting canines from digging into her flesh.

She feinted, leaning against a wall and allowed it to charge, ramming its head into the wall in place of snatching her in its mouth. Nevia dove past it and broke into a sprint. If she could just climb a bit further, to reach the narrower path where it could not fit—

Force smashed into her rib cage, sending her flying several feet to eat a mouthful of dirt, its spiked tail flicking violently behind it. Warm blood soaked her bodice and spread along the length of the fine fabric. She whimpered, scrambling to regain her footing, snatching up her tattered skirt in her arms as she tried to scale the slope upward. When Nevia started to bolt she was again flung back, the night creature's clawed hand throwing her against the wall.

By then the fight was almost out of her. She allowed her body to crumble down the cavern's wall, too crippled, too pained to try to get up again.

The reeking breath assaulted her nostrils as it approached, snorting as it drew nearer. She inhaled sharply, grasping it, trying to exude all of her hate, her anguish, and pain into her touch. If she was able to utilize her death magic before, surely she could inflict this monstrosity that threatened her life. And yet, its scaly flesh remained unchanged, the tingling of dark magic nowhere in her body. It was not working. What component was missing? How could she inflict death upon her best friend and Renault by accident and yet fail to do so when her very life was being threatened?

She forced her eyes closed, readying herself to die. Its sharp teeth pressed against her right cheek, snorts blasting putrid air into her face. A massive clawed appendage reached out to grasp her torso and pin her, plastering her to the ground.

The night creature whined sharply—a pathetic, high whimper—when the sound of steel biting flesh met her ears.

Daring to crack open an eye, Nevia was stunned to find none other than Qirin standing over her, snarling up into the face of the night creature. In his hand was a katana, its honed, sharp blade dripping with blue-black blood.

"You came." Nevia's shocked mind was still processing what happened, her statement coming out airy and confused.

Not being graced with ample time he did not turn to glance at her. The creature swept its tail and Qirin leaped back, readying his blade to strike if it came any closer. Choosing to ignore the blade wielder, it turned its attention on Nevia again. It barely managed a single step before a thrown spear embedded itself between shoulder blades. Emerging from the shadows stood none other than Ardan, who gave the night creature a swift kick in the face and vaulted onto its back. Dark hair flowed freely across his face, features hardened by fixation on ending the life of the monstrosity. Briefly their eyes clashed, hazel eyes unreadable.

What he was doing here, she had no idea, but if they survived she knew she would have to make it up to him.

Ardan grunted, barely able to maintain his balance atop the night creature's back. "Nevia, get out of there!"

Qirin and Ardan worked as a united front, together warding off the beast to protect her. Something warm enveloped her heart at the thought. She staggered out of the corner, holding her injured side.

The foul beast jerked in her direction again, wholly devoted to attacking her for some strange reason, but did not succeed in getting far. Qirin slashed out, his blade striking true a second time and severing its hand from its wrist. Nevia choked back bile upon witnessing blood spurt from the clean cut.

"Hang on!"

Ardan wrenched his spear free from the night creature as it fell forward. It arched its back in agony, and in a swift motion, he forced the spear tip directly into the creature's neck where the vertebrae connected back to the head. Letting out one final cry, the creature fell forward before going still.

As suddenly as it started it was over, leaving the trio gasping for breath. Nevia straightened herself, relying on the cavern wall for support. Her entire body trembled, from blood loss or exhilaration of the fight, she was unsure.

"Ardan."

The chieftain lifted his head at her soft voice, tossing his spear aside. They both made a move for each other around the same moment. Nevia threw herself into him. Arms encircled her, crushing her against his chest as he pressed a kiss to the top of her head.

"Thank the gods you're okay," he murmured, nuzzling his chin into her hair.

Before Nevia could backpedal them, her emotions spilled out of her in a rush. "I am so, so sorry. You were right. I was a fool. This is all my fault. Please forgive me, Ardan. I didn't mean—I shouldn't have said—"

An irritable sigh broke her from her ramblings. From the corner of her peripheral vision she noticed the Feishin king step closer, wiping his sword clean with the hem of his kimono. "This is very touching, and I'm *so* glad that you two are patching things up, but can we get out of here first? Who knows if more are going to find us down here." Qirin sheathed his blade, taking the initiative to charge ahead in the direction of the surface.

"But I don't understand," Nevia blurted, stumbling after him. "What are you two doing here, anyway? I didn't tell anyone where I was going, how—"

Ardan shifted to Nevia's side, allowing her to lean on him for additional support. She braced an arm around his shoulders while she nursed her injured side. "Orla told me you were coming to the Feishin Kingdom in search of the core," Ardan explained. "And trust me, I have some choice words to say right now but it's going to have to wait. You're losing blood and we need to reserve your energy for getting the hell out of here."

Nevia wanted to argue but could not. The weakness in her legs was becoming too apparent to ignore. Ardan slid his arm under Nevia's knees, sweeping her off her feet and cradling her close.

"Ardan?"

"Not now," he murmured. "We'll talk later. Save your strength."

She kissed his cheek, his stubble scratching her lips, before tucking her head in the crook of his neck. Never was she more glad to see him. His comfort was just enough to allow her heart to lie to her: for one moment believing that somehow, in some way, everything would be okay.

33
ARDAN

They weren't too late. She was still alive. She was here. He was holding her.

The thoughts continued to trickle into Ardan's mind even over the hours they walked. He had feared the worst possible outcome when Orla unveiled what she knew and had discovered on accident: the intentions that Saava had for Nevia. He arrived in the Feishin Kingdom within the same day as the empress' ship with the expectation of bringing back Nevia's corpse. But to be holding her, alive—it was a relief unmeasurable. He found himself continuously stroking her hair, breathing in her warm scent of earth and rose. It was out of great reluctance that he lowered the empress to her feet after a while of carrying her, reassured at least for the moment that she was not going to collapse under her own weight. The bleeding had stopped, and she was insistent that she felt strong enough to go on.

They rested only briefly, all too eager to escape to higher ground, and went on again. For how long, Ardan could not be certain, though it felt like they were walking for the better part of two days.

It was a blessed relief when they were at last emerging from the tunnel, back into the shrine that Ardan could not have been happier to see. The two men carefully helped Nevia up the final flight of steps, where they awaited the burst of fresh air and relief —

Only to find the grass along the hillside was brown.

The surrounding cherry blossom trees were withered and dead, shriveled leaves cascading in the wind. An eerie fog rose from the ground, suffocating, destroying anything in its path. Qirin's lips tightened in a thin line, entire body going rigid beside Ardan. The chieftain turned to him, wanting to offer words of comfort, but Qirin had already began walking, not once glancing at either of his companions.

They silently tread toward the palace, the entire kingdom feeling more like a cemetery than bustling and booming with life. To their left lay the city, once aglow with glittering lanterns now cast in darkness. A faint wind blew, rustling their hair and garments, and with it came the reeking odor of death. A horrid gasp rushed from Ardan's throat as he saw two guardsmen collapsed on the ground. Upon closer inspection he found their flesh darkened and shriveled, dark mist oozing out from beneath their leather armor.

Qirin's face was a mask of stone, yet all the color drained from his face. They approached the palace to find bodies littered on the ground, all afflicted in a similar manner to that of the guardsmen.

All was silent. All was dying. Perhaps they were too late, after all.

"This cannot be." The words came as a dying prayer on Qirin's tongue, barely audible from where Ardan stood. The chieftain drew a few steps forward to stand alongside him, to offer comfort, support, consolation, yet no words seemed appropriate.

The Feishin king whipped around, horror converting wholly into something feral and filled with contempt. His face turned purple with rage. "It was her doing!" He jabbed a finger in Nevia's direction. "This must have something to do with why she entered Gaia's Core."

"She was deceived, Qirin."

"Don't try to defend her! She sentenced us all to death!"

"Of course she didn't."

Qirin tilted his chin, jaw clenched so tightly his teeth ground. "Then what do you call this?"

Nevia's feeble response echoed from beside him, her voice so soft, so frail, that something in Ardan's heart broke just hearing it. "He's right. I did do this. All of this."

If Ardan had not been more concerned about her condition he would've given her a stern shake by the shoulders, but instead he settled for wrapping an arm around her as she shuddered. He wanted to support Qirin, knowing full well what it was like to have more than half your society killed by a disaster, but seeing Nevia broken and panicked made him feel torn.

Qirin threw his arms out, disgusted by Nevia's answer, and made the decision easier for him, marching ahead past fallen lampposts and uprooted hedges towards the palace steps. Perhaps he was searching for survivors, or maybe he was merely seeking a place to be alone. Ardan followed, albeit at a slower pace, though was soon about to be left behind when Qirin threw open the palace doors to enter within.

"I'm finding Liana."

And he disappeared around a corner before he could be reasoned with. Ardan let out a long, haggard sigh. He hoped, for his sake, that Qirin wasn't too late, and yet he followed, not out of hope, but the desire to comfort him when the worst-case scenario was upon them.

34
QIRIN

The king's hopes were shattered upon witnessing the guards collapsed at their posts outside the throne room, the odor of death insulting his nostrils. His pace didn't slow as he roamed through the palace, searching, hopeful, delirious. Seeking any form of life.

He was left wanting at every turn.

A frustrated cry broke through his lips as he punched a wall, breaking the skin on his knuckles and painting them with fresh blood. It didn't make sense. How did he survive when everyone else was dead? It was unfair, and he hated drowning in his own powerlessness to help the situation.

This was genocide of the worst kind. Worse than any war that could have rippled across his home. No amount of steel or stone could protect them from this terrible plague that claimed all and saved none, this blight that the Androvich empress brought.

And yet in the back of his mind he questioned his innocence in it all. Did it have to do with his continued distribution of Nephyl, despite the commandment to cease production? Even still, all signs pointed to Nevia's presence in Gaia's Core with Saava, especially when she reportedly cursed her own handmaiden.

Perhaps they both played a role in the untimely demise of so many.

The creak of a floorboard above restored hope. A sound so faint, so obscure, and yet one that was music to his ears.

There was life! Someone had survived the blight, which meant Liana could, too. If he never got the chance to set things right with her, he did not know what he would do with himself.

His footfalls grew lighter as he sprang across the palace, taking the stairs two at a time and emerging onto the second level. Hope was what propelled him forward, which only grew upon witnessing a servant girl staggering across the hall toward him.

But something was not right. Her movements were jerky and unnatural, and within moments she grasped for the nearest wall and slid down it. It prompted the king to approach her, kneeling down and offering a hand.

"Are you alright, miss—" Any further words died in his throat as she turned her head to face him. Darkened eyes, ashen skin, black blood oozing down the length of her mouth. She rasped incoherent words and reached for him, only for the king to recoil and yank himself out of her reach. She writhed, letting out a horrific shrill wail before going still. The poor girl did not move again.

Any warm sensation remaining in his chest sank back within, dying with her. Wherever Liana was, he could not imagine her fate better than this. In his outrage, he grasped the nearest vase and threw it, shattering it upon impact.

He was going to make the gods pay. All of them.

A shrill cry, a woman's agonizing wail, shrouded the hall.

Liana.

Panic dug its claws into Qirin as he slid across the smooth bamboo floors and skidded around a corner, following the wails with a pounding heart. It led him directly to Liana's quarters, where the queen herself stood. One hand braced the doorframe, the other clutching her swollen belly.

She was alive. Qirin let out a sigh of relief, moving toward her and placing his hands on her shoulders. Her raven hair parted as she lifted her head to meet his gaze, and, to Qirin's horror, her eyes were inky black. Just like those infected by the blight.

It took all of the king's willpower not to recoil, instead allowing his knees to hit the ground before her, forcing the tears away that threatened to flow. He clutched at the hem of her silken gown, the material flowing like water between his fingers.

"Qirin," she rasped, choking the words with great effort. "How are you alive?"

Qirin tilted his head upward, forcing himself to look into those dark eyes no matter how much it pained him. "Same as you, most likely."

He, too, wondered how the four were the only ones alive in an entire city of death, but he would have to seek answers later. After he was able to get Liana the support she needed, when she was brought back to full health. When she was happy and hale—

Yet when he stole another glance at her blackened eyes and cracked blue lips, he knew she was beyond saving. While this was the case, he preferred to continue lying. It was easier that way. In the depths of his soul he felt that, in uttering it long and hard enough, he would eventually even make something entirely unreasonable true.

The lies became more difficult to utter, however, when Liana only affirmed his fear. "I'm fading fast, Qirin. Best go, now, before you—you get it, too."

The scene was unfolding something akin to a nightmare. Only try as he might, he could not force himself to awaken out of it. The king sprang to his feet, giving Liana the truest embrace he ever had over the course of their entire marriage. He cradled her close, tucking her head beneath his chin. It was impossible to keep the tears away, then.

"We'll get you out of here. You'll be fine. You'll both be fine. You'll see—"

To his relief, Liana either believed him or decided to play along with his distorted reality. She folded herself in his arms. "Thank you, Qirin. For coming for me. For our child."

He swallowed hard, unable to think of a clever or less tragic response than the ones playing through his mind. He settled for stroking her hair absentmindedly, taking in the silkiness of each strand. Gone were the days that he took her love for granted. Even if not drawn to her as he was Rito, he could still love her, and love her he did. He would have her live, even if he had to give his own life to do so.

He made this vow under his breath to all the gods he could think of.

The king slipped an arm beneath her knees, hoisting her and his unborn child into his arms. Carefully he placed a tender kiss on her forehead. "You will be fine," he said sternly, perhaps more to himself than to her.

Retracing his steps, Qirin gravely tread toward the palace doors, ignoring the bodies of servants and soldiers around each corner. He clung to Liana as if he willed the life to stay within her, as if, perhaps, he loosened his hold she would slip away from him forever.

Outside the palace steps awaited Ardan and Nevia, hands clasped as they both wore stoic expressions. The king's jealous gaze flickered to their conjoined hands and up to Nevia's face, lip curling in disgust. How was it fair that she stood, perfectly fine, while his Liana lay dying?

Whether Ardan noticed remained uncertain, yet he broke the tense moment with an inquiry: "Is she . . . ?" Ardan couldn't finish, instead jerking his head toward Liana. A haggard breath escaped her at that moment and she let out a whimper.

"It's happening again," she moaned.

Nevia's eyes widened in surprise, slowly treading toward the royal couple. Qirin tried to shield his wife by turning to the side, which conveyed the message clearly. The empress halted in her tracks.

"She's in labor, Qirin." Her words were tender, and yet took him a moment to process.

Foolishly, childishly, he turned to Ardan, who approached him alongside the Death-Bringer. Qirin dared to utter in a whisper, "Tell me she will live."

Ardan's face was set into hard lines as he placed a hand on her clammy forehead. He took note of her ashen flesh, the dark circles beneath her eyes with a somber downturn of his lips. "I don't know."

"Tell me!"

The chieftain blinked, pity in his face despite the anger that Qirin lashed him with. The king's nostrils flared.

"She has to be okay. She must. I asked the gods to—"

"You're a smart man, Qirin. You know it doesn't work that way." Instead of chiding, Ardan's tone held only compassion.

Qirin sniffed, turning his gaze downward into the woman in his arms. His wife, whether he wanted her or not. The woman he once resented, blamed, and yet loved him despite his mistreatment and wavering loyalty. Tears streamed down his cheeks, silent at first, until he gave away to the sobs that shook his entire form.

"It should've been me."

Ardan bit his lip before clapping him on the shoulder. "Believe me, I've said the same myself, many times."

No further words escaped Qirin. He just held her and cried. Ardan stood there patiently, supporting, observing. There was little that he could do. That anyone could do.

"Let's leave the island and get her far away from here," Nevia said, extending her hands to reach for the queen. Qirin snatched her further away, out of the empress' grasp.

"You've caused enough harm already," Qirin spat. "Don't get your hands anywhere near her."

Nevia's jaw shifted, looking as though she wanted to argue, hurt flashing across her face. Perhaps Qirin should have felt remorseful, but no pity could he surmise for the woman that caused the death of his kingdom.

"Let's settle this another time," Ardan said. "For now, she's right. We need to leave."

Qirin looked down at Liana, so still, so frail. He rested a hand on her swollen belly, the unborn child within.

"Fine. Lead on." He jerked his head in Nevia's direction, eyes narrowing to slits. "Don't you get anywhere near Liana. If you must get aboard my ship, do it far away from me and her. Understood?"

Pain etched itself on to Nevia's face in response, hugging her arms to her chest. "Yes. Yes, I know, and I will. You have my word."

35
NEVIA

The voyage from the Feishin Kingdom was long and lonely, and Nevia felt very useless. She sat alone in her bunk, secluded to the same room since boarding the small steamship. Qirin wanted to ensure she got nowhere near his wife, thus deciding to lock her away for good measure. Something which Nevia deemed wholly unnecessary; she had no interest in getting near enough to run the risk of infecting anyone with her death magic. She had already caused enough harm.

She threw her head back against her pillow and stared at the ceiling, gaze tracing the same grooves ad nauseam. No news came regarding Liana's condition, and she wondered how the pregnant queen was faring. If her illness progressed as Elante's had, she feared how she would ever manage giving birth. Yet the arrival of the baby was imminent. She wished there was some way that she could offer her assistance without risking mother or child.

Her rumbling stomach reminded her of the passage of time, and how long it had been since she had a true meal. They had set sail yesterday, and no refreshments had been brought to her. Perhaps part of Qirin's plan was to lock her up to die. Or, worse yet, Nevia feared the startling reality that they may not have any food or water aboard the ship. Given Liana's critical condition, they wanted to leave the Feishin Kingdom and fast, not sparing enough time for preparations before setting sail. Despite the circumstances, they should have thought to pack food and water. They would die at sea, at this rate.

And yet, what were a few more deaths when Nevia had caused so many, perhaps even the death of the very planet? It made no sense, not the way that so many were rendered dead, while others, such as Qirin, Ardan and herself, remained untouched from the blight's hold. There was no rhyme or reason to the madness, yet Nevia was certain of three things: it was in connection to the blight resulting in Saava's freedom, the core shards, and her.

A shudder coursed through her as she brought her knees to her chest, still wearing the tattered remains of her filthy gown. This was worse than the Nephyl War. Perhaps fate couldn't be changed, after all. All those years ago she thought she was saving the Feishin people from genocide by stopping Darius from framing them, but it turned out they were annihilated just the same.

Her thoughts shifted toward Elante and Renault. Poor, sweet Elante. Her best friend, her confidant. She was probably dead thanks to Nevia, as well. If not from the blight she hand-delivered, then the one she'd inflicted on Gaia's Core. And now it looked as if Qirin's child would be killed before he or she was even birthed into the world.

Her throat tightened painfully as the tears streamed down, beading at her chin and falling to soak her leggings. So much pain with nowhere to channel it. She was horrid. Saava was horrid. Nothing felt good anymore.

A knock came at the door. The first in the voyage, yet she was in no mood for company. When she did not answer, a key was inserted into the lock, and in moments the door swung open. Boots clicked on the smooth floorboards, forcing Nevia to lift her chin. Relief and surprise flooded her to find that the newcomer was not Qirin, but Ardan.

The chieftain scowled darkly, holding up the key. "Didn't realize he locked you in." He extended it to her, yet she did not reach to take it. "I am so sorry. He's being an ass, but he knows it's not really your fault. It's just easier to blame someone for one's grief than to suffer with it. He'll get over it eventually."

"No." Nevia shook her head vehemently. "You're wrong. I *am* to blame, and this is my fault. He has every right to lock me away and be angry. I'm a danger to you all." She burrowed her face into her knees and waved a hand toward the door. "You should go away, too, before I hurt you."

Instead Ardan merely drew closer. "You could never hurt me."

This man was unbelievable. She lifted her tear-stained face, unable to keep the incredulity out of her voice. "I killed our planet, Ardan! How could you say that?"

Sadness washed over his face, but instead of turn away, as any sane person should, he sat alongside her and snatched up her hands in his. His thumbs massaged her palms, a familiar, comforting sensation, numbing a fraction of the hurt deep inside her.

"You were tricked by a monster who claimed to be a goddess," Ardan reassured. "She forced your hand. She said you needed to save her, and, well, she wasn't lying. You *did* save her, but not how you thought. This was her trickery. This is what she wanted. If you want to hate someone, hate her. You have every right to."

"But no one should have this"—Nevia wrenched a hand free to gesture at herself—"this death magic. This darkness. It's dangerous, Ardan. It's horrible. I should not live."

His hands fell from hers, retreating to the bedspread on which they sat. When she ventured to glance into his beautiful bronze face, she was shocked to see the pathway of tears streaming down it, looking nearly as miserable as she felt.

"Never say that," he choked. "Please. You are my world, Nevia. You mean everything to me. You're the greatest person I've ever known, and the world would be much darker without you."

A bitter laugh escaped her. "Sorry, but technically it probably wouldn't, considering the darkness I wield."

Slowly he lifted his gaze, hazel eyes clashing with her chips of ice. "What will it take to convince you otherwise?"

"I don't think you can."

It surprised her when his response came: a sudden pressing of his lips against hers, with an intensity and need that burned deep between them. Nevia devoured it just as eagerly. Thoughts surfaced of sparing him, of pushing him away to keep him safe, but she needed his touch, affection. Needed every ounce of the yearning that he poured into that kiss, with every fiber of her being.

He wrapped his arms around her, sitting on his knees to get close enough to hold her. She then pulled him back, bringing them both to lie within the swaying bunk. His hands knotted up into her hair, and hers continuously caressed his back, seeking the hem of his tunic to press her palms up against his warm flesh beneath. She needed him. Wanted him. Wanted his warmth to penetrate the ice that encapsulated her heart.

And it seemed he was very willing to give it. More than willing.

"Nevia," he murmured, brushing her hair from her face and neck, allowing his fingers to linger along her collarbone. He pressed a kiss to her lips before locking his gaze onto her. "I love you so much."

Tears prickled her eyes. She wrapped her arms around his neck and linked her legs around his waist, drawing him even closer. "And I love you, Ardan, even if I don't deserve to."

"Oh, stop." He pressed a kiss to her lips to silence her, and she accepted it, slipping her tongue between his lips, feeling the grooves of his teeth. A moan escaped her, savoring the taste of him.

Their hands searched, eagerly devouring one another. His hands roved over her hips, gently caressing them in circles. Her hips buckled as she nipped his lower lip, gently, which only elicited a groan from deep in his throat.

She did not recall feeling so alive, so ablaze. Her hands traced every curve and muscle, while Ardan rubbed her in places that ignited her. When she felt his own hardness beneath her she nearly lost herself in the ecstasy as she ground herself against him. He rolled her onto her back as her fingers fumbled with his belt buckle, undoing it and allowing her own hands to travel down, down.

Her fingers met with his length, causing a moan to escape him against her lips. Any restraints Nevia had shackled herself with had dissolved. Nothing mattered in that moment. Just them—their two hearts beating as one. Even if everything else perished, their love lived on. Something she desperately needed to remember, to cling to.

The contact she craved and anticipated for so long made her arch her back, as he at last lowered himself into her. She did not want to stop, had no care to. She imbued her fingertips into his hair, one hand running along the short-cropped side of his head and stroking him tenderly.

Once they were finished they both laid back, panting, her breasts pressed flat against his chest. She held him as tightly as she could, refusing to let go.

"I'm so sorry for everything that happened. I was confused, and I—" Nevia murmured, to which he promptly silenced her with a kiss.

"I'm not, if it meant that we came to this." He stroked her cheek tenderly, locking eyes with her. "I would wait many lifetimes if it meant that we could be together, Nevia."

In response she clung to him tighter, burrowing her nose into the crook of his neck.

"Me too."

36
ARDAN

Amidst the ruin and despair, Ardan felt himself to be the luckiest man alive. In his arms was his sleeping empress, eyelids swollen from all her fallen tears. He caressed her thick hair before pressing a kiss to her temple. How precious she was to him; he did not realize quite how much so until the promissory threat of losing her forever.

At long last, finally she was his and he was hers, their bond consummated after they made love the night prior. That incredible bond with her was more than he ever fantasized it to be.

A part of him wanted to stay in that uncomfortable bunk, never leaving Nevia's side as he clutched her close to his heart, and yet his thoughts strayed to Qirin, who was probably feeling the polar opposite of himself. Somewhere on that ship he knew the

Feishin king was mourning the loss of a family he would never get to have. Liana's condition had not improved, the darkness taking hold of her body harder and faster than before. While her contractions had ceased, her health still declined, and Ardan feared the worst: that it was only a matter of time before her—and their unborn child—slipped away into the afterlife.

Guilt threatened to crush the weightless joy that welled in his heart. How could he stay there, blissful and happy, when others around them were suffering?

When Nevia began to stir, however, he thought he could probably manage it, wrapping her in a tight, warm embrace and kissing her again.

"Is it morning?" she asked sleepily, throwing a leg over him.

He wrapped his other leg over hers and folded her in to himself. "Yes, though it's still quite early. Are you hungry?"

"More thirsty than hungry." She kissed him, the sweetest sensation to grace his lips, before sitting, blonde waves tumbling over her exposed shoulders. "But beyond that I'm worried."

A heavy sigh escaped Ardan's throat. "Yeah. I am, too."

"We should check on Qirin." Nevia threw off the covers and started to rise, though before she got far Ardan snatched her wrist.

"Wait." Ardan sat up, covers bunching at his waist. "Let me talk to him first. He may go wild if he sees you anywhere near Liana. He was a bit irrational yesterday, and he may be even more so because I disappeared and left him in charge of the ship."

"He knew where to find you if he wanted to," Nevia scoffed.

While it was true, he doubted that Qirin would wound his pride so much as to seek him out, but Ardan did not state such. Instead he interlocked his fingers with hers and drew her back into the bunk. The warmth of her flesh in the chilly room was almost enough to unhinge him, his body awakening to her touch as she pressed herself against him.

And yet, things needed to be done, things which would not occur if he remained down here with her. He was no stranger when it came to self-restraint with Nevia, and he reminded himself he could do it again. Ardan ran a hand down the length of her back before rising, this time being the one to leave her in the bunk.

"Feel free to wander around—you're not trapped here, you know."

Nevia nodded, yet there was a darkness behind her eyes, one that had been extinguished over the course of that night. He wanted to wipe away her anguish, distract her with his affection and promises, but he told himself he would have to do it later. First, Qirin needed him more.

Quickly he threw on his plain trousers and tunic before bounding out of her room, marching back up the stairs to the deck. The salt air stung his nostrils, the scent of decay a familiar one. One quick glance at the control room, a small compartment filled with gears and gadgets, told him all he needed to know: Qirin was not there, and so he went back below decks in search of him.

At last he found him where he'd left him: at Liana's side in a small room, coincidentally on the opposite side of the ship from Nevia. In the bunk along Qirin's chair lay the the Feishin queen, a woman hardly recognizable. Her face, once round with life, was now hollow. She was swathed in several blankets, beneath of which her chest barely rose and fell in shallow breaths. The only sign that she still lived.

Her dark eyes snapped open at the sound of Ardan's footfalls, and she turned in his direction. Ardan wished he could flash her a smile, if only to offer her some amount of solace in her darkest hours, yet he could not.

"Hello, Your Highness," Ardan managed instead, swooping down to kneel at her bedside. "How are you feeling?"

Probably a stupid question, but he did not know what else to say to someone actively dying.

"Better," she said, slowly turning her head to face the ceiling. "The labor pains have ceased, but the baby still thrives. I can feel him kicking."

Ardan quirked a brow. "Him?"

"We believe it is a boy," Qirin explained, waving a hand.

The young king looked as though he had not slept. His eyes were rimmed with red, complexion ghastly pale. Ardan wondered briefly if he was the only one relatively okay given their current predicament.

Qirin directed his attention to his ailing wife, lips drawn into a thin line. "It's good you came. You can take my place at her side. I should check on our trajectory."

"Right, yeah." Ardan jerked a thumb in the direction of the door. "I tried to look at the gears, but I have no idea how this thing operates."

"I wouldn't expect you to," Qirin said, stifling a yawn with the back of his hand. "Feishin technology. Not exactly like those crude boats your lot crafts."

Ardan shrugged, folding his arms over his chest. He would let the Zenochian insult slide—for now. "I see."

Garments rustled, the long cloak Qirin wore sweeping the floor as he bent over Liana. Not to dote affection, Ardan soon realized, but to whisper something softly in her ear. The chieftain desired to give them some privacy and retreated to the doorway, turning his back to give the illusion of disinterest. Ardan knew that they did not have a relationship birthed from love and that their marriage was strictly political, though given how distraught Qirin was when they found Liana, he had no doubt the king must somewhat care for her.

The floorboards creaking signaled Ardan that he could turn around, and found the Feishin king leveling him with a wary expression. "Keep an eye on her," he commanded. Always the ruler, even among equals.

It took great willpower for Ardan to keep the bite from his voice. "I will."

Qirin grunted in acknowledgement and disappeared around the corner, leaving Ardan with his ailing wife. The fear was real that she would die on his watch and be held responsible, as Qirin was proving to be irrational when distressed. The chieftain stretched, stealing a glance around the sterile room. Padlocked cabinets lined the ceilings, with counters that were relatively barren except for some rolled bedclothes atop them. There were plenty of drawers without exposed locks, though Ardan did not feel particularly curious to inspect them.

"Ardan."

He jerked his head in her direction, startled to find Liana's alarming black eyes fixated on him. He moved toward her and knelt, dipping his head both in respect and to avoid her unsettling gaze. "My lady."

"I need to tell you something," she whispered, tone urgent.

A simple nod was all he offered, prompting her to continue.

"And you must promise me that you won't tell anyone."

His throat momentarily seized. "Not even Qirin?"

"Especially not him."

His heart hammered in his chest. He was being drawn into affairs he did not think he wanted to get involved with, and yet how could he refuse this poor woman? "Then why tell me?" he dared venture.

"Because someone needs to know before I pass." She swallowed coarsely, and in that moment she looked so weak, so frail, that Ardan could not help his desire to ease her suffering.

Even if that meant swearing secrecy in whatever she wished to confide in him, reminding himself that Qirin was not his sovereign, and his actions were not treasonous.

"You can count on me," he reassured, clasping her clammy hand.

The moments ticked by, Liana appearing hesitant, frazzled. "When the blight spread," she started slowly, carefully forming the words with cracked lips, "I noticed my ring's light grow vibrant before fading. Dark lines like living tendrils spread through it. I was quick to discard it, but the damage was already done."

One of Ardan's brows lifted. "Your ring?"

"It was made of Nephyl."

This gave more context to the blight's spread, confirming their suspicions that it was linked to Nevia's reaction to Gaia's Core and the already-harvested core shards. Ardan was about to question why she did not want Qirin to know about this, but she then further elaborated on how she was personally affected.

"But while this happened, something happened *inside* me. I can't even describe it. There's something different about my child. He changed somehow." Her eyes fluttered closed. "I-I felt the blight—this horrendous disease—consuming me, and it was as if the child. . . ." Her words trailed off, gaze staring off into space. At first Ardan feared for her health, wondering if she was at her end, until her lips moved again. "It must sound ridiculous, this child saving me, but something about his energy. His light—"

Ardan took up her hand in his: a small comfort and the only he could provide.

"Why don't you want Qirin to know?" he asked quietly.

The words that next escaped Liana's lips made his heart sink, yet he could not blame her at all.

"I don't trust my husband not to use our child for evil."

37
QIRIN

The wind whipped Qirin's face above deck as the ship cruised ahead. It was a rather small vessel, albeit a fast one. Despite the steamship being a decade old, it had seen little use before Qirin was crowned king. The secluded island nation they once were had no demand for such a ship, but since Qirin opened borders and trade he was finding the small motorized ship to be exceptionally useful.

Especially in times like this, when he had no living crew to pilot it.

He drew his cloak tighter around his shoulders to stave off the inner chill consuming him. This was not a particularly new feeling; it had been ongoing since Rito left, and it had only increased in severity since. And now, when he had only started to appreciate and care about Liana, her life was in danger. Soon even she—and their child—would be ripped from him, and his biggest fear would become reality.

He would be truly alone.

The sharp waves tossed the cruising ship, slapping at its walls. Had it not been so loud he would have perhaps heard Nevia's approach, and not been so startled when she tapped his shoulder to garner his attention.

His cloak billowed around him with the movement, eyes narrowing in on her. The woman who caused all of this. Problems always seemed to dog her footsteps, and here she was: standing before him now. It took every ounce of his willpower not to grasp her slender throat and haul her over the deck into the choppy waves.

"Nevia." He spat her name like a curse. "I thought I locked you away."

Her lips thinned, color rising into her cheeks. "I was. But even a wild animal chews free of its cage if unattended."

Qirin had no response for that. It was not his intention to deprive her; he simply had not thought to nourish her. He scoffed, turning to redirect his attention to the calming waves. "Yes, well, this is all your fault, and I wanted to keep you from harming anyone else."

She moved closer, much to his annoyance. "You're right."

Nevia, admit to her faults? Surely he misheard. "What?"

"I said you're right: this is all my fault." She lifted her chin in resolve. "This plague of death. The darkness. All of it. You have every right to be furious with me, and that's why I wanted to find you."

She procured a dagger, and at first Qirin feared she was ready to do away with him. It surprised him when she placed it flat in her palms instead, extending it out to him in offering.

"Exact your revenge, if you want it," Nevia said. "Kill me. Watch my blood spill over this deck. Cleanse this world of my existence, and make me pay for what I have done to you. To your people. All of Gaia."

His eyes flickered uncertainly from the blade to her face. He could not deny that the offer was tempting, and that somewhere, deep down, the bloodthirsty part of him was considering it. Finally he accepted it, running a finger along the leather-bound hilt of the blade.

The empress stepped away from the railing and spread her arms wide, leaving herself vulnerable to his ultimate judgment.

"Make it as slow or as quick as you like," she continued. "You don't need to spare me. I've had this a long time coming. This— this is the only way I can make things right to you."

Qirin snorted. "Do you really think ending your pathetic life is going to make things right?" He threw the dagger in his other palm and stormed over to her. "The entire planet is dying because of what you've done. My kingdom is ruined, my people dead. My wife and child dying beneath our feet as we speak. How could your death do anything to fix that?"

Tears streaked her cheeks as she lifted her eyes. "It can't."

"Exactly." He chucked the blade as hard as he could, over Nevia's shoulder to burrow deep in the wooden plank. It swayed upon impact. "You're just going to have to be in it for the ride."

Qirin strode past her, pausing only briefly to offer a condescending smile. One filled with all the cold malice that he could muster. "Enjoy the ruined world you created."

38
NEVIA

The voyage lasted three arduous days. Rations were found below decks: plenty of fresh water, nuts, and dried rice to last them weeks. Their meals were bland and flavorless, but no one complained, as it served the purpose of filling the yawning hunger that carved holes in their bellies.

Somehow Nevia thought she would be relieved after offering her life to Qirin, only she walked away feeling even more helpless. To live with the guilt was becoming intolerable, and she desperately sought some escape, a secret reprieve. Ardan's reassurances that it was not her fault only went so far. While she did not mean to do this, it did not change the end result. Her death magic went rampant and cursed their planet, and there was no way she could take it back. Countless died by her hand, lives that would have been spared if she had not selfishly gone to Gaia's Core to save Elante's life, an attempt, she was certain, that was now futile. Now that Saava displayed her true colors, revealing herself not to be the benevolent Goddess of Creation that everyone thought she was.

She had been duped, and now she sentenced everyone to pay the ultimate price.

The air was absolutely frigid when they arrived at Yona Shore, the port on the easternmost coastline of Zenoch. Theirs was the only ship of its kind along the dock, the rest being skiffs of crude make. Zenochian ships were generally much smaller and slower, the ports being evident of this. It became even more apparent when Qirin found that their vessel would not fit into the allotted space, not that this deterred the Feishin king, as he chose to dock it anyway. The screeching sound of wounded metal assaulted Nevia's ears as they pulled in, materials shifting below decks. While she feared that the Feishin steamship sustained substantial damage, Qirin was wholly nonchalant as they walked away. Perhaps Feishin ships were made of something different than she was accustomed to.

They bundled Liana in Qirin's arms to stave off the northern winds, the mountainous climes of Zenoch already in its colder phases of winter. Perhaps choosing to dock in the north was unwise, but they reasoned it was the nearest and safest option. Given the blight's connection to the core shards, they risked wasting time if they arrived in imperial territory only to find it met with the same fate as the Feishin Kingdom.

Day turned into night, and night turned to day. This happened twice, before finally they came upon the Thomani clan. Nevia knew very little about them, despite originating from the north. Katsao commonly intersected with the Kohari and Sanen clans in their migratory routes, but never had she spent time in the easternmost region of Zenoch. She did know, despite their similarities, they bore many differences from the western clans. Most eastern Zenochians were red-haired and fair-skinned, something which Nevia reasoned had to do with their proximity to the ocean shores and migrants from other countries.

A cluster of clansfolk bearing sheepskin coats sat before a fire, chirping merrily to one another as they roasted a meal on spits. Immediately Nevia took notice of their thick red hair resembling Risanna, Ardan's former chief. Perhaps she had originated from Thomani.

They turned their gazes on to the party at their approach, expressions drawn and wary. Not that Nevia could blame them. While two of their number were clearly Zenochian, they were underdressed for the weather and far from home. It was no wonder they looked at them with suspicion.

Wind kicked up a flurry as Ardan approached, the clansfolk cloaked behind a screen of arctic wind and snowflakes. The wind's howls drowned out his already soft voice, making it impossible for Nevia to hear what he said to them. Their response, however, was animated and jubilant, and so she could only assume they offered a warm reception. She dared to draw closer and was met with wide smiles and outstretched hands.

"You are Nevia Bylilly?!" one said, accent thick. Before she could answer, the man drew her into a crushing hug, his bristly red beard catching fine strands of her hair. "A hero!"

Others quickly joined in as Nevia was spun around from one set of arms to the next. Her instincts told her to flee, to warn them what kind of a destructive force she truly was. Did they not know about the blight she unleashed on Gaia's Core?

No, she realized. They must not know. News naturally spread slowly in the mountainous regions of Zenoch; their only means of outside communication relied on tourists, merchants, and messenger pigeons. Everyone surrounding her seemed healthy and full of life. It seemed the blight had not taken hold here, furthering their suspicions that Nephyl was indeed a correlation to the blight and its spread. Nephyl was scarcely used in the north, and would perhaps not have been for many decades.

She threw a pleading glance in Ardan's direction, hoping to be wrenched free from the jubilant clansmen. Instead of offering a helping hand, however, he stood there wearing his usual lopsided grin, as if reveling in Nevia's being passed around like a celebrity. Qirin, however, wore the exact opposite expression, his lips downturned into a frown as he hoisted Liana further in his arms. "Hate to break this up," Qirin interjected, "but do any of you know a medic or healer? My wife is dying and with child."

Their contagious joy was snuffed out like a flame. Murmurs spread, and finally a woman with a hard-lined face and plaited hair rose from her perch by the fire. She jabbed a finger in the direction of the encampment beyond them. "You're in luck! Maestra Annika is here."

A chill found its way into Nevia's torso. Maestra Annika. She was notorious in the empire, the most sought-after woman for her dabbling in sorcery and passing her gifts to other women who displayed an affinity for magic. As a result, her and her kind sought refuge in the north, despite their differing beliefs on religion. While Maestra Annika was referred to as the "Mother Seer" and believed to have strong ties to Saava's will, the Zenochians were dubious about Saava's existence at best. Even still, they had coexisted for many years. That was some beautiful coexistence, if Nevia ever saw such.

Most cringed at the whisper of the head shaman's name, but Qirin merely blinked, fixing the clanswoman with a coarse glare. "Who's that?"

"That would be me."

A middle-aged woman clad in emerald robes emerged from the tent nearest, blonde hair plaited high atop her head. She brought her icy eyes to scan the empress, warming in recognition, before sweeping over the woman cradled in Qirin's arms.

"So this is the one I touched," she murmured, voice husky. She brought a wrinkled hand to Liana's cheek and cupped it, before allowing her hand to trail toward her swollen belly. Before she could lay a hand on her, however, Qirin jerked her away, his eyes narrowing into slits.

"And *what* are you supposed to be?" His voice couldn't have held more contempt, yet the woman only had pity in her eyes.

"Most know me as Maestra Annika," she responded. "Head Shaman of the Seers and former servant to Saava."

"Well, I think your Saava's done enough for a lifetime," Qirin snapped.

Sorrow clouded her eyes. "I am well aware of what Saava has done," she said gravely, "and I regret the role I played in it." Her gaze fell on Nevia then, her icy stare leaving her so vulnerable that it forced her to look away. She had her own reservations when it came to the seer, chiefly the ill omen she uttered when blessing her union with Darius all those years ago. A premonition, one that unfolded in the most devastating of ways.

"So you admit to conspiring with that woman," Qirin spat, glaring daggers at the seer, "yet you still think we would accept your help?"

Annika's lips were drawn into a thin line. "If only it were as simple as that." She dug her wooden walking stick into the snow, breaking clumps with its end. "Come with me if you want me to explain it all to you."

She turned around and lifted open the nearby tent flap, waiting for all to enter before she followed them inside. Nevia was hesitant, but obliged. They all did, whether to hear her story or to escape the chill of the elements.

The Zenochians, having lived in the harsh north for generations, knew how to survive the most brutal of winters. Their homes, consisting of leather circular tents wrapped with extra furs on the inside, were lifted inches from the ground to allow for ventilation for the open fire pits burning within each one. Plumes of smoke rose high, wafting through the opening in the center above where the wooden poles structuring the tent met. Nevia loved the scent of the wood burning over the open fire. It was comforting, cozy, and smelled of home.

Within this particular tent an array of cushions were tossed around the fire for seating. There were four in total, and a bedroll spread out just a short distance away. It was the perfect setup.

Almost as if she were expecting them.

"Lay her there," Annika instructed, inclining her head toward the bedroll as she stopped before an iron kettle and masonry.

With witty retorts whispered under his breath, Qirin complied and set Liana gently down on the prepared resting mat. The king clasped her slender hands in his own, kneeling before her as his lips moved, in whisper or perhaps prayer. His voice caused her eyes to flutter, a rare smile touching her darkened lips before she grew still and lifeless again. From her position in front of the fire, hands outstretched to absorb the fire's warmth, Nevia watched the scene. Her heart sank at the defeat on Qirin's face, the sorrow that she was certain threatened to break his heart. Pained to look at him any longer, she turned her attention to Annika.

"It's bad, isn't it?" Nevia asked.

Annika whirled around. The head shaman had finished assembling a tray of steaming mugs to waft in the frigid air. She wore a half-crooked smile "My child," she said, "Fate smiles upon us today."

39
ARDAN

The shaman's words were not ones Ardan expected to hear, nor Nevia as expressed by her slackened jaw and widened eyes. Behind him he heard Qirin make a choking sound, though he had the wisdom to hold his tongue and actively listen.

It was for the best. The king was heated at the moment, and Ardan understood, but Qirin's sarcasm was not going to assist them in resolving the matter, nor save his dying wife.

Nevia's face was aglow from the warm light of the fire, yet her eyes remained cold and hard as they met his. She ran her tongue over her bottom lip, hesitant. "Pardon, but I don't see how Fate is smiling on us today at all. The planet is dying, as well as so many of its inhabitants."

Annika settled herself on Nevia's other side, dropping the tray between them. "Yes, both those things are true."

"So what could possibly be good about this situation?"

"I never said there was anything 'good' about it," Annika said, tone soothing. "But it is as it should be, and you have Fate on your side."

Her roundabout responses did little to placate them. Ardan decided to try prying information from another angle. "I think you're going to have to explain, Maestra Annika. Because the way we see things, it's looking like only a matter of time before we are all snuffed out."

A slight smile stretched her thin lips. "That would have been the case if I hadn't interfered."

They waited patiently for her to continue, but she did not, instead holding out a steaming mug to Ardan. "Would you like a cup of tea to warm your spirits?"

"No, we want answers," Qirin spat, while at the same time Nevia answered with, "that would be lovely." The two glared at one another, seemingly unnoticed under the shaman's watch. She instead hummed a merry tune, handing Nevia the second mug while dumping the contents of a third on the ground beside her.

Ardan pinched the bridge of his nose; this was the oddest tea party he ever did see.

"Once upon a time," Annika started, as if she were sharing a bedtime story to a gathering of children. "There were two sisters of clashing powers. One was revered for her death magic in an eternal world, while the other was ungifted."

Death magic. Ardan's gaze flickered toward Nevia, who refused to lift her head, instead taking a particular interest in watching her tea leaves swirl on the surface of her mug.

"The sister's rivalry stretched on for aeons, and always the Goddess of Death came out on top. The little sister was mistreated and cast aside, and it broke my heart to watch."

Did this mean Annika knew Saava? Ardan started to interject, but Annika continued. "Finally things went too far, and the Goddess of Death had her little sister banished. The sister made her chrysalis a home in the massive dark universe, and it was there that she discovered her magic. It was the power of creation.

"She could not stop creating, and so create she did: that is why you are all here. Some of it was intentional, as you may have discovered with her pets, the night creatures. However, much of it"—her somber gaze flickered toward Liana's still form—"was not. At first she did not mind, but then she began to notice her creations growing limited, and having to rest between creations. She discovered her magic was finite, without having the everlasting source of her home world to fall back on. Her chrysalis was intended to circulate her magic to ebb and flow within her, not to expend it on other living beings without gaining anything back in return. What's worse is that her creations learned how to take her magic for themselves, to provide their own energy for their lives."

It was not difficult to ascertain the source of which she spoke.

"So she needs the core shards to live?" Nevia asked.

A dip of Annika's head was all the confirmation they needed. "Now that an entire society discovered the core shards, thanks to the Feishin Kingdom's efforts, her life force is waning rapidly. Her creation, once an amusement, became the recipe for her ultimate ruin. That is why she reached out to me, and I came to help her."

A frown deepened Nevia's brow. Ardan, however, spoke first. "Why you?"

"Because we were friends, many, many ages ago." Annika repositioned herself, as if the topic itself made her increasingly uncomfortable. "I sympathized with her plight, and therefore found a way to join her. Here, in this world that was not meant to be."

A stunned silence fell over them all.

"So you're just like them," Nevia whispered. "You're from Aeterna."

Annika lowered her head. "I saw her suffering, and I wanted it to end." The head shaman's shoulders slumped. "We therefore came up with a system, seers that could exude her will onto her creation through self-fulfilling prophecies, plausible futures when the future itself has yet to be written. Only a child touched by Gaia's second moon's light would receive the magical affinity to harness power in this world, and I would be the one to change them so that it could be so."

The second moon . . .

Nevia's face blanched. "You don't mean—"

A heavy sigh heaved from Annika's face. "Yes, child, I do: the second moon is Aeterna, far, far away from us. When it is clearly visible, a direct path to Gaia, our magic is at its strongest." She lifted a finger, pointing it directly to Nevia. "Including yours."

It made sense to Ardan. He did not know much about Aeterna, but he did know the second moon functioned differently than the larger one in the sky, was only full once every year. Was this the reason for Nevia's death magic, the reason behind all of this?

"But why did she need me?" Nevia asked, voice barely audible. "By tainting the core, which somehow seems to have afflicted all of the shards, would that not kill her eventually?"

"She can repurpose the shards and remove the blight, which is why she was not killed when you unearthed your blight upon the core. Others that the afflicted core shards touch"—she stole a pitiful glance at Liana once more—"not so much."

Ardan nodded in understanding. "So she can undo the damage that has been done."

The shaman's breath fogged the air. "I think so, but I don't think she will. Her desire is to annihilate the population, regain her lost magic, and return home."

Annika bowed her head, allowing this information to sink in before continuing, "Now then, what do you know about fate?"

The trio threw glances at one another. "Why don't we just skip this part and you can tell us what you want us to know about it?"

Qirin offered sardonically. "You're going to just correct us anyway."

"Young one," she murmured, closing her eyes, fine wrinkles lining the smoothness of her cheeks. "I know you're concerned; you want your wife healed, your nation restored. I must tell you none of those things will happen, and they are out of my control. I'm sorry."

"But aren't you like that witch from the depths?" He slammed a fist into the packed ground at his side. "Why did we come to you if you're so useless?!"

The shaman looked to Qirin with surprising calm. "You sought a healer, not me, though there is some veracity to what you said, because I planted the seed," Annika said. "And seeds have a tendency to grow if nourished properly."

Qirin gritted his teeth, fists clenching at his sides.

"And why did you plant the seed for us to come, then?" Nevia asked. "Was it just so that you could share your story, and unveil that you're at Saava's beck and call?"

Darkness clouded Annika's expression. "I was once her friend, back when we lived in Aeterna and she was the poor mistreated princess. After living with the people, getting to know them, sharing food with them . . . I realized these weren't like the simple drawings that she created back at home, but people, full-faceted people with true lives. I despised the notion of her annihilating them all, but it was too late. At that point she already had you, and there was nothing I could do to interfere. The sweet girl that I once knew has descended into madness. Revenge is all she cares for now."

Annika drew a long sip from her cup, while all watched her furiously, eagerly, hopeful, and breathless. "When Saava was awakened and the false Goddess of Death cast her blight on Gaia's Core, it spread like a disease. The core shards are a living entity. Even if separated from the parent, they all respond in kind to the mother."

"You said that they had to have direct contact," Ardan murmured. "But in the Feishin Kingdom everyone was dead, and I doubt they all were sticking their fingers on a core shard at the precise moment that Nevia's blight went out—"

A cough resounded from behind them. Qirin shrank back, sitting alongside Liana and as far away from the others as possible. "They were all touching Nephyl," he said quietly. "Each one of them. My men and women wear the Feishin emblem encrusted in Nephyl, and Liana"—his eyes fluttered painfully closed—"Liana had a ring. A Nephyl ring. It has become commonplace to utilize Nephyl for more than just energy. I had no idea. I didn't realize...."

"You could not have known this would happen," Nevia soothed.

Qirin folded his arms and remained silent, processing or sulking was difficult to discern.

"Anyhow," Annika continued, "Without any source of energy left, the planet would have eventually withered completely and all life would cease. I just added a gambit to keep it alive."

Ardan raised a brow. "*You?*"

"In this world I am known as Maestra Annika, the head shaman of the seers"—she shoved up her sleeves—"but in Aeterna I was Freya the Fate-Bender. Therefore, I did the one thing that could save this world. Not alter its path, for that has already been set in motion by Sable's replica"—she gestured toward Nevia—"but I was able to give this planet a new life force. Replacing Saava and her energy, a new Light of Gaia will be born, and all will be as it was before."

"And Saava?" Nevia further pressed.

The Fate-Bender's face could not hide the sorrow. Perhaps she willingly chose not to. "Something will have to be done with her. She cannot return to Aeterna, no matter how greatly she yearns for it, but I fear she won't stop trying until she burns away everything she has. She . . . is not the girl she once was."

"That's great and all," Qirin said, ruining the sentiment, "but when will this Light of Gaia restore the planet?"

"I'm afraid I don't know," Annika responded.

"How can you not?! You're the one that wrote him into existence, didn't you?"

"I merely changed fate," she reminded him, not unkindly. "He will harness the ability of rebirth and bring light back to the planet, but in due time."

"But everyone could be dead by then," Nevia said somberly.

"Yes, yes they could."

"So what's the point?!" Qirin cried, a vein bulging at his temple. "This was all a stupid, hopeless waste—"

"No."

Annika rose from her position, crossing the tent to return with a mortar and pestle. Its ingredients had already been prepared, herbs freshly crushed, scent putrid as it passed by from Ardan's position by the fire. She extended it to the anxious king with tenderness.

"It was not a waste. Because you needed to come to me."

Qirin took it, sniffed, and wrinkled his nose. "What do I do with this?"

"Give it to your wife," she said. "It is a medication I prepared for her before you arrived."

Wordlessly Qirin took the mortar and swept away from them, returning to his wife's side with the herbal remedy. Ardan watched them somberly, something in his chest constricting as he witnessed Liana barely able to choke down the contents that Qirin tipped into her mouth.

"Will this help her?" Ardan asked, concern contorting his brow.

Annika merely brought a finger to her lips, considering. "In a matter of speaking."

They were awoken in the night to screams echoing from the shaman's tent. Ardan snapped up with a jolt, brusquely disturbing Nevia, whose head had been resting on his chest. She tugged the woolen blanket to her nose, eyes wide and glossy.

"That's the queen, isn't it?" Nevia whispered, to which Ardan didn't answer. She pressed a hand to his chest and sat upright, reaching for her nearby coat.

"Maybe we shouldn't—" Ardan blurted, causing her lips to turn downward in disapproval. He paused, realizing he sounded selfish, so continued with: "I mean, I'm sure Qirin's with her. I don't want to hurt your feelings, Nevia, but he wouldn't want you there. And I-I'm not sure she would, either."

"But she needs help!" Nevia insisted.

"She has it," Ardan reassured.

He saw her thinking it over, gaze flickering toward the tent flap. It seemed she relented, lowering herself back into bed and into his embrace. He drew her closer, allowing a hand to stroke her back, the motion soothing to them both.

"This is all my fault," Nevia said weakly, voice cracking.

He pressed a kiss to her forehead. "No," he reassured. "It's Saava's."

Ardan lost track of how long they lay there, and how long it had been since the shrieks died down. He had only started to doze when a gust of cold wind entered their tent, the leather flap opening to unveil the Feishin king. In the dim light of the moon he appeared unwell before the tent was cast back into darkness with the close of the flap.

"Come with me," he said hoarsely.

Nevia and Ardan exchanged glances, dread settling in the pit of Ardan's stomach. Qirin left them to dress, both wordless as they scrambled out of bed and greeted the frigid arctic air. Quickly they donned tunics and trousers before following.

They found Qirin waiting outside the tent, moonlight unveiling his tear-streaked face. His raven hair, normally sleek and perfectly pinned was disheveled and unadorned. One look at his face told Ardan everything he needed to know. As if to confirm his suspicions, Qirin dipped his head.

"Qirin—"

The king remained mute and forlorn. He inclined his head in the direction of Maestra Annika's tent and led them up the snowy hill.

The tent was warm and well-lit, a fire still kindling in the pit. Soft murmurs could be heard across the room as two clanswomen carefully draped a white cloth over the Feishin queen. Ardan managed to steal a glance of her face before it was concealed: pale, ashen, and lifeless. Her ink-black eyes had been closed, her hair smoothed and fanned around her. The smell of birth lay heavy in the room.

A choked sob escaped Nevia at Ardan's side, her fingers digging into his bicep painfully. Her pitiful reaction only made the situation worse. They knew—or at least Ardan did—what they would find, but foreknowledge did not make it any easier.

"The child lives," Qirin said quietly, voice strained.

In that moment the tent flap opened, unveiling Maestra Annika. In her arms rested a small bundle. A child, Ardan soon realized, as she approached the trio slowly. The child's face was a healthy pink, and Ardan did not think he was imagining the hint of a glow surrounding him, akin to a halo of light.

"The life of this baby is what kept her alive for so long," Annika explained. "After birth, there was nothing left keeping the blight from consuming her."

Her words struck a chord within Ardan, a memory resurfacing of his conversation with Liana aboard the ship. She asserted that something changed within her after the blight spread, but Ardan had not thought much of it at the time. Now, though. . . .

The Light of Gaia. The gambit to save them all.

Could this man that Annika spoke of be the same that Liana carried in her womb? It all made sense. It was perfect. He would be their savior.

Annika tenderly placed the bundle in Qirin's arms, planting a kiss on the child's forehead. She clasped Qirin's shoulder and smiled.

"It's a girl."

PART 2
IN THE
END

40
NEVIA
ONE MONTH LATER

*D*earest Nevia,

Thank you for your kind correspondence. This has been a challenging time for all of us. I want you to know, however, that I don't discredit what the loss of my sister has been like for you. She always spoke so very fondly of you, and I know that she loved you with all her heart.

Rest assured, our family doesn't blame you for her loss. Fate is at times cruel and unfair, and it is that which took Elante. I know that you would never wish her harm.

I hope you one day find peace and solace, and forgive yourself for what went wrong. I know that Elante would want that for you.

Warmest wishes,

Bianca Kovalik

A heavy sigh heaved Nevia's chest as she reread the letter time a third time. The news of Elante's death came as no surprise to her when she returned to the empire, yet it did not make the blow any less painful. She locked herself away in solitude for a week after her return, refusing each guest and every audience that came to her door.

Time may heal all wounds, but that did not mean they couldn't reopen. Receiving the letter from Elante's elder sister, Bianca, succeeded in doing just that.

Nevia sniffed, blotting the dampness beneath her eyes with a kerchief. A steady hand rested on her shoulder, firm and reassuring amidst the sea of insecurity.

"May I see it?" his familiar warm voice asked.

There was no reason not to share. The empress surrendered the letter to Ardan, watching as he shook out the folds and read. His brow furrowed deeper with each line. Eventually he handed it back, dipping his head somberly. "I think she is being honest," he conveyed. "And she's right: Elante wouldn't want you to beat yourself up over this. I didn't know her well, but even I could tell that much."

Mutely she folded the letter and shoved it back in its envelope, refusing to meet his gaze. They argued over this time and again, and she knew that nothing good would come from another round of debate. They were at an impasse. While she could imagine Elante showering her with forgiveness, Nevia could not extend the same to her best friend's murderer. If anything, she wished to bear the scars of her dear friend's death on her heart for as long as she lived, right alongside those of Darius, her father, and the countless others she found deceased when returning to the capital.

Breaking her attention from self-flagellation, a knock sounded at the door before its hinges squeaked open. Footsteps scuffled along the wooden floorboards as Orla emerged, one of the few in Nevia's court that she still trusted.

"Your Highness."

Nevia nodded, beckoning for her to enter as she thrust Bianca's letter into the drawer of her vanity. If Orla was anything, it was curious, and she did not feel like going over the contents of the letter *again* with another person. Her heart could not bear it.

"Good evening, Orla. What brings you here?"

The seer fumbled with the lace hem of her sleeve. "I just . . . I just wanted to see how you were doing, honestly. Maybe I'm also kind of lonely."

It came as no surprise to the empress. Orla too had lost those she loved when the blight swept across Danaeca, friends and peers that she mingled with; the first she ever had. Since Nevia had been wholly unavailable in her grief they spent much less time together. Nevia bit her lip, feeling guilty anew for her lack of empathy. The girl would never admit to it, but Nevia was certain that worry for her family crept in as well. Orla had written to her father in Asturia weeks ago and had yet to receive an answer.

The chair alongside Nevia squeaked as the Sanen chief rose, seemingly taking Orla's arrival as a sign to leave.

"I'll give you two some time," he said. "Gonna head out to clear my head for a bit anyway."

When he leaned in to give Nevia a soft peck on the lips, she returned by deepening the kiss. Since her return she began to care little about what others thought about her personal life or whom she decided to affiliate with. However, the talk it garnered met her ears loud and clear, specifically from one particular noble in town —one with the wealth and influence needed to march his rebellion in her streets in protest.

With a deft thud Ardan closed the door, leaving the two girls alone to converse. Nevia reached out for Orla's hands.

"Do you want to go to Asturia to check on them?" Nevia offered, as if detecting her thoughts.

Orla appeared startled. "You mean leave?!"

Both were silent. Orla's mask of bravery faltered slightly. Nevia could tell that the girl was considering it deeply, eyes flickering about the room as if searching for something. Finally she shook her head. "No, my place is here. There's nothing I could do for him even if the blight affected home. And I'm sure we'll hear from him soon. Father is a terrible communicator. He always takes forever to write back."

A forced laugh escaped Nevia. "That he really is."

"Let's give it another week," Orla said finally. "And if I still don't hear from him I'll go knocking on his doorstep."

"I think that sounds very reasonable," Nevia agreed, perhaps too quickly. Truthfully she was relieved the seer was going to stay with her. Someone she knew and trusted by her side. Perhaps most importantly, she was someone who understood Saava as wholly as herself, if not more so. Orla had, after all, been the recipient of her projections for years, a witness to the possible outcomes and futures Saava wanted her to observe and convey to others.

Orla had not been the least bit surprised when Nevia recounted how their meeting with Saava went down, having suspected as much from her own revelation when traveling the bond of her goddess. The same could not be said for the rest of the empire after the world died. To denounce their goddess and call her a farce was not taken kindly. Some were in shock, others in pure disbelief and tending towards gushed vitriol, accusing Nevia of blasphemy and refusing her as their empress. Having brought Ardan home with her from the north only further worsened matters. If Xander Bakalov didn't have a case against her before, he certainly did now. Protests were organized in his name, and Nevia could not help noticing that their numbers for their cause only grew with each event.

The rejection from her people was a disappointment, albeit expected. Negative outcomes were fairly expected now. If anything, she was surprised that no one tried to assassinate her as they had the last time she told them something they did not like.

"Hey, while you're here," Nevia started, eager to change the subject. "I was wondering . . . have you, um, seen or heard anything from Saava?"

The young seer flung herself on the bed opposite Nevia and kicked off her slippers. She had a certain disdain for footwear. "Nothing." Orla let out a long sigh. "I have communed with the other seers, and their experience is the same. Seems like she has no further need of us anymore."

Nevia slumped back into her chair, nails digging into the velvet armrests. She figured as much, assuming the seers' role was complete and she would have no further use of them. The visions, after all, were Saava's own wishes for a future. They were not any more real than her imagination, which made the situation even more pitiful. Nevia had based many decisions on these visions, and to know they were self-fulfilled prophecies as Darius once acclaimed brought her no small amount of disappointment.

"I do, however, have a little bit of information."

Nevia's ears perked up at this. "Oh? Which is?"

"I think I know how we can stop her."

Nevia's hands balled into fists. As much as she wished it, she knew Saava would not be satisfied to coexist with her creations on this dying planet. If Maestra Annika was correct, she would seek to annihilate them all to return to her full strength. Saava could not create death, but she could cause it through her own creations. Perhaps disasters didn't work in a prosperous world, but in a dead one . . . .

Nevia shuddered at the grim possibility.

"How?"

Orla lifted the worn leather satchel from her shoulder and chucked it in her direction. Unprepared, Nevia failed at catching it, its contents spilling all over the floor. The girl scoffed, throwing herself from the bed to snatch up a heavy aged volume bound in a navy-blue cover. It looked far older than most within the palatial library.

"I'm assuming that isn't from our personal collection," Nevia observed.

The girl chose not to answer, tongue sticking from the corner of her mouth as she flipped through the worn yellowed pages, many dog-eared and chipped. She leaned over, hair aglow from the candle beside her head. Now that Nephyl had been tainted with death magic it was considered unsafe for use. The initial surge of death magic unleashing the blight seemed to have subsided, yet the core shards didn't return to their former state. They remained darkened, and no one wanted to find out if further blight would spread through its usage. So, they returned to coal and wood for heat and energy. Their supplies were not in abundance, but that proved to be less of a problem than it had before the Nephyl War. Many were in direct contact with Nephyl when the blight unleashed, leading to the loss of many, many lives.

No society had suffered as great as the Feishin Kingdom, however. Nephyl had become a fashion statement and status symbol, insofar as every Feishin soldier bearing a shard within medals upon their breasts. The results were catastrophic. Other societies that had very little Nephyl, such as Zenoch, were relatively unscathed.

At last Orla settled on a page, finger tracing a line of slanted scripture Nevia could seldom make out.

"I was taught some basic magic circles during my training with Maestra Annika," Orla explained. "Basically they're ancient magic, but aren't really used anymore because they just aren't that useful. Few can do more than transmute a few frogs or teleport a few steps, but that's basically it. I tried some, but I was not able to do much. We don't have the magic potential for these kinds of things."

Her finger roved across the page to a sketched hexagram detailed within a circle. "This here is a death circle," Orla explained. "Anything in its path, when activated, would be rendered lifeless."

The empress frowned, leaning in to further examine the page. The concept of such a circle was not anything particularly unique or special; Nevia had read of such spells within literature, and they had been rumored to exist. Such was the origin of banning witchcraft in the empire to begin with. Never did she think they could use this as a weapon against Saava.

"But you said that all the circles you've seen have been useless," Nevia reminded her.

Orla looked up from the page. "I don't think anyone's had the magic to channel it. But you. . . ."

Of course! Nevia. Her death magic.

It was perfect, and brilliant.

And lethal, and a positively dreadful idea.

"Absolutely not."

There was no way that she would attempt to unleash her death magic again, what with after everything it had cost them thus far.

Orla slammed the book shut with a snap. "But your magic will be controlled by the circle!" Orla encouraged. "No one will be in any danger."

"Yeah, only those that are within a thousand foot radius," Nevia countered sardonically.

The imperial seer rolled her eyes, throwing herself down on the floor at her empress' feet. "Come on, you can do this! What if it's our only chance at stopping Saava before she finds a way to end us all?"

"There's always another way," Nevia stated flatly.

But Orla was not willing to accept her refusal. She continued the pressure, resting her chin in her hands and putting on her best pout. "Maybe, but this is the only one I know."

The topic was akin to a heavy blanket weighing Nevia's heart. So far it was their only plausible option, and time was not their ally. Saava had only roamed Danaeca for a single month, and already cities had been overrun by night creatures, their populations annihilated. The attacks would persist until the human race was merely a blip in the history of Gaia, returning to being the lonely chrysalis floating in the void that it once had been.

"I know Maestra Annika denied it," Nevia started, "but is there a way for her to get back to her world?"

Orla made a dismissive noise in her throat. "I haven't the faintest idea. There's nothing in my books about it, obviously." She shook her head. "If there was a way, though, I know Saava would do it, no matter what it cost her."

This was nothing like the Saava that Nevia had come to know, both through legend and her own visions. She was a woman madly in love, ridiculed and mistreated by those who claimed to love her. But everyone had their breaking point, and perhaps Saava had been pushed past hers. If only there was some way to get her to see, to understand how far she had fallen.

"The problem is that I don't think she sees us as real living creatures," Orla said aloud, as if she'd read Nevia's thoughts. "To her, we are just figments of her imagination, projections of her thoughts and dreams. She doesn't feel she's hurting anyone by annihilating us all, not really. Or at least, that's what it seemed when I had gotten a glimpse into her inner workings."

Nevia's eyes fluttered closed. Despite everything Saava did, and all the chaos and cruelty she unleashed . . . she did not want her to die. The woman had suffered so much, and Nevia did not want to resemble her counterpart and mistreat Saava *again.* "We can't have her out there if she wants us gone," Nevia affirmed, perhaps more to herself than to Orla.

"I would agree, which is why the death circle is our best shot."

The death circle. A title alone worthy of a shudder.

"Not a chance," Nevia declared. "And I don't control my death magic, remember? All the times I've inflicted someone it has been entirely coincidental, without intention."

At this Orla merely shrugged. "All magic can be harnessed eventually. Just look at me. Remember how much of a wild card I was when we first met?"

Nevia did, the imperial seer's gift being out of control and nearly driven mad until she received training under Maestra Annika. It would make sense if Nevia could eventually harness her magic, too, yet a part of her wondered if this was something she truly wanted. After all, did anyone really want to wield the power of death? Even if it were the only way, Nevia loathed it.

"We'll practice," Orla said finally.

Panic clawed up Nevia's throat. "No."

"Safely," Orla reassured.

"I'll think about it." Nevia finally relented, before jerking her head toward the door. "Now then, why don't you go? I need to change because I have a meeting."

It seemed like a convenient way to exit an uncomfortable conversation, but Nevia spoke truth. She did have an important meeting, one that would change the fate of Velspire—and her life.

Orla scoffed, folding her arms over her chest in clear disbelief. "A meeting. With whom?"

The empress strode to her cherrywood wardrobe and threw open the doors, unveiling her abundant wardrobe of fine wares.

"The head of the rebels himself: Xander Bakalov."

41
NEVIA

The rebel leader was pacing when Nevia arrived in the study, wearing the threadbare carpet of her late husband's study even thinner. She closed the heavy oaken doors carefully before stepping into the room, clasping her hands regally in front of her.

"Xander."

The young man halted, lifting his head and leveling Nevia with a paralyzing glare. "You sent for me, Highness?" His tone was bored, twinged with a hint of irritation. Not that she could particularly blame him. Everything transpiring was her fault—and they both knew it.

"Yes, I did." She gestured toward the seat in front of the grandiose desk before sinking herself into the oversized armchair opposite. "Thank you for coming on such short notice. I know it's a trip."

"Barely half a day's ride," Xander said dismissively.

The empress swallowed dryly, nerves suddenly seizing her. She had been running possible outcomes through her mind, and this was the soundest one she could make. Even still, it was going to be difficult, and once she made the declaration there was no going back.

She steeled herself by clasping her hands on the desk, so tight her knuckles turned white. "I wanted to discuss a proposition with you," she said finally, with as much certainty as she could manage.

Tension filled the room and ticked his smooth, youthful jaw. "What do you want?"

"I am planning to make some changes within the empire," she said slowly. "And I want to give you something you've always wanted."

His interest seemed mildly piqued. "Go on."

"The empire has struggled ever since its inception," she stated plainly. "The first emperor did his best, and yet our people have always been in a perpetual state of turmoil and suffering. He died trying to defend us and bring peace, as did Darius. I'm coming to the realization that peace simply cannot be attained."

"Only now coming to that, are you?"

At this Nevia merely lifted a hand to silence him, which he had the grace to oblige. "We have tried many things, and I myself have attempted much during my reign as empress, but none of it has helped. People are still dying, starving, and suffering, and crime still surges outside the capital's walls. No one can truly be pleased with the arrangements that have been ordained years upon years ago, and so I plan to make some major changes myself."

She drew in a sharp breath, steeling herself for it. This was it. There would be no going back. It was something she mused over since joining Darius' side. And now, with the sovereign power in her hands to do it, she was about to make it a reality.

"I am disbanding the empire."

Xander's hand went still, the lines he was tracing in the dusty desk's surface ceasing. His lips parted, yet he could not form words. Nevia took this opportunity to continue.

"It might sound crazy, but I think it necessary. No one can agree, no one can get what they need. This way, each of the Five Lords can govern the way that they see fit, and we can all work as equals toward a common goal than an imperial sovereign to rule over all."

"You're a fool," Xander murmured.

Nevia's lips twisted. "I might be."

"And what makes you think the Five Lords would agree? How do you know that they want to disband?"

"Why would they dispute it?" Nevia shot back. "I'd be giving them more power by sacrificing my own."

"Then they would kick you out faster than you can blink," Xander shot back.

"No, they won't, because I am stepping down."

Silence.

Nevia's heart hammered in her chest as she held her breath, watching as Xander's expression shifted from confusion to shock and, finally, glee.

"Had enough of the turmoil and tribulations, have you?"

"No." A heavy sigh escaped her lungs. "I just realized that I'm not where I'm supposed to be." When Xander didn't inquire further, Nevia added, "I gave up everything when I married Darius. My life, my family, my heritage. My home. And now that Darius is gone, this empire is all I'm left with, and, honestly? I don't want it. Any of it.

"Sure, it gives me power and riches unimaginable, but the responsibility is not for the faint of heart. It isn't for me, and"—she lifted her gaze to meet Xander's and offered him a genial smile—"I've learned that's okay. It's not for me, but it might be for someone else, especially as I am about to appoint the District of Velspire with its first mayor."

His dark eyes swept across the room, flickering quickly between the three long windows at Nevia's back. "You mean me?" His voice was soft, barely more than a whisper.

Nevia nodded. "I do."

"But you're disbanding the empire," he interjected, "and you'll have the Five Lords. Why would you need me?"

"Someone needs to govern Velspire, the people that Darius loved more than anyone." Nevia's eyes fluttered closed, thumb brushing the ridged surface of the imperial signet ring passed down from ruler to ruler. With all-too-eager fingers, Nevia slipped the burdensome ring off, and suddenly, as if by magic, the weight of the world felt lighter. Borne ever since her rule, sensations and responsibilities of her office were finally being passed on.

She extended it to Xander between thumb and forefinger. The young man merely stared at it briefly, speechless, before looking back up at her.

"No trick?"

"No trick," Nevia reassured. "You have control of the District of Velspire, now, its own independent society. Gaia is in trying times, and the people here need you to govern them. You're one of them, Xander, and I willingly give this to you."

Xander ran his tongue along dry lips, contemplating, considering. "I have done terrible things to you."

"I know."

"And you would still surrender your power to me?"

"We have all made our mistakes, Xander. I myself am guilty of plenty." She heaved a sigh, before gesturing out the window. "This blight is one of them."

A gray sky with a thick blanket of smog concealed any trace of the sun outside. The gardens, once lush, were now withered, the grass reduced to dry blades. Trees, once fruitful, were now gnarled and brittle, clearly dead.

His gaze followed hers to the window. "But you said it will change."

"It will," Nevia reassured. "We have been given hope that it will."

"So this isn't all for nothing?"

"No."

Finally Xander drew a sharp breath and quickly, as though fearing he would be snared in a trap, snatched up the ring from Nevia's grasp. The relief of handing it over was insurmountable. She would not be sad to leave it all behind. Not at all. A life awaited her outside these gates, even if it appeared bleak right now. And she could walk away knowing that Darius' people were going to be well taken care of.

"As you might already know," Nevia continued, "everything we believed about Saava was a lie."

"Pretty much, yeah."

"And"—Nevia drew a sharp breath, realizing there was only one path forward—"I'm going after her to put a stop to her."

A laugh, soft and smooth, escaped Xander, and it was perhaps the first time she'd seen the light, more tender side of the rebel figurehead. "You are just full of surprises. I can see now why he fell for you."

He meant Darius, she realized, the statement causing a pang of sorrow to clutch her heart. She bowed her head. "It's the only way. Saava is an immortal being, and she wants the planet to herself again. Our existence drains her, and she can't have that. Even if we stop the blight from consuming and restore Gaia to what it was, she will just create others like me and repeat the cycle, again and again."

"She must have limits, a weakness," Xander murmured darkly.

Nevia gritted her teeth. "She must, but I don't know what they are."

"Find them," Xander insisted. "And exploit them. I will do whatever I can to support you. Just send the word and I'm there."

It was Nevia's turn to be surprised. Xander, the young, obnoxious youth of a rich warlord. She had thought very little of him except for a thorn in her side, but to see him support her, even offer his *aid*, was stunning. This was a new side to Xander. Perhaps he would indeed have the makings for a decent ruler.

"Thank you," Nevia said, and she didn't have to feign the sincerity.

"No, thank *you*." Xander dipped his head in gratitude. "If anyone can undo what has been done and stop that bitch with a god complex, it would be you, Nevia Bylilly."

42
NEVIA

Packing her essential belongings was harder on her heart than she anticipated. Perhaps she should have taken this opportunity to supply herself with items of monetary value for resale, but she was tired. Tired of the privilege, the power. The jewels and gold were left behind, ready to be divvied out in any way that Xander saw fit once he laid claim to the district. Among the objects that Nevia stashed away in her satchel were the remnants of Darius' handcrafted engagement gift, the pendant belonging to her mother, and a set of leather working tools that once belonged to her father. Reminders of those she once loved that were no longer with her. Her hands hovered over a golden locket resting within her jewelry box, fingers running the length of the clasp. Elante's. The tears fell then.

"I'm sorry that I couldn't save you," she murmured, unclasping the latch to place around her own neck. Elante's death weighed heavily on her heart. Her handmaiden had been lost to her once during the war, but now she was lost to her forever.

And it was her fault. As was Liana's death. As was her father's.

Her fault, her fault, her fault.

She swallowed back the painful lump in her throat. Dwelling on such thoughts would help no one, nor would it bring back the people she loved. She shoved a few simple outfits in her bag and drew the drawstring as tight as it would go. She was sick of this. The guilt, the thoughts, all of it.

She drew one final look around the room and inhaled sharply.

So many memories lingered within these walls. A pivotal chapter of her life was coming to a close. Once she left those palace gates, she knew there would be no coming back. The memories of her marriage to Darius, the manipulation and invisible scars he inflicted on her. The plenty of teatimes she had shard with Elante, the music she had played in the bay window to an audience of birds. These memories and more were being tucked away for good. Her current life was being left behind forever.

And yet, in her bones, she knew this new path was good. It was right, even if it felt uncomfortable now.

Her door creaked opened and closed, a rush of air tousling her curls. She did not need to turn around to know it was Ardan. He was given his own quarters in the palace, though they were seldom used with the open invitation to hers. It was now simply second nature to retire in her quarters, leaving his own untouched.

She lifted her head, watching as the Sanen chief dropped a couple of satchels upon the smooth wood floor, only to stare wide-eyed at the packed bag alongside her. "Where are you going?"

Nevia let out a slow, labored breath. She hadn't told him about this part of her plan. No one knew. Well, Orla probably had at least some idea, but that was the extent of it. She sat back on her heels, left leg tingling painfully from sitting in the same position for a prolonged period. "I've disbanded the empire and appointed Xander as mayor of Velspire."

She could practically see the cogs turning in his mind as his jaw worked, his expression befuddled. "Explain."

And so, she told him everything, from the discussion she had with Orla, followed by Xander, and the bittersweet decision she came to. They undressed as they spoke, Ardan freeing Nevia from her restrictive corset so that her lungs could expand freely again. Soon they were lying in one another's arms in Nevia's canopied bed, the cozy duvet serving to stave off the winter chill. Nevia inhaled sharply, taking in his scent of earthy pine as she burrowed her nose into his chest.

"I'm scared, Ardan."

He brushed a hand over her hair, fingers ensnaring in her curls. "I know. I would be, too."

She lifted her head, trying to make out his face in the darkened room. He just held her there, his hand straying from her hair to her exposed back. She concentrated on the feel of his calloused palms along her smooth skin, how every neuron seemed to fire off at his touch, but her thoughts betrayed her, lingering on one burdensome thought alone.

"Orla thinks my death magic might be the only way to defeat Saava."

His hands stilled, heartbeat quickening beneath her ear.

"So I'm going to have to practice," she continued.

"You really sure you want to?"

She tilted her chin to look into his shadowed face. "Of course I don't, but what other choice do I have? We're running out of time, and it's probably the only way."

Moonlight reflected on Ardan's eyes, which were locked steadily on hers.

"I trust you," he said finally. "Whatever you decide to do, I'll be with you."

This made her heart skip a beat, finding herself returning to the security of his warm embrace. Savoring the feeling of closeness, of connection, especially with the uncertain future that lay ahead.

"I just don't want to hurt anyone else that I love," she whispered.

Ardan kissed the top of her head. "You're not going to."

The tenderness of his words, his faith in her, made hot tears sting her eyes. "Thank you."

"For what?"

"For always believing in me, even though I've royally screwed things up multiple times now."

"Imperially."

It was Nevia's turn to raise a quizzical brow. "What?"

A chortle, deep and throaty, escaped him. "Well, you would've imperially messed things up, seeing as you're not a royal, but—"

She playfully slapped his arm away, to which he only laughed harder, grasping her sides and flinging her onto her back. He propped himself on an elbow, smiling down at her, as sheets of dark hair tickled her cheek. Even in the inky blackness, with only the moonlight from her bedroom window radiating on them, she could make out the smile upon his broad lips, the softness of his features. She wrapped her arms around his neck then, pulling him down into a kiss.

At least, with whatever came next, she would have Ardan by her side through it all.

Until the bitter end.

43
NEVIA

Ardan left earlier that morning, parting ways with kisses and promises that everything would be alright. He felt it best that she do this next part on her own, and she agreed. This was a chapter of her life she needed to close herself. It started with her and would end with her.

Nevia closed the door to her suite for the final time, footfalls heavy as she followed the familiar halls out of the palace. This time she was in no imminent danger, so she left casually, pace agonizingly slow as she took the spiraling steps, one at a time. A gathering awaited her outside the gates to bid her farewell, compacted like sardines in a tin to be near her, to extend a hand in farewell. Some thanked her for her service, others—specifically women—said she forever changed their lives. It made her stomach twist into knots to be thanked for the very actions she viewed as problems, but she offered gratitude anyway. It was the expectation, and she would follow customs—one last time.

Before long she would be home in the north, but was wise enough to know it would not have been the same as it was before. It never was, but it was a step in the right direction. Nothing was left for her in Velspire. There had not been for a while.

Orla's suggestion was the best they had so far at stopping Saava —seek out Maestra Annika and attempt to harness her death magic—and thus this was Nevia's goal. The thought terrified her, but if Orla could hone her gift and keep it from driving her mad, then maybe Nevia could rein in hers, as well.

She barely made it past the newly-repaired gates when she heard her name chanted from behind. At first she thought nothing of it, and did not even bother to glance back, until her wrist was caught in someone's grasp. She turned to greet the pale-faced imperial seer, eyes wide, fiery hair wild and unruly.

"Please, Your Highness, wait."

"Just call me Nevia now, Orla." Nevia patted the seer's hand. "I'm sorry that I didn't say goodbye. I guess I just didn't—" *Didn't what, think Orla cared?* The words died on her tongue, left unsaid, and it was Orla who thankfully broke the silence.

"That's okay. I never wanted to say goodbye. I actually was going to come along with you."

It was then Nevia noticed the pack slung over Orla's shoulder, her usual flowery apparel exchanged for a rugged dress and modest cloak. Nevia's mouth snapped open to protest, but Orla quickly interjected before she could.

"If you leave, who is to say that Xander wouldn't redact your verdict and sentence me to my death? He's openly displayed a hatred for magic, after all. I'm much safer with you."

A sound argument, and yet Nevia doubted Xander had any intention of imposing such a law with the world in such a state of upheaval. "I think we've all seen enough death to last us a lifetime," she asserted. "But if you feel unsafe I think it would be reasonable for you to return home. Asturia is independent now, and your father can instill his own laws. He would never impose anything that could do you harm."

Orla slipped her thumb between shoulder straps. "I'll go home one day to check on my old man, but not today. I'm coming with you."

"You can't," Nevia protested.

Orla tilted her chin in defiance. The girl exuded such confidence that Nevia at times forgot she was merely thirteen years of age, and was only at the same level of maturity as her peers. "I can, and I will. Who else will keep you safe out there?"

The sentiment was touching, and Nevia tried to hide her amusement by covering her mouth. "You think you'll be the one to keep me safe?"

The redhead bristled, but refused to be deterred. "Besides," she continued, trying from another angle, "I owe it to you. You saw me as something more than just a cursed, frail girl. You saw me worthy of your court." Her pale eyes were wide, pleading. "You are more than just my empress. I admire you, Nevia. Whatever happens next, please, let me be by your side."

Nevia's throat and tongue grew thick. For so long she had viewed herself as the source of anguish and despair. But to be admired, looked up to by a young girl who was only now finding herself? It was moving something cold and hard that had been frozen in Nevia's heart for a while. She clasped Orla on the shoulder, running a hand down her arm. "Then I thank you for your service and companionship."

Color returned to Orla's cheeks, posture visibly relaxing as her shoulders slumped forward. She snatched up the folds of her skirt and proffered Nevia a small curtsy. "I am forever yours, milady."

Nevia had to look away lest she start to break into her own set of tears. Again.

"I'm going to back to Zenoch." A lift of Orla's brows had Nevia further elaborating, "I've decided that your theory is the best we've got. I'm going to practice my death magic, and I think Maestra Annika will be able to assist."

"I could help along the way," Orla offered.

The thought alone sent a shiver to course down the empress' spine. "While I appreciate your offer, I'm going to have to decline. I'm not like you seers, Orla. I'm different, defective. But Annika is something like me, her magic raw and foreign. If anyone can help me hone this curse, it would be her."

Nevia tilted her head at the phantom sensation of a raindrop landing on her shoulder. Instead of rainclouds, however, her gaze met with a thick layer of fog. Smog was not uncommon for the industrial city, but this cloud of death was distinctly different, carrying with it an ominous odor reminding of decay.

A carriage had been drawn in wait at the end of the imperial drive below them. Two well-groomed horses were hitched to their ride: an ebony carriage with the imperial crest emblazoned on its doors. Leaning against its side, plagued with boredom and sleepiness, stood Ardan, strong arms folded over his chest. Nevia wondered how long he had been there waiting for her. Perhaps this was what he had been up to that morning when he gave Nevia time to say goodbye.

Nevia offered him a smile before trudging off to join his side. She looped one of her arms through his, her fingers clutching his muscular biceps. "I guess we're doing this, then."

His hazel eyes bore into hers, threatening to swallow her whole. "Looks like it."

Boots shuffled over to them, kicking up dust from the street as Orla made her approach. Her arrival made Ardan tense. "I thought it was going to be just us."

A chuckle escaped Nevia's throat as she smacked him playfully on the shoulder. "What, so we would have the privacy of the carriage to ourselves?"

The grin he threw her said it all, reaching over and drawing the carriage door open for her to enter, the young seer close at her heels.

"So this is really okay then?" Orla paused in the doorframe, admiring the golden decal adorning the interior.

Nevia tucked her skirts beneath her, shooting the seer a quizzical glance. "I thought I already said yes. Besides, it's not like you gave me much of a choice but to bring you."

Orla guffawed, waving a hand at their surroundings. "No, I mean *this*. I'm surprised you're able to take imperial property when it's no longer yours." Orla arched a brow. "Unless this, too, was written into the agreement?"

The insinuation brought a chuckle from the former empress. "No, they're just dropping us off at Port Kyanos and heading back. Xander knows, too—he gives his blessing."

"Xander? Give his blessing?" The girl flung herself into the seat alongside Nevia, tucking her arms behind her head in a leisure fashion. "Now I know you're really a witch if you were able to get a blessing out of him."

Nevia's lips thinned. "I don't know whether to take that as an insult or compliment."

Orla grinned. "Oh, a compliment. Definitely."

44
NEVIA

The journey to Port Kyanos spanned a few days by carriage. Little sleep graced Nevia on the road, but she was easily distracted from her compromised mental state by Ardan and Orla's antics. The young seer had a lot to say over the course of their journey, perhaps more than she had said in the entire duration that Nevia knew her. In those three days they learned more about the teenage girl than they ever cared to, from her true thoughts on the staff in the palace to gossip on who was dating who, to even suitors that Orla fancied.

"Are you going to eventually ask to court them?" Nevia asked, genuinely curious, which only garnered a snort from Orla.

"Absolutely not! They wouldn't be fit for a bar maid, let alone the lady of Asturia. I just think they're kind of charming and adorable."

It was odd to think of Orla as the lady of Asturia, but that title meant a great deal, especially now that Asturia was its own independent territory, free from imperial rule. "That's right. I guess that makes you essentially a princess."

"Essentially," Orla agreed, grinning widely. "So you'd better be nice to me or I'll see to it that you suffer."

"Sure." Nevia sounded more bored than concerned.

Port Kyanos was a small city off the coast of Malabria. Many of its original structures were still erect hundreds of years after their construction, easily marking the port one of the oldest in Danaeca. Brightly-colored rooftops greeted her vision as the door to the carriage was swung open by their footman, a stark contrast to the bleakness of the sky.

The air smelt salty, complimented by the familiar reek of decay, this time not only from the death ozone but the ocean's waves lapping at the nearby coast. The air, once filled with the shrill cry of seagulls, was sightless. A bleak and unattractive variety of grays concealed the brilliant blue sky above.

Port Kyanos was small, and yet it was one of the largest tourist attractions in Danaeca. As such, the streets were congested, buildings tightly clumped together. In the days prior to the planet's death it was often hard to find places to stay in the tourist attraction. Now, it had become a ghost town.

Chilly winds blew loose debris across the streets as they made their way further into town, dustdevils swirling fallen leaves. It was normal for the trees to be dormant at this time of year, but these went beyond dormancy. They were dead, devoid of life, never to reawaken at Mother Nature's natural cycle of rebirth.

"Think we'll manage to stumble upon anyone?" Ardan eventually whispered as they traipsed into the city, footsteps pronounced by the crunch of dried leaves.

Nevia took a moment to pause in front of an ancient cathedral, a place once a worship site for Saava in Danaeca's earlier days which now stood as a dilapidated building. Its stained glass windows were shattered, and nary a light shone through the fragmented windowpanes. "I don't know."

The trio strode further through the decrepit city, hope slowly dwindling in Nevia's heart as no signs of life were found. Eventually, however, a light flickered, followed by the creaking hinges of a door. Heart-hammering, Nevia followed the sound, steeling herself for more tragedy so as not to be disappointed when it was found. The rustling, though—that must've indicated life. It had to be someone.

But alas: it was instead a bobcat, its coat glistening in the pale moonlight as it stalked the streets. It was scrawny, muscles sunken beneath its tawny coat. It padded its way over to a cluster of homes, extending itself upon hind legs in search of something to eat inside a fishing barrel. The sight made Nevia's heart break with sympathy. Normally these animals wouldn't leave the wilderness. Clearly hunger drove it out.

Sensing her distress, Ardan wrapped an arm around her shoulders, the stubble on his chin snagging her hair. "We're doing everything we can," he said. "Finding Saava and ending this."

She swallowed the lump in her throat, allowing herself to be guided alongside her companions. In truth, she was not so certain ending Saava was going to end the blight—their suffering—as much as halt the further demise of humanity at the hands of new night creatures, but she digressed.

Their pace quickened, bringing them to the docks and borrowing a ship to set sail to the coastline of Zenoch. This time of year was abhorrent to traverse the mountain range; Nevia recalled this all too well when she and Ardan had done it not once, but *twice* during the Nephyl War. Sailing would be simpler by far, even if cutting through the mountains would have been faster.

None accompanied them aboard the simple sailboat, which they rented with a handful of coins and promises of return. The steward did not seem particularly interested or concerned. Whether it be because the leaser was the former empress, the steward did not care about sea travel, or both was unknown, but he lent the boat with no qualm nor required deadline for its return.

Nevia loosed a heavy sigh as she eased herself on the deck, staring up into the blackened sky. The stars twinkled brightly, and at night Nevia could almost convince herself that the world was still perfectly normal. This night seemed as such. She stared up at the stars, gaze tracing the constellations that guided many a traveler for millennia.

Did they have stars in Aeterna? Nevia could not help wondering. Perhaps not, if visions of her alternate life were any indication. Night did not exist, thus stars were not visible. She wondered, then, where Saava found inspiration for the stars in Gaia's night sky, or if these things were not part of her creation.

Perhaps she had less control over her surroundings than she liked to think.

45
NEVIA

The temperature had dropped significantly in the six weeks that Nevia had left the north, and yet the snow was far from fresh. Its surface, normally smooth and glistening, was disturbed and rock solid. It was clear the region was receiving far less precipitation than usual, which could result in many complications if weather patterns did not improve. Was this, too, an aftereffect of the blight?

The clans' lifestyle was otherwise unaffected by Gaia's death. Hunting parties still returned with plenty of fresh meat, stories were still told around campfires, and the children's laughter still carried through the valleys of the encampment. Nevia couldn't help noticing the number of women pregnant within the Thomani clan, as well, something she hadn't strongly noticed the last time they visited. Another reminder that life went on in their otherwise fallen world.

She brought this up to Ardan as they took up residence beside an open fire with others, trying her best to ignore the deer being skinned a short distance away from them. Ardan flipped up his collar, covering his exposed neck. "The clans have been trying to rebuild our populations," he explained. "No one was under any obligation, but it was mutually beneficial to us all, and the women agreed."

It relieved her to know they consented and were not coerced, though she wondered if they were receiving the medical support they needed. Clanswomen often relied on the experience of other women, most of which were mothers themselves, to guide them through childbirth. But things happened, and poor outcomes did follow as a result. Only after moving to the empire had she learned most women were tended to by physicians during childbirth, and were able to help women have safer, easier deliveries.

The uncomfortable conversation was thankfully interrupted, however, when a pair of arms encircled her from behind, plastering her against someone's chest. If Ardan wasn't grinning at her side, she might have been afraid that it was an attack.

"She still lives!" a deep feminine voice broke out, accent rich and hearty. "Been avoiding me, have you?"

That voice. Immediately she recognized it. Memories of comfort and times, which, while difficult, were still better filled her with warmth. Nevia wrenched herself around as the embrace loosened, turning to meet the sharp emerald eyes of her dear friend.

"Khatalia!"

Nevia threw her arms around the woman's neck, burying her face into her shoulder. She often wondered about the well-being of her friend, knowing only the tidbits that Ardan offered from his correspondence with her. It was a relief unmeasurable to find her healthy and hale, to surrender herself in the former Kohari chief's strong arms.

A chuckle, deep and throaty, escaped Khatalia as she returned her embrace, threatening to suffocate Nevia amidst her furs. "Good to see you, too, Empress." She turned a sharp glare toward Ardan, who busied himself with crunching into a carrot. "And you!"

Ardan began to gag.

"You say that you're leaving me in charge for a few weeks, and then you flat-out disappear for *months*? Who even does that?!" She punched his shoulder, a gesture which may have looked friendly but Nevia knew better than to buy it. Ardan didn't react, but she could tell that it must have smarted.

"But Tani gave you messages," Ardan protested, raising his hands in surrender.

Khatalia's glare was sharp enough to slice through flesh. "Not the same as hearing it from your mouth."

The casualness of their conversation made Nevia's heart considerably lighter. For a moment she could almost convince herself they were living in different times. It struck her, then, that they were in the Thomani clan's region, and Khatalia had been appointed to care for Ardan's people.

"But, how are you here?" Nevia spoke out suddenly, causing both Zenochians to turn. "I thought you were with the Sanen clan?"

Khatalia absently brushed her shoulders free of flurries. "I am. You see, our migratory paths crossed, and so we are sticking together for a couple of weeks. We figured we may as well, especially with the fewer members of our hunting parties."

From the avalanches, Nevia soon realized, not the blight that crossed their lands.

"Thankfully we never got mixed up with that accursed core stuff," Khatalia explained. "So we weren't affected by the disease."

That alleviated a fraction of the guilt that consumed her, at least.

Ardan, recovering from his encounter with the carrot, rose and reached for Nevia. "Let's catch up inside," Ardan proffered, beginning to steer Nevia in the direction of the rows of tents. "We've been out here so long, and I'm ready to thaw out."

Nevia certainly was ready, as well, the warmth a welcome promise away from days upon days in the bitter cold. Most especially, she wished to get Orla out of the frigid climate, the young girl not accustomed to it as they were. Mostly she traveled without complaint, though her silence spoke volumes when the girl was otherwise quite chatty.

Ardan inquired about Annika's whereabouts, locating a few of his own clansmen amidst the sea of Thomani redheads. After chatting with them several moments he returned to the three women, shaking his head with a sigh. "She is supposed to be coming back. Said she had some business to tend to. Might be days, could be weeks."

Days or weeks were not available, Nevia wanted to remind him, but any argument was left to die in her throat.

They traced their way around camp and slipped inside a nearby tent, the warmth of the open fire struck her like a wave, stinging her cheeks and causing her eyes to water. The pack at her shoulder found its way to the tent floor as she approached, falling short by the fire and savoring its warmth.

As they settled, Khatalia took it upon herself to fetch them something to drink, and Orla had begun a series of jumping jacks to warm herself. Things certainly felt normal, and for a time Nevia chose to set aside her worries for the future, basking in the warm presence of Ardan leaning into her side, in the companionship of the people she loved.

They were chatting about Khatalia's progression of food storage capabilities when the tent flap opened. Standing in the doorway, face hard and cold, stood none other than the Feishin King. His dark eyes flickered across the room, before at last landing on their target.

"So it's true, then," he said. "You did come back here."

Despite the hostility he conveyed, Nevia could've leapt up and embraced him for as grateful as she was to see him alive and well.

"What are still doing here?" she blurted instead, sounding more aggressive than intended.

Qirin waved a hand dismally. "Everything? Nothing? It depends on your definition of 'doing.' There's nothing left of my kingdom to return to. Perhaps one day I'll venture back, but I'm in no hurry. Consider it my paternity leave."

A choked sound escaped Orla's throat from behind them, as if to stifle back a laugh. Wariness flashed across Qirin's face as he noticed her. "Who's that you brought with you?"

"A good friend. We can trust her." Nevia gestured toward Orla, who was sitting on her knees across from her. "You remember Orla, don't you?"

Qirin's eyes narrowed, as if trying to recall. "Can't say that I do. Care to refresh me?"

"The imperial seer." Orla stated, flourishing a bow for dramatic effect. "Right hand to Her Imperial Highness, and daughter of Lord Torquil of Asturia." She dared a glance up, half-expecting the Feishin king to be impressed by her title.

He merely blinked. Twice. "Fascinating," was all he offered before turning his attention back to Nevia as he crossed the threshold into the tent. "Anyhow, as I was saying: I know next to nothing about raising children, and Maestra Annika has been so kind as to give me some pointers for Akari."

Nevia's expression softened in the glow of the fire. "You named your daughter Akari."

Qirin lowered his dark cloak from his arm, and it was then that Nevia noticed her: the wiggling bundle tucked perfectly against his chest. A baby, which could have been easily mistaken for a porcelain doll. Her black hair was perfectly plastered against her head, dark lashes long. Her cheeks were rosy and full, one hand balled into a tight fist resting just above Qirin's heart. The sight warmed her spirit as much as the fire before her heated her physically.

Despite the losses they endured, she was grateful that Qirin, at least, had his daughter, and that he was not left entirely alone in the world.

Qirin's dark eyes flickered across the room, assessing all that were gathered, and rested on Nevia in the end. "Well, I suppose now that we're all finally together we have much to discuss. Particularly why you decided to do away with your crown and what you plan to do now."

46
NEVIA

Nevia's mouth fell agape, expression shifting from surprise to horror in an instant. She turned her attention from Qirin to her steaming cup of tea. Heat rose in her cheeks.

"How did you know?"

"Did you not think that news would spread like wildfire?" Qirin shook his head.

Nevia bit her lip. She sought Ardan's gaze, as if pleading, seeking validation or assurance. He only briefly held it before dipping his chin. It was her story; she was on her own.

"Well, let's hear it from Nevia first," Khatalia said, forehead pinching into a frown. Her eyes were aglow with an intensity that made Nevia shift uneasily on her cushion.

"I did abdicate the throne," she admitted. "But for good reason. I disbanded the empire, and left Xander as mayor of Velspire."

"You gave that bastard power?" Qirin asked, tone flat in disbelief.

Nevia flinched. "It was the right decision."

The king rolled her eyes. "I suppose you didn't think about the very valuable resources that are now dead to us since you've sacrificed your namesake?"

"It was Darius' namesake, never mine," Nevia countered sharply. "And I was reminded of it daily. I am sick of being criticized, sick of being judged. I'm done. I think this is a satisfying end to an empire that never should've been brought into being."

"I bet Rufus Androvich is roiling in his grave right about now," Qirin grumbled.

A very loud sigh escaped Ardan's lips. "Well, no use in crying over spilt milk."

"What a curious expression," Orla mused, fidgeting with a salt shaker and tipping it to watch fine pink crystals land on the mat in front of her. It caught Nevia's attention, and she had to fight the urge to not grasp her hand and get her to stop. The others seemed mesmerized by her eccentric nature, as well.

It was Ardan who first broke free from Orla's distraction. "While I'll admit that I'm not sure how this move was a good one" —he shot a glance at Nevia, a lethal calm swirling in his gold and green eyes—"Nevia thought it so, and at this point does it really matter? Our world is dead anyway."

No one could argue with that. Well, except perhaps Qirin, but Akari started crying the moment he opened his mouth, diverting his attention.

"I have a plan, actually," Nevia said, timidly, quietly.

She had been giving it some thought over the journey. How they could actually put a stop to Saava. She had shared the details involving her magic with Ardan and Orla, but they did not know the rest. As if sensing her discomfort, Ardan reached for her hand and clasped it, giving a slight squeeze.

Nevia swallowed dryly. It was dangerous, and she was loath to do it. But it was the only way; she knew that now.

"Well, this has to be good," Qirin said. "What is it?"

"We have to kill Saava, by using my magic to do it."

An eerie silence fell over them, an uneasiness thick in the air. Perhaps it was the discussion of deicide that made them uncomfortable, or, worse: their fear of Nevia wielding death magic again, especially after what happened the last time which resulted in the death of the planet.

Ardan again pierced the silence. "What do you need from us?"

"Well, the plan involves you, specifically," Nevia admitted.

Ardan's brow rose in surprise. It was certainly not a part of the conversation she shared, and a part of her was putting this part off because it made her nervous. "Me?"

"She, um, well, was in love with you."

Both brows rose now. "Go on."

"An alternate version of you." Her tone heightened, and she began speaking more animatedly than she had all evening, mostly from nerves. She explained the visions she'd witnessed, as well as those she experienced with Orla. How Ardan had taken the likeness of Niall, Saava's former lover and Sable's husband, and how Niall's death is what spurred Saava's punishment.

"So that's why you two were at such odds with one another for so long," Qirin mused aloud.

Ardan shot him a dark look, before turning back to Nevia and the important planning at hand. "So, she would probably hate me more than anyone?"

A heavy sigh escaped Nevia, eyes fluttering closed, the very harsh reality paining her. "No, she is probably still in love with you."

"This is taking a weird turn," Qirin murmured around the rim of his cup.

Ardan blinked. Once, twice, before blurting, "And she wouldn't think it suspicious at all that I somehow side with her?"

"No, she probably doesn't even know you exist."

"And we do know she doesn't always create on purpose," Qirin murmured darkly under his breath. "Her dreams take forms on their own accord. Though now that she's awake I think it is safe to assume her creations will be more deliberate." Qirin's lips narrowed into a thin line. "Another reason I am choosing to lay low."

A laugh bubbled up in Nevia's throat before she could rein it in. "You, lay low? That would be the first."

His dark gaze flickered to her, cold wrath kindling within his eyes. "I'm not taking any chances with Akari."

Nevia bit down on her lower lip till she tasted copper.

"So, what do you expect me to do, woo the goddess?" Ardan chortled, but quickly silenced himself when no one joined in.

Nevia met his gaze evenly. "Yes."

She could think of a million reasons why he should not, in fact, woo the goddess, but none were reason enough when they were already looking death in the face, their race on the brink of extinction—and everything else with it.

"I suppose waiting for Akari to fulfill her task is off the table?" he instead asked, to which Nevia merely shook her head sadly.

"Saava's not going to stop as long as we're alive. And, if she discovers Akari, she will try to kill her, or simply wait till Akari's dead and do it again." The bluntness of her words made Qirin flinch, but she chose to ignore him, instead proceeding. "This is the only way to do away with Saava. You need to coax her to let down her guard, to get her into a place of vulnerability."

"Okay, hold up"—Khatalia lifted a hand, silencing all of them —"suppose you're right: Akari in danger, Saava pursuing her destruction bullshit till the end of time. What's Ardan supposed to do once he seduces her? If you haven't forgotten, she's immortal."

"But she can still be killed, and that is where I come in."

She told them about the magic circles, and how Orla suggested she ensnare Saava in one using her death magic. "It's just a matter of my learning how to control it," Nevia admitted.

Qirin scoffed. "And not cursing us all to death this time?"

Ardan began to rise from his seat beside her, a tick in his jaw. His striding over to the king and getting physical seemed highly plausible, considering the hardness of his expression. She snatched his sleeve to tug him back down beside her.

"Not if I can learn to control it," Nevia admitted. "Look, I don't like it either. It's full of risks—"

"You bet it is," Khatalia grumbled under her breath.

"But I think it's the only way. And we would be a fool if we were to let this opportunity slip by."

Qirin narrowed in on her, eyes as sharp as knives. "And you're willing to take responsibility should your death magic meet a target other than the one you wish?"

This was the part she feared most of all. She swallowed, panic sinking its claws back into her chest. She looked about at each person—at Khatalia, who had lost everything, at Qirin, who held his daughter in his arms. Everyone paid a heavy price already, and would only pay more if Saava were left to her own devices. Nevia's fists balled in her lap, resolve unwavering as she ground out. "Yes."

Her trembling hand wrapped around her cup, the tea having gone cold with the chill in the air, despite the warmth of the fire in front of her. There were a lot of pieces on the board, and a lot of ways that their plan could go wrong. But at least they had one, and it was the best they had.

"So when and how do you start practicing?" Khatalia inquired. "Need anything from me?"

"She's going to train with Maestra Annika, like I did," Orla piped up, reminding them all of her presence.

Qirin lifted his hands to absorb the fire's warmth. "She left about a week ago and should be back soon, so you came at just the right time, I daresay."

That was an improvement from the days or weeks that they were offered earlier. Nevia would take it. She turned to Ardan with a question in her gaze. "And you're really okay getting Saava into the death circle for me to set it off?"

Ardan tossed his head to the side. "If you're being brave, then I can, too. Even if it means I have to reap the curse alongside her."

A harsh breath drew in to her lungs. There was that risk—she had known it from the start—if her death magic would extend beyond Saava and afflict him, too.

"That will not happen."

She did not want to believe in the possibility, and thus did everything in her power to deny it.

Ardan arched a brow, but she averted her gaze from his after her rejection of the possibility. "Orla?"

Hearing her name, Orla stopped mid-motion as she draped her napkin over the structure she'd engineered on her saucer. "What?"

"You can help us find Saava, right?" Ardan prodded.

"I—" Orla's face suddenly went pasty white. "I mean, I think so. Connections are a two-way street, and I was able to see through our shared bond before. I should be able to do it again. I think. I just—"

Nevia placed a hand on her shoulder, slender fingers caressing the young seer in comfort. "I believe in you."

Orla blanched, palms resting on the table. Her face became half-hidden by her fiery locks as she bowed her head. "Yes, Empress."

"I'm not your empress anymore," Nevia reminded her.

"Milady, then."

That would have to do for now. They had a plan, and that was the best they could do for one night. Nevia rose from her position on the mat, allowing her legs to stretch after having sat in conversation for hours. Others began to follow suit.

"I will show you around," Khatalia offered, "get you guys a tent, if we can find a spare one around here somewhere."

Nevia was ready to accept, but Ardan spoke up before she had the opportunity. "It'll be all right. Why don't you help get Orla settled? I'm going to let Nevia stay in the chief's quarters." Ardan offered her a wink. "Just this once."

47
NEVIA

The chief's quarters had belonged to Khatalia as acting chief while Ardan was away. She grumbled her disdain, but when Ardan's expression remained hard and unmoving she eventually relented, muttering under her breath that she did not want to be in the same tent with them anyway. Therefore, the second-in-command took Orla by the hand and showed her to a tent where they would be staying together, leaving the couple alone. A smile played on Nevia's lips; Orla needed more friends, and she knew that the girl was in good hands.

A short trek led them to the chief's private tent. Ardan held open the flap to grant Nevia entrance first. The accommodations offered comfort without luxury. She allowed her coat, shrugged off, to fall to the floor as she kicked off her boots.

She wondered how her companions took all the news she shared.

She wondered what she'd just condemned herself to by agreeing to train with Maestra Annika.

She wondered many things about their uncertain future.

"Make yourself at home," Ardan offered, oddly casual, despite the fact that he was bringing Nevia into his intimate space. The tent he'd probably lived in for years before joining her in Velspire, the space where he'd slept, where he'd dreamt, where he'd—

She didn't allow her mind to wander further, instead shuffling further into the room. As far as Zenochian homesteads went it was rather standard: a bedroll in one corner, baskets of clothing and personal effects in another. Some pottery lay on the far wall, as well as a very small table only large enough for one chair. Otherwise it was rather neat and tidy, cozy, without the frills.

Nevia allowed herself to slink on to the sheepskin and flannel bedding, rolling her ankles as she watched Ardan kneel before the fire pit, broad muscles taut in his back. She closed her eyes to the striking of flint against steel, again and again. Finally the sound of crackling flames sprang to life, and he set the tools aside. In three strides he was next to her, crossing his ankles as he stretched out his long legs.

"You know, I was thinking back to our meeting back there," he said, chortling. Nevia's heart sped up, expecting something negative, but what escaped his lips was beyond shocking to her. "Everyone was so gods damn focused on what you were saying, but all I couldn't get over was how you kept fawning over Qirin's baby."

Embarrassment crept over Nevia's face. She knew so little about children, having never been around many. She had no siblings, no cousins, and only the clan's children to play with. They were all peers, equals, and as an adult she had spent very little time with children. Being in such close proximity to one, especially one as small as Akari, piqued her interest. She would have been lying if she said she never wondered what it would feel like to hold her and cradle her to her own breast.

"And I couldn't help thinking, in that moment, that you would make an excellent mother one day."

Nevia felt her cheeks grow warm. "Oh."

"In fact"—Ardan tilted his head to the side, long hair brushing her shoulder—"it surprises me that you and, well, *he* never had children." When she offered nothing he dared to further press, "Do you not wish to be a mother?"

"It wasn't the right time," Nevia said shortly.

"Ah." He waited, seeing if she would offer anything else. But she didn't, fists clenched tightly on her thighs. A gentle smile quirked the edge of his mouth, his cheek dimpling, a trait Nevia so loved. "So do you think it could be in your future, then, becoming a mother?"

She swallowed dryly. "It could. Definitely."

The words spread warmth through her chest, easing the heaviness that constricted her moments ago. Ardan, her beloved, a father. She could see it now. A cottage, somewhere warm and cozy in the mountainside, a basket of fresh herbs slung over her forearm. The door to the cottage would open before she could even reach it, and there he would be, Ardan, her husband, a child in his arms looking like the perfect blend of the two. It was a beautiful vision and a lovely future, something she never ventured to think about before.

It never felt safe enough to think about it before. She moved to cup his cheek, her fingers gently caressing his freshly shaven face. "If we survive this, I think I just might like to see what parenthood would be like—with you."

He made his move, then, as if unable to resist her any longer. He pressed his lips to hers, and she savored them: their warmth, their fullness, their taste.

The kiss was gentle, nothing as fiery and passionate as their previous exchanges, or as demanding. But slow, tender. Loving. She brought in his lower lip between her teeth, eliciting a moan from him as he allowed his tongue to flick against them.

Her arms snaked across his back, drawing him as close as humanly possible without getting beneath his skin. Her fingers traced his broad, muscular shoulders, hard beneath his linen tunic. His hands were equally as venturous, first cradling her hips before bringing them snug against him.

His hardness for her made her purr in delight, kissing him hard, fingers entwining into the fine hairs at the nape of his neck.

Her breasts ached, yearning for touch, their heaviness only lightened when Ardan's palm cupped one. Then the other.

Soon they both shed garments and laid alongside each other. To explore every curve, every smooth lining of flesh that they yearned for. Nevia lined his collarbone with kisses, pausing at the hollow of his throat, pulling skin between teeth and causing his breath to hitch.

"I've never been more proud," Ardan started, breath ragged, as he gazed up into her face, "to call something mine than in this moment."

A smile curved her lips as she threw a leg over him, straddling him between her legs. She could feel his manhood in her sensitive area, causing her to drag her hips along him once, twice. Finally she arched her back, pressing a palm to his chest as she leaned in close to his lips.

"And you mine."

48
NEVIA

It was barely dawn and positively frigid when Nevia marched across the snowy landscape, ice crunching underfoot as she made her way down the slick cliff face. Why Annika wanted to meet her so far away from the encampment, she had no idea. Perhaps she wanted to secretly punish her for the sins she'd wrought against Gaia.

Not that she was undeserving. In fact, she would have found it quite fair.

The sharp winds rustled the pale dreadlocks of the head shaman standing several paces away atop the hillside opposite her. Her back was to Nevia until she came within earshot, turning the older woman around with a harrumph.

"You're late."

Annika sprang backward, with an agility and finesse that was entirely unbecoming of the middle-aged woman that she had come to know. It must have something to do with having the build of an immortal.

Nevia flipped up her collar to cover her exposed neck. She was freezing. It was a particularly cold day in the dead of winter, and the night prior had been so toasty in Ardan's tent, with the chief himself keeping her warm and safe in his embrace.

Annika had returned the next day, true to Qirin's prediction, and she wanted to waste no time to start training Nevia in her magic. She appointed their first session to commence at the crack of dawn, and it was perhaps ten minutes past.

If that.

"Sorry to disappoint you," Nevia murmured. "How would you like us to start?"

The Fate-Bender did not respond right away, her gaze instead tracing the faraway mountainside. "Three years ago an avalanche shook those mountains."

A shudder coursed down Nevia's spine. Of course she remembered. But why was Annika bringing this up now? Did she blame her for that, too?

"As dreadful as the casualties were, the end result would've been so much worse." She threw Nevia a sideways glance. "Had you not intervened, done what you did, all of the Feishin Kingdom could've been annihilated, and had I not intervened, all of Zenoch could've perished."

Nevia's jaw fell. "You intervened?"

"I am a Fate-Bender, child," Annika reminded her. "It should come as no surprise that half the clansmen left on their migratory path a day early, missing the disaster by a miracle."

She had not known that, never once gave it thought. Her shoulders slumped. "Thank you. You did far more than I could have—"

"You would do well to stop feeling sorry for yourself," Annika interrupted, tapping her staff into the snow, one which Nevia hadn't realized she was wielding until then. "Start focusing on what you can do, and what you will do by getting your magic working. What can you tell me about the previous instances where you've been able to cast?"

Nevia drew in a breath of piercing cold air. The question was one she had been wondering herself, and had yet to draw any definitive conclusions. "It has been when my emotions were sharpest," she offered. "Generally when my heart has been meddled with."

A hum of acceptance escaped Annika. Nevia hoped she did not ask for clarification, because she did not want to delve into the specific incidents when her magic flared. It was embarrassing, really, to think back on how fickle her heart had been months ago, and that her magic had reared its head over losing Ardan, and then later Renault's betrayal. Gratefully Annika did not press further, instead pointing her staff again at the mountains.

"I want you to focus on those peaks," she said, "and recall the day your father died."

More than the cold stung her eyes. She would take almost any memory over that one. Almost. Resurfacing memories of watching silently, helpless as Darius ordered her father's execution pained her. A means of clearing Nevia's name, while simultaneously punishing her for her betrayal. That Darius would charge him falsely with sorcery for his assistance was an abhorrent act, despicable in every way.

A tear rolled down her cheek, hot against her cold skin.

So much pain. So much loss.

"Good, good," Annika affirmed, watching her from the side. "Now keep feeling those emotions, and draw them out from deep within. How raw it makes you feel, how much you wish to hurt those who hurt you."

"But I don't want to make anyone hurt," Nevia complained, concentration snapping from the memory and on to Annika at her side. "Goddess knows enough people have already been hurt because of me. I don't want any more suffering."

Frustration contorted the folds of Annika's face as she tossed her staff into her other hand. "Then you will never succeed in unleashing your death magic against Saava and do what needs to be done."

The words were a cold slap to her already frigid face. Nevia, however, felt like snapping back. "I'm just being honest! You wanted me to visualize wanting to make people hurt, and I can't when there's no one I want to hurt."

Annika clicked her tongue, "Which is exactly why you won't be able to control it."

"Fine, then!" Nevia threw her hands in the air and stormed off, fuming. She made it only a few steps when she heard Annika's voice fill the space between them, cold and sharp.

"I did not dismiss you!"

She didn't even turn around, much less respond.

Session one of harnessing her magic was a complete failure.

49
NEVIA

The days turned to weeks, and Nevia was no closer to harnessing her magic than when she first arrived. Her episodes of storming off in a rage became fewer, but that was the extent of her progress.

They had tried so many things. Tapping into her emotions proved ineffective, so Annika came up with the brilliant theory of exhausting her physically to see if her magic would manifest.

It was one such afternoon of physical exertion. Sweat froze on Nevia's forehead as she panted, bracing a long wooden pole in hand. She wiped at her runny nose as she and her opponent slowly circled one another in the freezing field, calculating, waiting.

She had been through several over the course of the week. Khatalia was quick to shove her to the ground, and after a broken rib it was deemed that Nevia wasn't quite ready to take on the barbarian in combat. Ardan was too soft on her, and, likewise, Nevia was too resistant about hurting him, thus their training sessions were ineffective.

This time her opponent was Qirin, circling her like a vulture ready to feast on its meal. He had agreed, perhaps too readily, to take her on in combat. Aside from the fact that both harbored animosity toward each other and neither held reservations about hurting the other, they were also more evenly matched. Qirin had the upper hand when it came to physical strength, but Nevia had the agility he lacked. His footwork was sloppy, his sword arm more so, being self-taught. While Nevia did not feign mastery over wielding a weapon, she had learned the basics when living in the empire, and there were times when Darius and her engaged in swordplay for fun.

Both marginally knew what they were doing. Which made them perfectly matched.

"What are you waiting for?" Qirin goaded, twirling the wooden pole in his hand. "Afraid I'm going to smack that ugly sneer off your face?"

"I'm not sneering!"

Still twirling, he charged, aiming the end of his pole to strike her sternum, but she deflected the blow, holding the stick with both hands in defense. They went on like this, striking, taunting, striking, until both were miserable and Nevia was ready to throw the fight so that it would soon be over.

Neither relented in the end. They continued to dance around each other, skirting around the issue that was really at hand.

"You're still angry with me," Nevia observed.

Qirin lashed out with his pole to strike at her right ear, only she rolled to dodge it. "Yes, of course I am."

"Then how can I make it up to you?" Strike one. Two. Three. All were body blows coming at varying heights. "How can I make amends?"

Qirin deflected all three. "You can't. Unless you can bring Liana back from the dead or restore my kingdom to its former glory, I'm afraid I'll go on hating you till the day I'm in my grave." A slow frown spread across his face. "Wait, no, scratch that. I will still hate you even after I'm long gone in the Nether Planes."

And they were back to circling each other again. Nevia partly wished to chuck her pole and start pummeling him, going hand-to-hand, but Annika discouraged such in the event Nevia's blight infected her opponent. Probably a good call, with her brewing anger for Qirin.

A frustrated cry escaped Nevia as she charged. She was tired of the pain she had doled out without intention, tired of being unable to make things right. She was frustrated beyond belief with trying to get her blight to manifest, and she sure as hell was tired of seeing Qirin's smug face despising her at every corner.

She just wanted to be understood. To be pardoned.

Forgiven.

A tingling sensation made the hairs prick up on the back of Nevia's arms, tendrils beginning to slither out from her fingertips. Excitement crawled its way up her spine and lit her eyes. Annika reacted, barking a command for Qirin to stop. He was already on it, his weapon held over his head and frozen in place. He stepped back. Just as quickly as the magic stirred, however, it faded away from view. The sensation, once potent and chilling, evaporated away with the elation going first.

"No," she growled, tossing down her stick.

Annika strode closer, jotting something down in a book she carried during all their trainings. "Interesting."

Nevia whipped to face her, hair loose and unyielding. "What, my failure?" she snapped.

"No, no, I think you're making progress." Nevia stared, stunned. Praise? That was new—the first she had been able to do anything marginally successful under Maestra Annika's tutelage. "It seems the emotion of regret is bringing about your magic. Though why did you stop when it surfaced?"

Nevia paused, giving it some thought. "I suppose I realized it was happening and it stopped manifesting, like it broke the emotion fueling it."

Annika dipped her head in assent. "As I thought."

"Are we through, then?" Qirin tossed the wooden pole on the ground at Nevia's feet and spat. "Because I need to go back to Akari. It's time for her feeding."

"Yes," Nevia gritted out, before the head shaman could declare a rematch with the newfound knowledge. "Thank you, Qirin, for your time."

He merely grunted in acknowledgement, shoving his hands in his pockets and storming off. The winds rustled between the remaining two, the unspoken tension unmoved by the gusts, Annika's stare burning holes through her. Unable to stand the scrutiny any longer, Nevia stooped to retrieve the staves, gloved hand stroking the smooth wood.

"You hate yourself."

Nevia lifted her head, still crouched on the ground. "Excuse me?"

"Your powers manifested when you were frustrated with your own shortcomings, your own failures." Maestra Annika fixed Nevia with one of her steely gazes. "So the key may be to tap into your own inner hatred, the deep-seated frustration of everything that you did wrong."

That sounded like a tremendous fuel for self-torture, but Annika had a valid point. Looking back on the scenarios of the past, she was frustrated with herself for rejecting Ardan when she cursed Elante, and she was frustrated by how gullible she was when she cursed Renault. She snorted derisively at herself. She had to push upon and embrace her own inner demon of resentment to unleash her magic? That was just plain sad.

But if that was the answer and what it would take to stop Saava, then so be it.

Saying goodbye to her life as empress was one of the best decisions she had made. When she'd left those gates she expected to feel some amount of remorse, but instead she only felt relief. She closed the door on memories tainted with sorrow, the joys that were short-lived due to the oppressive nature of imperial scrutiny and judgment. The politics that she loathed, the hatred she had felt emblazoned on her back by sneering noblemen whose gazes lingered when they thought she was not looking. And Darius, her first love. Her toxic relationship. Through him she learned so much about herself and the nature of humanity. She would always be grateful, and a part of her would always love him. But she always reminded herself that he mistreated her, and she could never pretend that he had not. Under no circumstance could she believe that their marriage was a healthy one. She was better without it.

Without all of it.

In the companionship of Khatalia, Orla, and Ardan she felt alive again. She was able to laugh and love, and through Ardan she was consistently reminded of what it was like to experience love of the truest and most unconditional kind, one which didn't rely on the performance of how well she behaved or how she made him look for others. He loved her for who she was. To have him in her life even if she felt unworthy—it inspired a gratefulness infinitely warming in her chest.

Their time together would be short-lived; Nevia knew this to be true. As soon as Nevia conquered her magic they would be on their way to encounter Saava. What was worse: they may never have this joy again. Sorrow tried to dig its claws into Nevia as she looked upon her found family around an evening fire, Khatalia waving about a roasted rabbit's leg as she retold a story while Ardan tried his hardest to look interested while on the verge of dozing off. Orla, sitting with her legs crossed and eyes wide with awe, was riveted by the outright barbaric stories that Khatalia told of war and raids. The girl was sheltered and loved to learn more. Even Qirin's company was a welcomed sight, watching Khatalia with an amused smile, tiny Akari tucked in the crook of his arm as if he were a dragon coveting its most prized possession.

This—all of this—could be gone soon, and it was all Nevia's fault. It was her brilliant plan that suggested Ardan put himself in danger and pose as Saava's former lover, and Orla to seek out the goddess' whereabouts.

As if sensing Nevia's attention, Orla's expression darkened, face lowering towards the fire. "I think there's something that I need to tell you guys." She lifted her chin, large orb-like eyes glossy. "Especially you, Nevia."

A tense silence fell upon the campfire, and the engagement that had once belonged to Khatalia's story, just as she began to reach the punch line, faltered.

Orla drew in a sharp breath, as if waiting for the sting, and finally blurted, "I didn't want to stress you, but I think that I would do you more harm if I don't tell you."

"Well, get on with it, then," Qirin snapped from his perch on a fallen log. "Tell us."

Yet Orla's eyes never left Nevia's, unflinching, unwavering. "I found Saava. She is heading to Velspire as we speak, and I fear what she has intended for the people there, if her past visits with previous towns are any indication."

Nevia arched a brow. "How do you know that Velspire is her destination? Is she already there or something?"

"The way our magic works is unusual, unique," Orla said. "It wasn't necessarily visuals that I picked up on, but feelings, intentions. Saava could communicate with our minds and I was able to reverse the process and take a glance into hers. Quickly I was shoved out, but, well. . . ."

"So she knows that we know," Nevia said, heart sinking as the realization hit her. "On the other hand, if you know she intends to march on Velspire, you know exactly what she intends to do there."

Guilty as charged. Orla turned her face toward the central fire, its flames bringing out the vibrant highlights in her hair. "I don't want to worry you, but I think we need to head out if we want to save as many people as we can."

Or to save Velspire from total obliteration, Nevia added mentally.

"Those bastards treated Nevia horribly during her time as empress." Khatalia waved her half-eaten rabbit leg around. "I'd say we let the bitch roast 'em."

"Khatalia!" Ardan cried, astounded.

"What? I'm just being honest," she said defensively. "Why stick our necks out for people that wanted her dead to begin with? Sounds like they had this long coming, don't you think?"

Nevia's hands balled into fists at her sides. Right or wrong, the people did not deserve to meet an untimely demise at Saava's hand. The empress in her would not allow it. "No one deserves to die. We *must* go."

The party seemed divided in this belief, however. Ardan was quite agreeable, not that Nevia would have expected anything less; he was reliably on her side through it all. Qirin and Khatalia, however, remained indifferent.

"Saava continues attacking wherever she goes," Qirin said at last. "I don't see why we should rush to the aid of the people of Velspire just because they're, well, the rich people."

"It's the right thing to do," Nevia countered.

Ardan offered nothing, instead stoking the fire with a stick, staring into it as if mesmerized. The jubilance that once surrounded the campfire had been snuffed as successfully as a fire in open rain.

"And what are you going to do once you get there?" Qirin sneered. "Fight her with a wooden pole? You can't even summon a shadow, much less set off this circle of death that you've been bragging about."

The former empress shook her head, not out of disagreement, but disbelief. It was true: she was no closer to unleashing her blight than she had been when she started training. "I will fight with my bare fists if I have to," Nevia retorted. "I won't let my people die."

Qirin sat back, smug. "Sounds like the imperials trained you well, then, if you're willing to die for their sorry hides."

Tears welled in Nevia's eyes, then. She couldn't help it, so consumed by the weight of the world, the shift of the universe crashing over her in a wave. She was so distraught that she hadn't noticed Ardan swoop up from his perch on a stump to sit over by her side, wrapping an arm about her shoulders. He leaned his head into hers, their hair intertwining. Light and dark. Opposites, yet they paired together so well.

"It's going to be okay," Ardan murmured, rubbing circles into her shoulder blade. "This doesn't need to all fall on you. We're in this together, and if we have to fight Saava off in hand-to-hand combat"—he shot a dark glare in Qirin's direction—"then that is what we will do. And for those of us complaining: you don't have to come."

Khatalia procured a handkerchief and extended it to Nevia. Heavens knew how clean it was, and perhaps that among other reasons was why Nevia politely declined. "Thanks, but I'm going to go for a walk. Need to clear my head."

Orla started to rise from the grass. "Let me come with you. I'll just—"

"No, I need to be alone."

Both Khatalia and Ardan watched the former empress leave their side, neither saying a word nor rising from their position. They knew better than to argue that she should not go alone, that she should be guarded. Ardan's hazel eyes locked on hers, somber and serious as he said, "Be careful."

She gripped the hem of her tunic and tugged. "Right."

The walk was short and free from danger. Not even a squirrel crossed paths with her. Nevia returned to find her companions exactly as she had left them, with the exception of Orla, who was curled up in a ball beside the fire, thick woolen blanket tucked to her chin. She appeared fast asleep.

Nevia couldn't refrain from kneeling beside her to tuck a lock of fiery hair behind the girl's ear. So brave, so full of courage, and yet so young.

"She reminds me of you, you know," Ardan said from behind her.

Nevia leaned back on her heels, savoring the feel of his warm breath and the rise and fall of his chest at her back. He wrapped his arms around her, cradling her close, both silently watching

Orla as she did not so much as twitch a muscle. Clearly she was a deep sleeper.

"Am I really this stubborn?"

"Gods, yes!" Ardan laughed. "Have you not heard yourself?"

A slight smile stretched her pallid lips. "Even still, Qirin is right. I'm marching us all to our deaths. I'm no closer to casting my magic than I was when we got here, and what then? We can't defeat Saava without it."

He didn't say anything, but he didn't let her go, either. He just held her, and she allowed herself to be held, listening as the fire extinguished at their backs and the wind blew through the dead trees. There was no answer for her question, and he didn't dishonor her by trying to forge one. Instead he gave her what he could: his strength, which she so desperately, earnestly needed for the path ahead.

50
ARDAN

Silence kept the group company for the majority of their journey south toward a port along the Black River, the goal to catch a trade ship to ferry them to Velspire. Ships were fewer and farther between thanks to the blight, but trade was still, thankfully, in operation. It marveled Ardan that, despite the bleakness of their reality, humanity was finding a means to survive. He did not know how that would apply in a dying world, but he hoped that they would always find a way to beat the odds.

At least until the Light of Gaia saved them all.

Even Qirin, as obstinate as he had been about saving ungrateful Velspirians, joined their crew, leaving Akari behind in the capable hands of Maestra Annika. He insisted she needed a mother more than a father, but Ardan knew that was not the true reason she was left behind. Perhaps Qirin expected that he was not going to make it out of this confrontation alive.

A fear that they all shared to an extent.

Nevia had been despondent since the night Orla had revealed Saava's location. Despite Ardan's faith that a good night's sleep would be enough to restore her emotional well-being, he was wrong. He caught Orla occasionally shoot a guilty look over towards Nevia, as if wishing to say something, but would instead strike up a conversation with Ardan, as if hoping Nevia would chime in. Ardan wished she would, too. But she did not, instead offering very little in contribution.

Khatalia, however, went on as if she had not noticed Nevia's muteness, speaking enough for the both of them. She also took to appointing herself as their navigator, despite only traversing this part of the country once. She steered them from the main path multiple times, through forests and over hills of would-be shortcuts, which resulted in getting turned around twice, and scaring away their prey as Ardan was about to loose an arrow and secure them fresh rabbit. Finally Ardan let out a sigh, clapping his second-in-command on the shoulder.

"Look, I appreciate that you're trying to help"—Ardan started, leveled her with an even glare—"but you are entirely distracted right now. If I didn't know better, I would think you're nervous."

The tall clanswoman harrumphed, folding her strong arms over her chest. "Look who's calling the kettle black. Last time I checked, *you* were the one distracted by your depressed girlfriend."

His expression grew stern. "She may be my girlfriend, but she's *your* friend. You can't tell me that it isn't affecting you."

Khatalia's gaze flickered over toward Nevia, who was meandering separate from the rest of the party. She carefully picked her way through dead brush, stopping occasionally to stare off into the snow-covered peaks in the distance.

"She has not been herself since we decided to set off for Saava," Ardan murmured under his breath, so only his second could hear. "It concerns me."

Khatalia slung her bow over her shoulder. "I'm going to go talk to her."

When Khatalia moved forward Ardan reached out and grasped her wrist. "Don't make it worse."

A mirthless laugh escaped her. "You think I'm that callous?" She yanked herself away. "Don't delude yourself into thinking you're the only one who loves her. I met her first, you know. I know how to get through to her."

He certainly hoped so, but he was not convinced. Khatalia, as well-intentioned as she could be, sometimes had a case of "tough love" when trying to help others. Even still, Nevia and Khatalia were close. Perhaps the woman would have a different kind of influence on her than he had been able to.

Ardan swallowed dryly as he watched Khatalia slip away into the fog, unable to protest or retort as she scurried through the trees to catch up to wherever Nevia had disappeared to.

51
NEVIA

H ey!"
The former empress heard Khatalia's voice boom over the rushing river at her side, but she did not deign to answer. Instead she knelt at the waterside, allowing the cool current to cascade across her hands. The scent of decaying aquatic life wafted in the air, but this was one of the few places such a scent was welcomed. Normal.

Nevia inhaled deeply, allowing the odor to permeate her nostrils. To embrace the death around her, as well as within.

"HEY!" Khatalia was louder this time, mostly from proximity. Nevia turned to see her friend sprint the last stretch toward her and grasp her shoulder, nearly wrenching it from its socket. Rage contorted the woman's features, spittle flying from her mouth as she shouted, "What are you, deaf?! Why didn't you answer me?"

A heavy sigh heaved from Nevia's lungs. "Sorry, I just need a moment. I"—she hugged her knees to her chest—"don't like what I'm going to have to do when we reach Velspire. I know it has to happen, but I don't want it. I don't." Nevia looked away, watching a hollow log travel downstream. "And if I can't do it, I'm leading everyone to their deaths *again*."

A growl escaped Khatalia as her grip on Nevia loosened. "The self-pity is getting old," she stated flatly. "We all signed up for this together, and together we will see this through. But your whining and complaining that you can't do it? Grow. The. Hell. Up. We're doing it. Period."

Nevia whirled to face her now, her sorrow morphing to fury. "You weren't there in the core when the whole world went dark because of me! And I casually just sentenced everyone that I love to their own deaths because I foolishly believed I could fix things!"

"And you can *still* fix things," Khatalia said, perhaps too calmly. "You're being ridiculous."

A fury unlike any she knew shook Nevia. She wanted a challenge, a screaming match, someone that she could yell and be angry at beside herself. Because she was very angry at herself. So. Very. Utterly. Furious.

"No, you are! This world is!" Nevia seethed, jaw clenched tight as her hands reached toward Khatalia's. "Now unhand me before I infect you too. I feel the power rising, and we all know I still can't control it. Don't make me add to my kill tally of friends."

"I don't care," Khatalia said, voice distant and hollow. "I'll defy death again. It doesn't want to take me."

A cold, despaired laugh bubbled in Nevia's throat. She had no idea where that feral part of her originated, but something deep inside came unhinged. Khatalia must've sensed it, too, for the wild-eyed look of panic flickering over her face made Nevia wish she could take it back. It caught her off-guard when Khatalia jerked her forward, throwing her arms around Nevia and crushing her in a chokehold disguised as a hug.

"Come back to us, Nevia," Khatalia said, her voice muffled from her face burrowed in furs.

Shock lay claim to Nevia as she just stood there, allowing Khatalia to plaster her against her chest, gently rocking her. Never had she seen this affection side of Khatalia, this tenderness. If the strong, at times brutal clanswoman was breaking to this point, something was desperately wrong. It spurred silent tears to roll down Nevia's cheeks and mingle with Khatalia's tangle of furs.

"I never left."

"That's not true," Khatalia retorted, not with fire but sorrow. "You left us the moment you cursed Elante."

The words stung, unfurling a spiral of emotions to overtake her. Nevia started crying, then, really truly crying. She cried for her dear Elante, her father. Her late husband. The death of the planet, the betrayal of Renault. The future death of Saava, a girl who was reeling herself after losing everything she loved. All of this death, all because of her. It was a weight she felt incapable of carrying, yet she knew she would have to a little longer.

And gouge out more lives in the process.

Gratefully Khatalia's grip was unrelenting, the woman clinging to her as if she were the only thing that mattered in the world. And maybe to Khatalia—a woman who had already lost her wife, son, and entire clan—she was.

"I'm sorry," Nevia choked out. "I just—I just want—"

"I know," Khatalia offered. "We all want so many things. Trust me, you won't believe the amount of wants I had when I stormed the Feishin Kingdom to make those bastards pay for what they did."

Nevia did not know how long the two were locked in that hug. That embrace which thawed the ice that encased Nevia's heart ages ago, dulling the ache ever so slightly. She was partly ashamed to show such fragility and weakness, but Khatalia did not care. She just held her, strong arms keeping her upright. It felt as if Khatalia were offering to bear that weight of all those deaths for her in that moment, and Nevia was so grateful for the momentary reprieve.

"I don't deserve you," Nevia mumbled, wrapping her arms more tightly around her.

Khatalia lifted a hand, cradling Nevia's head as if she were soothing a small child. "You're right, you don't. But then again no one does."

Nevia laughed a note and lowered her arms, and Khatalia took it as a sign to loosen her grip. Their eyes locked, and Nevia was partly taken aback to find the glistening of tears roll down Khatalia's cheeks.

"There. Feel any better?"

Loads. The weight still bore on her heavily, but she no longer felt alone in carrying it. "It's going to be a rough road, but I can do this. I will do this." Nevia let out a sigh, folding her arms over her chest. "Thanks."

"Don't mention it." Khatalia winked, before treading back in the direction she came. "Now, I'll leave you to whatever it was you were doing."

The offer was tempting. Nevia could not deny that solitude sounded pleasing, especially with so much plaguing her. She was not looking forward to facing Ardan when there was so much she didn't want to divulge. "No, I'll come back with you. It's time that I did."

Khatalia threw an arm around Nevia as she joined her side, tossing her cheek atop Nevia's platinum hair. "I'm glad that you finally see some sense and are ready to kick that bitch's ass back to the core."

Despite herself, Nevia couldn't help but give a soft smile in response.

52
ARDAN

Ardan didn't know what happened on the walk between Khatalia and Nevia, but something changed. Neither shared what happened down by the river, and Ardan was wise enough not to ask. They instead continued as if nothing happened, enjoying the roasted rabbit Ardan was successfully able to hunt without Khatalia's assistance.

The next day they arrived at the port that Nevia claimed would soon ferry materials down to Velspire, and she was right. The vessel was simple in contrast to the one they boarded on their journey to Asturia, devoid of bunks save for that reserved for the crew. A ferry to transport wood, the ship offloaded a portion of its cargo to merchants hungry for the raw materials which stocked stores and cured meats. The delightful smell of hickory was pleasant to the nose, as well, which Ardan confirmed to be better than the stench of soldiers amassed in preparing for war. Also pleasing was that they did not have to conceal their identities or risk being denied a ride. One glance at the former empress secured them a ride post-haste, the trade ship crew's only regret being the accommodations were unbefitting of nobility.

The ferry was part of newer Feishin technology that entered the Danaecan market over the past few years. The steam-powered engine would shorten the duration of an otherwise day-long journey to arriving in Velspire's city limits by the day's end.

The sun was high in the afternoon sky, having reached its zenith half an hour ago. Haze served as a barrier, yet the sun's rays still managed to penetrate through: a reminder that life still went on, despite the blight's aftermath.

Ardan had left the party to walk around the ship, curious to learn more about the mechanics that propelled the ship forward, as well as get a bit of fresh air. Tensions had been high with the upcoming encounter, and spacing himself from the others was beneficial with what lay ahead.

He arrived above decks to find Nevia sitting at the starboard railing, the highlights of her braid aglow in the pale sunlight. How lovely she looked in that moment, and how he wished to etch this image forever into his memory. Despite her peaceful exterior, he knew a torrent of emotions flooded her. She would have to exercise her dominion over death soon, against a goddess that she once worshipped. Nevia, his tenderhearted love. The woman who refused to condone the killing of any living creature, even if out of necessity. The irony that she was the reincarnation of the Goddess of Death was not lost on him.

If he could take that burden from her, he would do so in a heartbeat.

Ardan swept over to sit on the deck alongside her, resting his hands on his thighs. Her face was a stoic mask, yet her tortured eyes spoke volumes as they lifted to meet his. He reached out to wrap an arm around her, to which she responded with resting her head on his shoulder.

"If we live through this," he murmured softly, "we are definitely building that cottage in the woods."

Earlier they spoke of their dreams and aspirations, and both shared the same desire to live a life of obscurity surrounded by nature and free to love one another—and a growing family.

A shadow of a smile crossed her face. "I would very much like that. But what about your clan?"

"Don't worry about them." His fingers toyed with the small ringlets at the nape of her neck. "Let me figure that out. Right now, it's just about us."

She turned to him, then, eyes glossy, lips upturned. They met with his, a tender kiss filled with their hopes, dreams, and aspirations for a future that may not exist.

"I'm scared, Ardan," Nevia admitted. "What if we don't survive this? What if, well . . ."

He placed a finger to her lips, silencing her. "Only happy thoughts about us right now, remember? So much of the future is unknown, our destiny's unwritten. You've said it yourself: even Saava does not know the outcome of our planet, our lives. Only we can write that. And me? I choose hope."

Nevia looked forlorn, yet dipped her head in assent, hand clasping his. "I don't know what it will cost me to cast."

"Whatever it is we will get through it." Ardan laid his other hand atop her. "I will be by your side until the bitter end."

Until the bitter end.

The words resonated between them, Ardan wondering when, exactly, this end would come. But he had to hold on to hope—had to, or else Saava had already won, and their fight would be for naught.

"About that." Nevia jerked her head away, gaze once more tracing the river's ripples. "We should discuss the plan, and how you will lure Saava."

"Simple." He puffed out his chest. "I'll go up to her, tell her how beautiful she is, and sweep her up into a dance across the death floor. How does that sound?"

Color rushed to Nevia's cheeks. "Good, except for the part that you won't know where the 'death floor' will be."

"So I'll just be dancing her all around Velspire. Works for me."

The former empress scowled, digging a sharp elbow into his side. He rubbed it ruefully, unable to contain his chuckle.

"We need a plan, then," Nevia mused, "where the circle will be."

Ardan nodded sagaciously in agreement. "Okay, tell me where."

A silence fell, Nevia appearing thoughtful. Not that he could blame her; there were plenty of places to lay down a magic circle of death that they could easily stumble upon.

"How about you just make multiples?" Ardan offered.

Nevia shrugged. "Not a bad suggestion. If there's enough time."

"Then just make one."

Nevia flung her hands in the air with unnecessary vehemence. "Why does it seem like you're trying to make this difficult?!"

"Because"—he twisted so that he was facing her, hips parallel to hers—"I think it's cute when you're flustered. That's all."

Nevia chuckled, shaking her head. "You are hopeless."

"Aye, that I am," Ardan agreed, unable to resist cupping her cheek, the pad of his thumb brushing against her cheekbone. Her eyes closed, dark lashes fluttering. He all too readily would have kissed her again, had they not been intruded on by a teenage girl more than willing to get a front row seat to their romantic display. Ardan turned to find Orla skipping over to them with surprising exuberance given their current circumstances.

"We're almost there!" Orla chirped. "Just wanted you guys to know."

A chuckle escaped Ardan, deep and throaty. His thumb ran over Nevia's hand gingerly as he called to the young seer over his shoulder, "We're at least several hours away. Not almost there, not by a long shot."

Orla hummed her disagreement, propping her arms over the rail with her back to them. "Well, not with that attitude."

Ardan offered Nevia a wink as he rose, extending a hand to help her. They would find their moment together later, ideally free from young prying eyes.

The hours went smoothly, and soon they found themselves standing on the riverbank in the district of Velspire. The depressing landscape looked very much as they left it: fields, once green and lush, were now dried and brittle, the blades of grass whispering omens with the rustling wind. The tall evergreens resembled gray silhouettes outlined by the fading sun, cold and unwelcoming.

The four continued wordlessly to the border of the industrial city—the birthplace of an empire that was no more.

Ardan shot a glance toward Nevia, wondering how she was faring at returning to her former home, no longer as empress but as a defender of humanity. Her lips were drawn into a thin line, keeping her ice-blue eyes trained straight ahead. Perhaps this was intentional. Perhaps she was afraid of what she would see if she looked hard enough. Not that he could blame her. This was likely not the homecoming she once pictured for herself.

The silence encompassing them was unnerving. Not merely from their party, but their surroundings. The only sound gracing Ardan's ears was their footsteps crunching along the stone pathway and the whistling winds.

At last they arrived at the gates to the city, tall and flanked with great, spiring guard towers that vaulted overhead, but they had been left wide open, with no sign of security in sight. Ardan's heart scaled to his throat, the sign less than favorable.

They tread carefully on, only for Orla to let out a small gasp once they arrived to the central square, hand fleeing to her trembling lips. The golden statue of Saava, resting within the enormous ornate fountain at the square's center, had been shattered, crumbled within the center of the plaza. The fountain had dried, no trace of water to be found. The buildings were dilapidated, bricks, debris, and shingles littering the lifeless streets. And speaking of lifeless—

Dozens of bodies littered the ground, their remains indistinguishable with as ravaged as they had been. Blood painted the cobblestone and adorned the siding of homes. It appeared they just missed the scene of a massacre.

Which meant that Saava had already arrived. They were too late to save everyone.

Ardan swallowed hard, gaze flickering from Orla and quickly to Nevia. The former empress stood tall. Aside from her face paling, he never would have guessed the sight of her fallen empire fazed her.

The wind howled between them, sending Nevia's platinum braid whipping across her back.

No, Ardan realized, horror clenching his chest as the pounding of footsteps met his ears. That was not simply a gust of wind.

It was the unhinged roar of a night creature as it raised its webbed, clawed hand to swat at Nevia.

53
NEVIA

The impact sent Nevia reeling before she could even process what happened, flying, then tumbling along the worn cobblestone street. Her back screamed in agony when it met stiff resistance from the wall of the fountain, both from the impact and where the night creature's claws raked across her flesh.

For a moment she lay stunned, the blow and sudden burst of pain sending her ears ringing. Boots striking the ground forced her eyes open to find Khatalia kneeling in front of her, brow knit in concern. Grunting, she heaved Nevia over her shoulder with a casualness suggesting she'd done this before.

"I'm fine," Nevia managed to rasp, flailing in her arms. All her vital organs were intact, and the bleeding seemed minimal. The pain smarted, but beyond the shock she was well. "Let me go!"

Khatalia shot her an assessing glance, but was interrupted quickly as the creature charged for them again, claws outstretched and the beast on a collision course for their heads. Forced to comply with the request, Khatalia dropped Nevia brusquely on her feet and readied herself to parry the blow. Before she could, however, Ardan leapt in front, planting the butt of his spear between cobblestones to have the creature plunge into it. Far from the chest, the tip of the spear stabbed low, erupting from the other side of the lower thigh. A bloodcurdling screech resounded in the square as it attempted to swat him away. Ardan proved quicker, spear sacrificed as he bound out of the way before claws met their mark.

Its attention was quickly detracted from Ardan as it was met with another weapon, this time the sharp blade of a katana running along its left side. Nevia barely saw the flutter of Qirin's turquoise kimono and dark hair as he bounded from the party, luring it away. He threw a glance over his shoulder, dark hooded eyes interlocking with hers. His lips formed words, and, while she could not hear him over the wail of the monstrosity, she was able to make out the one word he uttered by lip synch: "go." She hesitated, not wanting to abandon them in the midst of an attack.

Her hesitation, however, was quickly remedied when she saw Orla run to her, white-faced and eyes filled with terror. The girl nearly tripped over the tattered hem of her dress as she made her way to Nevia, unable to keep from grasping on to the former empress. Nevia brought an arm comfortingly around her, recognizing the child that Orla still very much was.

She could fight. The trainings with Qirin and Maestra Annika had made her more physically fit than ever. And yet she knew she would merely serve as a distraction, a liability that the others could not afford. Without her the death circle couldn't come to fruition, thus leaving Saava to prosper and make them all suffer for it. She sucked in a sharp breath, jerking her head in the direction of the Velspirian palace. Its spires soared high in the air; a beacon promising the hope of salvation amidst a city in ruin.

"The circle," Orla rasped, clinging to Nevia's arm. "We need to go create it."

Nevia wrestled in Orla's grip as she tugged her in the direction of the darkened streets of the capital, silhouettes of tall factories blotting out the moon's light. "But we never made a plan," she blurted, stumbling as she nearly tripped on Saava's broken head and the remains of a wheelbarrow. "We didn't decide where to put it."

But her concerns fell on deaf ears, the young teen no longer listening. Instead Orla laced her fingers with Nevia's and dragged her deeper into the imperial city.

Not just deeper—to the palace itself.

The familiar sight gave Nevia pause. The gate, like most others, was mangled beyond repair, its center bowed and cast aside. Armored bodies littered the gardens and lay facedown in puddles of blood, a horrific sight that required Nevia to cover her mouth to contain the scream threatening to rip out of her. Dread clutched her throat, forming a knot. This massacre was worse than anything she had seen since the war.

But it was more. It was Saava's assault on the capital, upon her own worshippers. Sending them to the Nether Planes in a mass grave.

Willing her heart to stone, the former empress marched on toward the palace, stopping before the tall oaken doors and craning her neck to peer up. Her gaze trailed the windows along the second floor, finding some cracked, while others—such as her bedroom—remained intact. "Tell me how to create the circle."

At this Orla protested. "But I thought you said—"

"I said tell. Me. How."

The seer's lower lip quivered, tossing a wary glance over her shoulder at the ruined gate. The deep howls and screams emanating from the city reminded the two women that they were not alone, and that more night creatures would join them within minutes, if that.

"All right. Let's try it," Orla relented, "but we have to hurry."

54
ARDAN

Ardan heard a shrill cry from the back alleyway to his left moments before being knocked to the cobblestone, his chin colliding with the rugged surface. Fighting against the searing pain, he rolled onto his back, saving himself from having talons run clean through his jugular. He clambered to his feet, rubbing his chin with the back of his hand.

It came back red. Expected.

Blinking amber eyes bore into him, belonging to a winged night creature reminiscent of an enormous eagle, or perhaps a twisted representation of a roc. Its dark wings stretched wide beyond its scaly body as it let out a screech, exposing razor-sharp teeth and a slitted, narrow tongue.

Qirin rushed past with the first night creature at his heels, blade sullied by black blood. He trusted the king smart enough to outrun it, though he wished their numbers were greater to offer easier backup. Akari needed him alive, even if Qirin thought otherwise.

Coming to his aid, Khatalia performed a running leap, successfully clambering onto the creature's back with a one-armed grab. Finding opportunity amidst the creature's flailing at an unwelcome rider, she jabbed her spear down into the thick scaly hide on the side of its neck. It should've pierced through had the creature been a true bird, yet its scales were tough like steel skin, and the clanswoman barely left a mark on its exterior. It shook her and the spear off, Khatalia frantically trying to make purchase with her fingertips and, having failed, was flung to the ground.

It was his turn now. Ardan patted himself down, finding only a remaining knife on his person. His spear was lying on the ground where the first creature had wrenched it out of its leg. Inconvenient for him, the avian night creature stood between him and it. He would have to get dangerously close to the bird-like snapping beak in order to reach it.

"Don't just stand there!" Khatalia barked, back on her feet in a moment. Aside from a cut on her lip and a gash exposing her shoulder, she seemed otherwise unharmed. She ran to leap up on it again, this time throwing her body around its neck and holding the beast three times her size in the strangest headlock Ardan ever did witness. It whipped and snarled, razor-sharp beak snapping and threatening to cleave her in two should it find flesh. Khatalia's arms shook violently in her attempts to hold it. Even her astounding strength was failing.

Focused now, Ardan surged forward and swept between the legs of the creature, with its attention focused solely on Khatalia drawing his spear from the ground. With a swift gauging of the soft underbelly, he plunged the steel tip into its chest, heart-seeking. It jerked its head back, and it took all of Khatalia's strength not to be thrown headfirst off as it reared.

To Ardan's surprise, the creature kicked off and flapped its wings, showering him with bloody droplets as dark as ink. He must have missed anything vital with the way the creature still moved, injured but unhindered otherwise.

Khatalia, still holding on to its head, allowed herself to free fall before it could get far, landing into a crouch at Ardan's side. They shared a solitary look before it charged back, talons outstretched as it snatched Ardan by the shoulders.

He wriggled and twisted, but could not get free. Its sharp talons bit into his flesh, threatening tendons if it had not torn through them already. The warm dampness of blood dripped from his arms, fingers tingling from loss of sensation.

The situation grew worse with every flap of the monster's wings. The creature was soaring high toward a building, so that even if he did somehow kill the abyssal creature there was a challenging distance between him and safety. From the looks of things he would not have been surprised to have been flung directly into the stone wall. To come back from that? Impossible. With this height and velocity he would be a dead man by the second impact.

He squeezed his eyes shut tight, not wanting to see the moment of his demise.

I'm sorry that I could not be there with you for the end, Nevia.

The winged beast halted suddenly, as if lassoed to a halt, having Ardan tossed around limply. Above him the shrieking wail of the creature flooded his ears as they together started to plummet. Faster and faster they went, the ground growing ever closer as they spiraled. He was going to be crushed beneath the massive bird on the cobblestone streets. It was nearly as bad an end as the one he predicted.

That is, until ropes shot out and bound around his wrists and ankles, yanking him free from the doomed bird's grip and suspending him midair.

Not ropes, Ardan realized as he fought and wrestled with his confines. *Vines*.

His savior stood beneath him far below, startlingly bright eyes lifting to meet his. Slowly his restraints eased, lowering him slowly to the ground to stand.

The woman standing before him was beautiful. Hair as black as night hung in loose waves down her back, skin so fair it rivaled Orla's. She stared, lips parted, and for a moment—just one—she felt familiar.

Ardan's gaze strayed from the woman to the night creature at her feet, its head efficiently severed from its body. She must have decapitated it from the air using said vines.

It was clear to him that sorcery played a role in the creature's demise as well as his rescue. The woman standing before him—her name escaped his lips easily, his heart knowing her even if his mind did not.

"Saava."

She turned, golden hoop earrings tinkling a melodious chime in the whispering winds. Her lips trembled, but aside from that she stood immobilized, stunned. Taking this moment while she considered him, he took the opportunity to approach her.

Her chest rose and fell. "Is it . . . really you?"

Up close he recognized the fragrances of morning glories, violets, and primrose. Of evergreens and honeydew. She smelled of life and all the goodness that ever existed. Ardan could not help but lean in closer, intoxicated by her presence. The goddess ran her tongue over her teeth, nervous, before she finished closing the distance, brushing her lips to his.

In a spinning whirl of chaos, it all came back to him in a rush.

The gardens. Her laughter. Their hands intertwined as they stared up at the moving clouds, pointing out objects in the sky. The festivals and finery. Their passionate whispers and kisses in the quiet of her bedroom. The moment they were caught that night, and the door opening to unveil her sister.

Her sister. She was in every way Nevia, yet she was clearly not the woman he loved. On her face lay an ugly sneer, eyes brimming with jealously and hate. Some primal part of him detested this woman, and yet was tethered to her by the invisible chain of nobility. He had no choice but to wed her, and yet every minute in the uncomfortable goddess' presence was loathed.

The Goddess of Death, the eldest daughter of the Supreme Lord of Aeterna. Saava was merely a shadow in the presence of her glorified sister, simply regarded by others as the dreamer, the artist, the curious child. But this was the very reason he loved her: she was all of the goodness her sister never could be, and yet they were forced apart because her father deemed it so.

Her father: a man cut from the same cloth and yet several times worse than the Goddess of Death herself.

As if shifted into a different scene instantly, he found himself in the mouth of a cave, water gushing forth at its entrance. He felt unbelievably cold, breath being snatched from his lungs. Nevia towered over him, a smirk playing upon her lips.

"Your beloved will go down with you," she whispered sinisterly. "Your heart has become your enemy, your love the curse that will bring you to the end. And I? I will have everything she had, all that you both ever wanted. If only you had remained mine, I wouldn't have had to do this to either of you."

Ardan breathed in sharply, returning to the present in a rush, and had Saava not been there to halt his momentum he would have collapsed to the stone. Tears drew streaks down the face of the woman he once loved, and somewhere, deep in his heart, he still loved her.

He shook his head, shaking himself free of her grasp. It was a mind game. Everything he witnessed was impossible. He loved Nevia, and Nevia was none of those things he just witnessed. And yet the cruel woman resembled the love of his life so wholly, so completely, it startled him. For perhaps the first time he understood why Nevia had been reserved toward him months ago; this startling new reality was perturbing.

And yet those *eyes*. He could not turn off the heart that pumped in ecstasy at the sight of the Goddess of Creation. It took all of his willpower to fight the urge of pulling her to his chest in the tightest embrace. A shudder coursed down his spine.

This was not a part of the plan.

A sad kind of smile played on Saava's lips. "No," she said somberly. "It's not really you."

"Saava," he whispered, as if he could not get enough of her name. He shook his head, finally placing his hands on her shoulders. "It is, and yet it isn't. I remember now, I remember everything, but you're wrong. Nevia, she's not—"

"You mean Sable," Saava scoffed, darkness touching her features. "My sister."

"Yes, Sable."

So that was her name. One which brought with it an insurgence of painful memories, the horrid recollection of her mistreatment of them both.

"See, Nevia . . . she's not your sister. She's a great person, a beautiful person. And what you're doing? This has to stop. You cannot kill this world."

The woman scoffed, tossing her head so that dark silky waves fell over her shoulder like inky tendrils. "This is no world." Her tone held contempt. "This was my chrysalis, my prison. Don't you get it? None of this is supposed to be here. You aren't supposed to be here. You're all just my dreams manifested, your existence has been a lie."

It did not take enough effort for Ardan to cup her cheeks in his palms, causing her pale throat to bob. "We are *real*, Saava. Just as real as we were in Aeterna. I am real."

"No, you're not!" Saava practically screamed. She backed away several paces, shaking her head frantically. "Niall is dead!"

The next words that escaped his lips scalded him, the thought of harming this already wounded woman unsettling. "I'm telling you I *am* Niall," Ardan said impatiently. "I am every part of him that matters."

"Then if you are Niall, she is Sable," she whispered.

A frustrated sigh escaped him. It was a good argument, one which he had no clear rebuttal. They were reincarnations, sharing the same memories, the same existence, yet they were their own people, making independent decisions and living their own lives.

"Saava, listen to me." His heart pounded so hard he feared it would break free of his ribcage. "We may have started off as your visions, but *you* made us real. You have always been a beautiful artist and made the loveliest creations. This is no different, only you brought *me* back, in the only way you could."

"Stop!" Saava was shaking, tears streaming down her elegant face. She held up a trembling hand. "Just please, no more. You're not the man I loved. Don't toy with my heart by pretending to be."

Ardan looked away, the next words hurting some deep innate part of his very being. And perhaps, some part of him wished this reality could be so. "If you could just see the truth, we could all live in harmony on this planet together. Screw your sister. Screw your father. Screw everyone that ever doubted you and thought they could break you. We could have a life here—you just have to allow it to happen."

"And you would choose me?" Saava whispered. "You would give your heart to me and not *her?*"

The way she uttered the last word with such vehemence, such absolute *hate* made him step back. The fury on Saava's face was hideous, morphing her from the woman he once loved and into the monster they had come to know.

He shot a sideways glance over his shoulder, wondering where Khatalia disappeared to. He hoped she was going to check on Qirin. Regardless, he was grateful she was not standing with him at that moment witnessing his wavering resolve. She would not have tolerated it for even a second.

He had a role to play. A duty he promised. And he would fulfill it, even if it killed him.

Saava watched him with anxious eyes as she awaited his response. Drawing a deep breath through his nose, he carefully moved to wrap an arm gently around her waist. To his surprise, she allowed it. In a rhythmic pace, despite the night creatures shredding buildings and eliciting frantic cries of civilians in the night, the two walked side-by-side. For a moment resembling the couple they had once been in another lifetime.

"I care for you, Saava," Ardan said at last. "We had a life together, we loved one another, but things were different then. I know I will always love you, and a part of my heart will always belong to you. But in the life I've lived, the life I've always known, I love Nevia. She's the bravest, strongest woman I have ever known."

Her eyes fluttered closed, visible hurt contorting her features. Tears beaded on her long dark lashes. "I knew it," she murmured. "Sable won. She will always win."

Ardan threw a glance ahead, catching the flicker of red hair disappear behind the gates of the Velspirian palace. It was a sign. A signal, if there ever could be one. That must have been the place. He was almost there. He just had to get her a little farther. Keep her distracted for just a few more minutes.

"Saava, listen to me." He swallowed dryly. "Your sister hurt you, yes. She hurt me, too. She hurt all of us."

"This is all her fault!" she cried.

Ardan's gaze didn't falter from hers as he pushed open the damaged gate with a single hand. "Yes, yes it is."

"And you're defending her," Saava said in disbelief, shaking her head. "I cannot believe it. I cannot."

Rosebushes long past their bloom lined either side of them as they strode further into the gardens. Frantically his eyes scanned the ground, searching for any sign, any indication for the place they drew it. "Saava, I—"

"Please, just go away and leave me now! I can't bring myself to hurt you, but you are hurting me."

Saava slipped out of his loose grasp and started to turn away. He hated himself for this greatest sin, the greatest move of deception he ever played. Grasping her forearms, standing before the ruined doors of the imperial palace, he jerked her toward him, bringing her into a kiss.

To his relief, she bought it, wrapping her arms around his waist, keeping the kiss she yearned for. Perhaps, for one brief moment, she concluded that her Niall had returned to her.

And that was when he heard his name being screamed from across the palatial gardens, and a blinding serrating light engulfed the star-crossed lovers.

55
NEVIA

Deep down, she knew. It became clear the day she nearly unleashed her blight on Qirin when he wounded her with harsh truths about herself, making her lose her own confidence in her character.

She had suspicions on how her magic worked before, but she could not bring herself to say them aloud because she did not want it to be true.

Yet now, it was confirmed, and Nevia knew exactly how to cast her death magic: she had to be ready to sacrifice something in return.

Whether physical or metaphysical, it all responded the same. But the stronger the snapped golden tether to her heart, the more death magic she would exude. She did not know if Sable went to such lengths to control her magic, but if she did, it was no wonder she became such a villain in Saava's story. With the amount of loss she would have to endure, Nevia felt that, in her position, she would either be near-powerless or her equivalent in cruelty.

Back in the forest she realized with profound clarity why her death magic varied in strength with each casting, and suspected what she would have to do once they reached Velspire. Only the greatest sacrifice would be enough to exude the kind of death magic needed to impact Saava. The resurfacing of painful memories or new wounds would simply not suffice.

She would have to sacrifice the love of her life. She would have to sacrifice Ardan.

Tears streamed down her face as the magic circle that Orla sketched in Nevia's own blood came to life, its surface, near invisible in the black night, brightening until it was white-hot and painful to look at. The light and heat flooded upward, completely engulfing Ardan and Saava, the radiant beam shooting into the sky like the sun's brilliant rays.

Orla, seeking to comfort her in any way she could, snaked her slender arms around Nevia's waist, but it was to no avail. Fury rose within Nevia as she screamed out into the night, the bright light she faced revealing her anguish. She hated herself, hated she had to do this. And yet she knew it was the only way to ensure Akari had a future. That Gaia would be saved. If she could have sacrificed herself, she would.

But magic didn't work that way.

Magic was awful, formulated by unspoken rules and grimly revealed secrets.

And she never wanted to use her magic again.

The moments ticked by excruciatingly slow, until at last the light slowly ebbed away. Nevia's eyes fluttered closed, her heart unable to assess the damage she had wreaked, to see the corpse of her beloved strewn over the stone path.

A slight gasp escaped the young seer at her side, soon followed by dark and airy titters across from them. Titters which morphed into hysteric, shrill laughter.

"Oh, you are so very original, Sister. I applaud your efforts."

Nevia's eyes snapped open, then, the haughty voice of her nightmares coming back to life. There, standing within the heart of the magic circle, still aglow from the circle's light, was Saava. She looked akin to a fallen angel, with the way her tattered dark dress barely hung on her slender form, the remains of the light outlining her body like a halo. Her lip quivered, blood trickling down the corner of the mouth. Apart from that, much to Nevia's horror, she appeared unscathed. The same could not be said, however, for Ardan.

Pain threatened to seize her heart as she saw his body in a heap, face down, entirely unrecognizable. His clothing had been mostly charred away, as well as his skin, and she did not need to approach him to know that his heart no longer beat, nor did his lungs draw breath.

A shudder coursed through Nevia. If it weren't for Orla still clinging to her, she may have fallen to her knees. "Why are you still here?!"

Without any rational thought or plan, Nevia charged. She unsheathed the dagger from her thigh, arching it high above her head in an attempt to thrust it directly into Saava's heart in one fluid motion.

Instead she found the cobblestone path crumble at her feet, causing her to lose her footing and sprawl hard on the ground. Grinding met her ears, the stone beginning to reform into a pillar, encasing Nevia within a sea of rock and soil similar to before. She struggled, throwing all her weight into the hefty stone that threatened to crush her lungs, yet her efforts were fruitless.

Saava rose from the ground, hovering on a dark cloud of mist a few feet from her. The goddess clicked her tongue. "So very pathetic. To think you, a knockoff of my sister, could bring the death of me!" She let out a manic laugh, throwing her face toward the heavens and allowing her black hair to stream around her, appearing much more like the real Goddess of Death. "Did you really think you could turn my own magic against me, you imbecile? You all are *my* creation, and this is *my* magic."

Saava glanced down at Ardan's corpse, shaking her head dismally. "What a waste of life. It's a pity, too. He really loved you so."

"Shut up!" Nevia screamed hoarsely, thrashing harder as fresh tears burned her eyes. A torrential wave of darkness overcame

Nevia, a rearing of her death magic from reliving the emotions of her fallen love. Its reach was subdued, limited. The circle did not come to life again. It was not enough. Nor did it seem to matter, if Saava spoke truth. Gaia's magic was hers, and no magic that Nevia summoned would scathe her.

A dark smile crossed Saava's lips as she lifted a finger to them, feeling the blood and tasting it. Nevia realized that her greatest wounding of Saava was little more than a split lip that cracked from the sudden heat, nothing more.

"Aww, but Sister, I don't want to." An eery green aura culminated in her outstretched palms. It continued to build until it threatened to swallow the space around them. "Instead, I want to tell you about your boyfriend's dying words, the way he professed his love to me."

In a thick lump of flesh, wings, and blood, a monstrosity was born, stretching its neck until it protruded from its grotesque, slimy body. A night creature, one that Saava birthed effortlessly into existence, sunken orbs eyeing Nevia in delight as if she were a delectable treat.

"I feel that such a demise is too simple for you," Saava mused, tossing her hair over her shoulder. "But I am running out of creative juice, quite literally, and I have a very important date with my worshippers."

Nevia thrashed hard until the tender flesh of her neck was chafed. They had failed. And they would all die after all. This was not how it could end. She refused to accept it. And as she stared death in the face, with its oozing odorous breath and bulbous yellow eyes, all she could think was that life was incredibly unfair.

"Nevia, hang on!"

Rocks tumbled beneath the former empress, causing her to jerk her gaze downward. There, scrambling up the stone tower that Saava erected, was none other than Orla, golden dress fluttering in the wind.

No, Nevia thought weakly, struggling fruitlessly to move. *Get away. Far, far away from this wretched fiend.*

But she did not have enough time to give her thoughts voice. Her time had come to a close—

As the creature brought a clawed hand to slash her throat.

56
NEVIA

For the first time in so long, Nevia felt nothing. No pain, no anguish. Just muted indifference, suspended in a body of water coursing over her.

No, not water, she realized, running a hand through shimmering rose-tinted particles. It was perhaps the opposite of material, but immaterial.

"You're not really here," a bored voice called to her. "And the more you try to break the veil between realities I'm going to have to throw you back to your demise."

Nevia turned, only to find her own reflection staring at her, albeit looking much less haggard than herself.

As if she had not just fought a losing battle with a goddess.

A smile, cold and calculated, stretched the lips of her reflection. "Hello, Nevia Bylilly."

"You're her." Nevia breathed, realizing that this, indeed, was none other than the culprit of the madness. Sable, the true Goddess of Death. The one who sent Saava down her twisted path of vengeance.

A harsh laugh, high and shrill, sounded. "Maybe. That depends on who you mean."

"But how?"

A shrug lifted Sable's shoulders. "I don't rightly know, but if I were to wager I'd say that Freya was meddling again."

Suddenly it all made sense. The Fate-Bender. Somehow Annika did it again. Perhaps this meant there was hope, after all. Maybe fate would smile on them one more time.

"Does this mean I didn't fail?"

Sable shook her blonde mane, her waves somehow less unruly. "Oh, no, you failed all right. You're literally moments from getting your jugular sliced open. But I was called to this liminal space, and who am I to ignore a summons?"

A frown furrowed Nevia's brow, as she took in the space around them. Shrouded with shimmering mist, warm, and yet devoid of substance. Devoid, truly, of anything. "Where is this?"

"The Nether Planes," Sable answered. "Or at least that's what I think it is. Even I'm uncertain. Never been here before."

"So you're not really here, either." It was an observation, not a question.

Sable dipped her head in assent. "No, I'm not."

A sigh escaped Nevia's lungs. The clock was ticking, and, if what Sable said was true, she was about to die.

This was it. The final gambit to defeating Saava, the one chance she had left to save Gaia. If she did not find a way to use this for Saava's ruin, all of this would have been for naught. All the struggle, all the sacrifice—

Watching Ardan die.

Nevia sniffed the air, unsurprisingly devoid of scent. "I'm not sure what I should do."

At this Sable tilted her head. "What is it that you *want* to do?"

Nevia blinked in surprise. How could she be standing there and not know? "Well, I want to stop your sister."

Sable scoffed, folding her arms over full breasts. It was in that moment she realized the goddess standing before her was completely naked, and so was she. The realization made her change her stance, crossing her legs and wrapping her arms about herself for modesty. "Well, that's simple enough. You're supposed to be me, aren't you? Just do what I do best."

"But I can't." Nevia couldn't prevent her voice from cracking, a lump growing impossibly hard in her throat. "I tried, and I failed. And I-I don't think I can do it again. Even if I had something to give, all my magic is truly hers, which can't be turned against her."

It surprised her at how casual Sable, the dreaded Goddess of Death, was with her, having expected something far more regal and demure. She rolled her eyes. "Oh, please! I could just breathe the word and she'd be dead. Don't tell me you can't kill her."

Nevia's nostrils flared. And before she knew it, with her remaining minutes ticking away on the suspended clock, she was pouring her soul out to the Goddess of Death and telling her everything. Ironic, really, how the villain of her story was her confessor in her final hour. To her surprise, Sable listened, nonjudgmental, and Nevia didn't think she imagined the flicker of pity wash over her elegant, sharp features.

"So she made an imperfect replica," she murmured under her breath.

It pained her to be referred to as a replica, as Nevia felt like very much her own person. The goddess tilted her head and considered her briefly, before letting out a sigh and floating in the ethereal space toward her. Nevia wanted to move, to get out of the way, but she found there was nowhere to go. Sable collided into her, bracing her arms on hers. Their foreheads joined.

"You've been doing it wrong, silly," Sable chuckled, closing her ice-blue eyes. "Here. Let me show you how it's done."

57
NEVIA

Nevia!" Orla's screech filled the entire courtyard as her consciousness came rushing back in a surge. She jerked, gritting her teeth against the sudden awakening of pain coursing through her entire body, a fresh awareness of the blood she knew ran freely from her wounds. She wriggled to break free, only to no avail. Hot, heavy breaths beat down in her face, the night creature's claw seconds from making impact with her exposed throat. But then—

The night creature stopped.

Not just stopped. *It died.*

It was as if Nevia merely thought it, and it happened.

Realization made her heart nearly give away. That was *exactly* what she did.

An image of Sable's smug visage flickered in her mind, lips upturned into a smirk. Memories of the Nether Planes flooded back to her. Was the goddess true to her word, and really by her side to support her in the battle that would decide all?

With a simple bending of will, Nevia managed to bring her confines crumbling to fine dust, allowing her to land atop the powdered rock unscathed. She fixed her penetrating stare onto Saava, who merely stood there, paler than she had been moments ago. Her eyes darted around the courtyard frantically, seeking refuge where there was none.

Oh, how the tables had turned.

"You're done," Nevia declared, voice haughtier and stronger than it had ever been. She could feel it, the newfound energy coursing through her veins, exuding from her every breath and seeping from her very soul. It was exhilarating, delightful, entrancing. She felt drunken on this newfound power, in the most wonderful way imaginable. In that moment she knew all could bow to her, every living thing forced to cater to her every whim. She would be the conquerer and bringer of death—

But then she saw Orla carefully climbing out of the rubble of the tower, frail and bleeding.

She came back to her senses with a jolt.

No, those were not her desires. They belonged to the grantor of this newfound well of energy. Perhaps Nevia started from Sable, but they were not one and the same. Nevia *was* different. She would forever be different, and she would do everything in her power to remain that way.

She could hardly move, every muscle in her torso screaming with the effort, but she would fight.

For Ardan. For Liana. For the thousands of lives who died in this sibling feud that started thousands of years ago.

Not by Nevia's hand, she realized that now, but Saava's. She was the mastermind of it all; Nevia merely served as her puppet dancing on strings. She was put on this path long before she ever knew it, and now she would forge her own path, cutting the lines of those that strung her along and manipulated her.

Fate would not dictate her any more. She was taking fate into her own hands.

She charged, thrusting herself forward until she fell into Saava, raising her dagger to strike.

Again. And again.

Bleeding and staggering, Saava swept her away with a summoned gust of wind, throwing her against the wooden palace doors, *hard*. Nevia yelped, flung aside as if she were a feather blown. She tried to lift herself but crumbled from the effort, momentarily unable to move.

Saava wiped her face with the back of her hand, smearing blood across her hauntingly beautiful face. She sneered down at Nevia, lip curled in disgust.

"You're just full of surprises, aren't you?" she hissed, summoning up a trident whose forks glowed with crackling energy. She stalked over to Nevia, tattered dress sweeping over a blend of debris, dirt, and blood. Nevia brought herself to her knees, yet was only thrust down again as Saava placed her foot on her back, forcing her to eat dirt.

"I may not be able to create death, but I *can* execute it. Fare thee well, my dear—"

Her words fell short, her trident coming to a halt mid-thrust. Nevia lifted her chin to witness a long, thin blade jutting through the goddess' chest. Her electric-green eyes widened, yet no cry escaped her lips. Standing behind Saava's back, hollow-eyed, dirt-stained, and bloodied, stood Qirin, hair hanging in clumped sheets of sweat and dirt along his back. His eyes flickered to Nevia's briefly, before he gripped Saava by the shoulder and murmured coarsely in her immortal ear: "Your reign of terror ends here, bitch."

Nevia snapped to it, recognizing her cue. As she had witnessed with the stab wounds, Saava could regenerate. The blow that Qirin dealt would not be fatal, but this—this would be.

Unlike the last time, the magic she wielded did not belong to Gaia.

Nevia threw herself forward, placing both her bloodied palms against Saava's chest. Her sharp gaze took in Saava's terror-filled visage one last time, the words escaping her lips startlingly not her own.

"Goodbye forever this time, Little Sister."

Energy roared through Nevia's body, coursing through her as a conduit, the death magic flooding from her outstretched palms. Qirin, wisely, leapt aside, Nevia not once even thinking to warn him, to spare him.

The death magic flowed in, and back out, darkness oozing out Saava's back in quantities of jet-black thorny tendrils that reminded Nevia of an enormous bonfire. Nevia trembled, fighting through the surge of adrenaline and raw magic to see the once beautiful face of the goddess twist in agony. Saava screamed, flesh rotting away as the magic from the Goddess of Death penetrated every fiber of her being.

Soon all that was left of Saava was a black shimmering of dust along the damaged cobblestone.

As immediate as the power surged, it was quick to fade, leaving Nevia to collapse to her knees, fingers digging into the loose dust. The tendrils of her death magic dissipated in the night sky, until only the faintest of wisps was visible outlining the twin moons above. One of them, Nevia now knew, housed her savior, who was probably looking down at them this very moment.

"Sable, thank you," she whispered, tears streaking down her dirt-stained cheeks.

The legacy of Saava was over. No longer would they have to live in fear of the monster she had become, wondering when she would next strike. They fought her, and, startlingly, they won.

They. Won.

The words could hardly sink in over the withdrawal of magic Nevia's mortal body suffered from, its aftereffects wholly taxing. She felt empty, hollow, and realized it was from more than the absence of magic.

It was loss, an absence of her heart. Of her love.

Ardan was dead.

She lowered her head, allowing the tears to fall and splatter the stone beneath her hands. They had won—at a very terrible cost.

Nevia allowed her eyes to close against the throbbing pain in her head. "Thanks, Qirin," she half-whispered. "I didn't know how to execute it. What to—"

"You hesitated too long, like you always do." The king grasped her hands and wrenched her upright. "And you ignored your right almost the entire time. That's your greatest weakness, but once you get that down you would probably be a half-decent soldier."

She met his eyes then, within his gaze a sadness that mirrored her own. They both suffered great loss, and Nevia realized in his soft, somber smile there was empathy.

Orla brushed herself off as she hobbled over to them. Blood dripped down her left side, and Nevia only feared it was from a wound to her core. She made her way over to them at a furious pace, despite the blood, frantically waving her arms before extending her hands out to them.

"I have an idea," she piped. "Quick, Qirin! Give me your sword."

58
QIRIN

Why?" Qirin demanded, defensively jerking the katana away from the eager youth's outstretched palms. An eerie smile stretched her lips, eyes glittering with an ethereal energy, as if she were staring directly into his soul. The sight unnerved him, and he was not going to ever, not even for a moment entertain surrendering his blade.

"I can save him."

That made him question his resolve. One look at Nevia told him that he would have to surrender his weapon to an unstable child if he did not want to brand himself her enemy for the end of time. If there was even the smallest chance that Orla could fulfill the promise she just made to them, it was worth taking the chance.

He would have to accept the risk of being de-gutted by the young Lady of Asturia.

"Thank you," she chirped, almost in song, as she hobbled back off, partly skipping, partly staggering further into the courtyard.

She lifted the blade, and Qirin cringed, watching as she thrust his sword—his beautiful, perfectly sharpened katana—between cobblestones with a sickening screech. He could not suppress his shudder, an internal scream welling inside.

The girl had no idea of the kind of trauma she was putting the Feishin king through. Instead she merely hummed a cheerful tune, dipping her fingers in the remaining blood staining the steel edge.

"Orla?" Nevia's voice rang high, as if in alarm. "What are you doing?"

But the young teen ignored all outside distractions, working furiously on the ground. It wasn't until Qirin leaned in a little closer, frowning as he watched her furious scrubbing at the ground, that he realized what she was trying to do.

She was rewriting the death circle, using the blood of the Goddess of Creation to do so.

Orla's fingers traced sigils on the earth, crawling around in a semi-circle around Ardan's remains and working as fast as she could, painting fine strokes with the blood that remained on the Feishin king's blade. Finally satisfied, Orla sat back on her heels, just outside the exterior line of the two-fold magic circle. A circle, Qirin suspected, that no longer spelled death. The young seer rose, waving at the two with a reassuring smile before she clasped her hands and bowed her head. Wiry red hair framed her head like a halo, her voice ethereal as she opened her mouth and began to chant.

It was unlike anything Qirin had ever heard. It was lovely, haunting, and foreboding all at the same time. The words made the fine hairs on his neck stand on end, as if he could feel the very earth answering her song. Nothing she uttered was coherent to him, yet the intent behind her words was abundantly clear:

Rebirth. Life. Recreation.

The two stood within a short breadth of one another, watching agape as Orla quite literally worked her magic.

"She can do this?" Qirin asked, stunned.

"I knew she and others could do lesser ones," Nevia murmured, "but with the blood of a goddess? Maybe she can."

The inscribed runes became aglow, lifting from the ground in a tangible form. They danced along the length of the circular border, a melodious hum coming not only from the seer, but the very circle itself. Soon the entire circle was bathed in a vibrant light, not unlike the ray which informed Qirin of Nevia's location.

He stole a peek at Nevia's face, awe on her gentle features. Awe, mixed with hope. It was a mystery to Qirin what overcame him, then. Perhaps it was his many losses, or maybe his newfound affection he gained through fatherhood. Whichever the case, he found himself reaching to grasp Nevia's hand, giving it a slight reassuring squeeze. A soft smile played on her lips, and he returned it. No longer did he find himself hating her, or holding her accountable for all the ill that befell him. She was just as much the victim in this story as they all were, and she did not deserve to have her heart broken.

To sacrifice more than they already had was not necessary.

The light ebbed away, leaving the three breathless, most of all Orla. She was now on her hands and knees, rasping for breath and shaking from head to toe. Qirin started to make a motion for her, to find out if she was okay, then halted, unable to believe what he was witnessing.

Ardan's body began to stir.

59
NEVIA

This could not be real. Good things did not happen to Nevia. There was no way that Ardan had come back to her after meeting his untimely demise.

Yet here he was. No one could mistake his distinct movements as he placed both hands on the ground, muscles working in his exposed back as he started to shove himself to his knees with a deep groan.

Nevia's legs nearly threatened to go out from under her. He was alive. Really, truly.

Alive.

"Ardan!"

Qirin, wisely, released her hand as she wrenched it free from his, running with every ounce of her remaining strength and colliding into the arms of Ardan reborn. It knocked them both to the ground, onto the circle that caused both life and death within an hour of each other. They lied there, embraced tightly in one another's arms where they laughed and cried away their anguish.

"Ardan, I'm so, so sorry that I—"

He silenced her with a kiss before she could continue, one that was slow, sweet and tender. Mixed with the saltiness of sweat and the metallic tang of blood. Despite it all, it was the most precious kiss they ever shared, and Nevia eagerly returned it. So happy, so grateful.

Ardan pressed his forehead to hers as they broke apart. "I'm so proud of you," Ardan murmured roughly, voice hoarse from lack of use. "That must have been so hard."

She swallowed the lump in her throat. "There was no way around it. In order to cast I had to make a sacrifice, to elicit a strong enough emotion powerful enough to end Saava." He tucked a lock of hair behind her ear as she swallowed. "It didn't work, but Orla brought you back and—"

Orla.

Nevia turned around, feeling sheepish for nearly forgetting the person whose quick thinking revived Ardan to begin with. When she lifted herself to steal a glance around she was relieved to find Orla standing alongside Khatalia, who looked filthy and bloodstained, but otherwise fine. Some of the colors looked odd on her furs. Most of the blood, Nevia horrifically realized, probably did not even belong to her.

The young seer, Orla, looked disheveled but otherwise hale. Nevia dipped her head, ingratiated, and Orla merely winked and mouthed "you owe me" before accepting the arm Khatalia wrapped around her shoulders.

"Something tells me things didn't go according to plan." Khatalia said. "Sorry for the delay, by the way. Got caught up wrestling a half-horse, half-monster with two heads thing. What did I miss?"

Nevia released Ardan only long enough to swagger to her feet and help the chieftain to stand once again by her side. His fingers interlocked with hers, palms pressed together. Nevia turned her attention back to Khatalia, and couldn't suppress the grin stretching from ear-to-ear.

"Everything, but the important thing is we won. Saava is gone, and we're all okay."

She had to take a moment to allow those words to really, truly sink it.

They were okay.

Fate smiled upon them again. They saved Gaia, and they survived.

60
QIRIN

Exhaustion consumed Qirin as he slumped into a chair before the hearth of a local tavern. Apart from the busted window, collapsed bookshelf, and an entire case of rare, expensive wine shattered on the far wall, the building was still in relatively good condition.

The Feishin king was just served fruit and cheese, the assortment far from Qirin's idea of standards. He wrinkled his nose as he picked through a bushel of grapes, seeking those that were unscathed and worthy of his consumption.

Two tankards came crashing down on his table, causing Qirin to lift his head with a scowl. He despised liquor, always had. It was a substance that could turn the most reputable man vile, and he hated the bitter taste of alcohol. Sliding into the chair across from him sat Khatalia, the clanswoman that had at one point slaughtered his people single-handed, and yet had somehow become a good friend.

"You look well, all things considered," Qirin commented, noticing that she had changed into a fresh sleeveless tunic, free from any traces of the battle they waged only days ago.

Khatalia scoffed, clasping her tankard with both hands. "Considering we had a narrow brush with death and watched an immortal die? Yeah, I guess so."

The king dipped his head, resuming his search for grapes. "You did well out there."

Khatalia plucked a grape from the top of his discards and popped it in her mouth, chewing thoughtfully. "You do realize this is only the beginning."

"I certainly do."

She tilted her head, turquoise beads woven into her dreadlocks twinkling in the firelight. "So, what now? I don't think the world is going to go back to normal anytime soon."

Qirin chose not to respond, his face scrunched into a frown. He was still riddling through that, and had made no sound, satisfying decision. He knew Gaia's restoration had to do with his daughter, but how remained a mystery to him.

"No, most definitely not," a bored male voice responded behind them.

Qirin lifted his head, glancing over Khatalia's shoulder to find the new mayor of Velspire himself, Xander Bakalov, hands clasped in front of him with an air of authority. Despite the recent attack on the capital he had recovered well, his clothing pristine and suggesting he was far underground taking shelter when buildings were being decimated and the entire capital was compromised. His boots clicked as he allowed himself to sink into an empty chair at their table, setting down his own glass that looked questionably like wine. Curious, as Qirin did not think Xander was even old enough to consume liquor.

"How is your new throne?" Qirin asked him, unable to stifle the chill in his tone.

Xander considered him, dark hair curling at the nape of his neck. "Stale. Prickly. It's not easy governing a nation in a world of death that we must learn to thrive in, but that's to be expected. Nonetheless"—he dipped his head—"I'm honored to have the opportunity to set things right."

"That's good," Qirin said, testing the tankard that Khatalia brought for him. It was putrid and vile, exactly as he had expected it. He tried to conceal his look of disgust by lifting his arm. At least wine held a sweetness of proper taste.

"I'm still surprised, though," Xander said, draining the contents of his glass, "that she let a couple of rebels ruin her reign. I'm disappointed in her lack of strength."

"Or maybe she realized the current system wasn't working." It shocked Qirin that he found himself vouching for her, when only weeks ago he wished her ill. His gaze fell to his tankard; maybe the drink was having an effect on him, after all.

"Whatever the case, she's abdicated and disbanded the empire," Xander responded. "And now we are trying to rebuild."

"What are you doing to help that move along?" Khatalia asked.

"I don't know yet. I did, however, recently learn that the effects aren't as prominent across the globe, Iddlegaard being one such place, so perhaps we can pool our resources and negotiate solutions to better our world predicament for our peoples."

Qirin tilted back in his chair, taking in the ceiling's broken tiles no doubt caused by a night creature clambering atop the roof. "Well, you have my support. The Feishin Kingdom is more than willing to assist in any technology that is needed to get through this dark time."

"Get through?" Xander barked a laugh, short and sharp. "Why, this is our new reality. We have to embrace it or die."

A soft smile played on Qirin's lips, face still upturned. "No, this is only temporary. There is light in our future. I promise you."

Xander looked dubious, eyes narrowing to slits. "Is there something I don't know?"

Khatalia and Qirin shared a glance, wordlessly agreeing that the fewer who knew of Akari and her role, the better. A simple response would suffice. "Yes. The Light of Gaia is coming, and, when it does, life will return to us."

The Velspirian mayor scowled. "How can you be so certain?"

It was Khatalia's turn to respond. She leaned across the table, emerald eyes boring into his with a level of intimidation, which Qirin hoped would at last shut him up. "Because we have hope."

61
ARDAN

Saava's demise increasingly bothered Ardan as the days went by. Reliving the newfound memories of a past life made her death particularly haunting, remembering how he once felt for a woman that, in the present, he had no feelings for except negative.

Sleep was something he found elusive since the final battle; he could not settle in to rest. He was fortunate if he got a few hours of sleep each night, but no more could be enjoyed. Some nights he would simply lie there, wide awake, staring into the ether and wonder what was next for them all. They were now living in a future they did not think would come, and it was a matter of deciding how to live out the rest of their lives in this ruined, rebuilding world.

It was during one such sleepless night that he sat up, carefully unlacing his arm from beneath Nevia's head where she slept soundly. She was angelic with the ways her curls framed her face, and a part of him was loath to leave her side. But sleep would not come for him, and he could no longer lie there to be tortured by his thoughts. Carefully he drew the covers over her exposed shoulder, stroked her hair, and slipped from the room.

They were staying in the tavern for the time being. Xander had kindly offered rooms in the palace, but they were quick to decline. Even if the once rebel leader was turning a new leaf, Ardan still did not trust him, and clearly neither did the others. Besides, he did not think Nevia was all too eager to return to the stifling walls of the Velspirian palace after everything she had undergone within them.

Advisories hung on the walls as Ardan traipsed down the hall of guest rooms, reminding patrons of the Velspirian curfew until dawn for fear of night creatures. Ardan did not think this applied anymore; now that Saava was gone, he did not suspect they would bother humanity with such drive. Unless the abominations could reproduce and learn on their own—but there had been no reports of such thus far. He would let that be a problem for another day.

He silently climbed down the stairs, running a hand along the splintered banister to the landing below. The usual raucous chatter echoing from the main dining hall was absent, suggesting patrons had already tucked in for the night. A candle, however, was aglow in the sitting room adjoining the dining area, which struck him as particularly curious. Perhaps someone else suffered from the curse of the insomniac like himself. Letting his curiosity get the better of him, he meandered over to find Khatalia sprawled on the floor, sheets of paper in a disarray in front of her. She glanced up, quill in hand and ink at her side, blinking up at him bleary-eyed.

"Why are you are spying on me?" she asked in way of greeting.

Ardan chortled, entering the space to join her. Books lined the walls in enormous stacks, the remains of a shelving unit piled in one corner. He stepped over strewn papers to stand alongside her. "I couldn't sleep, so spying on you seemed like a better pastime than staring at the ceiling."

Khatalia made a dismissive sound with her tongue, tossing her head and writing on. She did not further reprimand him, or ask him to leave, so he took it as an invitation to drop down alongside her. "What are you doing, anyway? You've never, ah, exactly been the bookish type." Ardan gestured to the scattered papers, many of which lay in crumbled ruins.

A bitter laugh rumbled through her chest, finally taking one of the papers next to her thigh and handing it over. "Just some scribbles. I'm telling Reiya and Ayan everything that happened."

Ardan swallowed dryly. For Khatalia, the losses resulting from Saava's mayhem started long ago, particularly her dear wife and son during the loss of her entire clan four years ago. Despite the time that passed and the nonchalant way his former chieftain carried herself, the pain was still with her every day. She just knew how to hide it well. Such loss, Ardan assumed, would probably last with her for as long as she drew breath.

Gingerly he placed a hand on her shoulder. "I can leave you to it, then." He lifted his gaze to the open window, drawn curtains fluttering with a chilly gust of wind. "I know that she's proud. Her and Risanna both."

Khatalia swallowed hard, deigning not to answer. Perhaps unable to. She let out a quivering breath, face tight as if on the brink of shedding tears.

Thoughts of Ardan's former chief left him reminiscing, wistful of a time when life was far simpler, and certainly more vibrant. "I wonder what Risanna would say right now," Ardan mused, shifting his weight into his arms behind him. "After seeing what has become of the world."

"She'd probably laugh hysterically and say that we had it coming," Khatalia offered vibrantly. Their gazes locked, and Khatalia finally cracked a grin. "But she'd be damn proud of both of us. We've done well."

"Yes."

Blonde dreadlocks brushed Ardan's shoulder as Khatalia leaned over, collecting her clutter and tucking them into her tunic. "Why don't you stay with me a while. I . . . kind of like the company."

Ardan threw her a sideways smile. "I do too."

They both sat in silence for a time, soaking in the chilly breeze and tranquility of the late night. Ardan watched as the candle at Khatalia's side burnt itself out, running out of wick to burn.

"So I've been doing a lot of thinking," Ardan said slowly, gaze boring into the weathered wooden planks beneath them, "and I've come to a decision."

"Oh? Going to finally propose to that poor woman and get it over with?"

A chortle escaped Ardan. "No. Well, maybe that, too, but that's not what I was thinking."

"You're cruel to her, Ardan Kyaroe." Khatalia nudged her big toe into Ardan's outstretched leg. "Can't you tell that she's hopelessly in love with you?"

He shrugged, yet he could not suppress his smile. He was hopelessly in love with her, himself, and knew now that Saava was no longer a threat they would have a bright future ahead of them.

"Well, this has partly to do with Nevia," Ardan admitted, "but it mostly has to do with you."

His second arched a brow in question.

"Khatalia, how would you like to be chief of Sanen?"

Her nostrils flared, a tick in her tensed jaw. For a moment Ardan misread her reaction as displeasure and thought he made a mistake. He was quick to continue. "Absolutely no pressure. I can figure out something else. It's just . . . the people were so happy under your leadership while I was away. You have far more leadership experience than myself. You would do amazing."

"Ardan," Khatalia interjected, leveling her green eyes to meet with his. "This is nice and all, but becoming a good leader takes time. You'll get there. You just need some patience, and I'm happy to give you some pointers if you need them."

The chieftain chuckled nervously. "Well, it's a little more than that," he admitted, lowering his gaze to the floorboards. "I-I want to be with Nevia. Wherever that might be. I know that she's abdicated her throne, but I don't want to force her to come back to Sanen with me if she doesn't want to. She's spent enough time shackled to one place out of obligation—now it's time for her to choose where she wants to be, and I'll be there by her side through it all."

There, he had said it. The truth that had been nagging at him. Nevia was the most important thing to him, and he would not allow any further absences between them, no more allowing Renaults to step in their lives. He wanted to be with her, forever, until the day one of them died. And perhaps after.

He let out a shuddered breath when Khatalia leaned forward, placing a hand gently on his knee. "I would be honored. I think that's a great idea."

A weak smile stretched his lips. "Thank you."

"You take good care of her now," Khatalia said, sternness overcoming her expression. "If you break her heart I'll waste no time in breaking your neck. You hear me?"

Ardan threw his head back and laughed, a true, sincere laugh, fulfilling emotions that had become alien to him in recent times.

"Trust me, I'd throw myself off a cliff and break my own neck if I hurt her."

Khatalia threw him a lopsided grin. "Well, so long as we're on the same page, then."

Good ol' Khatalia. Yes, she was the perfect person for the job. While he was saddened to say goodbye to the people he had known all his life, it came as unmeasurable relief to surrender the task he resented. He never wanted to be chief.

He dipped his head in gratitude. For the first time in months, things seemed to be looking up.

They would get their happy ending, after all.

62
NEVIA

Y ou don't need to come with me," Nevia repeated for the fifth time. And again, her words fell on deaf ears. Orla busily packed up the contents of her new rucksack which consisted of objects she retrieved from her room back in the palace. Most of her prized treasures were lost through their travels and the battle.

"I want to make a difference in the world," Orla said at last, finally meeting Nevia's gaze with a harsh resolution. "I want to help. It's going to be hard to start over with the way that things are now, and the least I can do is help ease the suffering of others wherever and however I can. Besides, I like your idea."

Nevia dipped her head. It was true, their goals aligned. Nevia wished to travel the world, to salve those heavily afflicted by the blight and help them improve their way of living in this ruined world. It would make sense for them to travel together in their efforts to aid humanity and bring them together, but she was loath to do so. It wasn't that she wished to be rid of the girl. On the contrary, she would welcome Orla at her side as she performed charity work. Chiefly she hated the idea of separating Orla from her father any longer, especially after having already kept them apart these past few years.

"I don't know where I'm going," Nevia explained.

Orla shrugged. "It doesn't matter. I want to come, too."

A defeated sigh heaved from Nevia's chest as she closed her own trunk with a snap. "Then I would welcome you, so long as your father approves."

"He doesn't need to approve," Orla scoffed. "I'm no longer a child."

This was absolutely untrue, in Nevia's opinion, but she was not going to wage that war. The stubborn teen was mulish at that moment. Instead she rose from her spot on the bed, folds of her simple dress unfurling. "I'll leave you to your preparations, then."

"I should be ready soon," Orla responded. "I won't keep you waiting."

Nevia hesitated at the door, only briefly, watching the young girl fold up the rest of her clothes and shove them mercilessly in the rucksack. So young, and yet so courageous. She owed this child so much, and yet felt that she had little to offer her. "And Orla?"

The redhead glanced up.

"Thank you. For everything you did out there, and then some. Without you, I don't think we would be standing here today. Ardan definitely wouldn't be."

Orla's grin was wide, gaze shyly faltering to the floor. "Don't worry, you'll pay me back later," she chirped. "I haven't forgotten that you still owe me."

Something warm bloomed in Nevia's chest, an emotion she could now properly label: love. "Of course. I will be waiting to see when you want to redeem that request."

The girl hummed a light note as Nevia closed the door, traipsing down hall in favor of getting some fresh air. The tavern's dining room had only a handful of patrons, mostly those who stayed the previous night, much like they had. It was still too early for other patrons to come for liquor, the only one capable of such perhaps being Vladios, the lord of Malabria himself.

A cold rush of air greeted Nevia as she stepped outside of the tavern. A gentle snow was falling, flakes lightly dusting the dilapidated streets and the tavern's sign around the corner. While peaceful, she knew it was not over. Saava was gone, that was true, but the world was still dying, and it was something that they would have to learn to live with until Akari fulfilled her role, whenever that would be.

Bundled in his woolen coat, hood drawn was Ardan, leaning against a nearby lamppost and staring out into the vacant street beyond. His gaze lifted to her as she drew a step forward, his lips curving up into a smile. His breath fogged the air, and she wondered if the rosiness of his cheeks was from the cold or her presence.

A painful lump formed in her throat. They did it. They survived, and now they would actually have that cabin in the woods together.

Eventually. Perhaps. Once she did what she needed to do.

"How is your back?" he asked her in way of greeting.

Nevia shrugged, shoving her hands into her coat pockets for warmth as she strode up to him. "It's mostly healed. Still sore, of course, but I'm tenfold better than I was when the field physician first patched me back together. I might even be able to lift again soon."

"That's good." He kicked off from the lamppost, footfalls crunching the snow underfoot. "When are we leaving?"

Nevia gave a start. "We?"

She hadn't discussed her plan with him, at least not yet. Suddenly she realized that he must have been assuming they would go through with their dreamed-up plans now that she had abdicated her throne. Of course that was it.

Guilt settled in her stomach, feeling shame that she momentarily thought otherwise. It would only make sense for her to return to the north. It was her home, her roots.

And yet her calling was elsewhere. She knew that with absolute certainty now.

"Ardan," she started, cold air stabbing at her lungs. "I'm sorry, but I can't return to the north with you, not yet."

He held out his hand to her, and she accepted it, allowing him to bring her close to his side. "My place is with the people here. Ending Saava was only the beginning. There's so many people still suffering. I need to help them, Ardan. I have to. I brought this about, and it's my job to help the world find a better way to live."

She waited, watching him process the information and expecting his rebuttal any minute. To her surprise he seemed unfazed by her confession. "I figured you probably wouldn't be able to settle down so easily. It's fine. I passed the clan over to Khatalia. I am yours until the end of time, Nevia. Wherever that takes us."

The words filled her with more joy than she thought she could ever feel again. Nevia wrapped her arms around his waist, cinching him close against her. Ardan absentmindedly ran his fingers through her hair, eyes interlocked with hers. "We have all the time in the world now."

"So you'll do it, then? You'll travel with me while we heal this dying world as best we can?"

He paused for a heartbeat, fingers catching on her braid before snatching up her hand, bringing it to rest against his beating heart. "I wouldn't have it any other way. We will travel until we're either shunned or we've made everyone's lives better, but my place is by your side, Nevia Bylilly. My love, my light." He leaned forward, brushing her forehead with a kiss. "Wherever on Gaia that takes me."

An invisible weight lifted from Nevia's shoulders. She felt lighter in body and mind. Happier. In Ardan's eyes she saw a reflection of her own emotions. A new hopeful energy, a new light. Her fingers pressed tenderly against his chest. "I'm excited to see what the future in this dying world offers us," she said.

Beneath the morning winter sun, amidst the flurry of snowflakes, Ardan leaned in, sealing her promise with a kiss, and she absorbed it, savoring his warmth. Absorbing it, knowing she would be graced with this for the rest of their natural lives. When they finally broke apart he ensnared a hand at the back of her head, his smile reaching his eyes as he said, "Me too, Nevia."

EPILOGUE
65 YEARS LATER

A chilly breeze woke the Feishin king early that morning. The sun barely peeked above the horizon, just enough to paint the sky in shades of pale-blue and orange. And yet, not enough sun to permeate his bedroom window in the Feishin palace. That had not happened in over sixty-five years. A chill in the air left the elderly man shuddering, reaching for his cane and clambering out of bed.

Without bothering for lighting, he drew a heavy robe over his shoulders, long silver hair cascading over his chest. His gaze trailed to Rito, his beloved sleeping soundly at his side. A smile wrinkled his eyes as he quietly made his way across the room, bare feet padding along the bamboo floor.

His long life had been a good one, despite the blight afflicting the world many years ago. The Feishin king just celebrated his eighty-seventh birthday, surrounded with his husband, his beloved daughter, Akari, along with her husband, and their five children and sixteen grandchildren. For all of his fear of living alone, such was not the case for him. Slowly the Feishin Kingdom rebuilt, learning to live in the ruined world with newfound joy.

Qirin trailed through the halls, passing the ornate tapestries that told stories both old and new. He paused briefly before one of the newer tapestries, strung together in honor of the Restoration Committee founded by Nevia Bylilly. At first he questioned her decision to leave her crown in favor of a vagabond life. And yet, he could not have been more proud of her decision. With her work she was able to improve the lives of millions across Gaia. She passed on to the Nether Planes ten years prior, but her legacy would live on forever. Through her work, she reunited bonds once severed, bringing bountiful prosperity and peace to the people despite the state of the world. The people sang her praises, and would indeed sing her praises for ages.

Despite that, he did miss her. He missed all of them, and would one day take his place among them in the stars.

But not today. Not yet. His purpose on Gaia was not yet fulfilled.

The Wind Palace was no stranger to strong torrents of wind, perched on the highest peak in the kingdom, overlooking what once was a city adorned in splendor and riches. Indeed, Qirin recalled a day when the city would glitter alight as the evening sky darkened. Those days were long gone, and still he frequented them in his dreams, as if it only happened yesterday.

The breeze rustled the elder king's robes, the chill not quite as intense as it had been that week. The sun felt closer, more vibrant. If Qirin closed his eyes, he could almost feel its rays kiss his face.

He strode slowly through the courtyard on his usual morning walk, taking in the barren soil and enjoying the feel of it beneath his feet. His sights were set on the cherry blossom tree up ahead, the very one that he proposed to Liana in front of so very long ago. Often Qirin would close his eyes, allowing his walking stick to bob along to guide him. With closed eyes he could visualize what this path looked like in its former glory, its lush green blades of grass whistling in the wind. The sky a brilliant blue, adorned with fluffy white clouds coasting gently along the horizon.

His walking stick struck the roots of the tree, signaling his arrival. He inhaled sharply, savoring the moment, a pleasant smile on his weathered face. Yes, he could still smell the sweet fragrance of blossoms upon his favored tree—

Light infiltrating his eyelids forced them to snap open to find a startling sight. The sun's rays pierced through the thick gray fog, the first time since the death of Gaia. The sky cleared, unveiling a canopy of blue once more. A shudder coursed down his spine, forcing him to lean into his walking stick for support as a lone tear rolled down his cheek.

"My Akari," Qirin whispered, warmth blossoming in his chest. "You did it. You fulfilled your role and became Gaia's new light."

A gentle warm breeze kissed his face, and with it the soft words caressed his ear: "I'm smiling at you, Father. I see now what the world was, and what it will be again. It will be beautiful. It will be light."

He felt her, then. Felt her everywhere. Akari was somehow Gaia, or, perhaps, Gaia was her.

"Akari?" he asked weakly, bracing himself against the old tree for support.

As if in answer, directly above Qirin's head, the petal of a cherry blossom formed.

ACKNOWLEDGEMENTS

Just two years ago I decided to take the plunge and enter the world of publishing, and what a wild ride it has been. It's hard to believe that I'm closing Nevia's chapter for good with the closure of the *Legends of Danaeca* duology, something I could never have done without the support from so many wonderful, amazing, inspiring individuals.

First, I want to give a huge thank-you to my street team. You guys are really so amazing, for your words of encouragement, support, and sharing my stories with others around the world. It has been such a joy getting to know and work with you!

Thank you to my cover artist, Christian Bentulan, for sticking with me to the end of the story! These covers truly shine and convey the story so well.

A massive thank-you goes out to my editor and husband, Ross, for his devotion in me, and making my crude manuscript really shine. He poured himself into the world and these characters, spending so many late nights tweaking my story and offering very sound constructive criticism (especially after I changed the last half less than two months before release—eek!). I really don't think I would've had the strength to publish books without your support, and I thank you tremendously.

Very special thanks to Teresa at *The Art Armature,* who did it again with creating gorgeous official art. Thank you for always being there and bringing my beloved characters to life!

Thank you to Eva and Jess for being such lovely people and encouraging me in all areas of life. Your support of my dreams means so much to me. And a huge shout-out to my book club girlies, Rachel, Stefany, Sarah, and Sierra! Love our friendship and our conversations—book-related and otherwise!

And thank you, dear reader, for sticking with me and seeing Nevia's story come to a close. It has been a pleasure and the greatest honor to have you along for the ride.

ABOUT THE AUTHOR

Madison had a passion for storytelling from the tender age of four, her first love being illustrating the stories near and dear to her heart. While she still has a love for drawing, she has gravitated more toward writing the words that make a story rather than the visuals that support them. She wrote her first short story at nine years old, and has been writing stories ever since.

The *Legends of Danaeca* romantasy duology is her first completed series, though she suspects that she will continue writing in the genre for many years to come!

Madison lives in New England with her husband, daughter, and two fur babies in the countryside. When she's not writing you can often find her playing Dungeons & Dragons, dreaming up her next trip to the beach, or doing arts and crafts with her daughter.

READ MORE BY MADISON RENE

LEGENDS OF DANAECA
#1 SHE WHO CHOSE WAR

Madison Rene's romantic fantasy debut and the first installment to the *Legends of Danaeca* duology. Read how it all began in this tale of self-discovery, sacrifice, love, and betrayal.

LEGENDS OF DANAECA
#0.5 HE WHO CHOSE LOVE

Sign up for my newsletter at:
https://mailchi.mp/38f7e6c12503/madison-renes-newsletter-list
to receive the free exclusive prequel novella told from Darius'
point of view. Find out exactly what happened when Nevia and
Darius first met, fell in love, and the hurdles they faced all for the
sake of fiery passion and forbidden love.

Find Madison on the Web

Want to know more about Madison's current projects and interact with her on social media? You can join her newsletter: https://mailchi.mp/38f7e6c12503/madison-renes-newsletter-list or visit her website at: www.MadisonReneAuthor.com

You can also find her on the following social media platforms:

Instagram: https://instagram.com/madisonreneauthor
Twitter: https:/twitter.com/madireneauthor
TikTok: https://www.tiktok.com/@madisonreneauthor
Facebook: https://www.facebook.com/people/Madison-Rene/61558765373669/